NIGHTBORN

JESSICA THORNE

NIGHTBORN

bookouture

Published by Bookouture in 2020

An imprint of Storyfire Ltd.
Carmelite House
50 Victoria Embankment
London EC4Y 0DZ

www.bookouture.com

ISBN: 978-1-83888-763-6
eBook ISBN: 978-1-83888-762-9

To my always hero

Prologue

The Prince and the Guardsman

Once upon a time a terrible plague known as the nightborn descended on the kingdom. Their magic was wild and dangerous, and nothing could control them. But legend had it there was a cure. So the three princes of the kingdom determined to go on a quest to find that cure.

The eldest prince – handsome, tall and fair – took the finest company from the army with him. They rode to the far south of the kingdom, where they searched the lakes, the rivers and the streams, but they couldn't find the cure. The nightborn surrounded them and drowned them all.

The second prince – broad, strong and tanned – took a hand-picked hunting party with him. They rode to the far west of the kingdom, where they searched the forests, the trees and the undergrowth, but they couldn't find the cure. The nightborn surrounded them and tore them limb from limb.

The third prince – slender, quick-witted and dark – took only one faithful guardsman with him. The two rode to the far north of the kingdom where they heard tell of the stronghold of the Hollow King, the god of the mageborn. Surely there, they could find a cure.

In the valley of roses the nightborn surrounded them and would have burned them. The prince fell from his panicked horse, but the guards-

man pulled the prince up onto his mount with him. He was faster than the flames which consumed all the flowers around them, leaving only the thorns behind. They galloped through the valley, hacking their way through the deadly brambles and barbs until they reached an ancient palace of black stone.

The prince loved his guardsman well. He knew he owed him his life. He bid him stay at the entrance and not set foot inside lest the Hollow King demand something of him in payment for the cure. But the guardsman loved his prince in return, and loyalty was written on his soul. When the prince did not return from the hall of the Hollow King, the guardsman could stand it no longer. He made his way down the dark tunnel that led into the bowels of the earth, where even the Hollow King hid from the nightborn.

The first thing he met on the way was the Deep Dark. It seized him in its midnight grip.

'Do not venture into the hall of our brother,' the Deep Dark told him. 'He will demand more than you are willing to pay.'

'I am willing to pay whatever the Hollow King demands, if only my prince goes free with the cure,' the guardsman said in reply, and with a growl the Deep Dark let him pass.

The next thing he met was the Little Goddess, wearing her gleaming black crown. She drew him into her soft embrace. 'Do not venture into the hall of my brother,' she told him. 'He will demand more than you are willing to pay.'

'I am willing to pay whatever the Hollow King demands, if only my prince goes free with the cure,' the guardsman said in reply, and with a sigh the Little Goddess let him pass.

Finally he stepped into the cavern where the throne of the Hollow King stood overlooking the glowing pool of the Maegen, the source of all magic. Its golden light danced on the cave roof and revealed his prince and the Hollow King.

The prince saw his guardsman and wept, for he loved him with all his heart. He had made a pact with the Hollow King which would give them the means to cure the plague and restore the nightborn. But every pact requires a sacrifice.

'Why did you not stay where I told you to?' the prince cried in dismay.

'I could not leave you,' said the ever-loyal guardsman.

'Your prince has given his word,' said the Hollow King as he drew his knife, a blade so wickedly sharp that it could cut through light itself. 'But I will give you a chance. One of you must die. You must choose. Are you willing to die for him?'

Without hesitation the guardsman bared his throat to the Hollow King.

'I am willing to pay whatever the Hollow King demands, if only my prince goes free with the cure,' he said in reply. 'It is my honour to serve.'

And so, while the prince was free to leave, the Hollow King took the life of the guardsman and never let him go.

Chapter One

The setting sun turned the sea golden. Grace leaned on the balcony of the house on Iliz, feeling the gentle heat of the evening settle around her. It was warm on the Valenti Islands, warmer by far than it would be in Rathlynn at this time of year. The breeze carried the scent of open water. The soft song of the lapping waves of the lagoon filled the air, marrying with the cries of seabirds, their white forms gathered below on the water, or circling overhead.

The peace was a lie. She knew that. None of them really understood peace anyway. They knew pain and struggle, danger and murder, and they knew suffering. This peace, no matter how blissful it was, wouldn't last. Three months had slipped through her fingers already. Each day with him was a blessing, but she still could not relax.

Rest was an alien concept to an Academy officer, especially Grace Marchant.

Down in the central courtyard, where water from the little fountain danced and glittered in the golden fading light, the harper played a mournful tune of home, loss, and regret. A song as old as the kingdom of Larelwynn.

Grace knew all about regret. And loss.

The building made a pretty picture, she thought. The white marble glowed, the filigree that decorated it delicate as spun sugar. It would never survive even a basic assault. It was a palace. Or at least it would have been, once upon a time. They called it a mansion here because it wasn't big enough for the Valenti to consider it a palace these days. Now it was a refuge.

Her refuge.

His.

Strong arms encircled her, his scent and his presence wrapping around her moments before. Bastien kissed her neck, murmuring softly as he did so, his lips warm, his words those of a lover. She'd never thought to have a lover like him. A king, even if he was one in exile. A god, even if he was one who had given up his power.

'Come back inside,' he whispered. 'Don't go out this evening. Let the others do it.'

'Don't worry, I won't be long.'

'Are you sure?'

She shrugged and leaned against him. 'Are you worried?'

'Worried,' he laughed softly. 'I'm worried about who you might run into. And what you might do to them.'

'I don't hurt people.' *Much*. But she smiled as she said it.

'Grace…'

'I'll be careful. I promise.' She turned in his arms and kissed him before he could argue any more. It was fun to argue with him. But making up was even better.

Bastien sighed and rested his forehead against hers. 'I have to go to these meetings, people from the court here, some from home, people who could help us. I'd come if I could.'

She kissed him again, lingering on his lips and teasing him a little. She loved doing that. Her hand strayed up his chest, brushing over the golden torc which rested against his collar bones, and then up so she could press her palm against his high cheekbone. He was beautiful. Beautiful to her. Strong, dark, golden, made of honour and duty… Her Bastien.

'I'll be back in no time. And you're safer here.'

'Are Ellyn and Daniel going with you?'

'Yes, of course. That was the deal, right?'

Bastien's late cousin, King Marius, had shown more foresight than she could ever have predicted in secreting funds here before his death, intended for the Lord of Thorns. The Valenti had offered them safe harbour, and any number of international treaties protected Bastien. Marius Larelwynn had made plans within plans and she loved him for it.

Marius's primary intention had been for them to go to Thorndale, to the palace of the Hollow King, where all this had begun. Perhaps the late king had thought it would bring some kind of closure to Bastien. Some sort of release. But they were safe here. As safe as they would be anywhere. Safer than Rathlynn anyway. Which wasn't hard.

They had discussed it, but Bastien had been dismissive. 'There's no need, my love. Not yet. It will be dangerous, especially travelling through Larelwynn land, so close to the Tlachtlyan border.'

She knew he wasn't afraid. At least, not for himself. But the kingdom held so many painful memories for him. Presumably, Thorndale did as well, although he hadn't shared them. He needed time, that was all.

Misha's voice rose from the courtyard, marrying with his tune, strong and clear, threaded with his magic. He was a Lyric, a mageborn able to make magic with music, but Misha was naturally talented too, dedicated to his art and something of a scholar. Valenti Islanders did love their music, and people were already talking about him. His voice, his music, his repertoire.

'*To spill my blood on the cold hard ground*,' he sang. '*Three times dead, twice entombed.*'

'Divinities, give us a break,' Ellyn yelled. 'If you don't play something more cheerful, I'll drown you in the canal, Misha. And Danny'll let me.'

The tune stalled.

'No, he won't,' the harper laughed.

'Yes, I bloody will,' Daniel replied. 'We talked about this. Happy songs, Misha. Now.'

At least they didn't sound on edge. Not the way Grace felt. Here, every day.

The Valenti Islands were different from Rathlynn. There was a freedom that was denied the mageborn back home. Despite this, she couldn't find comfort here. She had not been made for palaces and peace.

Bastien wanted to go back, too. Rathlynn was his home, his kingdom, and he had left people behind. The guilt was eating him up inside. His sister might be insane, and might hate him with every fibre of her being. The new queen, Aurelie, might want to control him and make him her mindless slave. But still… his home and his people, especially the mageborn people, called to him.

Grace reached out, ruffling his jet-black hair. It fell over his dark brown eyes and, when he closed them, his thick lashes brushed the skin below.

'I'll be back before you know it, I promise.'

'Stay safe, love,' he whispered.

A shimmer of warmth slid up her spine, a fire inside her that blossomed at his touch. His gift to her, making her inner magic strong and sure, something she could rely on for the first time in her memory. She'd spent so many years without her magic, a Flint without the ability to conjure fire. She didn't even remember the trauma of its theft but now, with Bastien, the magic was back and it made her stronger than ever. Instincts and reflexes that had always been quick and sharp were now truly magical.

'You too,' she told him. She slipped away from him with a smile.

'I'll pick you out something pretty to wear for the Dowager's Carnaefal ball tomorrow night,' he called after her.

'Well, you can try. If you can get me into it.'

'What if I promise to get you out of it too, Grace?'

He would, too. She couldn't wipe the smile off her face as she made her way down to the side entrance to their new home. Misha was still singing – a much merrier tune this time – and Daniel and Ellyn were waiting for her at the door, dressed as she was in leather armour without markings. Nondescript. Designed to blend in with the night.

Something pretty, indeed, she thought. Did he know her at all?

'Ready?' she asked.

Her squad just nodded.

Ellyn took charge of the little punt. She'd been born to this, she'd told them once. Born to the water, the little canals and a life spent only half on land. All that time in Rathlynn hadn't changed her so very much. She'd taken to it again immediately, even though she couldn't have been much more than a child when she'd left here.

'We came from Desima, one of the northern islands, not here. But we… we visited the court when we came to Iliz for Carnaefal.'

'What were you doing in the court?' asked Daniel.

Ellyn ignored the question. 'My family used to rent a house down by the Temple plaza. It's where the best parties are. Not as nice as our fancy mansion now, but nice, you know? It had a garden.'

Grace noticed the quick change of subject but she didn't say anything. If Ellyn didn't want to share her past, that wasn't any of her business. They were holed up here because the Larelwynn name still counted for something in the Valenti court. There had been a couple of marriages years back. A little bit of Larelwynn blood, barely a drop at this stage. But it was blood all the same. That was what Bastien had said.

Blood meant more to the nobility than anything else. More than honour, more than gold. And Larelwynn blood most of all. Even here.

The punt moved silently through the water, and they sat in the base, cloaked and quiet while Ellyn manoeuvred them down the canals towards the port. There was a party in one of the nearby mansions, music and light spilling everywhere, but they slipped through the shadows, ignored and out of sight. Entering the Lower Divi Io canal other boats joined them, jostling along against each other. Shouts and laughter rang out around them but they pressed on.

'Carnaefal makes everyone insane,' Ellyn muttered. 'End of winter and all that... It'll go on for days yet. There won't be a barrel left unemptied.'

She'd pulled her hood right over her head, casting her face into shadow. Grace gazed up at her, and said nothing. She didn't look like herself. More like a ghost of herself. A harbinger of death.

'Are we late? I think we're late,' Daniel replied. They both sounded nervous.

'We aren't late.' Grace stared ahead. 'It's fine. Just keep going. Don't rush.'

The Grand Harbour opened up before them, a thousand other narrow canals spreading out like a great spider web across the city, linking all the little plazas and buildings by water as well as the cobbled streets. They travelled more by boat here than foot. The harbour itself was more elaborate by far than the twin ports of Belport and Adensport at home. But Valenti was a naval nation, with trade routes that put Rathlynn to shame. And Iliz was the centre of it all, its beating heart. People at home liked to say the Valenti had water in their veins. They meant it as an insult. But that wasn't true. There was more to them than met the eye. You only had to know Ellyn to know that.

The sounds and smells of the harbour reminded Grace of home. Rathlynn reeked, far worse than the canals here, and it was much more dangerous, especially around Eastferry or Belport. The dark alleys of Iliz were a stroll down a poorly lit laneway by comparison. Try strolling in Rathlynn at night and someone would have the boots off your feet. All the same, Grace missed it, the feeling like a knife in the heart.

Although it was risky to go back, one day, she knew, they would have to. Face Aurelie and Asher Kane, face Celeste, face all the people they had left behind. Some of the mageborn had made it out of Aurelie's clutches, but by no means all.

Grace still heard stories. Tales of mageborn rounded up and locked away. Living in hiding. Killed or driven insane. Queen Aurelie and Asher Kane, her lover and the commander in chief of her Royal Guards, were still trying to use them, to harness their magic and enslave them. And they had left others behind, too. Others who didn't have magic, to make them targets or serve as weapons. Just people. People who had no one left to stand up for them.

The trading ship sat high in the water, her cargo unloaded, sails furled, her flag hanging limp at the stern.

They pulled up alongside and a rope dropped down. They were expected, after all. Securing the punt, they climbed up and boarded.

'About time you got here, Duchess,' said Kurt Parry. He was lounging against the main mast, his eyes half closed.

'We're busy people, Kurt,' Daniel told his brother and a moment later the two of them embraced. 'Did you have any trouble?'

'No trouble, don't worry. I'm good. Business is… well, not good, to be honest, but not much is at home. How's the Lord of Thorns?'

'He's safe,' Grace said. 'And you risk too much coming here yourself.'

Kurt laughed, because that was Kurt. 'Concern, Duchess?'

She wasn't fooled. 'Always.'

He grew solemn then. Just for a moment. Then he sighed and shook his head. 'It's getting tighter. The mageborn we got out are gone now. Larks on the wind. Even taken off their collars so they can pass for anyone. They're safe. And what's left in Rathlynn? Aurelie is trying to round up anyone she can. Leeches especially, and Ateliers. There's talk of torture, naturally. But without Mother Miranda or that crazy woman in the Temple, she can't get to their magic. We get them out when we can. Some won't leave. They want to fight back too. Can't blame them. You know what they're calling us? The people of Rathlynn? *Thorns*.'

Grace laughed. She couldn't help herself. What would Bastien say to that? She reached out, held Kurt's shoulder for a moment. 'It's good to see you. But you're needed at home.'

'Got to keep tabs on my little brother somehow, don't I? Anyway, just a flying visit. We'll sail back tonight, be there before nightfall tomorrow. They won't even miss us. They never do.'

'And your delivery?'

He knocked on the door to the cabins. His smug grin got even smugger. 'We're ready for you, Lady.'

The woman who stepped out was in her middle years, but had no sign of age about her. Rather she was honed and refined like steel. Her eyes were the same grey as her hair and she stepped out onto the deck with the grace of a dancer. Behind her was a tall, slim man, dressed in black and dark grey. It wasn't a uniform, but he wore it like one. Hazel eyes studied Grace from a delicate, aristocratic face. He wore a chain around his neck. She had to drag her attention away from him and back to the woman.

'Lady Kellen,' Grace said solemnly, careful with her words, because it paid to be careful around Lara Kellen.

Bastien and Grace had been expecting her. She had been Marshal Simona Milne's second in command. She was Commander Craine's widow. Grace still missed the commander of the Academy, the woman who had taught her everything she knew. Craine had told them with her dying breath that Lara would find them. And now here she was.

Lara Kellen had been a diplomat for the Larelwynns, a spy, and, in all probability, an assassin. And now, she worked for Bastien.

'Captain Marchant,' she said. 'This is Jehane Alvaran, my second.' Her second what? Grace shared a glance with Ellyn, who didn't look any more certain of this than she did. When Grace didn't reply, Lara swept by her, heading for the ship's rail. 'Shall we?'

Lara settled herself in the punt without complaint and Alvaran sat behind her, watching her back, no doubt. If she thought their transport was unsafe or beneath her, she didn't give any indication. Perhaps, Grace thought, she didn't care. Transport was transport. She could have travelled in worse ways. Grace had no idea what Lara Kellen had done in service of the crown; she didn't want to know any details. The woman was an enigma and probably best left that way.

And as for her second? He didn't speak. Just watched them, all the time. His close attention made her skin shiver, and she was sure she could feel magic drifting from him, as tantalising as a half-remembered scent. The delicate silver chain he wore could be a form of a collar. But no one had mentioned a mageborn would be accompanying Lara Kellen.

Especially one who didn't say a word. And wouldn't stop watching her.

The moment they reached the narrow waterway of Divi Io, they merged with the other traffic, inconspicuous and unseen. Carnaefal raged on. There were fireworks in the sky, explosions of light overhead, reflected in the dark water beneath. Music came from buildings and from the plazas and every so often a heaving boat full of drunken partygoers would lurch by them.

They made it back towards the mansion on the water almost without incident. Almost.

Ellyn had just steered them down into the quieter section of canal, away from the parties and the celebrations, when the attack came.

Grace saw Lara glance up, towards the rooftops, and moments later, something hit the bottom of the punt, crashing through it and throwing them all into the canal.

Dark water closed over Grace's head, freezing cold, stealing her breath and her strength with the shock of its embrace.

She sank like a stone.

Chapter Two

Water… she hated water.

A surge of panic shook through her, making her heart thunder in her ears. She couldn't drown. Not again. Not like this. It had happened in her childhood, and in the Academy, too many times. Water hated her.

She struck out for the surface, breaking it at the same time as Daniel and Ellyn. Lara surfaced a moment later.

'Up above!' Ellyn yelled. 'Look out.'

The arrows followed, slicing through the water around them. Grace managed to grab a board from the shattered punt, using it as a shield.

The low arched bridge was only a few yards away. Grace swam there in seconds, shivering. The water sucked the strength out of her, the fire in her smothered and drained. Ellyn appeared, fishlike in the water. Divinities, Grace envied her. Small steps led up onto the bank, cut into the stone of the canalside. They pulled each other to safety.

For a moment. Just a moment.

'To your left,' Lara shouted and Grace jerked around, drawing her sword, just in time to deflect an attacking figure as it launched from the nearest alleyway. She lashed out with her own blade and felt a sword rise to meet her. They clashed, and she let his blows drive her back at first as she assessed him. It took only a moment. He was quotidian, not magical. Valenti too, a cut-throat perhaps but good with a sword. Too good. She planted her feet and came at him hard.

There were more. Ten or twelve. They came from the narrow alleys and dropped from the rooftops. They surrounded the Rathlynnese, trying to cut them off from each other.

'Grace! Down!' Daniel called and she ducked, trusting him. A crossbow bolt passed over her head and punched its way through another attacker. He learned fast, Daniel Parry, and he had a mean streak that should never be underestimated. Another bolt slammed its way into a third assailant.

'They knew we were coming,' Grace said. 'They knew—' More of them appeared, far too many.

A hard body slammed into her, knocking her to the ground, and a knife pressed to her throat, its curved edge like an embrace around her neck. She fell still, frozen as she looked on a face she barely knew. Handsome, determined. Sharp eyes on either side of that aquiline nose and a mouth like a sword slash. Alvaran. Lara's man, Jehane Alvaran.

Shadows came up like a wall around them, dissolving the world into some dark and terrible realm of nightmares. Grace sucked in a breath and her head ached as Jehane's magic unwound. It rolled over the attackers in a wave, a tsunami of darkness, licking up the walls behind them and falling again. There were screams, sobs, running feet. In seconds they were gone. All of them.

'Don't move,' Jehane whispered, soft and quiet, like a sigh. He flicked aside the collar of her shirt with the edge of the knife, revealing the chain on which hung the gleaming coin, the royal warrant. If he tried to grab it, he'd be dead. The warrant protected itself and she'd seen it kill those who tried to take it. Even with the power of a goddess, Bastien's sister Celeste hadn't wanted to touch it. But Jehane didn't reach for it. He was smarter than that. 'I'm here to help. Ease up or this will end badly.'

'For both of us,' she replied, her own knife digging into his side not quite hard enough to break the skin, but there all the same.

'Then it will end.' A bitter smile infected his voice. 'I'm on your side.'

'Yeah? Then why the knife?'

He glanced down towards her blade and grinned. 'I thought you might react badly to my shadows. I was right.' His blade drew back, followed by the weight of his body. Grace could breathe again. 'I'm here to help, Captain Marchant.'

'Really.' She picked herself up and faced him. He didn't seem in any way apologetic. 'And why do we need *your* help?'

'You seem to get yourself in a lot of trouble.'

Bastard. It wasn't just a smile in his voice, but a smirk. 'Bastien won't be amused.'

'The Lord of Thorns is hard to please, I believe. Just remember. You owe me your life now. One day I'll collect.'

He went back to Lara, and nodded to her. She didn't look impressed with either of them. Had it been some kind of test? Grace didn't like the interest in the warrant.

Daniel was at her side in seconds. 'Are you okay?' He didn't look at her for more than a moment. He was searching the dark quay and surrounding alleyways with his frantic gaze. But their assailants were gone.

'I'm fine, Danny. Really.'

'I hate this place. It's made for ambushes.' The fact he had grown up in the rabbit warren that was Eastferry in Rathlynn didn't count, clearly. He didn't put up the reloaded crossbow. And Ellyn…

'Danny,' Grace asked in sudden alarm. 'Where's Ellyn?'

There was no sign of her. Ellyn was gone, as if she had never been there.

*

'What do you mean, they took Ellyn?' Bastien asked in disbelief. 'Why on earth would they want Ellyn?'

He wasn't just confused. There was a kind of anger simmering in him that Grace had rarely seen before, usually only when she was under threat. He'd come out of his diplomatic meeting to greet Lara, not to face news like this.

As the Valenti representatives filed out behind him, he fell silent, waiting. Grace felt their curious stares. And more. Knowing smirks.

Bastien didn't spare them so much as a glance and Grace tried to keep her gaze distant, focusing on the wall behind them while at the same time taking in faces, dress, weaponry…

Daniel wasn't handling it much better. Mainly he was turning the blame on himself. He stood like a statue in the courtyard until the main door to the mansion closed behind the visitors.

'Someone explain to me exactly what happened,' Bastien snarled once the Valentis were gone.

'I should have been watching her,' Daniel muttered. He started to pace back and forth, hands on his weapons as if they'd somehow help now. He couldn't stop. He needed to get out again, she knew that. Grace felt the same way. Get out of this place and find Ellyn.

Lara said nothing, watching in silence, taking in the dynamics. An old hand at this, clearly. Grace would have to watch her. Even if she was meant to be on their side – Bastien's side, at least. She would, by courtly tradition, wait until Bastien acknowledged her, which he didn't seem in any mood to do. Jehane stood against the wall, silent and watchful as ever. If Grace hadn't heard him speak she might have thought he couldn't.

'I'll find her, Grace,' Daniel said. 'I'll go and get the word out. Someone must know something.' They'd looked. They had searched the whole area for clues, for anything that might show where Ellyn had been taken. But it was useless. She was simply gone.

'Enough, Daniel,' Bastien said. 'It's not your fault. This may be beyond your network.' It wasn't a cruel tone. If anything there was an understanding, a comfort. Grace knew when he was trying to be kind, even if he was impatient. 'There are other ways, aren't there, Lady Kellan? Or should I call you the marshal now?'

Lara peeled off her gloves and then undid the clasp at her throat to remove her cloak. It was all done with practised ease, a diligence and grace which made it seem nonchalant. But it wasn't. There was a minute trembling of one hand, the deliberately even breath.

'Lara is fine, your royal highness. I've never set much store by titles. They can vanish so easily.'

'So can those around me, it seems. De Bruyn is part of my household. More than that. She's my friend. I want her back. Are you, or are you not a spymaster?'

Lara froze for a moment and a smile flickered across her lips.

'I was… relieved of that duty.'

'Fired, you mean.'

'I left before there could be actual fire… or whatever way the queen might have chosen to deal with me. Aurelie didn't trust my loyalties. Luckily I wasn't close enough to protest about it or I'd have ended up on a spike like my superiors.'

Grace frowned at the brutality of her words. Simona Milne had been the marshal, Bastien's guardian and the king's right hand. His housekeeper Lyssa was dead too, and any servants thought to have been loyal to him. *All my friends*, Bastien had said as he stared at the bodies in the distance. Who else had Aurelie murdered in her purge?

Grace sighed. 'Danny, take Misha and start looking for Ellyn. People talk to him and he's made friends already. But be careful. I'll be with you shortly.' He nodded, grateful to be given something to do. Moments later he was gone and she stood there with the Lord of Thorns and his new marshal, feeling hopelessly out of her depth and desperately trying to hide it.

'How was your meeting?' Lara asked Bastien.

'The usual. Promises. Most of them empty. A few rather ridiculous suggestions. Join me.' He gestured to the room he had just come from. Happy to leave them to it, Grace started to follow Daniel. 'You too, Grace.'

'But I—'

'If you will.' It wasn't actually a request. She knew that. The tone said it all. It was the Lord of Thorns again, not her lover. It was the voice of a prince, a king.

Lara gave him an arch look as she followed him inside. 'And are these suggestions from the Dowager Queen directly? If so, I doubt they're ridiculous. I know her of old.'

'This isn't a chance for you to catch up with old friends,' Bastien snapped.

'Oh she isn't. A friend, I mean. Although, she is old. Desperately so. And more cunning than you could imagine. Jehane, guard the door.'

Grace felt a ripple of magic again and cast a suspicious glance at Jehane. Bastien's gaze followed.

'A Shade?' he said.

'Yes, my lord.' Jehane bowed deeply. 'It is my honour to—'

'No. Not here. I'm not… I'm not that person any more.'

A flicker of confusion passed over the Shade's face. 'Your majesty?'

'No.' Bastien turned away, the movement brutal and final. He closed the door in Jehane's face.

In the meeting room, papers were strewn across the table. Family trees, lists of names, and a series of documents which appeared to be akin to contracts. Grace didn't like the look of them. Lawyers were far from her favourite people. Lara dragged her fingertips over the pages, parting them and glancing at them. Then she fixed her piercing gaze on Grace. 'Now, can I see it?'

Grace frowned, confused. 'See what?'

'The warrant.'

The silence that fell over the room was complete. Bastien was the first to move. He stepped closer to Grace, wrapped his arms around her and pulled her close. He'd given her the warrant. He had yielded up godly power to be with her and handed over the one thing that could bring it back, the one thing that could control him, to her.

The warrant looked like a gold coin. When fitted into the torc Bastien wore around his neck, it became once more the crown of the being he had once been, the Hollow King. Lucien Larelwynn had been the first bearer of the warrant, and he had made the pact with the Hollow King to end the Magewar. His descendants had then proceeded to wipe Bastien's memories every time he came close to discovering the truth.

That had been Bastien's existence, his past stolen from him whenever it suited his captors, wiped out as if it had never been. It was strange to think of him as hundreds of years old, unchanging, his memories not his own. He wasn't a god or a king, not to Grace. He was just the man she loved.

But now the former king, Marius, Bastien's beloved cousin, was dead, the last of the line of Larelwynn. Marius's wife Aurelie had taken the throne he had meant for Bastien to inherit, breaking the curse and the spell holding him.

'You don't have to,' Bastien murmured as he kissed Grace's neck. Lara didn't look away. Nor did she look impressed. Perhaps she didn't think Grace had any business with the rightful heir to the throne of Larelwynn. She was nobody, an orphan mageborn without anyone to speak for her. Grace's hand shook and she curled it into a fist. Bastien's fingers closed over it, warm and gentle. She closed her eyes and leaned against him. At least she had this. Him, his support.

'It's okay,' she said quietly and reached up to pull the chain from beneath her shirt. 'Here. It's just a coin, an old coin. So old you can't even see any markings on it any more.'

The buttery yellow metal was heavy, too. Heavier than any other coin she had ever handled. It dangled from the chain and Lara's eyes latched onto it, fixed and knowing.

'Ah,' she said. 'So... it is true. I almost didn't believe it. My wife told me he'd done it and I said no. Not to Grace Marchant. We had such plans for you, Craine and I. But here we are. I'm sorry, pet. I really am.'

'Sorry?'

But Lara turned away, all her focus on Bastien again. 'You didn't tell her what the Valenti want?'

Bastien scowled. Oh he definitely knew, whatever it was Lara was alluding to. 'It isn't happening.'

'What isn't?' Grace asked.

'They want him to marry one of their princesses. To be a member of the Valenti royal family. To reclaim his throne.'

It was like the floor fell out from underneath her. Grace locked her gaze onto him, but Bastien wouldn't make eye contact with her.

'Marry.' Her voice was an empty echo. 'Who?'

'King Roderick's daughter. His youngest. She's a good match. Intelligent, beautiful, graceful.' Lara's attention returned to Bastien, fixed and pointed. 'The noble families at home have agreed, the Hales, the Rosses, the Reeves… I sent letters to you. It is all arranged in line with the royal accords and just needs your agreement. The Valenti will support your claim to the Larelwynn throne. Rathlynn will be yours again.' Was Lara watching her as she spoke? Grace could feel the woman's knowing gaze on her. She couldn't bring herself to confirm it. 'You need Valenti support, my king. This is their price.'

Bastien had pulled that royal mask of disdain over his features once more. 'Well it's too high a price. I thought I made that clear already. I sent letters as well, Lara.'

Grace frowned at him. 'They asked before?'

His face froze, guilty as a child caught with his hand in the jar of sweets. 'I told them no.'

She shook her head. He'd been keeping things from her. Of course he had. She had once thought Bastien was full of secrets. He hadn't changed that much. 'That's not what I asked.'

'Yes, they asked before. Demanded, more like. The Dowager is forthright when it suits her.'

'When, Bastien?'

'When we first arrived,' he said, more soberly now. 'Three months ago.' He still wasn't meeting her gaze. This was a bad sign.

Grace had always known this would happen. Whether Bastien wanted to admit it or not. He was a prince, he should be a king. She, on the other hand, was no one. A guard. An orphan. A nobody.

She closed her eyes, trying to push back her emotions and think. If she wanted him to be safe, if she wanted to protect him as she had sworn to Marius she would, she would have to let him go.

'Grace,' he said, his hand on her shoulder.

She pulled away. She had to. She needed to find Ellyn. That was something she could do, something on which she could focus. Something within her power. Politics and negotiations, and her royal lover… they weren't so easy.

Chapter Three

The royal palace at Sa Almento rang with life, with laughter, crowded with all the nobility of the Valenti Islands. The Dowager's Carnaefal ball was legendary. It was not the biggest – that was reserved for the Royal Ball which rounded off the festivities – but politically speaking, this was the one to attend. Grace had looked appalled when Bastien had pulled her away from the search for Ellyn and told her she needed to make an appearance with him.

Bastien had reverted to his usual black. It was expected of him and he knew he had to make a show for this difficult audience. Grace had once told him that his clothes cost more than half the city had to buy food. But here, in this room, he was not out of place. Neither was she. The pale green silk of her dress contrasted with her red hair and perfect skin. She was beauty in physical form, although she couldn't see it. To him, she was perfection itself. Her only adornment was the warrant and a sigil threaded on a chain. She wore them like a threat.

If only she'd stop looking like she wanted to murder anyone who so much as glanced their way.

Servants with glistening silver trays walked among the nobility of Valenti and their many guests. They carried food and drink, delicate canapés and confections, sparkling liquids in a multitude of colours. As Bastien and Grace entered, and Bastien's title was announced, the entire company turned to study them. Grace almost shrank back behind him, before she caught herself and that familiar steel tightened along her spine. Divinities, she was magnificent, his lover. He didn't tell her that enough. Whenever he tried, she blushed, looked away and clearly didn't believe him. But it was true. In all his years, all those fragments of years he could now remember, he had never met anyone like her.

A queen? He could think of no one better suited to the role. But all logic said he had to marry someone else. Lara was determined. He wasn't thinking, she told him. Not like a king. And maybe she was right. His outright refusal did them no favours. But how could anyone compare to Grace?

Her strength and compassion, her sense of justice, her pursuit of truth…

'Don't hide,' he told her and she scowled at him. 'Don't scowl either.'

'Am I allowed to breathe?' she hissed.

Bastien allowed himself a smile. 'It's a good idea. It stops you passing out and causing a scene. I don't think swooning is in fashion.'

He caught a glimpse of her grin from the corner of his eye and understood the unspoken amusement. The thought of her swooning… the thought of her *allowing* herself to swoon… 'Well, the heavens forbid I'm out of fashion, Bastien.'

He couldn't picture her swooning if his life depended on it. Passing out from blood loss perhaps. He'd seen that. She'd died and it had almost destroyed him. He had done the unthinkable to save her, drawn on powers that should never be held in a single form to do it. But swoon? No.

He led her into the throng. There were a few faces he knew, diplomats and courtiers who had visited Rathlynn on occasion, who had courted him since he arrived here. They stared at him, the never-king

of Larelwynn, the Lord of Thorns, the monster behind Marius the
Good. They had no idea what else he was. He could count on one
hand those who did.

'There you are, Larelwynn,' said a booming voice. 'Divinities, man,
it's been too long, far too long. Look at you! The Lord of Thorns right
here in my humble home.'

Bastien flinched, just a little. It was the name that did it. He stopped
himself before it was obvious, but he had no doubt Grace had registered
it. Her hand on his arm tightened, almost imperceptibly, and then
she released him. It would be easier for her to get to her weapons if
she wasn't holding onto him. If she needed to protect him, it wouldn't
matter where they were or who they faced. He knew that. He felt the
same way about her. It was unspoken.

The speaker shouldered his way through the crowd. There was
nothing humble about his home. Not with marble floors, and gold-
framed mirrors on the walls. King Roderick of the Valenti Islands was
smaller than Bastien remembered, fatter too, and much older. Six years?
He looked more like fifteen years had passed. Bastien thought he was
only in his late forties but this man looked nearer sixty.

'Your majesty.' Bastien dipped his head. A king did not bow to
another king. But that didn't mean one did not show respect. Grace,
meanwhile, was trying to fade into the background. Not an easy task
when all eyes were on them now. She had trained all her life to be
unobtrusive, to slip back and watch, to guard what she was told to
guard, to hunt what she was told to hunt.

'My word, look at you,' Roderick said. 'Just like your father. And is
this your famous captain we've heard so much about? I see why you've
been hiding her away. A beauty. A veritable beauty.' Roderick leered at
Grace in a way that, if it was anyone else, Bastien would have lashed

out. It took everything he had to hold back. 'Has someone got you a drink yet? Here, over here. Come now.'

The servant with the drinks tray nearest to them swerved in their direction and they helped themselves, Roderick downing one before grabbing another. Bastien just held his. He didn't want to drink anything now.

'We're thrilled you're here. Simply thrilled. I told the Dowager you would be an excellent addition to our court. I told her that we'd be cursed if we turned you away. And she listened. Of course she listened. She may be my mother, but I *am* the king, you know.'

'Of course you are, your majesty,' Bastien said as courteously as he could. An excellent addition? He had agreed to nothing yet.

'Come. Come and meet her. She's my youngest, of course. She's studied with the finest scholars. She's been trained in this court all her life. Oh, you'll love her. Everyone does. Beautiful girl. The beauty of the age, you'll see. She even surpasses that Aurelie girl. Oh yes, come with me, son.'

Son? Oh, divinities. Lara had already signalled agreement. Bastien hadn't even really made up his mind to go through with this evening and Lara Kellen had decided everything for him. He hadn't even had a chance to discuss it with Grace. She'd been out looking for Ellyn all day, trawling up and down Iliz.

The king glanced at Grace again, an assessing expression, lewd and unpleasant, and once again Bastien felt a bristle of… not jealousy, but something like it. Protectiveness. Possessiveness. Grace would be furious if she found out. But he had enough survival instincts not to tell her.

He only hoped Roderick didn't make the mistake of acting on his lusts. That would be a diplomatic incident he couldn't clean up. Not even Lara Kellen would be able to do that.

The Dowager Queen, however… well, she could do anything. But he didn't fancy the thought of how she might manage that.

Bastien looked up and saw her gazing at them. Still dressed completely in black, still mourning a husband forty years dead, she had none of the fat of her son. She was a skeletal figure, her pale skin and silver-white hair a stark contrast, but her eyes were what grabbed attention. Pale and grey, and hard as steel.

Her expression was furious.

No one seemed shocked or appalled, so perhaps that was her usual look but Bastien wasn't sure. Beside her sat a young woman, no older than twenty, with the same pale, sharp features, and the same grey eyes. A beauty, yes, if you preferred ice to fire.

More beautiful than Aurelie? Perhaps, but that was a dangerous statement. Only a king in his own kingdom, drunk on power, paternal affection and far too much wine, would say something like that to a member of Aurelie's family. Even one in exile. What one of her infamous brothers might have done didn't bear thinking about.

Bastien might hate Marius's widow, but he was not so foolish as to agree, especially not when he was here to navigate such a politically charged situation. Grace was right. If she could set aside her feelings in this, so could he.

He had to. Otherwise he would never be able to go through with it. But most of all he had to remember that this was his choice, his decision. No one else's, no matter what Grace and Lara thought. He would decide. He took a steadying breath.

The Dowager Queen beckoned once, a curt and commanding gesture. Roderick grinned like an idiot. And Bastien followed him towards the thrones. What else could he do?

Grace moved as his shadow, her footsteps matching his.

The Dowager Queen, Rhyannon of Gellen, was a legend in her own lifetime. Her husband had been the kindest man, ruling an impoverished archipelago of islands, and somehow he'd persuaded the daughter of one of the richest houses in the land to marry him. Rhyannon had transformed the Valenti archipelago. She had taken control of everything, made her husband rich in his own right and built everything for the two of them. Word was she'd loved him beyond reason. So when he died after only ten years of marriage, she had plunged into mourning. And into something else.

She'd built a network of spies and now traded in information. She was the spider at the centre of the web. She knew everything about everyone, playing kingdom against kingdom. She was the power at the heart of the world and no one dared to cross her. She had brought down kings.

Rhyannon had eyes that looked right inside him. And the mind behind them was a trap from which no one could escape.

'The Lord of Thorns himself,' she said and offered him her hands. He dutifully bent and kissed her fingers. A king might not bow to another king. But to this woman... survival sometimes made the unthinkable necessary.

'Your majesty, you honour us with your invitation.'

Us. That was the word that did it. She looked up past him and her mouth was a flat, hard line.

'Captain Marchant.'

Grace couldn't have looked more like a startled rabbit if she had tried. Her face froze and her eyes had that wide, panicked glaze to them.

The Dowager saw it, no doubt about that.

'Grace,' Bastien said and held out a hand to her. She joined him, beautiful by his side, strong and elegant. His beloved.

'We have heard great things about you, young lady. And not so great. Your queen seeks your extradition. She has made numerous accusations.'

Bastien was sure she had. Aurelie had sent threats to him as well. She wanted him, but she wanted revenge on Grace more.

'We… we did not part well, your majesty,' he said carefully.

'Rival claimants to a throne seldom do,' she said with a sly chuckle. 'But enough of this. Have you met my granddaughter? Rynn, step forward, girl. Curtsey.'

Bastien glanced at Grace again to gauge her reaction, and caught a flicker of annoyance cross the Dowager Queen's wrinkled face. Damn. He should have hidden that better. Now she thought he was comparing them. Yes, Princess Rynn was beautiful, exquisitely so, but in his mind she would never compare to his lover.

He would always choose the fire in Grace Marchant over anything.

Colour crept up the princess's cheeks but she looked angry rather than embarrassed. Oh great, he had upset her as well.

'Your royal highness,' he said in as calm and courteous a voice as he could manage. His magic simmered beneath his skin and he used it carefully, winding Charm around himself and hoping for the best. It wasn't the princess's fault. And if he used a little mageborn power to smooth over the rough beginning, so be it.

'Your highness,' she murmured in response. No one quite knew how to address him. He wasn't a king. Or at least not a king in the way Rynn's father was, with a throne and a crown. If they knew what kind of king he really was, they'd never be so friendly. They certainly wouldn't be parading their daughters in front of him.

Rynn would never sit on her father's throne. She had several older siblings. She'd never be the woman her grandmother was, either. Bastien knew that just from looking at her. Her duty was to marry well, into another royal house.

Did the Dowager have her sights set on the throne of Larelwynn? That would be a mistake, too. He didn't want it. It was not his.

And the throne that was his… well, no one would want to share that. But they didn't know the truth of the Hollow King, and what the Larelwynns had made of him.

'You will dance with her, Prince Bastien,' the Dowager Queen said. It wasn't an invitation but an order. She was still looking past him at Grace. Challenging her.

'Grandmother,' Rynn interrupted suddenly. 'You can't ask him to abandon his companion. It would be rude.'

She genuinely looked appalled. As did Grace. Although in Grace's case it was more likely to be because the attention of the Dowager was back on her presence there. If Grace could fade into the walls here, she would, this very instant. Bastien felt like joining her but knew that would never be possible. For either of them.

'No one asked your opinion, girl,' the old woman snapped. Rynn flinched and bowed her head. 'You'll do as you're told. Or face the consequences.'

Consequences? What did that mean? Was she threatening her own grandchild? It shouldn't surprise him. She had that reputation and she wasn't afraid to wield it.

But Grace interrupted before he could reply. 'The Lord of Thorns is free to dance with whomever he wishes, your royal highness. And I am not much of a dancer. I'm here for his protection, nothing more.'

Well, they all knew that was a lie. Bastien turned to her, ready to tell her otherwise, but her face was like granite.

'Grace?' he said, his confusion getting the better of him. It probably saved him from making a severe blunder.

She gave him the blandest smile in her arsenal. 'We discussed this before, *your majesty…*'

A warning. He was doing something wrong. Making a mistake. She could see it and she was right. Damn it. She was always right. Her survival instincts were so much better than his. Years of surviving on Rathlynn's streets rather than in its palace, hunting the worst of the mageborn. And yet she had navigated the palace at Rathlynn as carefully. This was no different.

He lifted his hands to Rynn in invitation.

'Well then, common sense prevails,' the Dowager Queen laughed. Everyone else tried to look anywhere except at him. 'But it is not time yet, *Prince* Bastien. You must wait a little longer.'

She smiled, a wicked, cruel smile. And he knew he'd been played again. *Prince Bastien.* The message in that was clear enough. It sent a chill through him. They wouldn't recognise him until he did what they wanted. He would be a king only when she decided that he was one. On her terms. Everyone here bent to her will.

'Rynn, you will dance with the Lord of Thorns as soon as the musicians are ready. You'll like them, Prince Bastien. They're mageborn. Enjoy yourselves this evening. We will speak again soon. I feel we have much to discuss.'

And like that, they were dismissed.

Bastien swept Grace to the edge of the room as quickly as he could. 'What happened? What was all that about?'

She didn't meet his gaze for a moment. 'Bastien,' she sighed, looking for an escape. 'You have to think. You said we can't afford to offend the Dowager Queen.'

'I remember.'

She leaned in close and her voice was a breath against the skin of his neck. 'Then think. *Think*, my love. What do you think is happening here?'

'Nothing is happening here. Not yet. Not now.'

She looked into his eyes then and the weight of sorrow in her gaze made him take a step back in alarm. 'You'd be safe. With them behind you. Safe from Aurelie and Asher.'

'But…'

'It was always going to come to this.'

He caught her arm before she could pull away, and he didn't think about the way it would look. Or about the many eyes watching them right now.

Grace didn't move. He released her carefully. She didn't appreciate being dragged around by anyone. 'You can't risk your position here for me,' she told him. 'I'd be derelict in my duty if I let you. I'll step outside if that's easier. I'm here if you need me but—'

'Grace please…'

This couldn't be happening. She couldn't let him do this. She couldn't be all right with it. She pressed a finger to his lips.

'Dance with the girl,' she said. 'I don't mind.' She was lying. He knew that. Her face flushed as she said the words. 'Do what you *have* to do.'

The music started up behind them and he didn't have a choice any more. He had promised and Rynn was waiting. So was the Dowager Queen.

He had to force himself to turn away from Grace. It was like walking to his doom.

The old woman looked so smug as Bastien crossed the floor to meet the princess. The crowd parted around them, everyone watching.

Rynn looked no happier about this than he did, but she was putting on a brave face. He could at least do the same. And she was the perfect partner, trained to perfection. She moved with him as if they were lovers who had spent years matching each other in every way. She was the epitome of grace.

Except the only Grace he was interested in had taken the first opportunity to slip through the doors to the garden outside.

The music paused, and so did they, the pair of them isolated in the centre of the ballroom with every eye upon them. There was no escape.

'My noble guests,' the Dowager Queen announced in a voice surprisingly strong for someone so old. She had all the power here, and she wielded it as the weapon it was. 'We hereby give leave to Prince Bastien Larelwynn of Rathlynn to begin formal courtship of our beloved granddaughter, the Rose of the Valenti, Princess Rynn Elenore Layna de Valens of Gellen. He desires that she will be the Rose to the Lord of Thorns.'

He'd made no agreement, and no such offer of courtship. This was Lara's doing. Or the Dowager's. It didn't matter which one. Arranged from afar or behind his back. Bastien couldn't help himself. He cursed under his breath, words Grace, Daniel and Ellyn had picked up in Eastferry, and he had picked up from them far too easily.

The sharp inhalation of breath from his partner made him turn his attention to her. Because she wasn't Grace, who would have rolled her eyes, or mocked him, if she'd felt like humouring him at all. Which she wouldn't right now.

'My apologies, your highness.'

'Don't,' she said, and the delicate little princess appeared to have evaporated. She gave him a look that was all steel. 'I need to talk to you and this is about the only chance we'll get. It can't wait. I have information. It's about Ellyn de Bruyn.'

Chapter Four

The wide silver mirror dominated the centre of the table, lying flat like a pool of water. It was older than the kingdom, or so Aurelie had been told. Older than her home, perhaps. It should be in the treasury, along with a hundred other magical objects, garnered by the Larelwynns over so many generations. Celeste claimed to have brought it with her when she first came here, back when she was the Little Goddess. When the Larelwynns had trapped her in the Temple – and that was where it had stayed. The problem was, as Aurelie was finding, the things Celeste told them could be true, or could be fantasy, or could just be lies told for her own amusement. She couldn't be relied upon, and the fact that Asher kept going to her for advice was driving Aurelie to distraction.

He was meant to be her lover, her servant, and her right hand.

But all he seemed to think about was the insane goddess locked inside the Temple, with her powers locked inside her. Not his queen, not their kingdom.

'Pour the water on it,' said Celeste, as if speaking to a particularly dull child. 'Slowly now. Slowly. Don't spill it.'

'It's pointless,' Aurelie said, but they both ignored her. Water from the fountain of the Temple gardens, collected by innocent hands. Those hands, and their innocence, were gone now. She hated the ravings of Celeste Larelwynn. A goddess she might have been, once upon a time, but now she was diminished, her power locked away by a sigil burned into her skin by her brother, the Lord of Thorns, Bastien Larelwynn. A parting gift.

Celeste couldn't even take magic from the mageborn Aurelie had imprisoned any more. Oh, she tried. But for every dozen they rounded up, she could extract barely the magic of one, and they took so long to recover now, if they recovered at all. She'd killed too many of them.

Aurelie's own cravings were not so easily satisfied. Celeste would not cooperate. She couldn't – or wouldn't – share the magic for which the queen hungered.

The mageborn were laughing at her, Aurelie was certain of that. So were the rest of them, all the quotidian, little commoners… the Thorns in her side. She could lock them up, torture them, kill them… it didn't help.

'There,' Asher said. Water covered the mirror to the edge of the ornate golden frame. Ripples spread out as they leaned over it, distorting their reflections. But there was nothing magic about it. Not yet. 'What next?'

'Blood,' Celeste murmured and a pang of fear shot through the queen. If Celeste wanted blood things could get very messy indeed. Very quickly. 'It's always blood. The oldest magic, the first spells, they were all born in blood. I bathed in blood.'

'Whose blood?' Asher asked. He didn't even sound particularly worried. If Celeste wanted his would he spill it for her? Probably. How much? What if she wanted it all? Aurelie stared at him, aghast, but he didn't seem to notice.

'For this?' Celeste sighed wistfully. 'Larelwynn blood would be best. Or royal blood.' She said it almost absently, distracted and only partially aware of her words. Aurelie took a step out of range. Safety didn't come into it. She wasn't sure anyone would ever be safe from Celeste.

'Don't even think of it.'

Asher laughed. 'No one is harming the child, my love,' he said in a suddenly tender voice. 'We need that little bundle of joy intact.' Then his voice hardened. 'Remember, Celeste?'

Celeste narrowed her eyes, working her way through whatever labyrinth of thoughts was jumbled together in her head. Then she sighed like a child herself. 'Very well then, but it won't be the same. Divine blood will do it. My blood. There's so much you can do with divine blood. Don't worry. I'll heal. I know you're concerned, your majesty. Here, give me a knife.'

All the same Aurelie stepped further away as Asher Kane handed over the bone-handled knife he carried at his belt.

'Divinity,' he said, and all but bowed. Aurelie pursed her lips, watching them together. He was lucky the crazy bitch didn't slash his throat right now.

How did one dispose of a goddess? There had to be a way. But then, why had the first Larelwynns imprisoned Celeste in the Temple? Had it simply been to keep her out of the way? It wasn't like she had ever been of any help. All she did was manipulate and control people.

Well, not Aurelie. She would not be used by anyone. Not any more. Celeste might influence weaker minds, like Asher, but she would never worm her way into Aurelie's head. She'd make sure of that.

She watched as Celeste sliced open the pad of her index finger and let her rich, dark blood drip into the water.

'Come here,' the former goddess said. 'Close your eyes. Let the darkness in.'

Asher obeyed and with all the formality of a high priestess Celeste anointed his eyelids with her blood. Then she drew a crescent on his brow. The final stage was a daub of blood on his lips.

'This is the oldest magic, Asher. My blessing. Once people would kill for the honour and I would make them mine.'

For a moment nothing happened but then he gave a shudder of pleasure. Aurelie didn't know what he was feeling but she recognised the rush of power as it rippled through him. 'My goddess,' he murmured. 'You honour me.'

Celeste turned to Aurelie, who glared at her. 'I don't need honours,' she said after a long moment. To her surprise Celeste just smiled, a knowing smile which sent another shiver through the queen's body. Jealousy of the magic coursing through Asher didn't mean she was willing to submit to Celeste. She wasn't that far gone. Not yet.

'No matter,' said Celeste. 'One day you'll wear my blood, Aurelie. I've seen that. And then you'll be mine.'

Aurelie narrowed her eyes, silently promising herself that she'd never do any such thing.

Celeste dropped the knife, a forgotten toy, and the cut healed itself.

The blood in the water swirled like ink, or a flower unfurling, spreading out, and Celeste murmured words in a language Aurelie didn't understand. It made the hairs on the back of her neck stand up, grating along the inside of her bones.

And slowly the water cleared. More than cleared. The reflection of the room drifted away and another scene appeared. In spite of herself, Aurelie drew closer once more, staring at the images moving in the mirror.

'That's the Valenti court,' said Asher. 'Well, he's resourceful. We knew that.'

'He's my brother,' Celeste purred. 'He's a shining star. He always has been. All kings and queens should bow to him.'

Aurelie scowled. She'd rot in the ground before that happened.

All the same she couldn't tear her eyes off him. Bastien Larelwynn had always fascinated her. She couldn't help it. Marius had been sick and wan, a weakling from the day they married. Bastien, on the other hand… Celeste was right. He *was* a shining star. He burned with the darkest fire she had ever seen.

Men didn't ignore her. They never had. She used that and relied on it. Asher had been an easy conquest, and an inventive lover. And in all things but his infatuation with Celeste, he was everything she could have wanted.

Except… he wasn't Bastien.

He wasn't a Larelwynn either. Oh, and he knew it. He was the last of his family, because he and his sister Hanna had murdered them all. She had become Mother Miranda, leader of the Temple and the keeper of Celeste Larelwynn, until her downfall, until Bastien had destroyed her. Asher had relatives in half the royal families that Aurelie knew of. He was rich beyond reason. But it was never enough. Not for someone like him. Nothing and no one was ever enough.

The crackle of magic in the bowl tugged at Aurelie, drawing her closer. She felt the same addiction he did. She'd never forget the feeling of stolen magic coursing through her, the power, and the sheer strength it lent her.

She longed for that feeling again. But some things came with too high a price. Coupled with an image of Bastien there, she couldn't draw away.

Images moved in the mirror. The ballroom, figures dancing…

'That isn't the charming Captain Marchant he's dancing with,' Asher said, his tone a mocking drawl.

'She's not a captain any more,' Aurelie snapped before she could stop herself. 'I stripped her of that rank.' It sounded petty even as she said it.

'Of course you did, my love.' There was a smirk behind his calm words. She could feel it. She didn't want to look at him, not painted with Celeste's blood, but she couldn't tear her eyes away.

All his attention was on the mirror anyway. She'd take another lover soon, she decided. Oh, she needed Asher and she'd keep him on side, but this time… someone dark-haired and golden-skinned, with eyes like pools of night. With a rush of satisfaction she imagined the moment Asher would walk in on *that*.

'We knew he'd gone to the Valenti Islands. It wasn't a big leap of imagination, Asher. But who is that girl he's dancing with?'

Celeste began to sing. The tune was simple and childlike and it twisted Aurelie's stomach. '*She's the prettiest girl in the world, the prettiest girl in the world. She's lithe as a gazelle, and graceful as well…*'

Aurelie couldn't take it any longer. 'Enough, Celeste! I asked a question.'

It was Asher who answered. 'She's a Valenti princess, King Roderick's youngest. Rynn Elenore Layna de Valens of Gellen.' The name came from his mouth like music. Aurelie remembered a time when people used to say her name that way. 'My third cousin once removed, or something like that, on my mother's side.' He leaned in conspiratorially. 'They say she's even more beautiful than you were.' She sucked in a breath and stared at him. His grin turned nasty. 'At that age,' he added, a final twist to the knife.

Two lovers. Both looking like Bastien Larelwynn. And she'd make Asher watch. And then she'd turn them on him as well. She'd have them overpower him and—

'The Valenti are playing politics in the oldest way imaginable,' Celeste said. 'She's pretty. She glows. I know that glow. If she marries him, we could bring her back here as well and play with her. The Dowager Rhyannon will understand, won't she?' She giggled and grabbed Asher's shirt, pulling him towards her. 'Can you imagine, Asher? Do you think she'll scream?'

'Enough,' Aurelie snapped and drew herself up to her full height, steeling her spine. She was the queen here. They needed to remember that. This was her kingdom now and she meant to keep it that way. 'He'll never take up with her. Not while he has his beloved Grace beside him. I know Bastien.'

Celeste laughed at her, releasing Asher Kane. 'Better than I do? My own brother?'

'He's not the brother you remember. Not any more. And you… you can't even get out of this room, let alone the Temple. You have no power now.'

'Aurelie…' Asher tried to intercede but that only made her anger burn all the brighter.

'I'm going. This fiasco isn't telling us anything we don't already know.'

'But it is,' Celeste crooned. 'Of course it is. Can't you hear them?'

'No, of course I can't. It's images in water. There's nothing to hear.'

Celeste glowered at her. 'Should have let me paint you. They'll be married. We'll have a new queen.' She turned to Asher like a child in search of a present. 'I want a new queen.'

Like a replacement? Or a toy?

Enough. That was enough. Aurelie slammed her fist down on the mirror, which shattered with an almighty crash. Glass and bloody water flew everywhere and beneath the cracks an endless darkness opened up. Celeste shrieked but Asher caught her in his arms as Aurelie swept from the room, slamming the door behind her. The carriage awaited her in the courtyard. One of the attendants offered his arm to help her in and she glanced at him. He fought not to recoil from her obvious rage, which only made it even worse. She shoved him aside and seated herself, spreading out her skirts and taking a deep, calming breath.

'Aurelie, wait,' Asher called from the far side of the courtyard. She heard him running. He jumped through the door before the carriage set off and landed at her feet. He tilted his head up to look at her and gave her that wicked smile. 'Going without me?'

The urge to kick him out was powerful. But when he looked at her like that…

She grabbed a fistful of his hair and dragged him up, face to face with her.

'Wipe that shit off your face,' she told him. 'Remember who is the queen here, Asher. It isn't her. It never will be. Nor that Valenti bitch.'

His pupils went wide with desire and he smiled, not that knowing smirk which so irritated her. This was a smile of relief. His face was a picture of pure lust. Slowly, deliberately, he brought his hand up to his face, smearing the blood into his flesh until all that remained was a flush of heated skin. He locked his gaze with hers the entire time.

'Only you, my queen. No one else.'

Perhaps she didn't need to replace him just yet. He had his uses. So many uses.

'That's better.'

But when she kissed him, she still imagined Bastien. And she wondered if Bastien pictured Grace Marchant when he kissed his princess. At least she had the satisfaction of knowing that if he had fallen under the power of the Dowager Queen of Valenti, he'd never be with the jumped-up Academy whore again.

She pushed Asher away. 'You're going on a trip.'

'A what?'

'A journey. To Valenti. As my representative. If Bastien Larelwynn is getting married there should be someone there from home, shouldn't there?'

Asher bowed his head, his smile so cruel she could almost forgive him his obsessions. Almost.

'Of course, and I'll bring them back. Celeste wants to meet her future sister-in-law. Isn't that sweet?'

Aurelie suppressed a shudder. She doubted if it was anything but sweet. Quite the opposite.

Chapter Five

Cold night air closed around her and Grace drew in a breath, the first that seemed to actually fill her lungs since she'd seen Bastien with the princess in his arms. They looked perfect together, like they belonged with each other. Their breeding, their education, their elegance… everything.

She dragged another breath in and leaned on the marble balustrade overlooking the lagoon. The water beneath her glittered with a thousand lights. It moved and swirled, rippling like the Maegen, the source of all the mageborn power, did in her dreams. But it was dark, entirely dark, beneath the surface reflections.

She had to be strong for him, for Bastien, because she'd always known this would happen. Well, not *this*. Not exactly this. But she'd known that they couldn't be together. That Bastien being who he was would tear them apart.

Because they didn't belong together. They were from different worlds.

And if he was to be safe – if any of them were to be safe – he needed to marry Rynn. It was the only thing that made sense.

Movement behind her made Grace turn but it was just another couple of guests stepping out into the night. They started when they saw her and then scurried off into the garden to the right, the woman casting a resentful glance at Grace as she went. The look the man gave her was darker by far.

Making friends wherever I go, Grace thought.

She stared down into the water and tried to persuade herself to go back inside. But she didn't seem to be able to move.

Something shivered down her spine, a warning, an alarm. She hadn't felt anything like it since they'd left Rathlynn. Not until last night.

Before they had been attacked and Ellyn had disappeared.

This time it was stronger.

She pulled out the knife she had hidden in the length of sea-green material wrapped around her waist. It felt right in her hand, perfectly weighted. She had only one sigil: the small metal disc etched with enchantments which had been masquerading as a pendant, hiding the warrant behind it. She couldn't afford to activate it without good reason, but she took it in hand anyway.

With danger so nearby, she felt the absence of Ellyn and Daniel keenly. They ought to be here to back her. And Bastien was busy wooing a princess. Or being wooed. Playing politics with people's hearts. Her heart.

She pushed that thought to the rear of her mind. This wasn't the time for that.

The thread of magic twisted out across the air and Grace sucked in a resigned breath.

With her magic restored, tracking mageborn was easier than it once had been, but it still made her head ache and her stomach churn. If she wasn't careful she'd have a migraine before she found the source.

All the same, she followed the trail of magic, like a scent, across the balcony, down the steps and into the garden. Roses bloomed all around her, rich and heavy with petals, their perfume thick in the air. In the darkness beneath them things rustled and shifted, furtive, dangerous, moving in shadows.

Goddess, she hoped Daniel had found Ellyn.

She forced herself to focus, to put herself in the here and now. Thinking like this could get her killed.

The garden rustled and moved. The scent of rich earth choked her but Grace pushed on. And in the furthest corner she heard a muffled cry. The trace of magic was stronger now, like too much wine or rich food. Her head pounded.

This was a bad idea.

A cry of alarm rang out like the cry of a night bird, sharp and terrible, out of place in this garden.

Magic flared white-hot, burning through her. Whoever wielded it had let it loose like a wave and it was strong. Far stronger than was safe.

The Maegen surged up inside her, the fire that was part of her racing through her veins in response. She reached the far end of the garden, where in a tiny bower decked with night-flowering jasmine, she saw the woman who had left the party after her. She stood over a pile of vines and roots. They moved like serpents, winding around a struggling shape. As they moved, she saw a gap, a face… The man the woman had left with.

A brief cry escaped his lips, quickly silenced as the writhing mass of vegetation squeezed tighter on his prone form.

The woman smiled and her eyes glowed with an unnatural light, golden in the darkness like twin suns.

Hollow. She was hollow.

The most dangerous of the mageborn: those overwhelmed by their magic, lost in that glowing light, unable to control what they were any more. It was the very thing that Bastien, as Lord of Thorns, had struggled to control in Rathlynn. It was the reason that, as the Hollow King, he had first made the pact with Lucien Larelwynn which had ended the Magewar. And led to Bastien and their people being effectively enslaved for centuries.

Grace didn't hesitate. She flung herself forward. She couldn't risk throwing the sigil. It was the only one she had. But before she could reach the edge of the bower, something huge and unyielding burst from the ground in front of her.

Dirt blinded her as she hit it hard. A root, an enormous root, which threw her up and then wrapped itself around her, dragging her forwards, into full view.

She was trapped. In seconds she could be dead.

The woman – a Loam, Grace now realised – her eyes still aglow, studied Grace impassively. The natural world over which the Loam's branch of the mageborn had power shivered in anticipation, waiting for her command. But she didn't move. Slowly, she tilted her head towards her shoulder, her eyes blazing.

'Well, you aren't what I was expecting,' she said at last. The root shook Grace. She kept her hands clenched around her knife hilt and the sigil. She couldn't afford to lose either.

'Let him go.'

The woman glanced towards her victim whose struggles were weaker now, fading fast.

'Him? Shouldn't you be more concerned about yourself? Do you know what he was intending to do to me? Do you know how many women he has lured out here? Alone? Defenceless?'

Grace could imagine. Her opinion of the so-called nobility hadn't improved much since meeting them. The Loam watched her former attacker with a kind of detached interest as his struggles weakened.

The root tightened around Grace, ready to slowly crush her, and the woman didn't seem to notice or care.

Grace was out of time. Her skills learned at the Academy weren't getting her out of this, not the mundane ones at any rate.

But she had other skills. Ones that didn't come from the Academy at all. She closed her eyes and reached for the otherness inside her. Now it was part of her again but she still didn't really trust it. Being close to Bastien, entering the Maegen, had brought it back. Not to full strength perhaps. Or maybe she had never been as powerful as all that. But it didn't matter.

It was all she had.

Fire roared through her, burning the enchanted vegetation binding her. The Loam screamed, the shock of her power being repelled sending her staggering.

Grace fell heavily, her handprints seared into the ground. Flames licked the area around her, blackening the earth and devouring the dry grass in hungry, glowing lines. Her hair spilled around her face and, as she looked up through it, she saw the woman backing away, concern suddenly flickering over her beautiful features. Fear.

'You're a Flint,' she said and licked her lips nervously. She straightened her clothing and took a step towards Grace. No Loam was going to feel easy around a Flint. Fire burned all living things. 'Of course… You're *his* Flint.'

'I'm my own Flint.' Grace dragged herself up to her feet and pushed her hair out of her face. She should have tied it back, regardless of balls and dresses and everything else.

The dress was ruined anyway. Great. This was why she couldn't have nice things.

'Grace Marchant,' the noblewoman said as she stepped forwards. 'You could be so much more. If you just had the courage to reach out and seize it. It's waiting for you. There's a sacrifice, of course. But everything worthwhile demands a sacrifice. Especially magic. Oh… it could make you so strong, little Flint. Little broken Flint. It whispers, the voices in the depths. I've heard so much about you.'

Grace didn't have time for this nonsense. 'Have you? Because I don't have a single clue who you are. Let him go.'

The vines smothering the man retreated. He lay still, unconscious, but breathing, albeit weakly. Would he live? Grace had no way of knowing. But if she didn't get out of this situation quickly, she wouldn't.

And the next moment there was another, greater problem.

'Grace?' Bastien's voice broke through the tense silence, fraught with concern. 'Grace, where are you?'

The woman started at the sound of his voice. Something flickered over her features; terror. Grace knew it at once. The mageborn woman was terrified of the sound of his voice. She retreated, baring her teeth, and the vegetation all around them recoiled, shivering, trying to draw up around her and protect her. The reek of fear was palpable.

'The Lord of Thorns,' the Loam whispered and then she froze. Abruptly, her glowing eyes faded to utter darkness, like holes in her head. The still burning patches of grass lit her up with an infernal light. '*Larelwynn*,' she hissed in a voice like a winter wind. The fear was gone. This was eagerness, and it was terrible. She didn't sound like herself. She barely sounded human.

Grace's skin tightened in alarm. The sense of magic roared through her, not a ripple now. An ocean.

Bastien burst through the bushes as if they recoiled from his touch, or he commanded them out of the way. Either was possible. The woman straightened still further, but now she smiled, like a jealous lover seeing an old flame in pain.

'*Hello, Bastien Larelwynn,*' the voice said from the Loam's lips and, this time, Grace knew that it definitely wasn't human. She wasn't sure what it was. It made her skin tighten around her bones, froze every scrap of moisture in her body. Her heart, trapped in her ribcage, hammered away at the base of her throat.

She knew it. From somewhere. Somewhere dark and terrible, somewhere she had seen in the depths between life and death…

She remembered it…

An answering something in Bastien, that bleak otherness, reared up to confront it.

'Grace, step behind me.' His voice was calm but empty and the glow that entered his eyes was bright and terrible. He was pulling on all the magic in him.

But it wasn't going to be enough. She didn't know how she knew that, but she did.

'*We remember her,*' said the voice. '*Fascinating. You made her stronger. Much stronger.*' The Loam stretched out a hand and Grace stiffened. Something ghosted over her skin, a breath of air or a cool breeze. '*How many times have you brought her back? A new sacrifice in the making, it seems. Is she three times dead, Bastien, twice entombed? Is she for us? Oh, Bastien, the things we will do…*'

It happened so quickly, so impossibly quickly. The scent of roses swept around her, through her, perfume so overwhelming that she couldn't think for a moment. It grew stronger, thicker, turning to the stench of mulch and decay. Grace choked on it, gagging as it smothered her. Bastien's arms tightened to pull her to safety but he was too late.

The Loam smiled, a strange, mad twist of her mouth, baring all her teeth, and she reached out and touched the warrant.

Just one touch, a fingertip. The metal went so cold against Grace's skin, it burned.

And the fire inside her was gone. Just… gone… A void nestled there instead, an emptiness.

Bastien turned on the Loam – or whatever she was now – with a snarl of rage.

The Loam didn't recoil this time. She opened her arms to him. '*We have missed you so much, brother.*'

For a moment she sounded so like Celeste, that same tone, that arrogance and superiority. That insanity. But it wasn't Celeste. Grace knew that.

Grace's eyesight swam as if she was underwater, as if light rippled through the shifting surface far out of reach. Tears burned in the corners of her eyes and the world blurred. There were tentacles, and eyes, and so many teeth…

She could see them, shadows contorting beneath the woman's flesh, coiling, writhing.

'What have you done?' Bastien growled, standing between Grace and the Loam like a dark star. Light surged in him, the power of the Hollow King, all the magic he bottled up inside.

From somewhere, Grace found her voice.

'Who… who are you?' she asked, forcing out the words through a tight throat that seemed to be blocked with her racing heart.

The Loam gave her a condescending smile, ignoring Bastien completely. She wasn't just a mageborn any more. She was something else.

'*Dear little Flint… you're not dealing with mere temporal royalty now. We are beyond that. And you belong to us…*'

'Enough!' Bastien roared. 'Leave her alone. Be gone from this place. Now.'

The Loam laughed. Stood there in the face of his fury and laughed out loud. '*You never change, do you? Oh, Bastien… it's so good to be free. Oh, how we will dance. And burn. And break the world apart. All those humans, all those fools… fragile little mayflies… But not her. She has been intimate with the darkness in her world and ours. She knows us. Celeste was right. She is perfect…*'

And then the Loam crumpled up like a rag doll, falling onto the ground with a dull thud.

Bastien rushed towards her, dropping to his knees beside her and rolling her onto her back.

'Breathe, please. Please breathe.'

But the woman stared sightlessly up at the night's sky without seeing a thing.

Grace's head swam; it was like she was moving through honey.

'Bastien?' She felt so strange. The warrant was still like ice and the void inside her had sucked away all feelings.

He took one look at her and, the next thing she knew, he was holding her, pressing his hands to either side of her head.

'Let me in, Grace. Let me help. Please. Before it's too late.' The words were urgent… desperate… and she nodded, too afraid to deny him.

The light in him rushed through her, golden and glorious, like sunshine, his power strengthening and stabilising her own.

Except her own wasn't there any more.

She was so used to the emptiness of her stolen magic since her childhood that it almost felt normal again to find it missing. It felt like her magic had been sucked right out of her. It wasn't possible. The woman was a Loam, not a Leech.

But she'd been Hollow.

And then... then she had been something else. Something Grace recognised, remembered. From the darkness beneath the Maegen.

She looked into Bastien's eyes, finally able to see again. He'd never looked so worried.

'Bastien? What did it do?' But she knew. Somewhere deep down, instinctively, she knew...

'Show me the warrant,' he said, his voice grim. Once again, she didn't dare to argue. It dangled between them, dull in the light from beyond the garden. It wasn't gold now. The metal looked tarnished, rippled with oily rainbows of light.

He pulled her into his arms, buried his face in her hair.

'This can't be happening,' he murmured.

She pushed him back, trying to ground him, to make him focus. 'What?'

'That... that was the voice of my sibling... or siblings... You saw it... aspects of it anyway, in the Maegen. A mind that is many and one, and utterly inhuman. That was the Deep Dark. And I think... Grace, I think it marked you.'

Chapter Six

The Maegen swirled, glowing with its own life, and Grace was lost in it. It swamped all her senses, covering her, filling her. There was no Bastien here, no one else. Just her and light and that pulsing warmth, the glow that never died.

And underneath it…

The darkness…

She was lost and empty inside. The ache was deep and endless. She could feel it clearly, a void inside her. Where her magic had been.

She knew it of old but she had never named it before. When Mother Miranda of the Temple stole her magic and her memories, back in her childhood, that space had been left behind. Hungry and dangerous.

She'd filled it with study, with the Academy, with her work. With hunting monsters and protecting the innocent. With her friends who had become her family.

With Bastien Larelwynn and a world of emotion she thought would never be hers. And her magic, although still weak, had come back to her. Because of him.

Dark threads whispered through the light, like ink in a boiling pool. She didn't know why but she stretched out her hand towards it. It threaded between her fingers, latched onto her and pulled.

She sank like a stone, unable to fight, unable to cry out. Darkness coiled around her, surprisingly gentle, each touch a caress.

It would be so easy to give up. So easy to let herself fall further into its embrace, to let it take her and be one with it. So very easy to pretend that it was Bastien holding her. That she was safe.

The Deep Dark tightened its grip, greedy and possessive, vicious now, determined to hold onto her this time. Grace dragged herself free, tearing it off her limbs strand by strand. But each time she thought she'd done it, there was more. There was always more, always shadows on her, always dragging her deeper.

She couldn't do it alone. They were inside her, in that empty place. Lodged there like parasites.

She needed Bastien. She needed—

Laughter shook around her, pulsating through the darkness and the light. 'He is us, part of us. And we are the same, eternal. You can be too.'

'I don't want eternity.'

It paused, as if allowing her the time to think about what she just said. 'Don't you? Not even with him? Beloved…'

Eternity with him? Yes. She would take eternity with him. She loved him. She hadn't really fathomed quite how much.

It gave her strength, strength she desperately needed to pull free.

But the voice was insidious. 'We can give him to you, forever, Grace Marchant. We can give you everything. Imagine it. You could rule with him. You could make everything right, care for the weak, seek the truth and mete out justice on wrongdoers. You can punish them. Stop the monsters. You can shine a light on the darkness. Beloved…'

Its myriad voices cajoled and murmured, rippled around her, caressing her, a choir of temptation. She could feel its desire for her… though whether to possess her or rend her limb from limb she didn't know. It wasn't love. It definitely wasn't love. It was possessive and greedy, determined to dig its grasping hands into every part of her. The Deep Dark wanted her. And it would give her everything she wanted if she just gave up and let it in.

What was she thinking? Was this her voice, or something else, something darker? Bastien trusted her. How could she betray him now? Join with the Deep Dark, his oldest adversary and let him go… No.

She reached for him with her body and her soul. The light above was everything and she yearned for it, for him…

Something vast and endless closed around her, something far greater than she could ever be, bright and blinding, all-encompassing. That power was more than her mind could fully comprehend but she gave herself up to him anyway.

Bastien enfolded her and pulled her to safety, into the light.

*

She gasped as she woke from her nightmare and he was still holding her, cradling her. Even though she was lying in their bed. Safe, warm, the bedclothes twisted around her. She curled around him, their bodies drawn together by gravity and a thousand other things. It was still dark. Bastien didn't look like he'd slept at all.

'Grace, my love, please… please don't… It's just a nightmare.'

She ignored his protestations and wrapped her arms around him, holding him close.

'I thought I was lost.' Her voice came out as a broken croak. It felt like she'd been screaming for weeks.

'You're safe. You're here. With me.' He didn't sound so sure. 'Oh Grace.'

'It had me, like it had that woman. That Loam…'

She'd seen the darkness in the woman's eyes, the void after the light. Those who were hollow were wild, out of control, but the Loam had known exactly what she was talking about. Or rather something inside her had. The same voices now lodged in Grace's own head.

Bastien held her tighter. 'Nightborn.' He said the word like it was a curse. 'The Deep Dark took one of the mageborn, drew on all her fear and pain, and made her nightborn. And then it killed her. Just to show us that it could.'

His touch, his warmth... she curled in against his chest. She could feel his heart, thudding away in harmony with her own.

But the warrant was still cold against her skin. Cold and empty, mottled with darkness.

She needed to focus. That was key now. Calm down, gather information, so she could understand. Think.

'I've encountered hollow mageborn before. This was worse. She was coherent. But her voice...'

'I know, love.'

He was watching her too closely, as if he expected her to... what? Attack him? Break down? Change?

'I'm okay,' she told him, even if she wasn't so sure herself. Something felt different. That dreadful emptiness... What had that woman done to her?

She struggled to sit up, even when he protested and tried to make her lie down again. Bastien still thought he could boss her around. Perhaps he always would. It was almost endearing.

Grace smiled at him and, instead of obeying, she got out of the bed before he could stop her.

Her legs felt wobbly but she hid it, steeling herself.

'Tell me about the nightborn,' she said. It was morning anyway, almost. Not quite dawn and the hour of Lauds. But she wasn't going to sleep now, not with those nightmares waiting. She should get up and start the search for Ellyn again.

She heard him move, slowly, carefully, like a stalking panther.

'Are you sure you're okay?' He stroked the skin of her neck, always sensitive, responsive, especially to him. Slowly, deliberately, he lifted her nightshirt and let his hands explore underneath.

'Trying to distract me, your highness?' she asked.

He kissed the place where her neck met her shoulder, then the nape of her neck, sliding his arms around her to cup her breasts. His thumb teased over the tightening buds of her nipples. It sent shivers right through her and she suppressed a sigh of pleasure and pushed the temptation away.

'Is it working?' That teasing tone, so knowing, so arousing… He knew exactly what he was doing.

'Answer me, Bastien. You know you'll have to eventually.'

He sighed. The rush of his breath on her bare skin almost made her lose her mind. But it was his final play, wasn't it? In other circumstances she would have smiled.

'Nightborn,' he said, as if he couldn't quite bring himself to voice the name. 'It was… it was long ago. I barely remember. I mean, I knew the stories but not the reality. I didn't remember at all for many years.'

She looked over her shoulder, met his gaze. The shame of it haunted his eyes. 'Not your fault.'

He smiled, or at least tried to. 'No. Not my fault. But still…' He fetched that soft, silken robe she loved so much. He slipped it around her and tied the belt. Then he sat down on the edge of the bed.

'During the Magewar we lost control. The Deep Dark rose from the depths of the Maegen, from the place where my sister the Little Goddess and I had banished it, and it took the mageborn, transforming them, so many of them. By the time I realised what the nightborn were… well…' He hung his head, unable to look at her.

Grace drew him back to the bed and sat beside him, tucking her legs under her and leaning against him. She wrapped her arms around him this time, her head on his shoulder, and she waited for him to find the strength to go on.

'By the time I did… It was too late,' he said on a shaking breath. For a moment, he choked, unable to continue. He inhaled, let the air back out in a rush. 'It infected people. That's the only word I've ever found to describe it. It wasn't their fault. It was… it was like a plague and it would strike at any time. Weak, strong, whatever branch of the mageborn, it didn't matter. First they went hollow. Then… then something else stepped into the space their magic had carved out inside them. Our siblings… Once the mageborn were empty, darkness filled them. Sometimes slowly. Sometimes all at once. Like the Loam tonight. And like her… they did terrible things. At first, perhaps, with some reason, in defence, out of fear… and then… then they just kept killing. Celeste even succumbed. I was the last one. Lost and alone. They burned the valley, trying to drive me out. That was where Larelwynn found me.'

'Lucien Larelwynn?' He'd never talked about that, about the pact and the boy who became a king. She stroked his hair. It was silky and thick, so dark against her skin. He leaned in to her touch, seeking out that comfort.

'Yes. Lucien. He was… he was a good man. Kind. They never tell anyone that. I wouldn't have trusted him otherwise. And I did, Grace. I trusted him until the day he died.' His voice suddenly tightened. Grief. She recognised grief. Divinities, she had heard it in enough voices and she should be used to it by now. But it still hurt to hear it in his. Even after so long. But then, part of the cruelty of all of this, of Bastien's stolen memories, was that he was reliving his losses over and over again. Every time he remembered, he lost his friends again.

'You loved him.' She wasn't naïve enough to think she was the first person he loved. He'd lived so many lives. She took his hands in hers and squeezed.

'I suppose…' He hung his head again, and then lifted her hand to his mouth, kissing her skin. 'It was long ago. Each of the nightborn was… is part of the Deep Dark incarnate. And the Deep Dark is legion, beyond counting, beyond number. It could overrun this whole world if it escaped. And that's what it wants. It was only because of the pact with Lucien that I managed to bring it to ground, to shut it away beneath the Maegen. And now…'

Grace sighed, suddenly understanding. It finally made sense. 'When you pulled me out of the Maegen's depths, out of its grip, we broke something. We let it out. We gave it a way of escape. But the Loam died.'

'Yes. It killed her. Deliberately. It only wanted me to know what it could do, I think. And to see you, and mark… mark the warrant…' *Mark her*, that was what he meant. Change her.

The chill void inside her stirred a little and the warrant felt strangely heavy. Grace closed her eyes.

'What did it do to me? To the warrant?'

'I don't know,' he whispered. He wasn't telling her everything. She knew that. She'd be a fool to think he'd share everything if he thought he was protecting her. Which he clearly did. 'I need to go back to Thorndale. Where it all began. The source of all the mageborn power is there. And… and it's where the Deep Dark comes from, too. I'll be able to undo all this. We can make a stand, keep you safe, stop whatever it's done…' He paused, and she looked up to find him staring down at her.

'But you don't want to go back,' she whispered.

He winced. 'I don't … I don't remember everything that happened there. Not really. What fragments I have are dark and terrible, a bleak place of pain and fear… But, Grace, there's no choice now. If going back there means stopping this, all of this…'

His hand lifted to the warrant, and he brushed it with a tentative finger.

Nothing happened. No reaction. It still felt icy against her skin. Like something dead.

'What do you mean?'

He closed his eyes and leaned forward, pressing his forehead against hers, forcing his breath in and then out again. For a long moment she thought he wouldn't answer and when he finally did, his voice was soft as a sigh.

'The Deep Dark is coming, and all the nightborn will be coming with it.'

'Coming?'

'For me. For you. And for everyone we love.'

Chapter Seven

Danny had always said Kurt would end up in more hot water than he could handle. Kurt had always told his little brother that he liked his water as hot as possible. The moment it cooled down he got suspicious. Because unless you were in trouble, how could you know you were truly alive?

It had always worked as a theory of life. For him anyway.

Sooner or later, he knew he would overdo it. But not yet.

The voyage home from the Valenti Islands had been peaceful enough. He'd enjoyed seeing his brother and surprising Grace Marchant. He even prided himself that there had been a bit of concern for him in her words. Just a little.

He liked his Duchess. Liked her fire and her fury, her straight-down-the-road attitude that always set his brother on the right path, too. It would have been far too easy for Daniel to have ended up in the same life as him. And he wanted better for the younger Parry than that. They had never had a dad. Or at least not one that stuck around for more than a year or so. Ma Parry had been tough as nails, too. Whoever fathered Daniel had left him something of a delicate nature compared to the rest of them.

Kurt had never bothered to ask if they had the same father, but he doubted it. It didn't matter. Daniel was all he had since Ma died.

And it was good to see him safe on Iliz, living in a palace with his pretty harper beside him, and if Kurt missed having Misha's talents at work for him, there were others. He could spare him. The harper had been the best envoy he'd had, but he couldn't begrudge Danny his happiness. Or his safety.

That was his one priority.

That and the remaining people of Eastferry. Mageborn and quotidian alike.

Melia was waiting on the quay. She'd been City Watch once. Before the Watch had been destroyed by the Royal Guard at Aurelie's command, along with the Academy and pretty much all law and order in Rathlynn. She'd been a godsend for him as it turned out – careful, pragmatic, hard as any of the Eastferry gang members he usually employed. But she had a way with people. They weren't terrified of her. That was useful.

He disembarked, paying off the final amount to the captain, who uttered nothing more than the usual grunt. Melia joined him.

'All good?' she asked.

'Not a single complaint. What about here?'

'Quite a number of complaints actually, but we dealt with them. Most of them. We have a problem. It's a nasty business, Kurt.'

'What's that then?'

'Mageborn.' She made a face. Melia didn't have a lot of time for the mageborn. 'Acting… strangely…'

He frowned. 'More strangely than usual?'

She shrugged. 'I'll show you. It isn't pretty. We trapped one of them. Held him for you. It wasn't easy.'

'There's more than one?'

Melia tilted her head to one side. 'Yeah. But they're gone now.'

The tone said it all. No humour there. Gone meant dead. This did not bode well.

She led him along the dock front, along a narrow lane only the rats would call home, to an empty warehouse. Ten of their toughest men and women guarded it. None of them looked happy, every nerve on edge, and no one would meet his eyes. These were hardened foot soldiers in his little makeshift army of Thorns. Whatever they'd seen had left them shaken. Kurt didn't like it. The feeling of uncertainty made his skin itch.

'What happened?'

'It's best you see first,' Melia said. There was a tightness to her voice he'd never heard before. 'We stopped him before it got too bad but… it took a lot to take him down. We weren't expecting anything, no sign of going hollow or what-have-you. It came out of the blue. And he's not the only one. Just the latest.'

With no Academy left in Rathlynn, everyone had to fend for themselves when the mageborn went hollow. It was happening more and more and they were under pressure. Kurt could hardly blame them. No Lord of Thorns to help them now. And if Aurelie's people caught wind of them, she had them rounded up and locked away in the palace. Divinities knew what they did to the mageborn in there. Nothing good, that was for sure. So they hid. Taking off the collars helped only so much, because the collars themselves, with their embedded sigils, served to mitigate the effects of the magic inside them scrabbling to get out. They were afraid and fear made people desperate. And dangerous.

Kurt understood all of this. He'd made it his business to know about the lives of the mageborn. He helped people hide, sometimes helped them escape.

When mageborn went hollow there was precious little that would bring them back. They killed themselves, their magic tearing through them, sometimes taking others with them. It was brutal, but it was over pretty quickly.

This sounded worse than usual. Much worse.

Melia opened the door to the warehouse. It was a huge empty space and in the middle there was a cage, the type used to hold livestock of a more belligerent strain.

The man sitting on his own in the centre of it was playing with something that, at first, Kurt took to be a doll or a puppet. He dangled it in front of him, made it dance, bow, sat it on his knees. He laughed and smiled at it, and then flung it as hard as he could against the bars.

It made a sickening, wet crunch.

'Shit,' Kurt said. It was about as articulate as he could manage.

'Yeah, don't get too close, all right? He used to have to touch people to control them but he seems to have got stronger. We almost lost two of our people trapping him. And we only managed to lure him in there with the body.'

'Whose body?'

Melia grimaced. 'His daughter. He'd already killed her. We were too late to save her life. He was a Gore. I don't know what the fuck he is now.'

Kurt couldn't contain his horror. He stared as the man picked up the small figure again, chastised her for whatever he believed she had done wrong and began to play with her again. The body wasn't going to last much longer. It was barely holding together as it was, only so much dead meat, broken bones and lengths of sinew.

Kurt Parry was not a man generally revolted by the grimmer aspects of his life, or life in Rathlynn, but he almost lost his last meal there and then.

Melia waited patiently while he recovered himself.

'What happened?' he asked.

'We got a message sent from Chandler's Row about noon. He'd gone insane, they said. But when we got there, no one was prepared for it. His eyes, Kurt, do you see his eyes?'

You couldn't miss them. They were black as night. You could see neither iris or pupil, just emptiness. Like holes in his head. Like someone had dug them out and filled the sockets with liquid tar.

And he was clearly insane. No one acted like that when they were in their right mind. Not really. But the magic… it was stronger than Kurt had ever seen in anyone mageborn. Except perhaps Bastien Larelwynn and he wasn't sure that really counted. If you believed Danny, the bastard prince was actually a god or something.

Plus, not insane. Not like this.

Maybe he could send word to them? Maybe Larelwynn would know something?

But that would take too long. And maybe Larelwynn wouldn't answer. Besides, Kurt didn't want to be beholden to the likes of him.

'We need to find out what the fuck he is now,' he muttered.

'Do we need him alive to do that?' Melia asked, matter-of-factly. He always appreciated that about her.

There was another wet crunch.

'Definitely not.'

She pulled out a brutal-looking sigil as a precaution, one of the super strong ones they kept for special cases. They were starting to run low and Kurt didn't like the prospect of running out, especially when faced with this new development.

'You two, with me,' Melia called, and grabbed a pike from the guards who joined them. The three of them circled the cage, but the

Gore kept on playing with his daughter's corpse. 'On three,' she told them, sigils ready in one hand, pike in the other.

It didn't take long. Kurt wasn't sure the Gore even knew what was happening and the pikes were long enough they didn't have to get close. He'd been gone for some time, lost in his own dream or nightmare. The little body lay as still as his.

Kurt didn't feel like food any more. He wanted the strongest drink he could lay his hands on at the Larks' Rest. And he wanted some answers.

He could think of only one place to get them and it was not an enticing prospect. He needed to be careful. He needed a plan. Danny might joke about improvisation like it was a badge of honour but Kurt believed in setting out everything meticulously, right down to the smallest detail.

Melia came back to him, her heart beating just a bit too fast. No one else would probably notice, Kurt thought. But it always paid to pay attention.

'You okay?' he asked.

'Yeah, boss. We'll torch the bodies, scatter the ashes. Nasty business, that's all.' She ran her hands through her cropped hair and shuddered.

Nasty business was an understatement.

'Tell Syl I want to see him, will you? I have a job for him. I'm going to need to get inside that bastard palace.'

Melia gave him a look that said he was insane. 'Why?'

'We need help, Mel. There are mageborn in there, ex-Academy, the ones we haven't got out yet. One of them has got to know something about all this.'

Chapter Eight

Bastien was woken by hammering on the door. He wasn't even aware he'd fallen asleep, watching her, waiting for yet another nightmare. Grace was up first, on her feet and armed, murderous in her half-asleep state.

'Stay there,' she told him.

He wanted to remind her that he was the most powerful magical being in this world and that very little could hurt him, let alone kill him. And he wasn't the one who'd been targeted in the last couple of days by unknown assailants or a host of dark gods intent on chaos. But she didn't look in the mood for an argument.

'Prince Bastien? Grace?' Daniel's voice from the other side of the door sounded frantic and that was enough to propel her forward to open it and let him in. He stumbled inside, Misha following him. 'You were right. We found out where Ell is. She's where you said she'd be.'

'Ellyn?' Grace's voice shook. 'Where? How?'

Bastien needed to explain and fast, before she did something rash. 'Rynn told me. She wanted me to find Ellyn. I don't know why. She told me when we danced. But then…'

He would never forget the moment, the feeling. He'd been dancing with the princess and she'd just told him what she knew about Ellyn and what she suspected it meant. And then he'd felt it – that terrible sucking emptiness, the void in the world and the threat to Grace. Most of all he'd felt Grace, the light in her flickering, going out…

He'd all but run from the ballroom out into the garden. What the Dowager thought of that he didn't dare ask.

He swallowed hard, pushing the thought of that away for now.

'Where?' Grace snarled.

'They locked her up in the most secure prison they have,' said Daniel. 'It's an island, too. Anyone trying to escape alone would drown.'

'Show me,' Grace interrupted. She was already pulling on clothes, ignoring the men around her. When she turned to Bastien, her glare was a warning. 'You knew. Why didn't you tell me?'

'I didn't know if there was anything to this. And besides…'

He didn't add anything about the Deep Dark, or whatever it had done to her.

'Besides nothing. You should have told me. Where is this island, Danny? Where is she?'

Daniel looked from Grace to Bastien and then back again, like a trapped rabbit. 'It's, um… it's not like…'

'It's a royal prison,' Misha answered for him. He still had that trace of nerves in his eyes, especially when faced with Bastien. Perhaps he saw the shadow of Celeste there, reminding Misha of the time she had spent torturing him. 'They use it for anyone in the Dowager's bad graces, usually her family. Other claimants to the throne, traitors, or the people they deem too politically dangerous to have in any of their normal prisons. They have more than you'd think. Ellyn's locked up in one of the most secure places they have. We couldn't get that close to her, but we talked to people. They bring in musicians for some of the prisoners, the rich ones. It's that kind of place. You get what you can pay for. Or what your family can pay for.'

Grace raised her eyebrows, realising what he meant a second before Bastien did himself. '*Musicians.*'

Misha swallowed hard and then nodded. 'Yeah, pretty ones. I only saw her from a distance. But it was definitely her. They weren't keeping her in the posh cells, if you know what I mean. And she wasn't making life easy for herself either. They were taking her down to the isolation cells, underground, the real shitholes.'

They owed him. Owed him big time. Misha might be a musician but he wasn't a whore. That he had played one to get close enough to identify Ellyn and her place of imprisonment spoke volumes. Loyalty came in many forms, Bastien knew that. And respected it.

'Then we're going to get her out,' Grace said. 'We can break in tonight—'

The woman was incorrigible. Bastien needed to protect her and here she was, planning a jail break with the least information available. 'No, Grace. Or at least not yet. This needs planning, and careful planning at that. Let me at least try something else first.'

*

The Dowager's private garden was enclosed in glass panels. Small, brightly coloured birds were free to fly about inside it. There was a fountain which also fed into various streams and waterfalls, forming an ingenious irrigation system. Plants from every land grew here, each more beautiful and startling than the last. And in the centre, on a small patio formed of interlocking tiles of many colours, the Dowager sat on a wicker chair, taking tea, admiring her own secret domain.

Bastien joined her there, with Lara in attendance. His request for a private audience had been given a prompt and courteous response. There was only one unused chair, a deliberate snub to his marshal, no doubt. As Lara had said, they knew each other of old. He wondered if the Dowager had expected him to bring Grace instead.

The old queen waited until pleasantries were exchanged and a servant hurried forward to pour him a cup of the delicately scented tea in a porcelain cup so fragile it was almost transparent in this light. He sipped it, savouring the exquisite flavour. No expense had been spared. Then he held it without drinking more, because drinking unknown liquids was not a mistake he intended to ever make again. Not after what the Larelwynn family had done to him for years, using a poison to steal his memories.

'Shall we get down to it?' the Dowager asked.

'By all means,' he replied, pleasantly enough. 'But before we go further, I require that my liege woman, Ellyn de Bruyn, be returned to my household.'

If the Dowager was in any way surprised, she gave no sign. There was no indignant denial, or argument. 'Your liege woman, is she? She made no such claim.'

'I'd be surprised if she spoke at all.' He could imagine some swearing, but she wouldn't talk, not Ellyn.

'Once the wedding is done, I'm sure her return can be arranged.' So they both knew where they stood. But still, Bastien wondered about her objectives.

'Why take her in the first place?'

'Young de Bruyn is still Valenti, Prince Bastien.' She smiled. 'We have questions for her. Family business, if you will.'

'Family?' Lara cut in with a hint too much suspicion.

The Dowager waved a skeletal hand dismissively. 'You know how we are on these islands, Lady Kellen. All related in some way or another. I'm not saying she's any blood kin of *mine*, you understand, but her family were of some standing once. Although all who would climb high run the risk of falling far. Right to the gutters of Rathlynn, it seems. A fitting end, maybe. I won't mourn her mother's loss.'

Charming. Bastien would have to ask Ellyn what on earth that meant. He fully expected her to swear at him and refuse to answer though. Maybe Grace or Daniel knew. It sounded like something they should know.

'Then you'll return her?' he asked.

'If you really want her back, yes. *After* the wedding.'

After the wedding. The wedding that was not going to happen. But he couldn't tell her that. Not yet.

Bastien stared down into his tea. It was the same colour as Grace's eyes, which made the next part all the more difficult. He left it to Lara. She could spin it out long enough so they could work something out.

'We should discuss dowry,' the marshal said.

The Dowager fixed her with a steely glare. 'We don't need to play that game. We all know he has what he has only by my grace and Marius's foresight.'

'Then why do this? What is your price?'

Rhyannon, the queen mother, put her cup down on the flimsy saucer with a distinct click and pushed it away, scraping it across the lacquered table. 'The name, the bloodline, and ultimately the Larelwynn throne, of course. You *do* want it, don't you?' Her gaze met Bastien's and, whatever she saw there, she didn't look too pleased. 'We will *get* it. I want my girl beside you. Her children after you.'

If only she knew, Bastien thought. He didn't want the throne because it wasn't his, no matter what Marius had thought. His throne was dark as night and long broken.

He replaced his cup silently on the table. 'I see.'

'Do you? You will set your Academy chit aside. Rynn is to bear your only heirs. No one else.'

The urge to just stand up and leave swept over him and from the corner of his eye he saw Lara frown. He gripped the arms of the chair instead, clasping them until his knuckles strained.

'Rynn's children would be mageborn then. Like me.'

The Dowager snorted. 'So be it. We don't have the same prejudices as where you come from. Mageborn have their uses. You've seen them here. Our own, and those refugees who followed you.'

'And I suppose you want a say in Larelwynn policy too?' So much for leaving this to Lara. He couldn't help himself.

Rhyannon smiled, her brittle yellow teeth on display. It was like looking into the maw of a shark. 'I'd gladly lend you my extensive experience, yes. Are we done?'

'That's all?' Lara asked. 'No land? No waters?'

'Come now, Lara. Don't be so tawdry. The boy and I would be family.'

It was one of the most terrifying statements Bastien had ever heard. Of course the Dowager didn't want any specific parcels of Larelwynn possessions. In time, she'd have it all.

'What about Queen Aurelie?' the marshal continued, unfazed.

'Oh, Aurelie.' The Dowager Queen smiled, as if talking about a foolish girl. 'She will come to see sense. She's with child. Women get so emotional at such times, don't you find?'

Lara had no children that Bastien knew of. Was it another dig? Probably.

'She doesn't carry my child,' Bastien interjected. It was hardly necessary. The Dowager already knew that or this whole negotiation would have been pointless.

Suddenly the old woman's eyes on him were very cold. 'Nor Marius's either, I believe. She always was a Tlachtlyan to the core, that one. They'll do anything, tell any lie, even the most transparent one, for power. But when the child is born and proved to be… well, the wrong sort of blood, it will all resolve. We'll see to that.'

A premonition tingled at the base of his brain. She'd use him as a figurehead whether he wanted it or not, and whether his home wanted him or not. He would return either as their saviour or at the head of an invasion force, backed by the Valenti and whatever mercenaries she would pay for. Rathlynn, if it resisted, would be sacked. His land would burn.

He walked a dangerous path with her as his guide.

He couldn't do this. He couldn't. 'And if I choose otherwise?'

She sighed and folded her hands together in her lap. 'It would be… unwise. In the current climate. And de Bruyn would only be the first to regret a change of mind.'

That was her threat then. Ellyn, Grace. And the rest of them.

She and Bastien stared at each other, the significance clear. She was a monster, a spider at the centre of her web. And her hunger for power was insatiable. The thought sickened him.

'Now,' she went on as if no threat had even been implied. 'Time runs short. I must get on. So many people are keen for audiences. You understand how it is. Come back tomorrow. It's almost the end of Carnaefal and the final royal ball will be magnificent. Rynn would so love for you to be here. You can give your answer then, either way.'

Either way? He doubted there was any either way about this. Not as far as she was concerned.

'A member of the Larelwynn line cannot be coerced,' Lara cut in suddenly. 'You know that, Rhyannon. With the threat their magic represents, the other realms would never allow it. There are treaties as old as the kingdom of Larelwynn itself. Valenti would lose everything you have built.'

'Lara,' she scoffed, as if talking to an idiot. 'No one is threatening the royal accords. They were signed by our legendary forebears and every realm holds them sacrosanct. I'm simply making an offer. If Bastien chooses to leave, so be it. How could we stop the Lord of Thorns? But he won't get a better offer than Rynn.'

Bastien rose to his feet and gave a curt nod of his head, the minimum necessary so as not to insult her. His skin crawled as he did it. 'I will… give it thought…'

It seemed like the only thing that might put an end to this.

'Rhyannon, a pleasure, as always,' Lara said. There wasn't a hint that she actually meant it.

The Dowager smiled. 'A short engagement is best, I think. Don't you?'

Bastien turned, stunned. He had imagined months of negotiations and preparations. What was she playing at? 'Short?' He hadn't agreed. He wouldn't agree. But it seemed that the Dowager Queen had made up her mind regardless.

'Propose soon. Tomorrow would be best at the Carnaefal ball. That would be romantic, don't you think?' She gave him the coldest nod, satisfied with her solution and heedless of his thoughts on the matter. 'Send in the other envoy on your way out. He should be waiting.'

The door to the conservatory garden clicked shut behind him. Lara let out a long sigh. 'Like we're servants to that old crone,' she snarled.

'I think that might be what she wants,' he muttered.

And then he looked up. The antechamber was empty except for one man who turned to look at Bastien. He didn't look alarmed at all, but smiled that all-too-familiar smile.

Asher Kane.

Magic surged through Bastien's system, the instinct to defend himself and Lara by any means necessary overriding all thought of where they were.

'Prince Bastien,' said Asher Kane, with all the false warmth Bastien had come to expect of him. 'What an unexpected pleasure.'

The Dowager had to be watching somehow. She probably had spies looking in on them right now, if she wasn't somehow doing so herself. She had the money to spend on any number of Atelier-wrought wonders to see whatever she wanted. Bastien tightened his fists at his side, his shoulders taut as wires.

'What are you doing here?' The air crackled around him. Lara's hand closed on his shoulder but he barely felt it. The things that man had done, to him and to others, the things he had attempted to do, had threatened to do…

'I'm here for the wedding, of course,' Asher replied as if he had lost his mind. '*Your* wedding. What sort of oldest friend would I be if I missed that?' He laughed, like he'd never drugged Bastien, or led him into a trap, or threatened all he loved. Like it was nothing at all. Like they were still old friends. *Your wedding*… Had the entire world lost their mind? Was he to have no say in this at all? He glanced at Lara. Had she made promises on his behalf? 'Our queen insisted,' Asher went on. 'The Larelwynn throne must be properly represented, after all. The Dowager is family, did you know? My great-great-aunt on my mother's side. Or something anyway. She demanded my presence, can you believe it?'

Before Bastien could move aside, Asher slapped his upper arms and pulled him into an embrace. 'I may even have the honour of escorting the two of you home,' he rasped in Bastien's ear. 'I'd like that. I believe she is quite the beauty, the Rose of the Valenti.'

The leer in Asher's voice sent a wash of icy water through him.

'You—' The words choked him and he tore himself free, magic kindling on his fingertips. All the things he could do to Asher Kane flickered across the forefront of his mind as a red haze descended.

'The Dowager Queen will see you now, General Kane,' Lara said, with a smooth, obsequious tone that Bastien hoped never to hear from her himself. 'My Lord Prince, we must go.'

She propelled him forward, and Bastien never looked back. He was sure he'd see Asher watching them go and grinning from ear to ear.

Chapter Nine

The Valenti Atelier she visited down the cobbled Iliz alley wasn't as good as the Master Atelier back at the Academy, Zavi Millan, had been, but few were. Grace paid her respects and examined the man's many sigils, beautifully wrought and cunningly fashioned but still lacking an indefinable *something*.

Careful planning, Bastien had said. So she and Daniel were scouting the approach to the prison, plotting ways in and out, and gathering supplies. She could plan when it was needed. It was just that plans tended to fall apart when you needed them to work.

'Where next?' Daniel asked when she came outside.

She didn't get a chance to answer. As they turned the corner into the little plaza, guards swarmed towards them. Twenty of them, all armed and all deadly serious, surrounded them both. It was so fast Grace didn't even realise she and Daniel were the targets until the trap was sprung.

She spun around, back to back with Daniel in a defence so well drilled into them that it was now instinctive. They could protect each other, circling slowly to take in all around them, weapons already in hand.

'In the name of the king, lower your weapons to the ground and stand ready to be apprehended.' The officer barked out the commands and Grace tightened her grip on the sword hilt, without the slightest intention of yielding. As warnings went, it was unequivocal.

'Ours is prettier,' Daniel muttered.

'Ours is for mageborn. They appreciate the poetry,' she replied, counting their number, assessing their armour and their weaknesses. Then she raised her voice, making it ring out clearly and loudly enough for the whole plaza to hear. Every gossip-hungry ear was their friend right now. If they were taken, publicly, at least she intended news would get to Bastien. Word had to have been passed along by now. 'We serve Bastien Larelwynn, the Lord of Thorns and heir to the Larelwynn throne. We've been granted royal protection in this kingdom.'

The officer barked out a laugh. 'Royal protection has been revoked. We're to bring you in.'

Shit, thought Grace. Shit, shit, shit.

'Danny,' she hissed. 'Can you make a break for it if I give you the opening?'

'I'm not leaving you. And no. Not a hope anyway. What happens if we kill a few of them?'

'Nothing good.' But possibly nothing worse either. And they might not have a choice. 'I don't think even Bastien could talk us out of this.'

'So we fight?'

'Of course we fight. Any second now. Wait for it.'

The nearest guard roared at her as he threw himself forwards. It was a showy and stupid act, designed to intimidate, but it was never going to work on either of them. They'd faced monsters, psychopaths, and a crazy goddess. One screaming man just wasn't going to cut it.

The clash of weapons echoed behind Grace in time with her own as Daniel fended off another attacker, and a third came in on her left.

She whirled around, driving him away, and twisted, kicking the first one so hard in the stomach the war cry died in a strangled sob.

Daniel snarled, ducking under her outstretched arm, and throwing one of his knives to take out another guard. Two more took his place.

Too many. There were way too many. It didn't matter. She wasn't going down without a fight. Neither of them would.

A chance blow took the wind out of her but she staggered up, recovering and forcing herself on. Another came at her, another went down, but it was only a matter of time.

Something took Daniel to his knees. He was still swinging, still trying to regain his feet, and she grabbed him by the back of his leather jerkin, hauling him up. But it left her exposed. The blade almost took her arm off but she turned at the last second, Daniel stabbing upwards and impaling the guard through the throat. The woman looked surprised as she went down.

'Fall back,' Grace tried to say, and she found her grip on the sword hilt slick with blood. Her own blood. It drenched her arm and the dull ache that went with it was bad news. The worst of the pain was dulled by adrenaline, but she knew enough to know she was in trouble. They both were. She was tiring, hurt, and so was Daniel. They fought hard and dirty, street fighters from Eastferry to the core, but it was only a matter of time before they would be overwhelmed. Fall back? Where did they have to go?

Suddenly a scream rang out. Not of pain, not of anger. This was a scream of pure panic.

Shadows swirled out of the gutters and the eaves, out of the sewers and the stones on the ground. They launched themselves forward like vines, twisting around their attackers and hurling them aside. Grace tried to pull Daniel out of the way.

She seized the advantage, taking down two more guards the shadows hadn't yet reached. The last guard lashed out, legs tangling with hers and bringing her down onto the cobbles.

Grace stared into a face with huge green eyes and long white-blonde hair like Ellyn's. But that was where the resemblance ended. The guard scrambled away from Grace, her skin bloodless with terror.

The tendrils snatched the woman up, dragging her across the plaza.

'Grace?' Daniel screamed her name. He was too far away. Where was he? Ahead or behind?

She rolled, coming up with her sword in one hand, the knife in the other, to face a horde of shadows now filling the square. It was a boiling mass of darkness, blacker than night, but it moved like a living thing.

At its heart, a figure resolved, drawing the shadows back into himself. He was clothed in black and grey, thin and tall. Like a shadow himself. Jehane.

Grace's weapons were cold and hard in her hands, though she barely had the strength to hold them. Her right arm was trembling and if she tried to do anything with the knife it held, she was going to drop it. She came up to stand in a rush of movement, putting all the force she could muster behind it in case she lost her remaining strength, but the figure didn't move. He didn't even flinch.

'Careful. You wouldn't want to hurt me, would you?' Jehane grinned. 'They're gone now,' he said. 'Let me help.' He lifted both his hands, empty of weapons. Grace knew that meant nothing. The hand itself could be a weapon. And that hand could wield shadows just as deadly. She'd seen what he'd done. But when the pain washed through her and she almost fell, his arms caught her. His touch was gentle but all the same she pulled away quickly.

'Where's Daniel?'

Even as she said his name, he appeared, clutching his side. Blood stained his hands and leather armour. That looked bad, worse than her arm. Grace grabbed him, holding him up, her own injury forgotten.

'We need to get out of here, Captain,' Jehane said, sliding Daniel's other arm around his neck and taking almost all of his weight. 'Before their reinforcements arrive. They'll do anything to make him go through with this wedding. Including use you against him. Your life could be at risk.'

He bowed to her. Actually bowed. Then the shadows roared up around them like a shield and they fled through the narrow lanes of Iliz.

*

Lara opened the door to the mansion herself. She gave them each a glance, unflinching at the sight of their wounds. She ushered them into the inner courtyard.

'What happened?' she asked, slamming the main door to the mansion and locking it.

'Retribution, I think,' Grace replied. 'Or an attempt to gain leverage. Where's Bastien?'

But Lara ignored her. 'Jehane, your report.'

Jehane shrugged. 'To be fair, they'd already dealt with most of them before I had to intervene.'

'You sent him after us?' Grace asked.

'Jehane Alvaran is one of my finest operatives. I sent him to find you and to look after you. A guard, if you will. I thought she'd try something like this. A bit obvious, but she knows the value of a blatant threat.'

Grace stared from Jehane to Lara in growing horror. 'I don't need a guard. I *am* a guard.'

The door from the parlour opened again. Bastien stood there and he didn't look amused. 'Grace? You're hurt.'

'We're both hurt,' Daniel muttered and Grace shot him a glare. This was not the time.

'You knew about this?'

'The marshal and I spoke about it earlier.'

Grace felt like growling in her frustration. They were all pulling rank around her and she didn't like it. Not one bit.

'May we have a moment?' Bastien asked. Lara raised her eyebrows, but then nodded and, with a curt gesture to Jehane, they both left.

Daniel rolled his eyes. 'Don't worry about me. It's not serious.' He had gone white with blood loss.

'Get that cleaned up and looked at,' Grace told him. 'We'll get a healer.'

But Bastien moved before she could finish. His patience apparently non-existent now, he stalked across the courtyard like a harbinger of evil. Before Daniel could react, he grabbed him in a vice-like hold and pressed his hand onto her friend's side. Daniel jerked away from him, or at least he tried to. As he went to move, all his muscles seemed to lock.

Bastien's frown deepened and the glow of magic entered his eyes, just for a moment.

Daniel let out a yelp. He snarled at Bastien as he tore himself free. 'Don't do that!'

'It's healed. You're welcome.'

'Yeah well… fine but… don't just do *that*.'

He pulled at his leather armour and shirt. Beneath the blood and torn material the skin was unmarked.

Bastien shrugged. 'It wasn't serious.'

Daniel looked up to Bastien's face and scowled. 'Yeah, like I said.'

For a moment Grace could have sworn Bastien looked shocked, as if Daniel had hurt his feelings. Then the façade slid back over his face, the royal expression, the Lord of Thorns. He straightened and gave him the most withering glance possible.

'Next time I'll leave you to suffer and deal with the probable infection yourself then. Grace, we need to talk.'

Bastien led her into the small sitting room. He closed the door behind them but she didn't doubt for a second Lara and Jehane would be looking for a way to eavesdrop on them. If they didn't already have one.

Not that it mattered. All Grace's attention was on Bastien now. He folded his hands behind his back – a sure sign he was up to something – and stood at ease, or at least as at ease as he ever got. He looked like a raw recruit expecting a dressing-down, defiant and resigned.

'Lara tells me Jehane is the best she has.'

'So send him to rescue Ellyn.'

'Grace…' He sounded defeated.

'What?'

'That woman in the garden, the attack on the canal… our position here has become untenable. The Dowager offered me protection. It should extend to my household. But now…'

Oh, she understood. 'If you don't marry Rynn, she'll take it away. This was her way of making sure you understand that.'

'Yes.'

Grace chewed on her lower lip, staring up at him. She hated this, hated that he felt this was the only way. That he was even contemplating it. And what would it make her? Part of his household…

He pushed a strand of hair back from her face. 'What are you thinking, love?'

It pained her to say it but she had to. 'That she'd be a good marriage for you. Politically speaking. That's what the Dowager wants, isn't it?'

'I don't care what the Dowager wants. I don't trust her.'

Grace frowned at him. Confused. 'Then what do we do?'

'We're leaving. We aren't safe here any more. Besides, we need to get to Thorndale. You are more important, you and the nightborn…'

Larelwynn was not a large kingdom. Thorndale lay in the north. And the border was unsettled, dangerous. Tlachtlya and Larelwynn had never been on friendly terms and the war between the two had been devastating. It was a mountainous region, harsh and unforgiving, and they'd left a wasteland of it during the Magewar. More recently the Great War had only made that worse.

'Thorndale isn't—'

'I know. It isn't safe. It has never been safe. But neither is staying here, or anywhere in between.'

He touched the warrant hanging around her neck. 'You are more precious to me than life itself. I don't know what lies ahead of us. We have to leave the islands; we have to travel to Thorndale across hostile lands. The nightborn are abroad.'

'*One* nightborn.' She remembered the cold touch inside her, the dark emptiness, and she shuddered. What Bastien said next didn't make it any better.

'There's never only one.'

'Bastien…' But he was determined. She knew that now. He was going to stick to his plan no matter what she said. All she could do was try to make sure he didn't cut her out in his misguided attempts to protect her. Bastien always thought he knew best. He was wrong. But he wasn't going to listen. 'They won't just let us leave, not when the Dowager is so close to getting what she wants. Timing is everything.'

He paused, his mouth open a little, as if he hadn't expected that. Good. She needed to be able to surprise him.

'I've told Lara to arrange passage for us off the Valenti Islands. She has a ship standing by in the Grand Harbour.'

That was good, wasn't it? It was time to move on, but… 'We need to get Ellyn out first. They can help with that, Lara and what's-his-name. Do you think they'd agree?'

'Jehane,' he said absently. He looked into her eyes, stared into them, it seemed, as if studying her, looking for something. Whatever he saw there, she wasn't sure she wanted to know. 'Yes. They'll help. I'll order them to. But Grace… you'll need a distraction if you're going to get Ellyn out. And there's something else you have to know.'

Something else? 'What's that?'

'Asher Kane is here.'

The cold ache came roaring back. The void inside her, leaving her stomach hollow and empty. For a moment her head swam in syrup and she felt as if something pulled her away from herself, deep inside her, and that same something seemed to look out past her, using her eyes.

Was it shock? Delayed somehow? Or was it the pain from her shoulder? Or just fear?

'Here?'

'On the island. In the palace. We have to be careful. Apparently he's related to the de Valens family.'

'Of course he is.'

Bastien huffed out a breath. He didn't like it any more than she did. The whole situation was a nightmare.

'We'll leave with the tide,' he said at last. 'Lara has arranged everything. I'll go to the palace and tell them.'

'You'll go to the palace? Just like that?' It sounded like a risky move. He read her uneasiness immediately.

'It's better this way. Look, it's their Carnaefal ball. They'll be busy with the celebrations anyway. If we vanish it will be a grave insult to the de Valens and there is every chance we'll need them again in the future.'

Divinities, Grace hoped not. But she couldn't argue with him. Why burn bridges if they didn't have to?

'Bastien…' She didn't know how to say it but she was not happy with this at all. 'What if they don't let you leave the palace?'

But Bastien leaned in, pressing his forehead to hers. 'They have to. I'm a Larelwynn. I'm the Lord of Thorns. All the treaties in this world protect me and my free passage to and from our home. Hold me here against my will and it would be a declaration of war. Not just against our kingdom, but against Brind, and Lean, even against Tlachtlya. They would lose all face, all standing. And the other kingdoms would love to fall on the riches of the Valenti Islands so I'd be the perfect excuse. They'll let me go. They'll have to.'

'I don't see them accepting that.' Grace sighed and nestled closer in his embrace. She would never let him go so easily. And to the Dowager, Bastien was a prize. With him came the throne of Larelwynn. 'But if you're distracting them at the palace, maybe I can get in and out with Ellyn.'

His grip around her tightened abruptly and put pressure on the wound in her shoulder. She couldn't stop the startled exhalation of pain and Bastien drew back, studying her in consternation.

'You're hurt too, aren't you? Can I help you?' he asked. 'Please?'

Her arm felt like lead. Much as she hated magic, she didn't want to put up with this for days. She needed all her strength to rescue Ellyn. Expediency called for healing and he could do it with barely any effort. Magic danced for him, sang for him. If she let him…

He only wanted to help.

'Fine…' she sighed. 'But be careful. You can't afford to have the Maegen overwhelm you.'

He smiled then, a brief, loving smile. 'Yes, ma'am.'

His hand was cool against her skin as he slid it under her shirt sleeve and found the gash. She winced in spite of herself and Bastien's expression became firmer. 'Why didn't you say how much it hurt?'

'Doesn't. Get on with it.' If he knew she was lying, he didn't say anything. Just gave her that look.

His magic flowed like honey through her, knitting her back together, draining away the pain, but still… that sense of something empty inside her persisted. There was something wrong with her, and Bastien, who she'd thought could look into her soul and knew her better than anyone else, couldn't see it.

When he'd finished he rested his forehead against hers, closed his eyes and held her.

'Promise me, Grace,' he murmured.

'Promise what?'

There were so many things she should be promising. And that she shouldn't.

Bastien tugged his gold signet ring off his finger, the one engraved with a circle of thorns, which he used as his seal, both mundane and magical. Before Grace knew what he was doing he took her hand and slid it onto her finger. It felt strangely heavy, like the warrant, but warm against her skin. Like his touch.

She stared at it. But she didn't know what to say.

'Promise me you won't do anything stupid.'

'I can't ever promise that, my love,' she replied, and closed her hand so the ring would remain where he'd put it. She didn't have the heart to take it off. Or the slightest desire. It was his, part of him. It was a promise, too. A promise exchanged, but unspoken.

Bastien kissed her lips tenderly and drew back a little, fixing her with that dark Lord of Thorns gaze that was meant to be stern. 'Then at least promise me you won't wait. Get Ellyn and get back to the ship. And if anything goes wrong… *promise me* you'll leave.'

Chapter Ten

As the evening light fell to darkness, Grace, Daniel and Jehane armed themselves and appraised Misha of what they were doing so he could let the others know – especially if they didn't make it back to the ship Lara had arranged to carry them away.

In the meantime, Bastien had gone to the palace with Lara. He was determined to make his apologies and take his leave. It was a stupid idea, as far as Grace was concerned, but he wouldn't listen to reason. Protocol protected him, or so he said. He'd gone on about treaties between the kingdoms signed when Lucien Larelwynn ruled, designed to protect his descendants and keep their magic safe. Lara agreed, which really didn't help. To simply leave would cause a diplomatic incident.

Grace hated diplomacy. She didn't trust it, not the way Bastien did. He thought it was inviolable but she knew better. It protected you only when you already had power.

The prison was on an island in the lagoon beyond the city. On the outside it looked like another of their ornate palaces. No one wanted to look at something ugly on Iliz. They were known for beauty and elegance, not misery and despair. That was reserved for the interior.

Vicious rocks guarded the approach and the small boat had to move slowly across the waves. Luckily Daniel knew what he was doing. He'd grown up with Kurt, half their childhoods spent in the alleys of

Eastferry and the rest in and around Belport. Apparently sculling a punt in near total darkness without making a sound was a valuable skill when someone was smuggling or creeping onto legitimate cargo ships to steal their goods.

Only a few lights lit the prison windows. They would be on minimum staff, or so Misha had discovered, most of them having been reassigned to the city for the final nights of Carnaefal. Musicians everywhere liked to drink, especially at this time of year, and when they drank they liked to talk. No one was coming or going from the prison tonight. Most of the guards had been sent to keep peace in the city itself, so the prison was on lockdown. No one in, no one out.

Except them. That was the plan. In and out without even the smallest ripple.

The jetty was overlooked by a watchtower, so they couldn't land there. Instead they had to come in via the rocky shore. It wasn't safe, and it wouldn't be pretty, but if Daniel could keep control, she and Jehane would leap for it. Then…

Divinities, she wished Daniel was coming with her, but if they left the boat on the jetty it would be spotted. She didn't trust Shades, but Jehane seemed different. He had skills, and more training, especially in something like this. Daniel wouldn't fail her. He'd wait out of sight, in open water, so he could spirit them away afterwards.

Ellyn was all that mattered.

Grace stared at the black rocks coming closer. The waves were growing choppier, the punt rocking in an unpleasant way. She hated water, always had and always would.

Focus on the rocks, she told herself. Focus on dry land. And make sure you get there.

'Ready?' Daniel said.

'As I'll ever be,' she told him. 'Don't be a stranger, Danny.'

'I'll be here. Just don't be late.'

She perched on the edge of the punt and jumped. The rocks came up hard and cold under her, slick from the water. She skidded forward and caught herself before she could slide back into the sea. Jehane's jump didn't go quite as smoothly. He came down neatly enough, but didn't get his balance right and stumbled backwards, arms going wide. Grace grabbed the front of his leather jerkin, pulling him to safety.

'Thank you,' he whispered.

At least he was polite. 'Don't thank me yet. Let's get going.'

He spun a web of shadows around them both. A useful skill, she decided. Even with the chill effects of his magic surrounding her, Grace had to admire it. But she'd seen other Shades and what they could do. Just because this one appeared to be on her side, it didn't make it easier.

They'd solved the first problem of getting to the island, but they still had to get inside the prison. The main gate faced the jetty, but there was a side gate too and they skirted the shoreline until they reached it. Locked, of course, but Daniel wasn't the only one who had picked up tricks from Kurt and his friends. She pulled out the lock picks and set to work, listening intently until she heard the click that told her they were in.

She pushed the door open a crack and Jehane's shadows slid inside, masking their entry. He shook his head and Grace understood. No one on the other side. They were relying on the impenetrable nature of the prison. She wondered how few guards were actually here. The fewer the better.

Jehane went in first and Grace followed. 'The shadows will hide us,' he assured her, his voice no more than a breath. 'But noise will betray us. As will bodies, do you understand?'

'Yes. Of course. Do you?'

He laughed that soft, melodious laugh. It was almost likeable. His dark humour called to something in her. Things they'd done, things they'd seen, in service to the crown. 'Let's go.'

The cells on the upper floors were home to the more affluent prisoners, but they weren't about to keep someone like Ellyn up there. Ellyn was an example, a message to Bastien. So was the attack on Grace and Daniel. The Dowager wanted to isolate him, use him and control him. They were the leverage. None of them were safe.

And Grace didn't trust her to keep her word. Not in the slightest.

The hallway was dank and miserable. It led to a central observation room with others leading off it like the spokes of a wheel. In the middle, two men sat in unstable chairs, playing cards on a desk. A spiral staircase led both up and down. Grace was about to signal their next move when Jehane slipped by her, shadows billowing around him. The guards didn't even see him coming. In a moment, he was on the nearest, grabbing his head and slamming it down on the table.

The other one scrambled away, opening his mouth in a scream, but Grace was already there. She kicked the back of his knees, bringing him down and putting him in a headlock before he could make a sound. He struggled weakly, gasping for breath.

Jehane let the guard he'd taken out slump in the chair. At least he hadn't killed him outright. When he pulled the knife, Grace shook her head, stopping him.

'If he wakes up he'll raise the alarm,' Jehane pointed out.

'We'd better get this done before he wakes up then, hadn't we?' She shook the guard she held. A boy really. Probably no more than seventeen. She could bet they gave him every shit job in the place. Right now he was crying, great silent sobs as he hovered on the edge of consciousness. She gave him another, meaningful shake and then let him go. He fell to his hands and knees.

'Please… please don't hurt me,' he stammered.

'Maybe you should do what I want then. Help us out. We're looking for someone. Her name's Ellyn. Ellyn de Bruyn.'

'That one? She's a psychopath. We can't even feed her without someone getting hurt.'

Yeah, that sounded like Ellyn. 'So you take me to her and I'll relieve you of the job. Sound good?'

'Y-yes? She's in the pit. The bottom, underground. Isolation.' It sounded charming.

'Good boy. Come on then.'

Grace didn't wait for the boy's answer, heading down the stairs with Jehane hauling him after them. It was even darker on the next floor, and things only got worse the lower she went. Sometimes she heard cries, sobs, or the ravings of people who had been there far too long. She couldn't save them. She didn't know if she'd want to.

When she finally found Ellyn, it was in the darkest hole left in the place. It was damp and freezing. No one would survive here for too long. Ellyn huddled in the dank recesses of the cell, her wrists and ankles in chains. There were bruises up the side of her face, layers of them. They vanished down underneath her torn shirt, all along her neck and shoulder. She looked up as they approached, glaring through her long, tangled hair like she would kill them the moment she got loose. Which, knowing Ellyn as Grace did, she probably would.

'I… I have the key…' the boy said, desperately trying to get it in the lock. Finally managing it, he turned it and jerked open the door to the cell. Jehane pushed him inside.

Ellyn eyed them all but she didn't move. For a moment Grace thought she was drugged or that she'd lost her mind already.

'Get up,' the boy told her. 'They've come for you. Get the fuck up.' He grabbed her chains, hauling her to her feet.

Grace gave a snarl of anger and started forwards. The guard took one look at her and basically flung Ellyn at her, an offering or a shield.

Ellyn fell into Grace's arms, wretched and weak, stinking. She clung to her for a moment, staring in disbelief. 'Grace?' she groaned, her voice broken and hoarse. 'Took you long enough.'

Grace tried to smooth her hair back from her face and Ellyn winced as she touched her. 'Dear goddess, what did they do to you?'

'You should have seen the other guys,' she said, almost falling over. 'Jehane? Take her.'

He stepped in and took her in strong arms. 'It's okay. We've got you now.'

'To be fair, mate, I don't know who the fuck you are,' she replied. 'But that little shit in there is lucky I don't make him sing soprano. So watch the hands.'

Grace turned, staring at the boy, her face a mask of fury. The darkness around her bled into her veins. She could feel the emptiness, that void inside her glorying in her rage, stoking it. Her fire might be gone but she could still feel it kindling in her blood.

'No one raped her,' the boy said, as if that made it all right. 'No one could get close enough.'

Grace waited a moment until he went silent again, aware what he'd just admitted. They'd tried. Of course they'd tried. Then she closed the cage door on him. The keys were still there, waiting. She turned them.

The stench of terror came off him in a wave.

'Wait, you can't leave me down here. No one comes down here for days. Please. Don't – don't do this. Don't leave me here!'

Grace leaned against the door, listening, and the void inside her surged with pleasure. Fear. Fear was good. She wanted him afraid. She wanted him to suffer.

'Do you know what else is in the dark?' she asked.

At the sound of her voice, he went silent. She waited. After a moment his voice came in a kind of sob. 'Wh-what?'

'Monsters. Jehane, show him.'

He smiled. It wasn't his pleasant smile this time. She didn't know what shapes the shadows took that Jehane sent flooding in there, but the guard's screams echoed after them as they helped Ellyn up the stairs and between them carried her back the way they'd come.

Chapter Eleven

There were so many ships in the lagoon and the Grand Harbour. So many little lights twinkling on the dark water, like stars in the sky. One of them held Grace, and Bastien fancied he could almost sense her out there. Somewhere.

Even if he didn't know exactly which ship it was.

But instead of being with Grace, making ready to sail away, here he was, in a little antechamber overlooking the lagoon, waiting for Lara so they could slip away into the night as the Carnaefal celebrations pitched headlong into their final day. Then he would finally rejoin Grace and leave the Valenti Islands far behind them.

Lara had gone to request an audience with the Dowager so Bastien could tell her that he was leaving rather than marry the girl. And it was taking far too long.

When the door opened, however, it was not Lady Kellen. It was Rynn, holding a glass of a deep red wine.

'I wondered where you were,' she said by way of an explanation.

'Rynn…' How did he tell her? He hadn't expected to see her at all, not really. He knew he wouldn't be breaking her heart. She was a princess, raised to marry where she was told, to be courteous to a visiting dignitary. She was doing her duty.

She swallowed hard, blinking in the face of his darkest look. 'Yes?' Offering him the wine, which he took with a brief thank you, she closed the door behind her.

Suddenly, the situation seemed awkward and uncomfortable. 'Shouldn't… shouldn't you have an escort or…'

'Why? To protect my honour?' She gave him a shy smile. She flirted artfully but he didn't believe a word of it. 'You're going to be my husband. I don't think it matters now.' She indicated the wine. 'Aren't you going to drink it?'

He'd expected a curt dismissal from the Dowager, not a young woman trying to salvage this disastrous betrothal plan.

'Rynn, I have to explain… I can't… I can't marry you. I'm leaving Iliz. I can't stay here.'

She just stared at him, her face unreadable. 'They told me.'

He set the glass down on the side table and his eyes flicked to the young woman, suspicion making him pause. She looked paler than usual. When she thought he wasn't looking she knotted her slender hands together, trying to stop them trembling.

'Please understand.'

She drew in a breath.

'What is there to understand, my Lord of Thorns?' she whispered. 'You chose another over me. It's… it's never happened before.'

When the door opened behind Rynn, the last remaining bit of colour drained from her skin and she turned away from him. Bastien hoped for a moment, for one desperate moment, that it was Lara this time.

But it wasn't. Asher Kane stood there, with four Valenti guards.

The Dowager followed. Still clad in black, like a skeleton, her eyes cold as stones. Bastien took an involuntary step back. He bumped into the table, knocking the wine everywhere. The glass smashed by his feet. Where was Lara? What was going on?

'Did he drink it?' the Dowager asked. Her emotionless gaze took in the broken glass and the liquid pooling on the floor, dripping down the legs of the table. Then she dragged it back to Rynn's stricken face. 'No. You couldn't even manage that. Well, no matter. General Kane, if you will.'

Asher shook his head ruefully and took out a silver hip flask.

'Finally learned not to drink everything that's handed to you, Bastien?'

The guards seized him, too many to resist. He was too shocked to protest as they shoved him down onto his knees, holding him there. One gripped a fistful of his hair and forced his face upwards. Another gripped his jaw, yanking it open.

'No,' Rynn tried. 'You'll hurt him. Please—'

The Dowager slapped her across the face, a sharp sound in so quiet a room. Even the guards holding Bastien stiffened in alarm. But no one moved to help her.

'Silence yourself, you useless child,' the old woman snarled.

Asher ignored them. All his attention was fixed on Bastien, his smile infernal. He walked forward, opened the flask and emptied the contents into Bastien's open mouth. It all happened so quickly that the stab of magic rising within Bastien was too little, too late.

Bastien choked on the burning liquid, tried to spit it out, tried not to drink… but Asher placed his hand over his mouth and nose and it was too late. The liquid scorched all the way down Bastien's throat as if he was swallowing molten silver.

He knew the taste, knew it far too well, sweet and sickly, burning down his oesophagus. He choked, his eyes blurring with helplessness.

Rynn backed for the door, her arms around her chest, tears covering her marked face.

'Don't you go anywhere, Princess,' Asher warned in a threatening tone. 'You're still needed here.'

The Dowager glared at her and Rynn fell still, standing there like a startled doe.

The guards released Bastien and he sank forward onto his hands and knees, gasping for breath, his head swimming. The sensation of drowning in the syrupy substance turned his vision golden and glowing. He couldn't focus on anything. The world was zooming in and out, like he was looking through the eyes of hummingbirds from the far south. Bits of his mind crumbled away like cracked eggshell.

'When I suggest a deal, Bastien Larelwynn, no one backs out,' the Dowager said. 'That throne of yours will be Rynn's. And you will obey. General Kane, begin.'

'You can't do this,' Bastien managed to say. 'The accords…'

'The others will never know. You'll agree to marry my granddaughter and do so with joy. Your sister's idea. And she was there when those wretched Larelwynn accords were signed protecting you and your line.'

Celeste? Of course it was Celeste.

Asher laughed. 'Celeste was most insistent. She wants you and a Larelwynn. Old magic, she said. Blood magic. And now we have you both. The Valenti have been most accommodating. Family, and all that.'

Someone laughed softly, a hissing, whispering sound. The Dowager, Bastien realised.

Flailing about wildly with his mind, Bastien tried to draw on his powers, some way to defend himself, to stop this. To stop him.

'You won't use your magic,' Asher said in a voice that shook its way through him. Something shuddered in the depths of him and just like that the constant contact he had with his magic was gone. 'You'll do exactly what you're told. Understand?'

Bastien couldn't help himself. He bowed his head, not because he wanted to submit. He didn't have the strength to hold it up any more. He couldn't focus, couldn't keep hold of himself. He was drowning. And Asher had bound his magic, the only thing that could save him.

Asher knelt down beside him. 'Now, this is what's going to happen, my old friend. It's all very simple. Listen carefully. Aurelie should have been specific the last time. She should have made sure you drank the whole lot and had very clear instructions and we would never have had any of that unpleasantness. So listen to me now, and listen carefully, because this is how it's going to be. Tomorrow you're going to marry that beautiful girl. She's the love of your life. She's all you have ever wanted. You worship the ground she walks on and you would never do anything to hurt her, understand? Then the two of you are going to come back to Rathlynn where we'll sort out this misunderstanding with Aurelie. She'll become the Dowager Queen and Rynn will take the throne beside you.' Rynn visibly shrank to avoid his look, but her grandmother grabbed her arm in a clawlike grip, holding her firm.

'You will watch this, girl,' she said, her tone sharp and bitter. 'You will learn and understand.'

For what? In case she had to drug him herself in future? In Rathlynn, with Asher in power, Rynn wouldn't stand a chance. She would have no choice but to do whatever he wanted. Asher and Celeste... Bastien wouldn't wish them on anyone. But where did Aurelie figure in this plan? Did she even know they were going to replace her?

Asher slapped his face, getting his drifting attention back to the threat at hand. 'Pay attention, your majesty.' Every word dripped mockery. 'I'm your trusted advisor. Everything I tell you, everything I suggest, that's what you're going to do, understand?'

This couldn't be happening. He could feel everything slipping away, his life, his memories, his magic. He was losing himself. He was losing…

'Grace,' he said hoarsely.

Asher laughed. 'You won't even know her. Not that I expect her to just give up. I'm counting on her determination. But she's no one to you from this moment on. In fact, the next time you set eyes on Grace Marchant, the moment you hear her voice, the first opportunity you get—' He grabbed Bastien's chin and jerked it up so he had to look into Asher's hateful face. 'You're going to kill her for me and then you'll take the warrant. It's mine, Bastien. She's a thief. Kill her and give the warrant to me. I'm your marshal from now on.'

'No,' Bastien whispered. But he didn't even know what he was saying no to.

'Oh yes. Welcome back, my Lord of Thorns. It's time to go home. And look at the prize you'll be bringing with you. Beautiful, cultured and so very rich, the perfect match. It was a most profitable trip.'

Asher jerked Bastien's head around to look at Rynn. She looked as if for the first time she truly understood the nightmare that she had stumbled into, that by helping Asher she was his accomplice and his pawn. That she, too, was in his power. The Dowager just stood there, entirely complicit in this.

Asher licked his lips. His grip on Bastien's jaw turned bruising. 'I'll look forward to entertaining her myself. As will your sister, I'm sure.'

The world turned to shifting golden light and coiling black shadows. Bastien couldn't hold on any longer. He crashed to the floor and everything went dark.

Chapter Twelve

Sunrise over the city of Rathlynn should have been beautiful. Aurelie knew that. Everyone told her it was. She hadn't watched it before. Not really. Not even when she had stayed up all night drinking and revelling. The sea, the red tiles, and the creamy walls, pale and washed-out at first then flowing with reflected light, surging into colour as the sun crept over the horizon. The long shadows of the statues, visible below her on the Royal Promenade leading from the Temple and its wide square and up the hill to the gates of the palace.

But all those statues had Marius's face. Or Bastien's. Or something in between. Every statue watched her with the same disappointed expression.

No child of hers would look at her that way. He wouldn't have those features. She rubbed her flat stomach and sighed.

Shame wasn't something to which she was accustomed. Tlachtlyan royalty did not feel shame. Or guilt. They acted and they dealt with the consequences. They bent the world to their will.

Her family had taught her that, from the time she could first listen to their stories, from the cradle. They had taught her well and she had been a dutiful student. When they told her she was coming here, to marry Marius the Larelwynn king, she had nodded, agreed and never thought twice about it. She hadn't wondered if there was someone else for her, if she would find true love or even a handsome prince. She'd done her duty.

Part of it, anyway. She hadn't been able to provide him with an heir. Not her fault, of course. It was never her fault.

Especially not now.

She stood in the window and gazed as the sun spread golden light over her kingdom. *Hers*. She deserved this. Marius had tried to be a good husband, she knew that. He had been kind but not interested in her. How could he be? He wasn't interested in women at all. That hadn't bothered her either. It wasn't something to be frowned upon like it was down in Barranth, where they forbade men to be with men and women with women. And Bastien, bloody stubborn stupid Bastien, was too brainwashed and loyal to do anything that might have been in any way useful. She had tried so hard.

And all for nothing.

No one would believe any child of hers was a Larelwynn. No one. And if she killed anyone who dared to say it out loud, it would be a bloodbath.

It wouldn't be her first.

So many of the mageborn had died. And they kept dying. In the city, in her dungeons… They'd die rather than submit to her, something they had proved time and again. The ones she had managed to imprison wouldn't give up their powers, and torture just broke them to pieces instead of making them comply. Some killed themselves, or each other. They refused to cooperate. The whole bloody kingdom defied her.

Those who had fled were called Larks. But there were others, determined to stay and make a stand against her. They called themselves *Thorns*, of course. The thorns in her side. Just like Bastien.

Celeste might make a scene, but she was as trapped as Aurelie. She couldn't leave the Temple and she had no power now. Bastien had seen to that. She was hopeless, a crazed psychopath playing her own game and running down the clock on her usefulness.

'Your majesty?' Her most recent lover came out of her bedchamber, his black hair tousled, his brown eyes blurred with sleep. Last night Aurelie had thought he had a look of Bastien about him. Now she couldn't see it any more. He was a pale comparison. 'What are you doing?'

'I couldn't sleep.'

'Come back to bed. I can help with that.'

She sighed again. Goddess, he was predictable – irritating and so sure of himself. It never ceased to grate. Men were all the same. Even Asher. Sometimes she thought it was a shame she needed him so much. She didn't have anyone else.

Not here, anyway. That would have to change. It was good she had sent Asher to Valenti. Well, not so much sent as accepted his going. She had the strangest feeling he had manipulated her. Again. And she hated that.

'Later. I have things to attend to.'

'What things?' A barb in his voice caught her attention. This one didn't like being dismissed. Too bad. He was a petulant child. She hadn't even bothered to learn his name. Why would she? She wouldn't have him back. He'd be lucky if he left here alive. Let him boast about screwing the queen and she'd have him castrated before she gutted him herself.

'None of your business,' she snapped at him and left him standing there.

He wouldn't follow. She knew that. Not if he had any survival instinct at all. Perhaps he'd slink out or perhaps he'd stay. He was pretty enough, she supposed, her march through the palace taking some of the edge off her temper. And he had been skilled. More than most. If he was still here when she was finished, maybe she wouldn't throw him out after all. Perhaps with a lover like him her child might even look the part.

Guards fell in around her as she swept down the corridor, past tapestries of all those ancient Larelwynns, all those dead and gone ancestors of her late husband, and Bastien. Bastien everywhere. Wherever she went. It was always going to be this way. Aurelie kept her eyes fixed ahead, ignoring them all. This wasn't what she wanted to see. This wasn't a time for regret.

This was a time for strength.

Down and down she went, her clothes chosen for this moment, her hair left long like a glory, her face fresh and angelic. And yet the path she went was anything but.

The dungeons lay deep inside the palace complex, buried in the hill above Rathlynn. No one escaped from this place. No one. She'd make sure they all knew it: mageborn and quotidian alike, if they crossed her, they'd rot in here for the rest of their days.

The nagging voices that said she couldn't do this, that she couldn't rule, that she would still be defied at every turn, needed to be quashed completely. She couldn't listen to them any longer. They sounded like Celeste. They sounded like Asher. *You need us*, they seemed to say. *Without us you're nothing.* Well, she'd show them. She needed to act. And this was the first step.

The warden stood to attention as Aurelie entered and her guards fell in around her. The commander of the Royal Guard stood with him, resplendent in his gleaming uniform.

'Your majesty,' he said with a low bow. The rest of them followed suit. Maybe she should get him to give Asher some lessons.

'Is he here?'

'Yes, ma'am. We took him coming out of Eastferry by way of Jewellers' Alley. Right where our informant told us he would be.'

'Just him?'

'Yes, ma'am. Just him. He was alone. His arrogance knows no bounds. But we've put him in his place.'

She graced the commander with a smile. Obedience was always to be encouraged. Perhaps she would reward it as well. Perhaps.

'Show me. I want to see him.'

'He's dangerous, ma'am.'

'Then you will obviously need to protect me, Commander,' she purred.

He stared past her head, clearly uncomfortable. Asher was his superior and he knew – as they all knew – about their relationship.

'This way, ma'am,' he said, in as careful and deferential tone as possible.

The cell was completely dark and it stank like something had died in there. Which, on reflection, something probably had. And something probably would again. When they opened the door, the pool of light spilled inside, revealing a man on his knees. Chains held him there, arms behind him, heavy black iron around his wrists and ankles. A bag-like hood covered his head.

He didn't have the grace to look defeated though. Oh no, not him. She nodded to the commander and he pulled off the hood so she could look him in the face.

Scruffy black hair fell over his dark brow, and deep brown eyes looked up at her with a murderous glare. The defiant line of his mouth just irked her.

There would be no begging, no pleading, not from him.

But he would break eventually. She'd see to that. If he didn't she'd give him to Celeste. She'd make him scream.

'Parry,' she said in pretty tones. 'What a pleasure to see you here.'

'The pleasure is all yours then,' he replied with an impudent grin. There was no 'ma'am' or 'your majesty' from him. Nothing of the sort. Not from Kurt Parry.

The word was he fancied himself as the king of Eastferry, ruler of that parasitic dungheap infesting her city. Reports said he had even defied Bastien, standing up to him and claiming Eastferry as his own.

Everything about Kurt Parry disgusted her.

Not to mention the way he looked at her. Like he'd chew her up and spit her out. She could have him flogged for that. Traitor, usurper, criminal… there were so many reasons.

But right now she wanted information.

'What were you doing in Valenti, Mr Parry?'

The reports sent to her said he'd met with Marchant and others; not Bastien himself perhaps but still. It was damning enough. She'd get the rest out of him eventually. She'd take her time. He was the scum of Rathlynn. She should have hauled him in here months ago to teach him a lesson.

'You can call me Kurt, love,' he said. 'Everyone else does. And as for Valenti? Never been there. Like the food though. Hear Iliz is good for a party. Much like you, I'm told.'

He grinned again. Aurelie glanced at the commander who took the hint instantly. The punch he threw hurled Parry over, his face smacking off the stone slabs. Guards hauled him up again. He spat blood onto the floor at her feet and smiled at her again, his teeth very white against the scarlet in his mouth.

'Going to be a long day then, love, is it?'

She narrowed her eyes in warning. 'You can make it shorter.'

Lewd savage that he was, he trailed his gaze up and down her body. 'Oh no, love. I can go for hours.'

Love? How dare he call her *love*? And in that tone. Well, she had another thing in store for him and love was the least of it.

She could have him tortured, of course. She'd enjoy it. But she had a far more effective way of dealing with him.

'Enough, we'll see what Celeste makes of you then.'

'Celeste Larelwynn? Isn't she crazy?'

More than crazy. Raving. Dangerous. Psychotic. But Aurelie could use that.

'I suppose your little brother told you about that. And she was so fond of him. She wanted him as her pet. Celeste is insane, yes. Almost entirely. She does like to play with the pets we give her. Like the harper your brother sold his friends down the river for. Oh, the things she did to him… She'll love you. She might even keep you as a replacement for the two of them.' She leaned in closer, even though the guards all stiffened in alarm as she did. She didn't care. She wanted Parry afraid. She wanted all of them afraid. For her. Of her. It really didn't matter which. She was going to make such an example of this one. 'Oh, Parry, the things she'll do to you. And as for your precious brother and his friends … just *wait* until you see what I'm going to do to them.'

He huffed out a laugh, like he didn't believe her. Oh, to have the arrogance of a man like him.

'Haven't you seen the mageborn lately? I heard you have a few still stashed away down here. Or have you killed them all yet? We've got a problem in Rathlynn, Aurelie. Perhaps all over the kingdom and beyond. They're losing control. Like, really losing control. Perhaps Celeste's crazy is catching. Mad black eyes, stronger than ever, batshit behaviour that'd have even a hardened bastard like me sending for help. They're powerful, too. Like something out of the old stories. They call them nightborn.'

She knew. She'd read the reports. The ones in the cells down here who had changed… well, they'd had to put them down immediately and burn the bodies. Not even the other mageborn had tried to help them. But she didn't want to give Parry the satisfaction of knowing that.

'Enough,' she said, his nonsense trying her patience. 'Just take him to the Temple and let him deal with Celeste for a while.'

She waited, relishing the sight of the guards dragging him out of the room, before she followed. Her foot hit something metal on the ground and she stared at it. A black bolt like the iron of the chains.

And then all the seven hells broke loose. She didn't know how it happened or what he did, but suddenly Parry was free, and those chains holding him had become weapons in his hands. Four guards were on the ground, bleeding or dead, and the commander had pulled a sword and was pursuing him down the narrow corridor.

Aurelie's own guards closed in around her, blocking her view, which only made her more enraged. She shoved by them and ran after the sound of the melee, heedless of danger. He wouldn't dare. He simply wouldn't dare.

But Kurt Parry was gone.

It was only later that they found the vault beneath them had been broken into and no one really had any idea what had been taken. Her lover, who'd looked so much like Bastien Larelwynn she now saw him for the lure he had obviously always been, was gone as well. And the cells below that were empty. All the mageborn, including the last of the Academy cadets who still resisted her, who refused to bow and serve her, to lend her their many talents. They were gone, every last one of them.

That was when Aurelie realised Kurt Parry had somehow played her. And then she really knew fury.

Chapter Thirteen

Ellyn sat by the narrow window of the cabin, overlooking the lagoon. A soft blanket was wrapped around her shoulders and she stared off into the distance at the morning sun on the water. She had barely spoken since they arrived back here and Grace was starting to worry. Misha played his harp, a sweet lullaby which Grace hoped would soothe her, but Ellyn hardly appeared to notice him. His magic wound around her, healing, comforting. Grace felt it trembling on the air, enchantment weaving itself around her friend, and for once she didn't mind. She trusted the harper, she realised. She'd underestimated him too many times.

The old stories about Lyrics said they could bring the birds to sing with them, heal with their song and make the sun shine on the darkest day. They could change moods, heal broken hearts and broken minds. There was a darker side in those stories too, of course. During the Magewar they had brought down castle walls and driven whole battalions insane. But that was long ago, wasn't it? Stories grew with time and maybe the Lyrics of today enjoyed building up their reputations. No one had seen one do anything so terrible since the fall of Thorndale, and Lucien Larelwynn's pact with the Hollow King.

Maybe those Lyrics had been nightborn. Until Bastien had confirmed they weren't just stories to frighten children, she'd thought that hollow was as bad as it could get.

Misha took a moment to notice Grace's presence but as soon as he did, his fingers fell still on the strings.

'Can you give us a minute?' Grace asked. Misha smiled and picked up his harp, leaving the two of them alone. Ellyn didn't react to that either.

Grace sat down on the end of her bunk. 'Want to tell me what happened?'

Ellyn shrugged but didn't look at her. 'They grabbed me off the edge of the canal. Must have been waiting for us.'

'Why you?'

'Why not me?' she snapped suddenly. It wasn't like her, not the anger nor the depression. Not like Ellyn at all. Maybe it was trauma. Grace wasn't sure. 'I'm Valenti, I guess. Less chance of an international incident. If they took you, Bastien would have dismantled the whole of Iliz to find you, brick by brick. '

The guilt almost choked Grace. She couldn't tell Ellyn that the Valenti had tried that as well. It would diminish what happened to Ellyn somehow. 'We… we looked for you…'

'I know. And found me.'

Grace got up and crossed to her, meaning to sit beside her, but Ellyn flinched so she sat on the end of the window seat, perched awkwardly just within reach.

'What did they do to you?'

She lifted her hand to her face. 'This? I tried to escape. I kept trying. They didn't like it. Nothing worse though. I mean, not for want of trying. I suppose I was lucky.'

'Are you sure? You'd tell me, wouldn't you?' The boy in the prison had implied that they hadn't managed to do anything but that didn't mean he wasn't lying.

Ellyn laughed humourlessly. 'I'd tell you. Sure. Also they would be missing vital body parts. I promise.'

That sounded more like her friend. The taut wires of Grace's shoulders relaxed a little.

'Talk to me, Ellyn. What's wrong?'

'It's being back here. That family, this life… I never realised when my mother spoke about it how… how *real* it was. The sense of oppression. The manipulation. They toy with lives. Did I ever tell you about my mother and my aunt, how they got to Rathlynn? They fled here because my father and his family tried to stand against the Dowager. When the king died. She killed every relation of mine who didn't flee, who didn't drop everything and run. She's grown even more powerful since then. Her spider webs are everywhere. Everywhere. Her spies, those she blackmails, the noble families she's brought under her control… All her own family – that pretty little Rynn included, I'm sure – she uses them like tools. And when they took me to that place… I thought this is it. They're finally going to finish the job. The de Valens will have finally killed all of us.' She shook her head, sniffed loudly, and brought her arm up across her eyes, wiping away tears. Grace stared. Ellyn never cried. Never. 'And it wasn't even about me, was it? It was about Bastien.'

Grace sighed and leaned in, wrapping her arms around her friend. This time Ellyn didn't fight her or pull away. She leaned in too.

'That's royalty for you,' Grace said at last. 'It's always about Bastien.'

Ellyn heaved in a breath, let it out slowly and relaxed into Grace's embrace. 'I can't stay here, Grace.'

'None of us can. Time to move on before the Dowager gets her claws in any further. Bastien wants to go to Thorndale.'

Grace didn't want to tell her why. The warrant felt very cold against her skin. And heavy. What would it do to her if they didn't make it to Thorndale? If the Deep Dark took her, what would it make her do?

Ellyn groaned. 'Where is he then? I can't wait to get going out of this shithole.'

'He's meeting us here.' But Bastien was already late. Grace was trying to ignore the feeling of dread rising in her chest. What if they had locked him up and wouldn't let him go? What if something worse had happened to him? She might have promised to leave without him, but she hadn't meant it. He had to know that.

'Thorndale… I've heard stories about that place. Not good stories. And I suppose that means we have to make sure he gets there alive.'

'That's the job.'

'Do we have a plan at least?'

Grace smiled, held Ellyn closer. 'No, we don't have a plan. We never have a plan.'

'Oh well, nothing changes. We'll improvise.'

A knock on the door broke through the silence that followed.

'Come in,' Grace said.

Daniel opened the door. 'Lara's back. We have a problem.'

Grace didn't even turn. She closed her eyes, resigned.

'Of course we do,' she sighed.

*

The Valenti, as Grace had noted when they first arrived on these wretched islands, loved a celebration. Any excuse. Any reason. This, the last day of Carnaefal, was the largest party in their year. There was music everywhere, streamers and banners hanging from all the buildings. Flower petals floated in the air and in the canals and everywhere there was music. It was still morning but the party went on and on.

People flooded the streets, but Grace noticed the Royal Guards as well. They stood on every corner, manned open rooftops and patrolled the plazas. Oh, they wore their finery too, but the weapons they carried were not for show.

Well, neither were hers.

It was the glimpse of sigils that unnerved her the most. Why did they need sigils?

Lara's return had thrown everyone into confusion. Bastien wasn't coming, she told them. He had vanished in the palace. When Lara had finally tracked him down, early this morning, he'd just said he was staying there and dismissed her.

There was more. Whatever he had said had Lara deeply worried but she wouldn't share it, especially not with Grace.

'They've got to him somehow,' said Daniel. 'Blackmailed him or threatened you. There has to be a reason.'

Grace wasn't so sure. She had a terrible feeling about this.

She ordered Ellyn to stay on board the ship, which, while she wasn't happy about it, she agreed to do. She needed to heal, and the Valenti clearly had it in for her particularly. Misha would look after her. Grace set out with Lara, Jehane and Daniel.

The Temple to the Winds shone in the bright sunlight, its polished marble exterior rippled with veins of different colours. They slipped through the hushed and reverent crowd gathered in the plaza outside, keeping their faces covered as much as they could, but Daniel's colouring and Grace's hair stood out like beacons among the pale Valenti. Anyone could spot her. The hood hid it as best she could. It would have to do.

A patrol of guards passed by as they joined the crowd and her heart beat a little too hard in her chest. But they kept going, laughing about something instead of paying attention, and she somehow managed to breathe again.

Suddenly the crowd roared, ecstatic.

'Shit,' Daniel said on a long, drawn-out breath almost drowned out by the cacophony. 'You're joking.'

Grace followed his line of vision across the crowd, to the top of the steps in front of the Temple. The carved wooden doors, twice the height of any man, decorated with gilt and mother-of-pearl inlays with images of the four winds, opened and a couple walked out to tumultuous cheers. All around her people cried out in delight, waved their arms in the air or jumped up and down. She felt like a statue, standing among them, frozen in horror.

Bastien was holding Rynn's hand. He was smiling broadly, a smile she had never seen on his face before, bright with delight and wonder. There was no trace of the shadows of his past or his many regrets. This was a man who had everything he had ever wished for, right in his hand. He was wearing clothes of white and gold, wedding clothes, and he gazed at his princess whose gown matched him in brilliance and beauty. His bride…

He'd never looked like that with Grace, never looked at her that way. She was scarred and cynical… and this girl…

She was just a girl, but she was so beautiful, like a goddess standing there, dressed in white and gold, a shining diadem on her fair hair.

But some instinct made Grace look at her a little more closely. Unlike Bastien, she didn't look delighted. She didn't even look happy. She looked terrified. It was the only word for it.

The priest followed them, holding the wide silver chalice from which they were to drink. And behind him, with the bride's family and the other nobles, Grace finally saw Asher Kane. He smiled, a nasty sort of knowing triumph on his face. Bastien had warned her Kane was here, but she still hadn't been prepared for it.

Grace swore loudly enough that several people turned and stared, so she ducked her head and turned away, Daniel, Lara and Jehane following her.

'Did you see him?' she asked as they walked away, making for the edge of the plaza and another laneway, which was empty. It led towards the harbour and no one else was going that way. They were too busy watching the love of Grace's life marry someone else.

It was a stupid question. Of course they had seen him.

'Couldn't miss him,' said Daniel. 'What the fuck is he doing?'

'Nothing good. Nothing good at all.' Grace leaned against a wall, trying to force herself to breathe evenly, to get control of herself, to hold her body intact and not shatter into a million pieces. This had to be a mistake. A trick. Maybe. Bastien had to have something planned, didn't he?

He always had something planned.

It was just that she had seen his so-called plans go horribly wrong before.

'We need to get into the palace, to find him. We need—'

'Grace…' Lara began and then went quiet.

'I'm not leaving him. Not unless he tells me to.'

'He already did.'

And go where? Thorndale? What would Grace do in Thorndale without Bastien? What was the point? She couldn't do anything about the nightborn or the Maegen without him.

If something happened, if something went wrong. That was what he meant. If he was dead or imprisoned or… but he had to know she wouldn't do it. Not if there was a chance to get him out of there.

Not… not if he changed his mind and chose Rynn instead. Chose power and a throne. Chose to give up fighting.

The ring on her hand felt unnaturally heavy. She shouldn't have worn it. She should have put it away safely and kept it secret.

'It doesn't matter.' She turned to Jehane instead. 'Get me in there. I have to talk to him.'

'Grace, are you sure?' he asked. 'It's dangerous. And he doesn't look like—'

This wasn't the time for a discussion. 'Just get me in there!'

*

Lara got them inside with relative ease, Jehane once more using his magic to hide them enough so they weren't recognised. The guards were on the lookout for magic, he said. They were watching all the mageborn for any sign of trouble. Grace could only focus on getting there; finding Bastien alone was going to be another matter. But again it was Lara who came through. She led them upstairs to an opulently decorated room, one with rose petals strewn on the bed and every luxury surrounding them. Their wedding chamber, Grace realised, as Daniel went a funny shade of grey and refused to meet her gaze.

What had happened to Bastien? Why would he have…?

The urge to vomit made her wrap her arms around her stomach, but she couldn't look away from the bed, the silken sheets, the furs, and the flowers. This was for him… for the two of them. And this was what he had chosen.

It had to be a mistake. She had to keep telling herself that. It had to be…

But the voice in the back of her mind said it was inevitable. He'd marry a princess, not an orphan dragged up in the Academy. That she had only ever been fooling herself.

A voice that sounded like Miranda. Or Celeste. Or Aurelie…

'I'll get him,' Lara assured her. 'Just stay here, out of sight. No one else will come in here, not yet. So stay put.' She cast a warning look at Jehane, who nodded solemnly. He'd keep them here then. Grace didn't have a choice. She couldn't do this herself. Not here.

The panic was getting the better of her. She didn't even trust herself to walk down a corridor of this palace without breaking down or attacking someone.

Instead, she locked all the feelings inside herself. She had to.

When the door opened again, Bastien was looking over his shoulder, laughing at something Lara was saying, perhaps arguing gently with her.

'And then Asher said, when we get back to Rathlynn, he'll have to order one the size of a—' His voice stopped when he saw the two men. 'Lara? What's the meaning of this?'

'Bastien?' Grace said, amazed she could even get her voice to work.

Something in his whole demeanour changed. It rippled over his skin, something violent and terrible, something so alien to his nature it was like watching some kind of possession in progress.

'*You*,' he said and the word came out twisted with loathing. He launched himself at her, so quickly no one had a chance to intervene. No one expected that they would have to. Before she even could react, his hands closed around her throat.

The force of the attack drove her across the room. She slammed into the far wall, striking her head, his grip crushing her throat as he lifted her from the ground. She kicked out desperately but his hands tightened around her neck. She stared in bewildered horror into his face, the face of a stranger, a monster, someone who clearly hated her. The world around her was turning to dancing lights and a darkening tunnel. Wind roared through her head. She could hear her own heartbeat, racing, thundering, ready to burst in despair.

Chapter Fourteen

The noise of the others shouting fell away. Grace tried to prise Bastien's hands off her, tried to draw up her knees again to get a kick in, to drive him back.

Shadows coiled up around him as Jehane, Lara and Daniel tried to pull him off her. Their hands dug into his shoulders, his arms, but he was like a statue, a rock, unmoveable. And he was far too strong.

And Bastien… Bastien… she didn't know him any more. He drew back his lips in a snarl. His eyes, so dark, so endless and black…

'Stop it! Bastien, please, stop.'

Another voice, one Grace barely knew. Rynn. She stood in the open doorway, still in her wedding gown, but she had clearly run from wherever she had been to find this scene of horror.

To Grace's shock, Bastien shuddered and then released her, leaving her to crumple to the ground and throwing the others off him. He looked at Rynn like a dog looking to its mistress and turned away without so much as a glance at Grace.

'Get them out of here, Lara,' he snarled, joining his princess. 'All of you, get out. I've made myself clear. I'm not leaving Rynn, not now. She is my wife.'

His wife. Grace's heart wanted to scream, but everything hurt too much. The words were like daggers. She gasped for breath and fought not to vomit as Daniel tried to coax her upright.

Rynn gripped Bastien's arm, stopping him from leaving. He looked down at her tiny form, clearly confused as she gently, but firmly, closed the door behind her, shutting them all away from the wedding, inside this godsforsaken room.

'Calm down. Captain Marchant, perhaps if you could… if you could be silent for a moment, and stay away from him.' It wasn't a threat. It couldn't be construed as that. Rynn's voice was still gentle music but it was a warning. 'He could kill you. I don't know entirely what that bastard implanted in his head but he can't help himself. General Kane was quite detailed.'

Asher Kane. *That bastard.* Rynn wasn't wrong about that. Of course. Bastien had said he was up to something.

'He *what*?' Daniel stared at them in horror, and Grace knew he above all others should understand. He'd been bespelled by Celeste to betray her too. His voice came out thin and disgusted.

But Bastien wasn't even looking at them any more, all his attention fixed on the princess. 'Rynn, this is madness. She's dangerous, I know that better than anyone. Call the guards. Let me defend you.'

She still held onto him, a tiny pale hand on his arm. Grace wanted to scream at her to stop touching him, to leave him alone. But right now Rynn appeared to be the only thing keeping him in check. If she released him, Grace wasn't sure what would happen.

'I don't need defending. Not from them. Try to understand.' She sighed and looked at Lara, begging her for support. 'There was a potion. A drug. They gave it to him last night. I didn't know what it was, or what it would do.'

'*You—*' Grace's voice was a wretched and broken thing, a hoarse croak of dismay and indignation, but at the sound of it Bastien swung towards her like an enraged bear, murder in his eyes.

'No!' Rynn cried out and when her hand touched him again, the spell seemed to settle once more. He turned to her, Grace forgotten, his only thought of Rynn. It was like Grace didn't even exist any more. His face softened to fondness. Grace wanted to scream but she didn't dare make a sound. Daniel held her, his face like stone.

'It's your voice, I think,' Rynn went on, as if it was some kind of hypothetical problem to be examined.

'How are we going to get him out of here now?' Daniel said.

'I'm not leaving,' Bastien murmured, gazing down at his wife in adoration.

Grace closed her eyes. It was easier. And it almost held back the tears.

She'd never felt so weak and broken in her life.

'I could knock him out,' Jehane offered, assessing Bastien with a critical eye. He didn't seem particularly put out by the idea either. In fact, he sounded like he would positively enjoy it. Knowing he had her back helped a little. 'Just hold him still for a moment.' The shadows rose from the floor and dropped like vines from the ceiling.

'We'd have to carry him,' Daniel said. 'Through his own wedding celebrations. That's hardly inconspicuous.'

Lara waved him back. 'Parry's right. Besides, it's no good if he attacks Grace again every time he hears her. It's lyriana root, it has to be. The Larelwynns used it on him in the past. Must have been a hell of a dose and Asher must have been very detailed. We're lucky he even knows who he is. If you don't give specific instructions…' She trailed off guiltily. She clearly knew far too much about the drug.

Grace sat down on the bed, dislodging a waterfall of rose petals onto the ground. The stench of them turned her stomach.

They'd won. They'd stolen him from her, wiped all his memories of what they had, and remade him as her would-be assassin.

He hated her.

Rynn meanwhile threaded her fingers with Bastien's, the way they used to do. She spoke so softly, as if cajoling a wild animal. Given what Grace had just experienced, that wasn't far from the truth.

This couldn't be happening. He was like a different man. Her Bastien, the one she knew and loved, was gone, wiped away. Instead here was a man who was by turns a besotted fool or a rage-filled murderer.

Asher had won.

Her eyes filled with scalding tears again and she couldn't blink them away any more. She couldn't bear to watch as he took Rynn in his arms and bent to kiss her.

But Rynn stepped back, awkwardly, turning her face from him like a demure temple virgin. He moved forward again but she put up a hand to stop him. 'Trust me,' she told him. 'Not yet. Wait.'

He looked so hurt.

Grace buried her face in her hands.

'I don't want to wait any more, my love.' She knew that tone. She could hear the arousal in his voice. She wanted to say his name, to tell him to stop this madness, to say something, anything, but she couldn't. Even if she could find the words.

Daniel wrapped his arms around her, holding her tight, and she gave up, turning to him so she could smother herself in his chest and try to block out the world. She didn't even dare let the sound of a sob escape.

'I came across a passage in Inariant's Alchemy about lyriana root,' Rynn said, her voice still shaking. 'Part of my studies, theoretical but… it doesn't matter. Lyriana works on mageborn, makes them… well…' She waved one elegant hand at Bastien, then caught Grace's glance and her expression grew placating. 'But there's an antidote. It's not… not difficult to make.'

'Are you the royal apothecary all of a sudden?' Jehane asked harshly. His gaze flickered to Grace, just for a moment. Whatever he saw in her face made his expression harden but nothing more.

Rynn narrowed her eyes and her voice took on a formal tone. It was defensive, Grace could hear that, but it was withering as well. 'I have many skills. My education is second to none. At least in that my family didn't fail me. I can make it.'

'And why would you make it for us?' Lara asked, her own shrewd mind more firmly on the subject in hand.

'I can't stay here. Take me with you and I can cure him. It might even be like he never took it. Or at least… we could try to make him like… like he was…' She didn't sound so sure about that. Hopeful but not certain.

'You don't know where we're going, Princess,' Daniel warned her.

Rynn rallied again and fixed him with a look that branded him an idiot. 'I don't care.'

Grace lifted her face. Bastien had turned to look at her again, but now he just looked confused, as if he was trying to recall something from a dream he had long ago. Or a nightmare. Maybe deep down he still recognised her, maybe there was still some way to get him back. She had to believe that. If she didn't, she'd fall to pieces.

Even if he was married to someone else. The very someone who now held his future in her tiny hands.

If someone had told her a few months ago she would fear she'd fall to pieces because of a man she would have called them a liar and punched them to unconsciousness.

Grace met the anxious gaze of the Valenti princess and nodded.

*

The apothecary's study was deserted, with everyone at the wedding celebrations. It was on the lower floors, servants' quarters really. Grace followed the group while Rynn led the way with Bastien by her side.

'You okay?' Daniel asked.

It was a stupid question and she could see from his face that he knew it the moment he uttered it. But what else could he say?

'No,' she told him, daring him to argue.

'We're almost there, almost out,' he assured her. 'There's a servants' entrance, not far from here, leads to an alley behind the palace. Their security is shit.'

'Because the whole bloody city is a trap,' she muttered in reply. To get out of Iliz meant getting onto the water and as far away as possible before the sea defences could be raised. They could close off the Grand Harbour and raise chains across the entrance to the lagoon. And if they didn't make it to the ship, the maze of the city wouldn't help them. They didn't know it well enough.

The candlelight danced around them as Rynn worked. Grace was aware of Bastien watching her, no matter how hard she tried to blend into the background.

Every moment she thought she saw a glimpse of him again, as if he might remember, his eyes glazed over and he scowled at her. She looked away. She had to.

'Here,' Rynn said, pulling the tome off the shelf and flicking it open until she found the page she wanted. 'I need help.'

'Of course,' Bastien replied, dutiful and attentive as ever.

'Not you. Make sure no one comes in. Stay there. I need Captain Marchant's help.'

'Not her!' Bastien blurted out, unable to bear the thought of Grace near his princess. 'It isn't safe. Please, my love.'

The words speared into Grace. This wasn't happening. Couldn't be happening. And yet… here she was.

Rynn's expression was as firm as her voice.

'She won't hurt me. We can trust her. Really. Kane lied, Bastien. He lied about everything. Please, just step back and guard the door.'

He looked uncertain, but obeyed her again, taking himself back to stand beside Jehane at the door, guarding the entrance. Part of whatever Asher Kane had said included his unswerving trust in the man who had betrayed him time and again.

Divinities, Grace thought, I should have killed him when I had the chance.

Not that she had actually stood much of a chance.

At least she had Daniel on her side. And the Shade. Jehane glared at Bastien fiercely as if he expected him to attack again at any moment, but Bastien looked defeated. She had never seen him look so lost. The urge to comfort him was almost instinctive, but she knew now that would only end in disaster and pain.

The princess met Grace's eyes, and beckoned her over. 'This doesn't take long. I promise.'

'Why are you doing this?'

At the sound of Grace's voice Bastien stiffened again, and Jehane stepped between them. It could be a suicidal gesture, but he didn't flinch. The Shade was made of more than shadows. Loyal to the crown, he'd said. But he was loyal to something else as well: his comrades.

'Stay there,' Rynn commanded. 'I mean it, Bastien. I need her.'

He stopped, glowering at Grace. She bristled and turned her back on him deliberately. Rynn tried to smile, a gesture of encouragement. It didn't help.

'Why do you need me?'

'You're a Flint, right? It's quicker with a Flint.'

'I *was* a Flint.'

'Well you'd better be again, and quickly because otherwise this will take hours and we need to leave before anyone comes looking for us.'

Great. The one thing Grace could do to help and she couldn't actually do it any more.

Rynn didn't wait for anything further from her. Nobility to the core, she just carried on as if Grace hadn't told her that it wouldn't work. The princess had decided it would be so and so it would be.

She poured three liquids into a vial and handed it to Grace. Then she grabbed something that looked like a nut but smelled of sulphur and grated it into her potion. Next came a single drop of another liquid that shone like gold and slid like honey down the side of the vial.

'Heat it.'

'I can't. Didn't you hear me?'

Bastien glared at her and she flinched. She couldn't help herself. Not this time. The hatred, the malice…

The darkness. The same thing she felt inside her, ever since the Loam in the garden had turned nightborn.

There was darkness deep inside her, the same darkness she had felt beneath the light of the Maegen. It wasn't safe, she knew that. But she could sense the power there. Beyond the emptiness. If she would reach down and take it.

What had the Loam in the garden said?

You could be so much more. If you just had the courage to reach out and seize it. It's waiting for you. It's a sacrifice, of course. But everything worthwhile demands a sacrifice. Especially magic. Oh… it could make you so strong, little Flint.

Just reach out and seize it. The void inside her beckoned, waiting for her. Grace closed her eyes, steeling herself for what might come. All she had to do was make a sacrifice. And that sacrifice was herself. It was her honour to serve. That was what she had been taught for as long as she could truly remember everything. Serve the crown. Serve Bastien. Do her duty. And here she was yet again.

She reached out into the depths of the deepest nightmare, back to the edge of life and death where she had almost been lost before. Some part of her had never left the place. Not really. She knew it from her nightmares. It haunted her. Deep in the darkness underneath the Maegen, where unknown things moved. Things with too many eyes, claws and teeth, things that were hungry, that dripped poison, that wound around her greedily, that pulled her in…

The warrant against her skin burned like acid. She winced, clenched her teeth and forced herself on.

The fire that had been stolen from her veins roared to life. She almost dropped the vial, blinded by the light that burst from it.

The liquid inside turned a bright blue and Rynn almost squealed with delight. The sudden noise broke the link of shadowy tendrils around Grace's heart.

'That's it, perfect!' Rynn reached out to take the vial from Grace, but the heat made her snatch her hand away.

Daniel and Jehane grabbed Bastien before he could launch himself at Grace again, pushing him against the door with a solid thud.

'She's a witch, Rynn. She's dangerous. Don't you see it? Don't you see the darkness?'

Rynn flinched, her face paling, and turned to Grace with a stricken expression.

'It's okay,' Grace whispered, pushing it from her consciousness. What had he seen within her? What had he recognised? 'Make it work. Please.'

Rynn nodded, swallowing hard. 'Not here. Not yet. If he… if he passes out we're stuck here. And we can't be. Not with Kane. I can't take that chance. We have to leave.' She grabbed the vial in spite of the heat and sealed it with a stopper, holding it close. 'Bastien won't leave without me and I can't stay here. Not if he goes.'

'Why not?' Lara asked. 'You don't love him. You don't even like him. Kane can't hurt you here, with your family and your people.'

Rynn heaved in a few tight breaths, looking from one to the other of them, as if deciding if she could trust them. Clearly she made her decision as her gaze alighted on Grace.

'My *family* will hand me over to Asher Kane without hesitation. They can use our marriage to make me a figurehead or… whatever they want… He'll take me to Rathlynn. Even if you take Bastien away, they'll use me, as his lawful wife. And then… then…'

And that was the thing. Grace couldn't do that to her. She couldn't do that to anyone.

Rynn retreated towards Bastien who pulled himself free of Jehane and wrapped his arms around her, holding her close and trying desperately to comfort her. He cast them looks which said he'd murder anyone who came too near or tried to part them. Grace didn't doubt it.

But right now he didn't seem to be aware of the power he could wield. He hadn't used his many forms of magic against them. She could thank Asher Kane for that as well, she supposed. It was a bitter kind of relief.

Grace glanced at Daniel. He tightened his mouth and then nodded at her. They couldn't leave the young woman behind, not to face that. But stealing Bastien was bad enough. Stealing the beloved Rose of the Valenti was going to see them pursued to the ends of the earth.

But what else was new?

'She comes,' Grace said. 'And we need to get the hell out of here. All of us. But if something happens to you, or that vial, he's stuck like that. Please, your highness. I'm begging you. I won't let you be left behind but we need Bastien back, if it's possible. I need him…' It was almost too much to say, too much to heave out of her heart. 'I need him in his right mind again.'

Or as near to it as he could be brought. Restoring him suddenly seemed too much to hope for.

Rynn stood there, holding the vial in both shaking hands, her grey eyes so very wide, Bastien still holding her in a gentle embrace. She looked like she'd burst into tears and Grace couldn't blame her.

Then, abruptly, she turned to Bastien, thrusting the vial at him. 'Drink it.'

He obeyed her without hesitation, and though Grace felt the same pang of shock that he would be so gullible, so easily led, this time she had to hope for the best. Because if it didn't work, she'd lost him forever.

Chapter Fifteen

Bastien couldn't tell what was going on. They ran down the luxuriously furnished corridors of the palace, ducking down back staircases and through servants' passages. His mouth was filled with a bitter taste, like almonds and vinegar, and his stomach churned. Whatever Rynn had given him, he should never have taken it. She must have made a mistake. This was meant to be the happiest day of his life. But Rynn wasn't happy and now they were surrounded by enemies, led by that red-haired witch. Asher had warned him. He'd told him she was dangerous and that he should kill her as soon as he saw her. Her voice alone drove him into a blind rage.

He'd almost killed her. It was almost done, as it needed to be.

Rynn had stopped him. Her heart was too good, too pure. She couldn't see them for what they were. The witch had her under some kind of spell.

Bastien couldn't see the magic binding Rynn but he knew it was there. It had to be. She was acting so strangely. Whatever it was, this invisible binding, he couldn't unpick it and set her free.

He reached out with his senses, with the tingling thread of magic, carefully, tentatively. There was something wrong, terribly wrong…

If only he could find Asher, get word to him. He'd help. Of course he would help. Rynn had to be mistaken. Asher was his friend. He had always been… but why did that thought set off another cold shudder of revulsion inside him?

The redhead was watching him again. The pain in her eyes made him uncomfortable in a way he couldn't define. It wasn't right. He shouldn't feel that. He loved Rynn.

Didn't he?

But he couldn't remember anything clearly. Couldn't remember a first kiss or any gesture of affection. Couldn't remember talking to her for longer than a few minutes. There was the dance at the ball. That had been magical. Like something out of a story… But…

He'd been looking for someone else the whole time. And halfway through, he had felt something… something terrible… like his world was falling apart…

Like the feeling sweeping over him now.

Grace. Her name was Grace. And she was—

He reached for the thought only to find it snatched away. He knew he was missing something. He reached deeper, into the darkness, into the depths…

Grace…

'*Bastien, remember.*'

The voice wasn't his. He didn't know where it came from but it sliced through the base of his brain like a blade. A man's voice. No, a boy's. Someone from so very long ago. Like a dream more than a memory.

Rynn's hand on his arm brought him back to the present. Her sweet face looked so concerned, so worried about him, and he blessed himself for that. That she cared, that she was in his life.

'Stay with me,' she said. 'We have to leave. It's the only way.'

'Rynn, we should check with Asher.'

Her face went pale and she shrank in on herself, fragile and delicate. 'No. Not him.'

'But he's my friend.'

'He isn't, Bastien. I don't know how to make you believe that but it's true. He lied to you. Asher Kane is not to be trusted.'

Bastien frowned. It didn't make any sense. Asher was his oldest friend. He had always been there for him. Always.

Except… he remembered kneeling, excruciating pain ripping through his body, Asher smiling at him, enjoying his torture. He came to a shuddering halt.

'*Bastien…*'

Rynn rounded on him, holding his shoulders and staring into his face. 'Are you… Bastien, are you remembering?'

'Remembering what?' The words came out in a defensive snarl. It was a dream, that was all. A nightmare. He tried to shake it away. He was a prince. This was his wedding day. His happily ever after.

Wasn't it?

'What's wrong?' Lara snapped. 'Why have you stopped?' The marshal's voice was all command and he couldn't believe she was going along with any of it. She was meant to help him, guide him, obey him. But this was madness.

'He's remembering.'

'As quickly as that? Maybe you have a vocation as an alchemist, your royal highness.'

Grace stopped in his line of vision again, trying not to meet his gaze, her face a veneer he couldn't read. She was attempting to hide her feelings now, to control them and do her job. Whatever that was. Kidnapping him and his bride… And that same thing reared up in the back of his mind. Like he knew her. From the moment he'd seen her wield magic… he knew her. Like they were connected somehow. As if her power called to his.

And within that connection there was a darkness, endless and terrible.

An image of his hands tangled in her hair, of her lips parting against his… He shook it away in horror. No, revulsion.

From outside he could hear the sounds of the city, but this wasn't the constant hum of Iliz. This had a different note, one of panic. Running feet, shouts of alarm, anger…

'Move, keep moving,' Lara said. 'We're almost out.'

By the cellar steps, the guardsmen kept cloaks and she grabbed them, making him put his own on while Rynn deftly wrapped herself in the scarlet fabric.

Outside, noise rose in a cacophony, sounds of horror, of rage, the sound of a mob.

'Something's wrong,' Lara said. 'Jehane?'

The Shade slipped ahead and vanished in the shadows beyond the door.

They hadn't even followed him out into daylight before the noise rose louder. Like a breaking thunderstorm, conflict and panic everywhere. Bastien felt it like a wave. It rose up from the ground itself, from the earth and water of Iliz. He shuddered to a halt as it swept over him and through him.

Magic. Born of horror and fear.

'What is it?' Rynn asked. 'What's wrong?'

'Something's happening. Something terrible.'

Another wave struck him and he staggered, this time unable to stand against it. Pain, terror, fear. And beneath it, rising up, feeding on it, an endless, ancient darkness.

'Keep moving,' Lara urged. But he couldn't. Every instinct howled it at him. He couldn't go out there. It wasn't safe. It wasn't—

Grace Marchant reached the end of the shady alley and stood there, silhouetted against the lights and chaos. The celebrations had changed to something else. The plaza beyond was still full of people, but not celebrating, not any more. Screams and shouts replaced music, a stampede of running feet, the crash of weapons, the smell of panic, sweat and blood. She was a void, a dark and empty unmoving space between him and whatever was happening out there.

'*She'll die for you. She'll always die for you.*' The voice was stronger, more urgent now. '*Remember. Remember everything. Or lose her forever. It's coming. If you don't remember nothing will stop it.*'

They reached level with Grace and the full horror of it all revealed itself. Everywhere groups of guards with naked blades were closing in on the mageborn. Not just guards. The people of Iliz as well, makeshift weapons in every hand. Others scattered across the plaza, crushing people underfoot regardless of their heritage or abilities. Blood spilled across the stones.

A man staggered down the alley from the other direction, clutching his side. He saw them, tried to reach them – looking for help, or a place to hide, or maybe even to warn them – and he fell to his knees, his guts tumbling onto the cobbles underneath. The Valenti who followed were a mob, diving on him before he was even dead, kicking and stamping.

Bastien barely caught sight of the collar around his neck before he vanished beneath them. He'd been mageborn, Rathlynnese, one of the Larks who had escaped Aurelie.

Rynn screamed as someone seized her from behind. In the same instant Bastien's heart seemed to stop inside him and he barrelled towards her, but Grace was there first, the sword and dagger already in her hands. The man went down in a heap without making a sound, the fury of her attack taking him – taking all of them – completely by surprise. The red-haired witch grabbed Rynn and thrust her towards Bastien before spinning around to fall in beside Parry, swords ready.

All around them a mob raged, tearing at one another. The mageborn fled, those still able to move, and the Valenti pursued them. Another pack raced at them but stopped when they saw the two Academy officers blocking them, fully armed and furious as they prepared to fight.

'Leave them,' someone shouted from the rear of the group. 'Come on. There's more of the mageborn bastards heading for the docks. They're trying to escape.'

And they were gone. The dank little alley was suddenly very dark and cold.

'They're Valenti,' Rynn whispered. 'They were…'

'They're killing the mageborn,' Jehane said, reappearing from his woven shadows, his features tight and bloodless. 'All over the city. They started rounding them up when the matins bell chimed, using those crap sigils on them… and then… something went wrong. Someone fought back. And the Valenti retaliated. The whole city has gone mad. We have to move.'

'She wouldn't,' Rynn said, as if she couldn't grasp what was happening. 'My grandmother wouldn't…'

But she would. The Dowager Queen? Of course she would. Rynn couldn't be that naïve. The deaths were probably not the Dowager's plan, not this many. But she had stoked the fear of the mageborn among her citizenry too expertly.

And fear, Bastien knew, could change the mageborn. Make them nightborn. The waves of terror he was feeling now, sweeping through the traces of the Maegen all around him, infecting it with the Deep Dark… It would take them all.

Grace watched him, her face so cold that it stabbed at something inside him. Why should he care what she thought? Why did it seem to matter so much? Her eyes flickered with darkness and for a moment the gold dimmed to something else, something filled with shadows.

His breath caught in his throat.

'Make for the ship,' said Lara. 'We can't help here. We need to get out of Iliz before they raise the sea defences and close access to the harbour. Move.'

'I can't just *leave* them,' Bastien protested, but no one was listening to him any more. Without someone to stop it, the Deep Dark would take every mageborn in Iliz. And then the slaughter would begin in earnest.

'I didn't know,' Rynn shouted. 'I swear it. I didn't—'

It was a retreat. More than that, it was a flight. They had to escape. Iliz was drowning in blood, ravaged by fire summoned by nightborn Flints. And the waters rose as Tides turned nightborn as well, and Loams shook the foundations of the city. Lara led the way. Jehane and Daniel brought up the rear, driving back those Valenti who came after them. Like being pursued by ravaging dogs. And behind them all, that red-haired witch slaughtered as she went, anyone who came too close, her sword a silver blur, her body as much a weapon as her steel.

Was she gone? Had the Deep Dark taken her? The thought made his heart stutter inside him, like a fist had clenched around it.

Rynn slipped her cold hand into his and stumbled along, pulling up the wedding dress when it hampered her. There was too much fabric – it wasn't made for practicalities. She stumbled, almost fell, but valiantly got to her feet and tried to keep going.

'Here,' Bastien said and scooped her up in his arms. 'Just hold on.'

'Don't stop,' she breathed in his ear. Her voice and her trembling form told him she had never experienced terror like this. When would she in her sheltered life? 'Please.'

The canal led directly to the lagoon. He could see ships out there in the Grand Harbour beyond.

Another memory reared up, gazing at the dark water and the lights last night. Standing by a window, looking at the same view from a higher angle, and wondering which light was the one. The one where Grace was…

The stab of pain came back, this time almost bringing him to his knees. Memory. It was a memory. *Grace.* Only the fact that he was still carrying Rynn made him keep his footing.

'What is it?' she gasped. 'What's wrong?'

Bastien's head was burning up. This wasn't right. He knew it wasn't right. 'Did you… did you poison me?'

Gods and goddesses, it hurt. Like a hundred sigils burning into his skin. Like someone rummaging around inside his brain and draining the magic from his system, ripping off the blindfold and turning his eyes to face the sun itself.

Grace stood alone behind them, facing a mass of rioting figures. Mageborn fire and darkness rose up in her to drive them back, transforming her to the monster he feared. She illuminated the palace square of Sa Almento, the bodies and the gore-streaked cobbles, the canals red with blood.

And then, a heartbeat later, the mob swept over her and she vanished.

'Grace!' Bastien howled, the word torn from him, ragged and bleeding.

'Get in the boat,' Lara said. 'She's fine. She's coming. Get in the boat with Rynn.' When he didn't move she grabbed him, throwing him forward.

He fell into the bottom of the low punt, hitting the wood so hard that he was lucky he didn't go through. The boat rocked as the others clambered in.

'They're coming,' he heard Daniel say. 'They've gone insane – mageborn and Valenti alike. We'd better make this fast.'

'It's not exactly a fast boat, is it?' Jehane argued.

Daniel wasn't in the mood. 'Well, do something magical then, you arsehole. Where is she? What's taking—?'

'Shut up, the pair of you,' Lara growled and pushed off from the quay. The boat lurched in the water, rocking sickeningly.

Bastien reached out, dragging himself up, and Rynn took his hand. But he didn't want Rynn. She wasn't there. Wasn't in the boat.

He looked back to the land. To Grace.

For a moment there was nothing, and then a figure burst out of the carnage, running for the edge of the quay.

She ran from the guards and the mob, red hair flying behind her, weapons in her hands, and she jumped at the last minute, even as the others began to row like their lives depended on it. Grace crashed into the water beside them and went down, swallowed up by dark waves.

Gone.

For a moment Bastien's life was over.

Then she broke the surface, coughing and spluttering, flailing around as she tried to swim with her weapons still clenched in her hands. She hated water. She still had nightmares and woke screaming. When she was a child they'd tried to drown her, to put out the fire inside her. Because—

He knew that. He knew every detail. Because—

He reached for her, almost flinging himself over the side of the boat to do it. At the same time he scraped together the remains of his magic and demanded the water return her to him, to give her back. He felt Asher's command still lingering. But this time… this time he tore right through it.

This was to save her. This was to save Grace.

The water bucked and kicked like a mule, an unnatural wave, and then something was flung up towards his reaching hands.

Grace was soaked and freezing. Hauling her into the boat with him, he wrapped himself around her, holding her against him, pulling the cloak around her shivering form. She gasped for breath, her chest heaving against him.

Not just from the cold water, he realised. There was fear too, shock.

And he remembered his hands around her throat. He remembered his attempt to squeeze the life out of her, the way she'd struggled and kicked, all in vain.

'Grace,' he said, needing to reassure her. 'Grace, it's me. It's really me.'

She twisted beneath him, her body rolling, her legs tangling with his and suddenly she flipped him over, her whole body her weapon as she pinned him down in the bottom of the boat. The punch to his face sent his head slamming against the hull, the pain blinding him.

When he could see again, her face hung over his, wild and furious, her wet red hair clinging to her skin like trails of blood. He was probably lucky she'd dropped the knife first.

'Stay down,' she told him. 'Stay the fuck down there and don't move.'

Grace kept him pinned in the base of the boat until they got to the side of the ship, so he couldn't see much as they arrived. His head pounded, and his body ached. Every so often spasms of agony would bring him to the brink of unconsciousness.

'Should it do that?' Lara asked Rynn.

'It'll pass. It's… the potion has to be driven from his blood. I didn't think it would be this painful.'

But it was. Asher had drugged him and made him Rynn's willing slave.

Bastien stared up at Grace, horrified, but she wouldn't meet his gaze. Or couldn't.

Divinities, what had he done?

It took almost all the strength he had to haul himself up the ladder and stumble onto the deck of the ship that awaited them. Thankfully, Daniel and Jehane slid in on either side to hold him up so he didn't fall flat on his face in front of the sparse crew.

The cabin was small but neat, a couple of bunks and a porthole window.

'Put him on the bed,' Rynn said brusquely. 'I need to check that nothing's wrong.'

He slumped back onto the bunk, his head pounding, stomach churning.

'Where's Grace?' he asked.

'Don't worry about Grace,' Daniel told him. 'She's fine.'

'Danny, tell her I didn't know what I was doing. Tell her—'

Daniel Parry had never taken to him, Bastien knew that. He didn't like the aristocracy and, given his experiences of the Rathlynnese royal family and their associates, Bastien couldn't blame him.

'Give her a break, Bastien,' he snapped. 'She's been through hell with you tonight, all to get you out. Just let her be. She could have died back there.'

Rynn stepped between them. 'And you let him be. He's ill and needs to sleep for the antidote to finish its work. Get some wine or whatever they have on board,' she said.

'Bit early in the morning for drinking,' Jehane said, a teasing tone attempting to lighten the mood. He didn't seem as shaken as the others. A Shade was always closer to the Deep Dark; maybe it didn't affect him as much. But Bastien had seen something in Grace's eyes. And the Deep Dark had already marked her…

It wouldn't be long before it took all the other mageborn as well.

Rynn didn't feel like joking. 'It's my wedding day,' she all but snarled at him. 'Get the bloody wine.'

And that was when it finally hit Bastien. What he'd done. What he'd said.

He'd married Rynn.

And then he'd tried to *kill* Grace.

He'd lost her. This time he had really lost her.

Chapter Sixteen

Grace made for the cabin where she'd left Ellyn, heaving in breath after breath as she went. She didn't seem able to hold air in her body. Her lungs ached and her head pounded. She was freezing cold, soaking wet and everything was wrong. As she fell into the cabin, she forgot about the raised lip of the doorway, tripping over it. She caught herself with shaky hands and hung there, wet hair dripping over her face, staring at the floor, unable to think, let alone move.

'Divinities!' Ellyn grabbed her and hauled her upright. 'What happened to you?' Grace clung to her, shivering. Where did she even begin to explain? How could she put it into words? 'Here, get this off.'

Grace let her friend strip her of the sodden clothes. They came off like ice sheets, but Ellyn wrapped her in the extra blankets from the cubbies under the bunk.

'I'm okay really,' Grace tried to say. It came out weak and broken.

Ellyn gave her a look which called her a liar and kept rubbing her limbs through the blankets, trying to warm her up. 'What happened? Divinities, Grace, your neck! Who did that? They'd better be dead.'

Grace almost laughed. She really did. She'd almost forgotten about that. Fighting for her life against a rampaging mob put some things into perspective. And then the laugh turned into something else. A great, long-suppressed sob of agony.

'Bastien,' she managed to say. And with that one word, it all came out, words rushing out of her, a torrent of information all jumbled together like the chaos she had seen unfold since she last saw Ellyn. The horror on her friend's face as she spoke made the reality of it slam into Grace once more. 'Daniel can tell you. He'll explain. He was there.'

For a long, painful moment Ellyn seemed unable to find words. 'For fuck's sake, is this what happens when I'm not with you for one mission?'

Was she joking? She was grinning. She was actually grinning.

'Ellyn, it isn't funny.'

'It's ridiculous, that's what it is.'

And Grace finally let go. The great racking sobs that she had been holding in finally broke free; sobs that made her ribs ache and her throat raw. Ellyn held her tight, letting her cry. She might call it ridiculous, but she knew it wasn't. She recognised shock, pain and grief. Finally, when she went quiet, Ellyn spoke again, her voice gentle.

'Where's Bastien now?'

'I don't know. The antidote made him… I couldn't… I couldn't…'

Grace couldn't help him. The magic in her had blazed and the Deep Dark had been there, within reach, laughing through her mind. All she could think of was him, his hands around her throat, the look he'd worn as he tried to throttle her. The hatred, the rage. It hadn't been Bastien, not really. She knew that.

But also, it had.

The Deep Dark whispered to her, assuring her it was true.

The fear it thrived upon, the terror, the deepest nightmares, it fed on them all and made her…

'Just take your time,' said Ellyn, her voice Grace's anchor. 'He assaulted you. You don't have to do anything, Grace.'

She wanted to say it wasn't his fault. But she'd heard those words so many times from other women, women who made excuses and shouldered their burdens and made the best of it. So had Ellyn. She couldn't say them.

Ellyn stroked her wet hair. 'Try to get some rest. I'll find something warm for you to drink. Go on, lie down.'

Grace did as she said, but when the door opened, she shuddered again. It felt like a threat.

'Ellyn,' she whispered and Ellyn stopped, looking at her. 'Lock the door behind you.'

It was only when she heard the little catch turn that she was able to close her eyes.

From the other side of the cabin wall, she heard muffled voices and groans. Bastien in pain, suffering as Rynn's antidote purged him of the lyriana root. It sounded like he was in agony.

And part of her wasn't sorry at all.

*

The ship rocked Grace like a cradle, her body finally relaxed enough to sleep. She'd heard nothing else. Ellyn had returned with a soup which she'd drunk and then she'd slept while the ship carried them away from the Valenti Islands. Grace had never felt so fragile or so pathetic.

She'd lost everything back there. Everything.

Who had they rescued? Who was Bastien Larelwynn now? Did they still head for Thorndale? Perhaps he would want to return to Rathlynn with his new wife rather than help find a cure for the nightborn. Grace shivered, pulling the blankets around her. He might be happy to let the Deep Dark have her now. Part of her ached to give in and let the darkness take her.

She knew she would have to get up again eventually but, right now, she didn't have the strength. No one needed her. She lay still, under a mound of blankets, while Ellyn came and went, locking the door behind her when she did. When the sun finally did rise again, it did so over the open sea.

Grace pulled on some dry clothes and wrapped herself up again. The blankets smelled of sea water and some were still a bit damp but she didn't care.

When Ellyn came back she wasn't alone. Rynn followed her, her anxious face peering over Ellyn's shoulder.

'I can tell her to go away,' Ellyn assured Grace. 'But she wanted to speak to you.'

Grace nodded carefully. The bruises on her neck had really come up now, black and ugly, tender to touch. She didn't bother trying to hide them.

'All right,' she said. 'Princess.'

'Rynn,' the young woman said. 'I don't think titles are going to help now.'

'Fine.' Grace didn't offer her own name. Her title – her rank – was the only shield she had, even if it wasn't really hers any more. Not since the Academy had been sacked. 'How – how is he?'

'Better. Much better. Almost back to himself, I think.'

'Himself. Good.' Whatever that meant.

Rynn leaned forward, desperate to explain. To justify what had happened. 'He couldn't help it. That drug is—'

'I know what it is.'

'He wants to talk to you.'

'I don't—' Grace wanted to say she didn't want to talk to him. Because she didn't. And yet she knew she'd have to. They were on a small ship heading to his home, facing the divinities knew what. She didn't have a choice. But what on earth was there left to say? 'It's complicated.'

'I know it is. But Grace…' When Grace glared at her, the princess's eyes widened in fear. 'Captain Marchant…' she tried again. 'This terrible situation…'

Unexpected anger flared in Grace's voice, in her eyes.

'You married him.'

The royal façade rushed back into the girl's whole demeanour. Grace loathed it in anyone, but in Rynn it was particularly galling. 'I had no choice. Nor did he.' The princess leaned forward, her elbows on her knees. 'It's a political marriage, Grace. And it wasn't consummated.'

Grace groaned. 'Too much information.'

It was Rynn's turn to smile, a sudden and more comfortable expression on her perfect face. 'But true nonetheless. You're not what I expected.'

'Thank you. I think.'

'Will you see him? He asked me to see if you would. He begged me. I think it will help. He's devastated.'

So was she. Couldn't anyone else see that? True, she made a point of hiding her emotions. She had to.

She'd seen it on his face, in the little boat, seen the horror of realisation at what he'd done written all over his features.

'Rynn… I don't—'

'He needs you, Grace. Needs you more than anyone else in this world. When he remembered, the first thing he remembered… that was you. Please…'

'I'm sure you think that. And thank you. Thank you for making the antidote, for bringing him back. But I can't just forget what he did.'

'No one is asking you to. But… at least talk to him.'

It wasn't going to stop. Grace wasn't going to get any peace. Everyone would tell her to talk to him, she knew that. Everyone.

And in the end…

'You don't have to,' said Daniel from the doorway. Eavesdropping. Because everything in her life seemed to be on public view these days. But at least Daniel was on her side. That was something. 'Grace, I'll lock him up for the duration of the voyage if you want. I'll stand guard here too if that's what you'd prefer. I can throw him over the side, but he'd probably just control the sea and walk after us.'

It shouldn't make her smile. But it did.

'Probably not necessary, Danny.' It gave her what she needed, the sense of normality to their conversation. It grounded her and she drew in a breath before she looked at Rynn again. 'All right. Tell him I'll talk to him. But not here.'

Not alone, she wanted to add, and hated herself for it.

That was how she found herself up on the foredeck, the wind blowing the shadows out of her head. There was no sign of land ahead of them yet. No sign of the Valenti Islands behind either, and for that she was grateful.

What was going on back there? Grace couldn't shake off the echo of what she'd experienced there. Not just Bastien's attack, although that was bad enough. But reaching into the emptiness inside her, finding the magic she needed to make the antidote with Rynn, the bleak black place that power had come from. And she still didn't know what she had done to make sure they escaped. She had been lost in the moment, in combat, in action. Like something else had taken over.

She was afraid of what she had felt. The sense that it was right. Just.

Danny and Ellyn promised they'd watch from a distance and they were as good as their words, waiting for her by the steps to the foredeck.

She didn't trust Bastien. And that scared her more than anything else.

A curly-haired boy leaned on the bow rail, staring ahead, and Grace could feel the shimmer of magic in the air around him. She could almost see it, like a heat haze, and she recalled how once, back in Rathlynn, Bastien had helped her see the tethers of magic binding the mageborn. She could almost do that by herself now. This boy was a Zephyr and he was taking them away from the Valenti Islands as fast as he could.

'Oh, sorry, ma'am… I didn't see you there.'

He'd turned, staring at her in something akin to wonder. What had he heard? The sailors were all gossiping, she knew that. She'd be a fool to think otherwise.

If she never set foot on those islands again, she could die happy.

But she doubted that would happen. Maybe the first part but definitely not the second.

The boy was still staring at her.

'It's okay. I need somewhere quiet,' she told him.

'It's good for that, up here, the quiet. For thinking. That's what the captain says.' He gave a bow, not as well practised as all the ones she'd seen in Iliz, but far more honest. 'I'm Larne Pardue. She's my aunt… the captain, I mean. Captain Pardue. You're the one they're all talking about, aren't you? The captain from Rathlynn.'

'A different kind of captain,' she told him, bemused. The boy smiled at her without a care in the world.

'They said that too. Like no one else, they said. His true love.'

Is that what they were saying? Grace had no need to ask who *he* was. The mageborn all seemed to refer to Bastien in that tone of voice.

Awe. Wonder. It was rather confusing to hear herself referred to in the same way.

She folded her hands behind her back. 'I don't know what I am. Not any more.'

He just grinned at her, his young eyes so very bright and full of faith. 'It's going to be all right, ma'am. I'm sure of it.'

Then he skipped on by, the breeze rippling behind him. A little Brindish child from a land of sun and spices. Nothing more. But his faith was so strong it left Grace speechless.

She would have liked to say she sensed Bastien approach, that her instincts warned her and her years of work and training had honed her ears to hear things others couldn't, but she didn't. Suddenly, he was there, behind her.

'Grace?'

His voice was so soft, so hesitant, that for a moment she thought it was part of the wind in the sails, or the creaking of timbers.

'Bastien.' It wasn't much by way of a reply. Perhaps she should have thought about it, found something witty or cutting, some perfect phrase to put him in his place.

'Grace, I'm sorry.'

'You couldn't help it. It wasn't your fault.' They were the right words to say but she felt as if she was just parroting them off because she was meant to say that. Wasn't she? And objectively, it *wasn't* his fault. He *couldn't* help it. But that didn't help her.

Bastien wasn't managing any better than she was.

'I should have fought harder. I should have been able to resist. It's—'

'Even as a god, you weren't able to withstand the effects of that drug, Bastien.' She sighed, leaning forward on the rail, taking almost her full weight on her arms. It took her mind off everything else. Just for a moment. The sea rushed by beneath her, crashing on either side of the bow.

'But still…' he said. He didn't touch her, though she could sense his need to do so.

'So Asher Kane got what he always wanted,' Grace said. 'To hurt us. No, to hurt *you*. I was collateral damage.'

He tried again, divinities bless him. 'I never meant to—'

Finally she relented. Just a little. 'I know that.'

'The marriage isn't even—'

'I know that too. Rynn explained.'

'Am I allowed to at least finish a sentence?' The irritation in his voice was real. It was much easier to deal with. She was about to tell him that when he went on and the tone was different – apologetic, tender, and careful once more. 'May I see?'

She didn't have to ask him what he needed to see. Closing her eyes so tightly she saw spots against the darkness, Grace swallowed hard and then turned to face him, leaning on the rail now, her arms out on either side. She let her head tilt back slightly, exposing her bruised throat to him, letting him feast his eyes on the full extent of what he had done.

When she could bring herself to look, the expression of agony on his face made her stomach twist inside her. She knew Bastien, knew him better than she had ever known anyone else. He couldn't believe he could have done such a thing, not to her. He gave a choked cry. 'Oh, Grace… I – I'm sorry.'

Her voice came out gentler this time, less accusatory. 'It wasn't your fault.'

'But it *was*. That's who you saw, who you felt… My hands, my strength. Grace, I – I can't—'

Part of her wanted to punch him again, to inflict on him what he had inflicted on her. But the rest of her couldn't have hurt him, not any more than he was already hurting. She couldn't move anyway.

'You left me, Bastien.'

'I never meant to.'

What could she say to that? It was the truth. She believed him, and she had stopped him, saved him. And now…

She let out a long sigh and it was like a weight lifting from her.

'Don't… don't do it again.'

The anguish he wore on his face bled into his voice. 'Never. I swear it. Never again.'

She frowned at him, waiting for him to touch her, to say something… *anything* else. In the past, he would have wrapped her in his arms, held her close, and she would have let him because he always made her feel better. 'May I?' he asked at last.

Confused, she shook her head. 'May you what?'

'I promised never to touch you without your permission once. I should have kept that promise. I should always have… Grace, I'll do anything, anything you want to make it up to you, to show you…' His voice shook. 'To show you that I wouldn't hurt you like that without – I don't know – outside influence. But if you need me to stay away, or—'

She had to be brave here. She owed him that at least. He was flailing, lost. Her cool and caustic Lord of Thorns, her always-in-control Bastien – but he hadn't been in control this time. Bastien didn't even trust himself any more. Asher Kane had stolen that from him too. And if Bastien wouldn't trust himself, Grace would have to do it for him.

'Do you want to?' she asked, afraid of the answer.

'Stay away?' He looked horrified. 'No, but – how can you bear for me to—?'

'Bastien,' she sighed, his name her prayer. She reached out a hand, ashamed of how it shook, but when he didn't move to take it, that made it somehow much worse. She let it drop. 'I saw you, your face, but it wasn't you. I don't know who that was. It may have looked like you, but it – your eyes…' She gazed up into his eyes now, so deep and dark, but so warm. Endless. She would gladly lose herself in those eyes and never be found. His eyes had not been like this in the palace, when he had attacked her. They had been cold and hard, the eyes of someone else. Her hand came to rest on his shoulder and his muscles tightened beneath her touch. 'We'll take things slowly,' she said.

His hand came up and wrapped around hers. His touch. Actually *his* touch this time. His tenderness.

'I don't think we've ever managed to take anything slowly, Grace,' he told her with a rueful smile. He almost looked and sounded like himself again.

Her heart gave a lurch, though she couldn't quite fathom why. 'We'll try.'

Grace wrapped her arms around him, held him again. His head bent down over hers, his cheek resting on top of her head. She could feel his breath, the movement of his chest. She stroked his back, the lines and angles of his body better known to her than those of any other man.

The drug had transformed him into someone else. There was no other word for it. Had that happened to him every time? Did she really even know the man she loved?

But despite everything, she didn't doubt that she still loved him.

Shame washed through his eyes. 'I – I wasn't strong enough.'

He'd loved another girl once, and the Larelwynns had stolen that from him, making him drink lyriana root until he forgot she ever existed. Grace had always wondered if he had really loved the woman who became Mother Miranda, whose pain and hatred had made her into a monster. Now she knew it didn't matter if he had or not. He would never know. That damned potion.

'Come with me,' she told him, and led him below decks, back to the cabin.

She closed the door behind them.

'Come here,' she said.

'Grace?' His soft, dark voice made something in her tremble. Not in a bad way. Not this time.

He stepped into her arms and she tilted her face up to his. He bent forward, kissed her, gently at first, a brush of the lips. And he sighed.

'I could have lost you today.'

'I *did* lose you.' She bowed her head, pressing her forehead into his chest, feeling his racing heartbeat. 'Bastien… You could lose me any day. You are eternal, aren't you? It will happen eventually.'

'You found your magic again, to make the antidote.' He didn't look happy about it though. If anything he looked concerned.

The warrant against her turned cold and she remembered the words of the Loam in the garden, the woman possessed by the Deep Dark.

If you just had the courage to reach out and seize it. It's waiting for you.

But it hadn't been courage that made her reach for it. It had been fear. It had been desperation, the very thing which turned mageborn to nightborn.

'We have to get to Thorndale,' Bastien said, his voice more certain now, more sure. Divinities, Grace wanted him to be sure. She wanted to cling to that. Thorndale might be the answer, if they could make it there. The Maegen, the source of magic, the seat of Bastien's power… he'd find a way. She knew that. If Bastien Larelwynn put his mind to it, he could do anything. He just… he didn't look so sure right now. 'I've lost too many people. I can't lose you, Grace.'

He could, but she didn't want to say that. That emptiness inside her, the cold emanating from the warrant… a thousand other things could tear them apart.

She pushed the image that taunted her in her mind, of him bearing down on her, of his hands around her throat. Of the stranger behind his eyes, the man she didn't know any more.

For a moment every instinct screamed at her to pull back, to push him away and defend herself. But if she did that, she really would lose him and Asher would finally win outright. Forever.

Grace lifted her face, gazed into his eyes, tried to smile. It was wavering and unsure, but it was all she could manage. The stranger wasn't there any more. It was only Bastien. Only her Bastien. And he looked so worried.

'Grace,' he whispered and his lips brushed against hers. 'Grace, it will be okay. I promise.' He couldn't promise that, not really, but right now she didn't care.

His kiss deepened, and he framed her face in his hands. Every time, she forgot how gentle he was. How perfectly gentle. He was so strong, so powerful in every way, but when he touched her, when he held her and loved her, he seemed afraid he might break her.

Grace pushed his shirt open and teased across his chest with her kisses. Bastien bit out a gasp but didn't move.

'I could lose you too,' she told him. 'Maybe not to death, but in so many ways. To Rynn. To Aurelie. To someone else.' *To Thorndale and the Deep Dark*, but she didn't dare say that. She paused, contemplating that. Technically she had already lost him. He was someone else's husband. But she couldn't think about that, not now. She didn't want to. Perhaps it was selfish. She wanted him. She wanted him to be hers again.

He kissed the top of her head, then lifted her effortlessly and sat her on the bed. Even his strength was tempered with that gentleness. That was what had been missing from him when he was that other man. She understood now.

The bed wasn't large or even terribly comfortable. The cabin was neat and functional. But she didn't need anything more. Nothing but him.

'Are you sure?' he said.

She knew what he was asking. 'Yes.'

Bastien helped her shed her clothes, following each touch with a kiss. He worshipped her and, for once, she let him.

The boat rocked gently and Grace lay back beneath his kisses, his caresses, his tender touch. He bowed over her body, his mouth on her skin, making her gasp his name until she couldn't stand it any longer.

'Bastien,' she whispered, hardly able to form the word.

'Are you sure? Grace, after what I did—'

'It wasn't you. Remember?'

Bastien rose over her, his body a pale gold in this light and beautiful, the lines like those of a sculpture, a god. She reached for him, pulled him down, claiming his mouth, his body. Making him hers again. Just hers. If only for a little while.

He was everything to her. Everything.

And he almost drove the shadows away.

Almost.

Chapter Seventeen

The screaming had been going on for hours. Kurt had locked the door because there was nothing else he could do at this stage. The girl wasn't coming out anyway and her family were already traumatised. When the flames came, licking under the gap beneath the door, turning the whole room into an incinerator, he just stood there, praying. He didn't even know who he was praying to.

The screaming eventually trailed off to sobs and coughs and then… Silence ate away at the air around him and for a moment he couldn't breathe. How could he still be breathing?

It wasn't fair.

It took an hour before the door was cool enough to touch, let alone open. He didn't want to. It took him a full ten minutes more to work up the nerve to do it.

The smell almost knocked him from his feet. Nothing remained inside. Nothing. Only ash.

'The iron held then?' Melia's voice came out of nowhere, making him jump and turn, ready for an attack. When he saw his second in command silhouetted in the doorway leading back to the inn, he relaxed a little.

'Just about,' he replied. 'Poor kid didn't… well, she wasn't getting out.'

It wasn't exactly a smile. More like a grimace. It passed over Melia's face like a ghost. 'You couldn't have let her out. She'd have taken all of Eastferry with her, if not the whole city.'

He sighed, leaning on the door frame, staring at the blackened iron-plated interior. It was a furnace, or as near to a furnace as they could make.

Behind Melia, Syl cleared his throat. 'But it held,' he said after a moment. He looked appalled, as if he hadn't really put two and two together about what he had designed until this moment.

Syl was a fully trained Atelier. He'd left the job, as he liked to tell anyone who would listen, for a carefree life of prostitution. But he had talent and skill. Kurt hadn't appreciated how much until now.

'Yeah, Syl. It held. Couldn't have asked for more.'

The mageborn kids they'd broken out of the dungeons helped where they could, looking for nightborn, trapping them, but they were only Academy cadets to begin with, nowhere near fully trained in their powers yet, green and inexperienced, not to mention traumatised. Kurt couldn't ask them to risk themselves.

'The Master Atelier could have done more,' Syl muttered and turned away.

'You don't know that,' Melia told him. 'Even if we could find him—'

'He's in there. I know it. They took him from the Academy, but they didn't kill him. They wouldn't dare. The cadets told me. Aurelie tried to use them to break him.'

'I gave you all the time I could to search when the royal bitch was trying to threaten me,' Kurt interrupted. 'You were meant to be distracting her, if I recall.'

Syl smiled his lazy, sultry smile, the one that worked on almost everyone, and his dark eyes glittered. 'She was plenty distracted until you turned up, then you were all she could think of. Maybe we should have switched places. Or don't you whore for Eastferry?'

Maybe, Kurt thought, he should have. But he wasn't sure he'd have left with all parts intact. Besides, while he was distracting the queen, Syl had been able to rescue the cadets and raid the treasury.

'Just as well I don't want you for your body, Syl.' He nodded towards the metal chamber. 'This was necessary. And it worked, thank all the divinities.' That didn't make him feel any better. Nothing did.

Syl swallowed hard and closed his eyes. 'I know. I'll get back to work.' He slid away, up the stairs. Whether it was Atelier work or his preferred profession, Kurt didn't have the heart to ask.

'Her family are still here,' said Melia. 'I've had Halyk pouring them ale and Scarlett's making some food, but they won't touch any of it. They need to talk to you, boss.'

'I know that too.' Kurt groaned and then made himself straighten up. He hadn't meant that to come out so peevishly. 'I know. Thank you, Melia. I'm coming up now.'

They needed to talk to him. They needed explanations he couldn't give, platitudes he didn't feel like saying, and comfort he just didn't have in him. This wasn't his job. None of it. But he went anyway.

Melia stood behind him the whole time. He didn't know how he would have endured it otherwise. The mother wept. The father sat there, his hands wringing together the whole time, and never looked up.

'Her magic did this to her?' the sister asked. She was mid-twenties, a Loam who made sure that Eastferry got fresh food even though the city was starving. They kept her safe, and secret. Her sister had jeopardised that as well. The mageborn succumbing to the darkness put them all at risk from Aurelie's guards as well as their own powers.

She looked very pale, dark shadows under her eyes. The stress of it was getting to her too.

'Mr Parry, Elsie wasn't the first. We've all seen it. We've all felt it. It's getting worse.'

Kurt felt the unfamiliar need to explain, to make some sort of amends, even if no amends were really possible. 'I'm doing everything I can.'

'It's not your fault.' Her mother stood up, stopped and choked on a sob. 'Thank you for trying. She was a good girl. Really. Such a good girl. So careful. It's not… not fair.' She trembled then, shook from head to foot. The sister – Bella, he reminded himself, her name was Bella – wrapped her arms around her mother. She pulled her away from Kurt.

'You have to stop it, Mr Parry. We can't trust the Royal Guards. They just lock people up and kill them. And that queen is useless—'

Kurt raised a finger to his lips, and the girl stopped. 'Those aren't safe words, love. Not safe at all.'

She glared at him. 'There are far more dangerous ones. *Thorns*, for instance. Isn't that what you call yourselves?'

Melia hissed and Bella flinched but didn't back down. 'We can't go on like this. It's imprisonment and divinities know what, or… or become like *that*… Where is the Lord of Thorns? The mageborn need him. You have to get him back.'

Melia started forward, ready to intervene, to throw them out if necessary. Kurt signalled her to stop. She glared. He didn't need to look around to see it. He saw the fear infect the girl's belligerent face, the knowledge that she had gone too far.

'What makes you think I have any way of doing that?'

'You know him. You know where he is. Your brother is with him. That's the word out there.' Bella nodded towards the door.

'So what?'

'Get him back here. Or there are going to be more. It's a plague. The nightborn, like in the old stories. Maybe they *are* nightborn come again, I don't know. Bastien Larelwynn is the only person with a hope of stopping it. Ask anyone. The mageborn – we know. We need him. Come on, Ma, Da. We have to go. There's nothing else for us now.'

'I'm doing everything I can,' Kurt told her and instantly felt pathetic. It wasn't a sensation he was used to. It didn't help that Bella was right. It didn't help that she was voicing his own fears. There was nothing he could do about the nightborn. Nothing but kill them. Or make them kill themselves.

She gave him a defiant look. Tears welled up, matting her lashes together like smudges. 'It's not enough. And if you can't get *him* back, what good are you?'

Melia showed them out and the moment the door shut Kurt sank onto the nearest chair. It wasn't the world out there he was worried about, at least he hadn't been until now. He was fending off attacks on every front. He didn't need his own people looking for the impossible. He couldn't ask Bastien Larelwynn to come back here, even if he wanted to. Even if he thought for a moment he would. The queen would kill him on sight, if he was lucky. And that was nothing to what she'd do to Grace Marchant, Danny and Ellyn de Bruyn – she'd made that more than clear in his dungeon audience with her.

Although it hadn't exactly been an audience. They'd snatched him off the street at dawn just as he had planned. A hood went over his head and the next thing he knew he was chained up on his knees on a rough stone floor. Exactly as planned. Kind of.

When they pulled the hood off him and he saw Aurelie standing there, surrounded by guards, he had thought this was it. He had miscalculated, gone too far this time. He was dead. Instead of execution, however, there were threats, and questions which he wouldn't answer. He'd talked his way out of it, played with her, and delayed her while Syl left her bedchambers and made his way down to the dungeons. They'd slipped out through the narrow secret passages and made their escape, all of them.

The jailbreak had been the stuff of legend, not that anyone would actually believe it. He'd emptied the treasury and her cells, all while a prisoner himself. A man in two places at once. And all he had to show for it were some bruises.

Well, Syl didn't want the credit.

Being roughed up by the palace guards was something Kurt could handle. It wouldn't be the last time. And it didn't compare to a good old dockside punch-up anyway. Melia had picked him up, patched him back together, even found him a Curer to sort out the worst of the damage, and Eastferry had rallied around him. Especially when Syl had brought those kids home.

The mageborn cadets he'd rescued hadn't been who he was looking for, but he broke them out anyway. Syl had been looking for his mentor, the Master Atelier, but he couldn't leave his former comrades behind. Not there. Kurt didn't blame him, the state some of them were in. They wouldn't have lasted much longer. After taking out the guards, they made their way to the treasury and rendezvoused there. Then they had loaded up everything they could.

Syl was a looker with a talent for fucking he put to excellent use. But he also had an eye for magical things, and a sense for what was worth nicking. It had made them a fortune in the past.

And Kurt had discovered the most useful bit of information of all. It turned out that Aurelie didn't know what was going on any more than he did.

The mageborn were out of control. The ancient pact between the Hollow King and Lucien Larelwynn was broken. They were changing, they were killing and they were dying. Their own powers were tearing them apart from inside. Their eyes went black as night and they lost their minds. Not like going hollow. This was calculating, malevolent, evil. Nightborn. Just like the stories.

And there was nothing he could do about it.

Melia came back in and shut the door. 'She didn't mean it, boss. They know you're trying.'

'All I'm doing is getting them killed. She's grieving. And she's scared she'll be next.'

They all were. Melia sat down beside him, stretched out her long legs. Another time he'd compliment her on them and she'd tell him to push off. Light-hearted, like.

'What are you going to do?'

He shrugged. 'I can't bring him back here. Aurelie with his power at her beck and call? No, thank you.'

Melia sighed, rolling her head from one side to the other to stretch out the tense muscles.

'What about the other one? In the Temple?'

'Crazy, Danny told me. Crazy and dangerous to boot. I think the words *psycho-bitch from the deepest pits of the seventh hell* were used. Besides, she doesn't have her power any more.'

'Are you sure?'

'That's what Danny said.'

'Has anyone… you know… checked?'

'Melia? Are you suggesting we break into the Temple now?'

'We've been everywhere else, boss. And if she doesn't have powers, maybe she has information. We could do with that at least.'

And damn it all, she was right.

The Temple was even more secure than the palace, for very good reason. Aurelie couldn't afford anyone getting near Celeste, or Celeste getting out. They opened the place only when the queen deigned to visit Bastien's crazy sister.

It was the most secure place in the city. Much more secure than the palace.

And that was when it hit him. 'Divinities… I know where the Master Atelier is… He's in the bloody Temple with Celeste.'

Chapter Eighteen

They were far out to sea when the noise started. An argument, quickly escalating, a lot of shouting. Grace roused, disentangling herself from Bastien's long limbs. As he woke he tried to pull her into his embrace but reluctantly she wriggled free.

'Something's happening,' she told him. 'Need to see what.'

He struggled up after her, his hair falling over his face, his eyes very bright beneath it.

Outside, the argument was louder, heading their way. She heard Ellyn challenge someone. This wasn't good.

Quickly they pulled on their clothes and then Grace opened the door.

'There you are!' Rynn shouted, her beautiful face determined. Ellyn blocked the approach to the cabin, and the princess, Lara and Jehane crowded the narrow passageway. 'I need to talk to you right away. This is unacceptable.'

She wasn't looking at Grace though. Her gaze was fixed on Bastien and she looked desperate. Ellyn had a knife in her hand and every nerve in her body was taut. But she didn't move.

'I told you not to come down here,' Lara said. 'I'll sort this out. I promised you.' Her voice came from behind the princess and Jehane was with her, lurking by the access to the deck. Grace couldn't see him clearly, but she could sense him, read the traces of his magic on the air. He was gathering shadows, ready to attack if needs be. In a very short period of time, in this very confined space, everything was about to go to hell if she didn't intervene.

Grace moved slowly, carefully, starting with the biggest threat to safety in the corridor. She stepped up to Ellyn and slowly mimicked her stance, bringing her arm in line with Ellyn's, reaching for the knife. She closed her hand over her friend's.

'Let go, Ell,' she whispered.

Ellyn shivered and then let her take the weapon. Grace breathed again.

'What the hell is she doing here?' Ellyn hissed.

But Rynn was oblivious to the danger Ellyn posed. Perhaps she wasn't even aware of what she represented, what her family had done to Ellyn and all her line. Rynn had to know. Her family had killed every de Bruyn they could find. 'I have every right to be here. I'm his wife. They're all gossiping about it up on deck, the sailors. About you, down here, together.'

'Enough, Rynn!' Lara snapped. 'Bastien, we need to discuss this. This could be an international incident of gigantic proportions if mishandled. It's bad enough what happened back there. I need you to think with the brain in your head.'

He was still half-naked. His shirt hung open over his sculpted form and he was barefoot. His dishevelled appearance made it clear how they had spent the night. Bastien glanced over at Grace, who was not wearing much more than he was. He actually had the nerve to grin, just for a moment.

When he looked at Lara, however, his expression might have been carved from stone, like one of those statues in Rathlynn.

'Perhaps we should speak in private,' the marshal said in firm tones, her glare terrifying.

But Bastien wasn't intimidated by Lara Kellen. Possibly not by anyone, Grace knew that. He'd been cast as a villain for most of his life and he knew how to use that.

'You can speak in front of my people.'

Ellyn looked over at him, eyes blazing as he said it. Then she nodded slowly and stepped back. *His people.* No one had ever claimed Ellyn other than Grace, Daniel and the Academy. Bastien signalling that Ellyn was *his* was a promise to always protect her.

'Very well,' Lara said, although it was clear that she did not consider it well at all. 'You have asked us to get you safely to Thorndale. Asher Kane will come after us, as will half of the Valenti.' She drew in a breath, clearly steeling herself before she could continue. 'It isn't far to Thorndale but the way is hard. Two nights at most, three days on the road. If we are to make it there safely you need to leave it to me to organise. There is no way we can avoid scrutiny. You are far too recognisable. Word will travel on swift wings that the rightful heir has returned to Larelwynn soil and we can do nothing to stop that. You need to play your part, *your majesty.*'

'And what is my part?' Bastien asked, so quietly. It was always dangerous when he went quiet. Grace knew it was a warning sign.

'A royal king, not a lovesick fool. A man ready to wear a crown and ride into battle if necessary. And it may well be necessary. Asher Kane may have thought to use you and Rynn, but we can use his own plan against him. We can—'

'Enough!' Bastien said. 'Why is Rynn here?'

The princess interrupted before Lara could reply. She all but stamped her foot. 'Because I don't have anywhere else to go. Thanks to you.'

A dozen emotions passed over his face, a man who masked his feelings more completely than anyone Grace had ever known. Disgust, horror, guilt and more. A ripple of all that had happened since he met the Rose of the Valenti. It wasn't Rynn's fault, Grace knew that, but she was a catalyst. And she still wasn't prepared to let him go. Even if her interest was political rather than romantic. She was playing with fire.

'*Thanks to me?*' Bastien snarled at her. Even Grace flinched at the sound, but no one was looking at her. Rynn shied back, eyes wide, and she suddenly seemed to realise that the greatest danger didn't lie in being left behind somewhere. 'What did *I* do to *you*? I was drugged,' Bastien went on in the coolest voice imaginable. 'You had a hand in that, I believe.'

But Rynn was not easily intimidated. She visibly pulled herself together, smoothing down the front of the gown and drawing in a deep breath.

'And I have apologised for that, and I tried to make amends... the goddess knows I tried... I cured you. But it doesn't change the fact you said the words in the presence of representatives of the aristocracy of your kingdom and all of mine. As far as anyone is concerned, I am your wife. No matter *who* you sleep with. Kings and queen have dealt with less and kept their marriages. But they keep it to themselves. Appearances are what matters and if anyone sees you with a mistress—'

'I'm no one's mistress,' Grace cut in. If her voice was harsh she didn't care. Anger was surging through her now. Anger and disgust. She shouldn't care what people thought of her, least of all Rynn. But being spoken to – and dismissed – like this made the rage inside her swell to fill the dark and empty places. She wanted to lash out. But she couldn't. She clenched her hands into fists and folded them behind her. Striking the princess now would solve nothing.

Rynn gave her a pitying look. It was the image of her grandmother's.

'I don't know *what* you are right now. But I need protection and he is the only shield I have. So I intend to use it.'

In that instant Grace completely believed her, and suddenly saw in her the queen she could become. Aurelie was an amateur in comparison. Rynn was royalty and it showed. Steel in her veins, determination in her eyes, and the utter inability to believe that anything would go contrary to her will. Divinities help whoever crossed Rynn Elenore Layna de Valens of Gellen. Bastien was raised the same way.

This wasn't fair. This couldn't be happening. Because Rynn was not wrong. Grace felt her anger turn white-hot and insurmountable.

The ship lurched beneath them. Grace barely kept her footing but Rynn wasn't so lucky. She lost her balance, falling forward, and all Grace could do was catch her. She was trembling all over and her eyes had gone wide, grey and helpless. Terrified. Suddenly politics, marriage and mistresses seemed like the least of their problems.

'Lara, get Rynn to the cabin and keep her there,' Bastien barked.

Cries of 'All hands on deck' went ringing out and, even though they were probably going to be of no help whatsoever, Grace and Jehane scrambled up through the narrow hatch to the deck first, followed by Bastien and Ellyn.

The wind had got up, tearing through the sails, and the waves crashed over the sides, drenching the deck. The ship pitched back and forth, the timbers groaning under the strain.

'A sudden storm, came up out of nowhere,' Captain Pardue yelled. She stood at the wheel, wind tearing at her long black hair as she wrestled with it. 'Out of clear skies too. You best get down below, out of the way.'

'This isn't natural,' Jehane shouted. 'Can't you feel it?'

Grace could. The air was tainted, trembling. No, not the air, because all the air was wind, a blinding gale. But something else. The energy around her felt different.

'Definitely not natural,' she agreed.

'It's mage-sent,' Bastien told them, as Daniel and Misha struggled across the deck to join them. 'There's a Zephyr somewhere. Powerful and out of control. This isn't good, Grace.'

'There's a Zephyr on board,' Daniel said. 'But he's just a kid.'

'Bastien, can you locate him? Stop him?'

'Perhaps. If I can—'

A terrible cracking sound shook the world around them, followed by a crash which sent them all to the deck. It hit Grace hard, wood splinters driving their way into her hands. Dirty white material wrapped itself around her, wet and smothering as a shroud, pinning her down. She struggled to tear her way free and heard more shouts of alarm, of warning.

Hands reached her, pulling her clear, out from under the thrashing sail and ropes, away from the broken mast. Misha hauled her to her feet and she leaned heavily on him from need and shock more than anything else.

'Bastien,' Grace shouted. 'Where's Bastien? He was right beside me.'

The sail caught in the wind again, snapping back with a crack like thunder. And she saw him, lying there, sprawled on the deck, not moving.

Daniel and Jehane were first to reach him. Grace tried to throw herself forward but the harper still held her, refusing to let her go. As she shouted and screamed at Bastien to wake up, her friends turned him over, lifted him gently.

Rain lashed against his face and blood turned it red.

Grace tore herself out of Misha's arms and grabbed Bastien, trying to wake him. He opened his eyes, stared at her groggily. He was dazed. She hoped it was nothing more serious than that.

'Get him under cover, now,' she barked to Ellyn. 'To safety. He needs a healer. He needs…' Damn it, someone needed to get things under control. They had a Zephyr on board the ship, one who was clearly out of control. Bastien was down. She had to fix this.

She darted over the fallen mast and sail, climbing up to the wheel deck and Captain Pardue. She was aware of Jehane on her heels and Daniel too. Misha and Ellyn grabbed Bastien, trying to get him below decks to safety. If this ship went down in a storm stirred up by a rogue Zephyr, it wouldn't matter where they were. They'd all end up at the bottom of the sea.

Pardue screamed her orders over the howling wind, her knuckles white on the wheel.

'Where's the Zephyr?' Grace shouted but the wind snatched her words away.

'The what?'

Grace grabbed her, more to pull herself in closer than to pull Pardue away from the wheel. That would be suicide. 'The Zephyr? On board?'

'Larne, but he's not strong enough to control this.'

'Where is he?'

'Bow! He always takes watch at the bow.'

At the bow. About as far away from Grace as he could be. That's where she had run into him earlier. She couldn't see him now, not with the amount of spray coming over it. She couldn't see anything. Just water everywhere. Water in the air and water coming to get her again.

'Daniel, Jehane, with me,' she shouted, unsure if they could hear her or not. It didn't matter. She was going anyway and she was pretty sure they'd follow.

She jumped across debris and struggling crew, people trying to hold the ship together, running as if her life and everyone else's depended on it, because it did. She could feel it now, the hum of magic, the touch of the Maegen, running through her. The dark tide beneath it shuddered out of synchronisation with the light. The hollow pit inside her gnawed away but she ignored it. She had to.

And then she saw him, the kid she'd spoken to yesterday, clinging to the bow rail, drenched to the skin. The power radiating off him bent the wind and rain around him.

'You have to stop this!' she shouted.

He turned, shocked and terrified, his eyes aglow and his hands still wrapped around the rail. His legs splayed out beneath him. He looked afraid, terrified.

'I can't! I've tried. It won't—'

Another wave hit, bursting around him and almost throwing him off the boat completely. But shadows surged forward, tangling him in their unnatural grip.

'Got him,' Jehane shouted. 'Now what?'

A blast of wind slammed into him and the Shade lost his footing and his grip. He slammed to the deck and slid towards the dipping bow but Grace dived on him, pinning him there so they didn't lose him to the storm.

The Zephyr shook himself free, terrified and overwhelmed with his power, the Maegen running wild inside him.

'You've got to get control of it,' Grace yelled. 'Larne, isn't it? Larne? Please, you've got to—'

Tears streamed down his face. 'I can't. I told you. The Maegen, I reached for it and it changed. It's dark and it's terrible. It's eating away at me. I'm empty inside. I—' He stiffened, his whole body going rigid, and then he threw back his head screaming. The wind joined him, buffeting the ship, waves crashing up over them.

The cry cut off and he jerked convulsively. When he opened his eyes, they were dark, dark and endless as the void. He smiled, a slow, wicked smile, and the voice that came from his mouth was not that of a boy. It clung to the wind, crawling over her skin, and she knew it.

'*Come to Thorndale, beloved. We hunger for you. We cannot wait.*'

And suddenly there was a chord. Music filled the air, drowning out the wind and the waves, a frantic, mad tune, rising up and down the scales and then plunging on into a melody which took sudden shape. The sound was all-encompassing, breaking over them all and driving the Zephyr to his knees. Grace staggered forward, looking for Daniel, and he was there behind her, holding onto Misha who stood, iridescent with power, harp in hand. He must have grabbed it from their cabin and come to find them. To help in the only way he could.

Misha was a fine musician, she knew that, but she'd never really thought there was much use to be made of a Lyric. He'd helped Ellyn, soothed her and comforted her with his music. But this… this was different. Now, the storm itself stilled for him, for his music, for the power flowing through him. The Maegen, which had been thrashing around her, unmanageable and terrifying, stilled abruptly. The wildness bled out of it as the tune turned softer, slowing as its rhythm slowed, and bit by bit Misha tamed the storm, brought the Zephyr back under some form of control. Not his exactly. Grace knew it wasn't like that. But his music soothed the world, and the boy fell, sobbing, to the deck. The storm abated, and the clouds overhead cleared.

Misha's tune tailed off and the sudden silence felt unexpectedly disorientating. There was only the sound of calm seas and a soft breeze. Behind them, the sailors shouted but their voices seemed so far away.

Grace picked herself up and stumbled across to where the boy lay. He was so small, lying there, limp and exhausted, his chest moving fitfully. But his eyes, when they opened, were his own again. She managed to pick him up and drag him to safety, other hands coming to help her.

'Be gentle with him,' she warned the sailors. 'It wasn't his fault. Take him below to the Lord of Thorns. He'll help him.'

And then she remembered Bastien, the blow to his head, the blood and that dazed look in his eyes. Divinities, she'd only just got him back.

She rushed by Misha, paused to press her hand to his shoulder and then thought better of leaving him there.

'Thank you,' she said. He looked exhausted now, having sent his power out into the world, quelling an unnatural tempest. 'I'll need to talk to you but – I've got to check on Bastien. And the boy. You… You should rest.'

Daniel held him close, arms wrapped tightly around his lover's waist. 'He will. I'll make sure of that. Interrogate him later, Grace. Go.'

Bastien… he was hurt. And the boy… he had spoken with the voice of the Deep Dark. How Misha had saved him, she didn't know. Perhaps Bastien would.

But she couldn't get those words out of her mind.

'*Come to Thorndale, beloved. We hunger for you. We cannot wait.*'

Chapter Nineteen

The light of the Maegen surrounded him, wild and furious. It was like standing in the heart of a storm made of light and power, a hurricane composed of pure rage. Bastien was lost in it, flotsam and jetsam in the tempest, buffeted and broken. The more he struggled for equilibrium, the more the world slipped through his fumbling fingers.

'Bastien,' said the voice. Not her voice, not the one he longed for. This was another voice. From another time. A voice he had never thought to hear again. 'Bastien, remember.'

The boy was only a teen, not even a man. Slim and delicate, thick hair falling over his face and a stupid, oversized sword in his hands. He had Rynn's nose and jawline. Or rather, she had his.

'Bastien, please.' Lucien Larelwynn fixed him with that look, the look that he always used, even when they were boys. Even when…

But they weren't boys. His memories were better but still scrambled. This was something new. Perhaps Rynn's antidote had opened doors to more than just the recent past.

'I remember, Lucien. I remember everything now.' It took a moment before he recognised the voice as his own. And the lies too. His memories were still scattered.

Lucien Larelwynn smiled, a half-hearted, broken smile. There was nothing more tragic. He always knew Bastien better than he knew himself.

'No you don't, Bastien. Not really. You remember some. But not all. You need to go back, right back. You can remember, if you try, but only if you really want to. We need to make it right. You have to remember.'

We? There was no 'we' about this. Lucien Larelwynn was hundreds of years dead. And go back? What did this phantom from the past think he was trying to do?

'I am going back.'

'No. Really. Go back. Right back.'

He didn't mean Thorndale.

Lucien reached out, his hand trembling, and he pressed it to Bastien's head. The pain was immediate and complete. It was agony. Something tore through him, a lance of betrayal and desperation, loss and misery, the feeling that the once-king had ripped something vital out of him and stolen it away.

'Someone always has to die. I'm so sorry, Bastien.'

The same force hurled him away. He fell; fell down into the depths, into the darkness.

Shadows smothered him, the Deep Dark swarming over him. He was trapped here, lost, drowning in the source of magic itself. And here below, the Deep Dark was stronger than ever. He could see it spreading, reaching out avaricious tendrils into the world beyond them. It laughed at him, stuck there and sinking. It was strong, so strong. Stronger than it had ever been before. He could see its escape routes, its ways out and the many, many lives it tainted, infecting so many. He shuddered, staring at the enormity of it. How was he to fight that?

How could something like that ever be contained?

He tried to still himself, to focus and remember, just as Lucien had instructed. Blood. Blood in the water. He could see it, spreading out like ink, dark and red. He could taste the thick coppery tang of it on his tongue and in the back of his throat.

Blood was the key. It opened the door. There was always a sacrifice. A willing sacrifice.

Not Grace. It would not be Grace.

He tried to breathe as that endless and terrible thing clamped itself around his throat. Long-fingered hands – too long to be human – closed over his face and pulled his head back, exposing his neck, the nails digging into his eyes, burrowing into his brain. A blade kissed his Adam's apple.

Remember.

Larelwynn blood.

The girl laughed. She threw her Valenti white-gold hair over her shoulder and smiled. Her blood glowed within her veins. Her laugh echoed around the cave like the light reflecting on the rough roof overhead and the water boiled before her.

'It's beautiful,' Rynn said.

Blood fell into the luminous pool, feeding the magic, transforming it.

A knife clattered to the stone floor, blood pooling around it. So much blood.

Bastien tried to cry out but his voice was gone. Another figure stood over him, something dark and terrible, eyes aglow with magic, a thing of stone and shadows with an implacable soul as old as time itself. Something he had no defence against.

It wore his face. Divinities help him, it wore his face.

And beside him there was a woman. Made of fire. Unmistakable.

'Beloved,' it said.

*

The cabin seemed smaller than before, the place where he and Grace had made love, where she had tried to make him whole again. But Bastien was more broken than either of them knew. Broken in ways that couldn't be explained. Blood stained the bedclothes and the pillow now. His blood, he realised. His head pounded more than he could ever remember. More than a hangover, more than a headache. More than lyriana root. It felt like his skull had been split open and glued back together. Right where Lucien had touched him.

Grace sat beside him, holding his hand, her eyes closed. But the moment he moved, she opened them, gazing down at him. There was a flicker of alarm on her face. Perhaps it would never go away. The shame of it washed through him like nausea.

'Take it easy,' she said. He could hear the exhaustion in her voice, see it in her face. 'You were knocked out.'

'By what?'

'One of the masts fell on you.'

He pushed himself up anyway. His body ached everywhere, his head most of all. But it didn't matter. The power behind that storm had been mageborn and out of control.

'Who was it? Who turned nightborn?' His voice grated against the inside of his throat and he swallowed hard. Grace brought a flask of water up to his lips and, after only a moment of hesitation, he drank gratefully. It was Grace, after all.

'A Zephyr. He's crew on the ship.'

What had happened to him? Had they killed him? Bastien had heard of that turn of events before. A Zephyr on board a ship going hollow and the crew hurling him overboard to save themselves. He'd seen the Zephyr on this ship. He was only a boy, but sailors were superstitious. And while a Zephyr could be a boon, they could also be a curse, especially if they lost control. Like this. Bastien had felt it in the air, in the wild wind, in the storm itself. Magic had whipped it, drove it, and made it tear at the ship, ready to drown them all. In the moments before the mast knocked him out, he had seen it all. After Iliz, he should have checked each of the mageborn present before they set off. He should have offered to balance their powers and do all that he normally did when a mageborn paid homage to him, the Lord of Thorns. But all he'd been thinking of was Grace.

Grace must have sensed his concern. She smiled at him. 'It's okay. He's safe. He's sleeping.'

He stared at her, trying to fathom it. What had she done? 'Is he… what happened? How did you stop him?'

'Not me. Misha, of all people.'

Her answer couldn't have surprised him more.

'Misha Harper?'

'Yes. He used his music. I've never seen anything like it. He calmed the storm and brought the Zephyr back to himself. I didn't even know it was possible. It's like something out of an old story.'

The air around him shook and a dreadful sense of foreboding swept over him. Lyrics couldn't do something like that, could they? It shouldn't be possible. His dream of the Maegen returned to him and the world shifted around him.

You have to remember.

Remember? Something out of an old story, she'd said. He remembered old stories. He remembered them as if they were yesterday. Memories of years ago, of Lucien, of the Magewar…

But the pact was broken, Marius Larelwynn was dead and Bastien had gone into the Maegen to rescue Grace, breaking the confines which had held the Deep Dark back for so long. He needed to get to Thorndale as soon as possible. He needed to find the source of the Maegen and find a way to purge it, to contain the Deep Dark again. More and more of his people would be infected. It would run from mageborn to mageborn, taking them over, turning them into nightborn and possessing them. And then the Magewar would be upon them, all over again. This time, he didn't know if he would be able to stop it.

The Lyrics of old could do incredible things. Those that went hollow were dangerous in the extreme. The power of music could bring down castle walls, reduce the strongest warriors to shivering wrecks, inflame tempers until people killed each other, or steal their will to live until they took their own lives. Lyrics had been feared. But since the fall of the Hollow King – since Lucien had bound him and the two of them had formed the pact – the power of all mageborn had been diminished.

Misha wasn't that strong. Not strong enough to calm a storm. He was a good musician, skilled and dedicated to his art. But his magic was only a small part of his talent. His magic wasn't powerful at all.

He wasn't strong enough to do that.

'I need to see him, Grace.'

'Of course. He's with the captain. She didn't want him out of her sight.'

'Misha?'

'No, the Zephyr. He's just a kid, Bastien, and he doesn't seem to be any threat now.'

No. She didn't understand. 'Not the boy. Misha. I need to see him now. Grace, he could be in terrible danger. We all could.'

Bastien slipped by Grace and headed for the cabin door, his legs unsteady. She swore and moments later she was beside him, sliding beneath his arm and supporting him. At least she didn't flinch this time when he touched her. He'd thought, last night, that everything might have been forgiven but now… now he wasn't so sure.

'This is a terrible idea,' Grace scolded him. 'You aren't up to this. You could have been killed when that thing came down.'

Bastien shook his head. He wasn't that lucky. 'Probably not. There isn't time, my love. This is serious. Misha could be at risk even now.'

'Misha? Why? He was fine. He didn't even seem tired.'

It was worse and worse. Bastien tried to sort through the scrambled memories that had reasserted themselves. If he was honest, he had shied away from examining anything too closely. There was just too much.

But Lyrics… since the Magewar they were the gentlest branch of the mageborn. They were artistic, creative, the ones who were most overlooked in the greater scheme of things. They made music. What could be wrong with that?

Until they went hollow. Then their power increased, their magic became unstable… It wasn't like other mageborn. Perhaps because of the nature of their magic. The way it played with emotions, stirred up memories, drove others wild with passion or despair.

The ship was peaceful now. At least there was that. Daniel and Misha were up on deck, which wasn't Bastien's ideal situation. Too exposed, too public. But that was beyond his control and he couldn't waste time.

Remember, Bastien.

Lucien's voice was an echo. Oh, he remembered now. It made him shiver… or maybe that was still the after-effects of a blow to the head. The wind and waves were calm and in the far distance he could just make out land, a ragged line on the horizon. They were almost there, almost back to his homeland.

Except that wasn't his home either. It never had been. There was only one place that he knew for sure had been his home and that was where they were ultimately heading. And what else did he remember about Thorndale? There had been roses and they had burned. A castle in a valley, standing watch over the most magical place in this world or any other.

Blood in the water. Hands holding his head. A knife blade at his throat. Three times dead, twice entombed.

Like in the song Misha had sung back in Iliz.

Misha and Daniel were sitting together, chatting, as he approached them. Bastien slowed as he drew near, not wanting to startle Misha. Daniel looked up and suspicion entered his glare. It always did. Daniel still didn't trust him. Which was ironic really as Daniel had been the one to betray Bastien rather than the other way around. Perhaps he was still waiting for retribution.

'Shouldn't you be resting?' There was that Eastferry tone of voice.

'I need to talk to your harper.'

Misha didn't look in any way alarmed. But from the defensive attitude of Parry, something was clearly wrong.

Misha still held his harp in his hands, cradling it close to him. 'What do you want of me, your majesty?' If his strangely formal address was unnerving, Bastien wasn't going to show it.

'How are you feeling?'

'Feeling?' His fingers strayed over the strings and a few notes hung on the air between them, haunting and ominous. A warning perhaps. 'I feel fine. There's nothing to be alarmed about. Music and magic go hand in hand. I've only just realised that. But surely you knew. Being who you are.'

Who he was? What did Misha know of who he was? He and Grace had agreed not to speak of the Hollow King and what he once might have been. He still didn't feel entirely sure of it himself. And now, with his memories tangled and unfolding so slowly…

'And who am I?'

Misha smiled. His eyes fixed on Bastien's and they were just his eyes. But the knowing in them… that was new. And they looked slightly darker… as if shadows moved through them. Darkening. His hands moved slowly over the strings of the harp.

'Who are you? Bastien Larelwynn? That's a question you alone can answer, is it not?'

Bastien couldn't say he liked this new attitude. He didn't like it at all. It was rubbing off on Daniel as well, or perhaps the other way around.

Grace looked awkwardly from one to the other. Her mouth was a hard line, which was never a good sign. She had always been defensive of her squad and this sort of dissent was guaranteed to make her uncomfortable. One could never tell which side she'd come down on. It would depend on how it happened, on who she felt was in the right. And she'd still give Daniel the benefit of the doubt until the day they both died. Bastien only prayed that one day she would trust him the same way.

Bastien never broke eye contact with the Lyric. 'Let me help you, Misha.'

'What if I don't need help?'

'I think you do. I think the magic is getting stronger, taking over. I think there's a risk that it will run out of control if we don't do anything. Please, you know more about this than you've shared. Let me help. What do you know about the nightborn?'

For a moment Misha smiled at him. But it wasn't his carefree smile. Not really. 'Nightborn? Just a legend, surely. Oh wait, no. Not any more. What did you two stir up this time?'

The nastiness in his voice didn't belong there. And it was too familiar by far, though it wasn't Misha. He didn't have it in him. This was something else. This was the voice from Bastien's nightmares.

'But you're all about legends,' Grace told Misha. Maybe she recognised it too. She had to know that this wasn't their friend. 'You love them. Danny says you can never resist the chance to tell a story.'

'Does he?' The tune rose from his harp, louder now, jarring a little. Daniel winced and stared at him in dismay. The expression Misha wore wasn't kind, wasn't his usual gentle air. This was something else. Someone else. A long-remembered darkness. 'Danny says a lot of things, Grace.'

'What sort of things?' she asked warily.

Daniel cut in before the harper could speak again. 'Leave him alone. He's fine. He's more than fine. He saved us all.'

'Danny,' Grace warned but her oldest friend glared at her. She ignored him, her expression firm.

But Daniel wasn't finished. His hands balled into fists. 'What? It's true. You were there. Misha saved us, and—'

But Grace's patience didn't waver.

'Misha used more magic than I've ever seen him use. He's a Lyric, Danny, not a...' She waved her hands around vaguely. Bastien wasn't sure what it was meant to mean, but Daniel seemed to.

He surged to his feet, his face distorted with anger. 'Not a what? Not a Flint like you? Not the Lord of Thorns? Not as powerful and important as you or your lover? What about me? I'm not even mageborn. I'm nothing. Is that what you want to say?'

'*Danny!*' Ellyn gasped, sliding into the space between them as she arrived. She grabbed his shirt before he could lunge at Grace, who stood there, exposed and shocked. She hadn't even moved to protect herself. Not from Daniel Parry. But she should have. 'What the hell is wrong with you?'

He shook himself free of Ellyn, his eyes wild as the storm had been. Spit flecked his lips. 'Wrong with *me*? He almost killed you, Grace, and now you're over it? One quick fuck and everything's okay? There's nothing *wrong* with *me*.'

Grace's features froze in shock, in horror. Anger flared, fire inside her blazing. But this fire was dark and unnatural. The surge of icy rage that swept through Bastien's body was nothing compared to what he sensed in her. For a moment he thought he'd kill Daniel himself, reach out with all his vast powers and stop his heart. It would take an instant, no more. For a moment, he wanted to.

But the thing in Grace... It could end them all in an instant. If she only let it.

And then he heard it, that sound on the edge of hearing, relentless, maddening... Fingers moved on strings, fast and deadly now, a dance that churned up emotions and wrung them out.

'Yes,' Bastien said. 'Yes, there is something wrong. With both of you. Misha, please. Think. Stop this. You can't risk hurting Daniel, can you?'

As if Bastien's use of his lover's name broke the spell, the harper stopped playing. The sudden silence shook Bastien more than he expected. The tune had been a constant, a hum at the base of his brain. It had been winding them all up, playing with their moods, their fears, their anger.

Now, without the music, the world swung back into sharp relief.

The ship was still and calm, all attention turned to the small group on the deck, ready to tear each other apart.

'Misha?' Daniel interrupted, unsure now. 'Misha, what are you doing?'

Suddenly the defiant expression on Misha's face wilted. His mouth opened just once but he didn't say anything, as if suddenly afraid to use his voice at all. Confusion made him seem like a lost child. He set the harp down on the deck gingerly and looked up at Bastien.

Bastien took Misha's hands in his, holding them and letting his own power unfurl. It was an instinct rather than a determined desire.

He sought out the source of the harper's power, the Lyric inside him, and felt the magic flowing in his blood. The traces of the Maegen threaded their way through him, part of him. Misha was a good man, an honest man. And he loved Daniel. Loved him more than reason.

Like called to like. It was the same way Bastien felt about Grace. It made no sense. It was terrifying. And yet it was wondrous. It was everything.

Thriving on that love, the magic was stronger too. So much stronger than it should have been. And within that magic…

Fear. So much fear. Fear of losing Daniel, of losing his lover and his friends. Fear that even being close to Bastien and Grace would kill him, perhaps kill both of them. Fear that they would end up like the mageborn in Rathlynn or even Iliz now… enslaved or dead. Or wild with magic, hollow, nightborn…

Bastien saw it now. The darkness, the Deep Dark, threads of it everywhere like an infection, stoking the terror on which it thrived. He mentally seized a strand and drew it away, only to find four more in its place. His usual techniques were useless here. He went deeper, searching out the source and finding only more. It wasn't an imbalance, not really, but the whole system seemed to be twisted. A spiral of darkness which took him too far into Misha's mind and consciousness. Too far through his body. Where had it come from? It was like an infection but every Curer could tell you, with an infection, there had to be a source.

The hands he held tightened abruptly, spasming. Bastien jerked back to see the harper shaking, his mouth open wide in pain, his eyes staring at the sky. His whole body shook as if he was having a seizure.

'What have you done?' Daniel shouted. Both Grace and Ellyn were holding him back but he tried to rip himself free of them, heedless.

What had he done? It was an excellent question. Bastien didn't have time to answer him. He did the only thing he could think of and plunged in again, gathering all of Misha's magic that he could touch and dragging it into his body instead.

Misha fell into his arms, still shaking but breathing once again. Bastien could feel his heart, beating frantically like a trapped bird. But he was safe. The magic wasn't gone forever. He would never cut anyone off from their power unless he absolutely had to. It would return, but slowly. There was time for him to find a cure for this infection. Time for the harper, at least. That was all Bastien could do for any of them now. Buy time.

'What have you done to him, you bastard?' Danny snarled as he dragged Misha away and gathered him into his arms, cradling him. His touch was so tender, so careful. That sense of love encircled the two of them and Bastien knew it. It could save both of them.

Bastien rose to his feet, his own body aglow with magic, his mind reeling from so much light and dark twisting away inside him. It took more effort than he would have expected to push the power back down inside him.

'Grace,' he said and reached for her. 'Please…'

She grabbed him, holding him to stop him from falling.

Her voice was matter-of-fact, the consummate professional. Everything was calmness and order, practical commands. 'Come on, let's get you down to the cabin. We need to sort this now.'

'No.' The magic made Bastien's voice vibrate, the sheer power inside him making it tremble as his heart did. 'The boy, the Zephyr. Got to check him too.'

She was right. Of course she was. She knew the signs as well as he did. Better, even, because she saw what happened when it swept over him. He could feel her pulse fluttering away inside him, just like he'd felt Misha's, feel the breath entering and leaving her lungs. Feel her magic, her fire, coursing through her veins. Not overwhelming her like Misha's had threatened to.

Bastien had thought that the Deep Dark had taken her power from her in the garden, when the Loam had reached out and corrupted the warrant. But her flames were impossible to kill. She was irrepressible. Every time her magic came back, it was stronger. It was part of her.

Something had happened to her on Iliz, when she had found her magic again to help Rynn save him. Her power was stronger than ever. And it had changed.

There will always be a sacrifice. He'd seen her made of fire, standing by an image of himself that was inhuman: the Hollow King, or maybe something worse.

He had to get to Thorndale. If he was at the source of the Maegen itself, he could stop the Deep Dark there, lock it away again. He had to stop the nightborn. He could save Grace. He had to. But there had to be a sacrifice…

'We'll get him, we'll bring him down to you,' Grace said. 'Please, Bastien. Let me help you. Ellyn? Will you—'

'On it, boss,' she said and strode off towards the captain and the Zephyr.

Leaning on Grace, Bastien let her lead him down into the cabin. She sat him on the edge of the bunk and rummaged in her packs, all business and determination. He wanted to apologise again, to beg forgiveness, but he couldn't. He watched as she pulled out sigils, already on a belt, which she wrapped around her waist before she found one of the jars.

'Here.' She shoved it at him and he took it willingly. It was smaller than the ones he had used in Rathlynn. But it was all they could bring with them.

'I'll be fine. There's no need to do it.'

'Hold onto it anyway, Bastien. Just in case. I don't want you going off like a firework in confined quarters, do I?'

It made him smile, although she didn't seem to appreciate that. Her hand slid across the sigils, and they started to glow. But she wouldn't use them on him. Not unless she had to.

He'd never imagined he'd see her afraid of him, but now she was. Afraid of his magic.

'All right,' he said. 'Just let me…'

Slowly he began to transmute the magic inside him, restrain it and bring it under his control. When he could breathe easily again, he closed his eyes and pressed the last of it down into a diamond-hard space the size of his heart. So bright and so warm, glowing like a new star. It moved and coiled in on itself, forming shapes like flowers and vines. He peeled back the exterior, the petals of light, searching through the magic he had gleaned from Misha. And in the heart of it was the blackest worm.

For a moment he couldn't move, couldn't think.

Then, all in a rush which brought Grace up to her feet, looming over him in alarm, he opened the jar and let the captured magic purge out of his body, falling like tears from his eyes, glowing and terrible.

He knew he sobbed as he did it but he had no control over that. It hurt, every time, like pouring the fire of the sun through his body and making it something else.

Her hand between his shoulder blades was so cold, and yet so welcome. One single comfort. She helped him breathe, helped him get through it. She always did. Maybe all wasn't lost after all. Maybe…

She didn't ask what it was. She knew. 'How did it get into Misha?'

Bastien drew in a shattered breath. 'It's in all the mageborn… traces of it…unless we get to Thorndale and lock it away again.'

A knock on the cabin door brought Bastien back to his senses. He put the lid on the jar and pushed it hurriedly under the blankets. The magic within it swirled and glowed, the image of a flower in the heart of it. And the dark speck coiled among the petals, the most dangerous thing he could have found.

'Come,' he said in a voice that almost sounded like his own.

The Zephyr shuffled in, Ellyn behind him to make sure he didn't make a break for it. And behind her Captain Pardue stood, her whole stance a threat. 'I'm here to make sure that nothing ill befalls him. He's just a boy and he's one of mine. He's family. He's never lost control like that before. Never.'

'No, of course not. It wasn't his fault. Please, come in, Captain.' Even though there was barely room for all of them. Even though the whole crew had seen Bastien perform what should have been something private between him and one of the mageborn, the very rite he had performed on every day of homage, for every citizen of Rathlynn born with magic for more years than he could possibly remember.

And in all that time, he'd never found the Deep Dark within like that. Never.

He'd thought it was trapped. Locked away beneath the Maegen. Safe.

But it had taken blood to trap them. A sacrifice. Just like the Deep Dark had demanded from him. It couldn't be Grace. It would not be Grace. He'd die first.

He had to protect her.

And Rynn with her Larelwynn blood. He had to protect them both.

Someone always has to die, Lucien had said. But that wasn't going to happen. He wasn't going to let that happen.

And right now he had to protect another of the mageborn. One of his people. A child.

'Come here, boy,' he said, as gently as he could.

'Larne,' said Pardue, still shielding him. 'His name is Larne. He's my nephew. Family.'

Bastien met her eyes, recognised the warning there, the implied threat.

He nodded. 'Larne.' He held out his hands, met the boy's eyes and tried to be comforting. He would help him, balance out the magic, make him safe again. He had to. 'Don't be afraid. This will help. I promise.'

Chapter Twenty

Aurelie hated the Temple. It was too quiet. Her footsteps echoed strangely in its emptiness. True, it was almost deserted these days. She had to keep some retainers here to keep Celeste fed and watered, amused and quiet, though it wasn't an easy job. She was going through carers like a scythe at harvest time.

But Aurelie could always find more willing to serve.

Well, they weren't exactly willing but whatever.

The former goddess was not in her rooms today. She was down in the cellars, trying to break her favourite obsession, the man who had created the sigil binding her. The fact that it was burnt into her skin now didn't seem to occur to her. Aurelie was fairly convinced that Celeste would slice her own flesh off if she thought that might free her. She had probably already tried.

At first Aurelie had been reluctant to turn the old Master Atelier over to her but Asher had insisted and, idiot that she was, she had let him persuade her.

It'll be fine, he'd said. *It'll keep her happy. And if she does find a way to break the spell, well then we'll have her power at our command. She can feed us again.*

If she could make the old man cooperate, so much the better. If anyone could replicate Mother Miranda's work, it was Zavi Millan.

Or so everyone assured her. Miranda had used her leeching powers and her knowledge of Bastien's research to harness the powers of so many mageborn, sharing that magic with Aurelie and those she had honoured. But nothing broke the old man. Nothing.

Divinities, Aurelie missed the taste of magic, the feel of it in her body. It was an addiction, she understood that, one she had been forced to quit far too soon. She longed for it again: the power, the strength, the ability to bend the world to her whim at will. And she deserved it. All of it. Magic wasn't something to be wielded by the weak and cowardly.

Now she had no one to source it for her. The last of the orbs containing raw, drained mageborn power were used up. She still had Celeste, and the mageborn prisoners, but no Miranda and no way of getting at their magic.

But if the price was letting Celeste Larelwynn free… Even Aurelie baulked at that thought.

Luckily, Master Atelier Zavi proved to be even more stubborn than Bastien, Marius and Grace Marchant put together. That was probably how he'd survived the fall of the Academy. His knowledge of how to access mageborn power had saved him then, the information locked away inside him invaluable. If they could only get him to comply.

But even Celeste couldn't manage it.

He wasn't screaming this time, that was a relief. Whatever she was doing inside his brain, she kept him quiet. But Aurelie could see the pain in his eyes, the way they flicked from side to side in panic. Celeste held his head in her small and perfect hands and pressed either side of his face, muttering words that didn't make any sense. They might have been a dead language or they might have been gibberish.

Who knew? Aurelie didn't exactly care.

She cleared her throat and Celeste turned, releasing her victim. Zavi slumped down in the chair, sweat pouring from his skin.

'What do you want?' Celeste snarled at her.

Charming. Just charming.

'I came to visit. I have news.'

'What news?'

'Your brother got married.'

Celeste threw back her head and laughed, a harsh, inelegant sound.

'Where's Asher? I need to talk to him.'

'He isn't back yet.'

'I want him back!' Celeste screamed suddenly, and Aurelie's guards stepped in around her, weapons bare.

At that the former goddess retreated, her rage subsiding, fear making her meek again. She was vulnerable. She knew it. So did Aurelie. She lived by the queen's whim, and without Asher to protect her, Celeste was running out of time.

Was it possible to kill a goddess? If she was clothed in flesh, why not? Aurelie was itching to find out. It was like reasoning with a goldfish. Even talking to her was a trial.

The queen smoothed down her skirts until Celeste was quiet again. 'They left Iliz – in chaos I might add, unleashing monsters if the reports are to be believed. Asher has gone after them. The Dowager Queen has armed him and given him troops. He will track them down, but he'll bring them here. Not to the Valenti. I've made it clear that if he does otherwise I will be most displeased. I need information, Celeste. About something called nightborn. Do you know what they are?'

Celeste stared at her for a long minute. 'Nightborn? There are nightborn abroad?'

'What are they?'

Her face broke into a grin like a naked skull.

'Oh, but this is *good* news, Aurelie. Wild mageborn, servants of the Deep Dark, my servants, don't you see? They're part of me and I am part of them, my wild siblings. They'll come and free me. They'll bring me my crown and then we'll see it all burn. All of it. Just like Thorndale did. I'll burn Rathlynn and the ports. All the ships on the sea. I'll burn the towers and the cesspit of Eastferry too… This is wonderful news!'

So… not good news at all. Iliz was still in pandemonium. The outer islands had closed their ports to all ships and the great Valenti trading empire would soon be on its knees. The few who had escaped spoke of the canals filled with corpses, the palaces crumbling, fire like an inferno. And so many dead. Mageborn… collared, sigiled, slaughtered. Thousands of them. It wouldn't stop until they were all dead or driven out.

Aurelie swallowed hard. They'd have to be culled, any in Rathlynn who turned nightborn. It was already happening, unofficially. And elsewhere in the kingdom. She'd have to issue an edict. There'd be some innocent mageborn casualties along the way, but maybe that was for the best. Were any of the mageborn really innocent? Kill them all. Purge her kingdom of mageborn entirely. Start anew.

That was what the Valenti should have done.

She left Celeste where she was and approached the Atelier. He was watching her with his most intent gaze.

'What about you, Master Atelier? Feeling any more inclined to serve the crown in its time of need? That was the vow you all took, wasn't it?'

'That was when the crown was worth serving,' he growled, in a low, broken voice.

With a curse of frustration, Aurelie turned her back on him. This was pointless, infuriating. Not even Celeste had managed to break him. It was a wonder he was still sane.

From the corridor outside she heard a scuffle, a shout, and then the guards outside the door fell like dominos. Figures in clothes the colours of stone and shadows rushed through the door. Aurelie threw herself aside as a weapon swung through the air again, sharp little blades slicing anything in its path. She scrambled into the nearest alcove, grabbing a knife from a fallen guard as she went. She held it in front of her. It shook wildly.

And she knew it wasn't going to help.

Kurt Parry stepped from the corridor, gave her an exaggerated bow while his men swarmed the room. There was only Celeste to protect her, insane and vicious Celeste, standing between Aurelie and the Rathlynnese scum who called themselves Thorns.

'How did you get in here?' Aurelie hissed at him.

'Trade secrets,' Kurt said with a laugh. 'Can't expect me to share that, can you? Couldn't have done it without you though, love.'

They only opened the Temple for her now, that was what he meant. He'd been waiting for her to visit Celeste then. Damn him.

The woman with Parry stepped between Aurelie and escape, her sword bare, as if daring the queen to make a break for it. Celeste snarled at her but backed up against Aurelie, trapping her in the alcove. The other woman stood there, waiting, not engaging, holding them there, while her friends unshackled the Atelier and dragged him out with them.

Celeste lunged at their guard, her nails out like claws. The woman bent to avoid the frenzied attack, fluid and skilful. But she didn't retreat and Celeste didn't even press her advantage. If it was really an advantage. She snarled and fell back again, shielding Aurelie. Protecting her.

For what? That was the question. Why was Celeste protecting her? There was no love lost between them.

'She's mine,' Celeste snarled, spittle flying from her mouth, all her teeth bared. 'Her and her child. Mine!'

Aurelie's stomach twisted. What was happening? What was she doing?

'Leave them, Mel,' Parry said, his voice completely uninterested now he had what he wanted. 'You don't want to tangle with that.'

No, but he'd happily leave Aurelie to Celeste's tender mercies. Bastard.

The woman murmured something that sounded like *psycho-bitch from the deepest pits of the seventh hell* and nodded. 'Yeah, I get it now, boss. Not really much of a conversationalist. We'd better just take what we came for and go then.'

Kurt Parry gave Aurelie another of those infuriating mock bows of his. 'See you, love,' he told her. And then they were gone.

Aurelie let out a howl of rage. How did he do it? Just come in and leave like that? Where were the rest of her guards? They couldn't have killed everyone.

Bloody Eastferry rats with more luck than the gods gave a three-legged mongrel.

Celeste had fallen to her knees. She crawled to Aurelie's side, crooning and muttering. She grabbed the queen's legs and pulled herself up as far as her belly, which she petted and stroked.

Aurelie froze, sudden horror sweeping through her, Parry forgotten.

'Mine,' Celeste said. 'All mine. It's going to be so good, you'll see. You and me. We'll get out of here. We'll be free. Just you and me. Together.'

She wasn't talking to Aurelie. She didn't even seem to realise that the queen was even there. She pressed her face against Aurelie's stomach.

'Mine,' she whispered. 'My little miracle. My little way out.'

And then she stopped, frozen, staring. Slowly her gaze dragged up to meet Aurelie's. At first the shock melted to disappointment, then betrayal, then rage. Her eyes burned.

And Aurelie knew that the ruse was over. And if Celeste knew, Asher would know, and the Valenti would know… *everyone* would know…

'Liar,' Celeste hissed. Spittle flecked her lips. 'You aren't with child…'

They would all know. She couldn't be a regent if there was no child. And there was no child.

'You liar!' Celeste's hands clawed at her hips, digging into the skin through the heavy material.

Aurelie didn't think. She just reacted. She would lose everything if anyone else found out. Everything.

She grabbed a fistful of the former goddess's hair and wrenched her head back. Without hesitation she buried the knife up under her jaw, directly into her twisted, broken brain. Celeste's eyes went round, bulged, and a choked sound came from her mouth, a wet gasp. Pulling the blade out, Aurelie plunged it in again and then sliced open her throat for good measure. Blood gushed from the wound, covering Aurelie's gown, but she kept on cutting and cutting, long after Celeste finally fell still, just to be sure.

Her remaining guards found her some time later, sitting on the ground by the corpse, still cradling the severed head.

Smiling.

Chapter Twenty-One

Grace didn't know what to expect when they set foot on dry land again, given that she was arriving back with Bastien Larelwynn, the Lord of Thorns, heir to the Larelwynn throne, who as it turned out was also the legendary Hollow King, the divinity who had once been all-powerful in this land. Earthquakes or whirlwinds, perhaps, towers of fire or the soil springing forth new life like an eruption of joy.

Nothing of the sort happened, of course.

They put in at a hidden cove, far from any towns or villages: herself, Bastien, Ellyn, Daniel, Misha, Jehane, Lara and Rynn, just the eight of them, on foot and lightly provisioned. It wasn't far to the road east which would eventually lead to Thorndale. There were few towns along the way, not much to speak of. The outposts on the border were dotted along the same road where it swung close to the mountains. Lara had a plan, or something like one, but she didn't seem very keen to share it.

And there was still the matter of Rynn. A Valenti princess was surely going to slow them all down. But all Bastien would say was that Lara was right about him having to play the role of rightful king. And they would have to continue this pretence that wasn't really a pretence, about who he was, about his marriage, and his place in the world.

So Grace tried.

'It's going to be hard on the road. There are no luxuries, no comforts.'

'I'll manage,' Rynn said. She'd found some spare clothes on the ship. They were all too big, slipping off her shoulders. The belt wound twice around her tiny waist. She even managed to make that look attractive.

To Grace's surprise, it was Ellyn who answered. 'I'll – I'll watch out for her.'

If that was a comfort to the princess, Grace wasn't sure. There was something about the way she watched Ellyn… almost fascinated. Like Ellyn was a mystery to be solved. Like their family histories needed to be unravelled and examined. 'Thank you,' she whispered.

Ellyn nodded and looked away from her, went back to shoving provisions into a pack. Every so often she pointed at something and barked out an order. Rynn meekly picked whatever it was up and put it wherever Ellyn said.

Grace grabbed her own pack and went to join Bastien. 'Tell me again why you think this is a good idea.'

Someone had found him clothes too. They were black, the garb of the Lord of Thorns just as she remembered him from when she'd first seen him. He was lost in thought, his eyes fixed on the far distance, and his thoughts on somewhere else, far away or long ago, or both.

'What's a good idea?' he asked. The bleakness in his voice should have been a warning.

Grace sighed. 'This. Any of it. Thorndale. Bringing Rynn with us.'

'We need Rynn.'

She rolled her eyes and then pushed his arm, not so much to get his attention as to fulfil the need to unsettle him in some way. '*Why?*'

'Would you believe I had a vision?'

'A what?' The thought made her stomach knot inside her and her whole body go cold. 'You… you and Rynn? In the Maegen?'

For a moment he didn't seem to understand her, as if she was talking nonsense. Then his whole face transformed in horror. 'No! Oh divinities, no. I didn't mean that.'

It shouldn't have been such a relief. The air left her lungs anyway. 'What was it then?'

'It was blood. It was always about blood.'

'What?'

'The vision. I saw blood in the Maegen. And I saw her. In the cave with me and something… something else, something I don't think I can stand against. At least not without her. So…'

She knew there was something he wasn't telling her. Something bad.

He needed *Rynn*. To do what? She didn't want to feel sorry for the princess but he wouldn't sacrifice someone's life, would he? Not even to save every mageborn under the skies. Not to save her. He couldn't. Not Bastien. At least not the Bastien she knew.

He had to know another way. Something buried in his broken memories, some way to trap the Deep Dark that didn't involve—

'Bastien?'

He was staring off into the distance, refusing to meet her gaze. Like it wasn't him any more. She felt a chill snaking down her spine. He was a stranger, like he was back in Iliz…

Not Bastien. The Lord of Thorns. Or worse…

'When we landed, did you feel anything?' he asked. 'Something in the air, maybe? Something in the earth? Something wrong?'

Grace shook her head and forced her breath to be calm. 'Another vision?' She didn't mean it to sound bitter, although it did. Bastien didn't react.

'Not this time. A warning maybe. Something is missing… or loose, unleashed… This is bigger than you and me, Grace. The nightborn, the Deep Dark… I sense it… Do you understand that?'

What was she, an idiot? Of course she understood that. And she understood what he was saying as well, what he meant.

He was staring ahead, down the road that would lead to Thorndale. She shivered suddenly as cold rippled through her even more.

'We head to Thorndale then,' she said.

'There has to be a way to stop it there. To trap the Deep Dark again. In the pool of the Maegen or…' He closed his eyes and an expression of distaste passed over his face, giving him the look of a man tortured and lost. Then he opened them again and gazed at her, his eyes seeing deep inside her. Seeing far more than she wanted him to see. Her fears. Her doubts… 'It's a long way. We should get started, shouldn't we?'

It was easier and safer to seal off her emotions, to just do her job. The same way he did. She could see him doing it, right now. And when the time came if she needed to stop him doing something unforgiveable, she would. She promised herself that.

She had lost him in Iliz. She'd thought for a moment that she had him back. She had been wrong. She couldn't shake off the memory of his hands around her throat, the hatred in his eyes. And now he was closing himself off from her. Just as she had to close herself off from him.

They could go to Thorndale. They might find the Maegen and he might find a way to stop the Deep Dark. He might even find a cure for the nightborn, and for her. If it was within his power, Bastien Larelwynn would save them all. But she had lost him. She had to accept that.

While the kingdom of Larelwynn stood, he would never really be hers.

'I suppose so,' Grace whispered, and turned away. She didn't like what she saw in his dark eyes. It left her unsettled, uncomfortable. Alone. There was no arguing with him. Not now. Lara Kellen had his ear. And whilst Grace wished she could bring herself to trust Lara, everything felt wrong. Whether it was her instincts or her emotions she couldn't say.

This wasn't Bastien. This was the Lord of Thorns. Or maybe worse. Maybe this was the Hollow King.

He wanted Rynn with him when they got to Thorndale, when he faced whatever he had to face in the Maegen. She was a Larelwynn, or as close to one as they had.

Blood, he'd said. He'd seen blood.

Whose blood?

*

Lara provided horses. Grace didn't want to ask too much about where she'd got them but she and Jehane left the group and returned a couple of hours later with eight mounts and a couple of pack ponies.

Daniel wasn't as concerned about offending the marshal. 'They don't look like farm animals. We don't need angry owners following us.'

Jehane laughed. 'There's a garrison up the road about three miles. We're borrowing them in the name of the Larelwynn line. They totally understood.'

'Quiet, Jehane,' Lara told him with a warning glare. 'We didn't steal them.'

'You wandered in there and demanded this many horses in the name of Larelwynn?' Ellyn asked. 'Do you want to write a letter to Aurelie as well, just to tell her where we are now? I could ride ahead and take it to her. If you want.'

It was Grace's turn to direct her own version of the warning glare at her squad member. But Ellyn, unlike Jehane, just shrugged and gave her a look of her own which said '*What? I'm right.*'

And she was.

'I'm still the marshal,' Lara replied. 'And still a member of the King's Messengers. I didn't have to give more than a sign and make my requests. The garrison commander was happy to oblige. Your majesty.' She offered Bastien the reins of the black stallion she led, a beautiful creature. It suited him, made him look like a man from legend. From the moment he mounted, Grace knew that Lara was setting a scene – Bastien Larelwynn, the Lord of Thorns, the monster he never wanted to be, coming to claim a throne, a crown and a kingdom.

Rynn ended up on a grey mare just as perfectly symbolic as Bastien's mount, just as complimentary. The pair of them were guaranteed to make an impact wherever they went. Oh, word would spread, all right. That was clearly Lara's plan. There were many more ways than one to wage a war.

They'd married in Valenti. Bastien was the Lord of Thorns and Rynn was a royal heir with Larelwynn blood. They were coming home.

Or at least that was the mummers' play Lara wanted the world to see.

Grace's horse was a bay gelding who resented everyone and everything in the entire universe and showed it at every possible moment. He fought her every stretch of the way for the next few hours. She was exhausted long before Lara called a stop for the night. The next day was even worse. Her body ached in every way possible. As she mounted up again on the miserable beast, she wished that just once in her life she had learned to ride properly. All she could actually do was hold on and hope for the best. At least Daniel was suffering alongside her. Ellyn, though, seemed as at home on a horse as she was everywhere else. It wasn't fair.

But when her friend pulled up alongside her, she didn't look happy – although, after a breakfast of black bread and porridge, Grace didn't really blame her.

'We're being followed,' Ellyn said.

That dispelled Grace's bad mood. Or rather transformed it from general misery to darkest suspicion. She glanced over her shoulder but could see nothing but the lonely road through a rocky landscape behind them. Stones broke like old teeth among browning ferns and brambles. The road wound up the hill beyond. That said, she knew to trust Ellyn's word implicitly. If she said they were being followed, that was that.

'How far back?'

'More than a mile. They're good. But they're definitely there.'

It could just be another traveller, but Grace doubted it. Of course they were being followed. Lara had as good as announced their presence and, although largely lawless, this was still Larelwynn land. Maybe they should have gone through Tlachtlya instead. At least then they would have seen the attacks coming and known to expect them at all times.

'How many?'

'Only one. Tracker probably. Could be more behind, of course. Do you want me to go and get rid of him?'

Ellyn looked a little too eager. And Grace was sorely tempted to join her.

'You'll get to punch something soon enough.' Grace half wondered if she should send Jehane instead. He'd be quicker and quieter. She didn't doubt his skills. He was still watching her, all the time, her appointed guard. He took the role very seriously.

'Let's wait and see. We're ahead of them for now and they seem happy to keep it that way. We'll reach this inn Lara is taking us to before nightfall. We can sit in the taproom and see who else arrives. Could be interesting.'

Ellyn nodded but as she lifted her face again, her gaze snagged on Rynn's. The princess was looking at the pair of them. She turned her face forwards instantly, ignoring them. Ellyn snorted. 'Can you actually picture her in a taproom?'

'Why don't you like her? Everyone else likes her.'

'You don't.' Grace flinched and Ellyn's face became instantly apologetic. 'Sorry, I didn't… I know why you don't though. Obviously.'

Grace sighed. She couldn't hide anything from her friends. 'I'm… it's complicated.'

'That's a word for it. You have reasons, so do I. Her family had me kidnapped. I'm an experienced Academy officer, Grace. And their mob of uneducated thugs snatched me off the bank of the canal while you were under attack and dragged me off to be nothing more than a bargaining chip.'

It stung Ellyn more than she liked to show, Grace knew that. All her experience, her knowledge, her fighting abilities, and she'd been taken just like that.

Grace let her eyes narrow as she thought about it. 'She's royalty. She has a way about her.'

'Yeah, she clicks her fingers and people jump to her whim. Even Lara Kellen is doing it.'

'And Bastien,' Grace murmured, thinking about what he'd said about blood, about his vision, about sacrifice. What was he up to? Time was she thought she could trust him implicitly. Now… now she wasn't so sure. A whisper in the back of her mind kept reminding her of what had happened in Iliz. Of his hands around her throat.

She couldn't help throw a glance at Bastien riding ahead with Lara beside him, their heads bent together in conversation. Rynn was right behind him.

Ellyn pursed her lips. 'She bothers me. That's all. She's always watching us. Every time I look at her, she's looking back. Her family wiped mine out. The ragged remains of us that made it to Rathlynn never recovered. I'm the last one, all that's left, and even I… Why is she even here? She agreed to marry him, after all. She can claim that they forced her, but we don't know that.'

Grace was starting to see it, her own bleak and miserable future stretching out ahead of her, without him. She didn't have it in her to be a mistress. She wasn't the sharing type.

'We don't know that she's lying.' Her throat tightened to a painful knot. She couldn't say anything more than that. But the marriage was binding. Whether Rynn wanted it or not. Whether Bastien wanted it or not. It was bigger than either of them, and out of their hands.

'She's hiding something,' said Ellyn. 'I'd bet an entire taproom of beer on that.'

Grace had learned long ago never to bet against Ellyn. In this case that didn't make her feel any better.

*

The sign hanging outside the inn had a crown on it. Grace wasn't sure if that was a good omen or not.

Probably not.

Lara arranged the rooms which meant that Grace, Daniel, Misha and Ellyn were in the guardroom – a barracks-like space – along with Jehane on the ground floor. The three nobles took rooms upstairs. Bastien didn't argue so Grace thought, fine. It didn't matter.

'How do we guard them if we're down here?' Daniel asked.

'Set up a watch rota, do a sweep hourly, you know the drill.' Grace didn't meet his eye as she said the words. 'Ellyn owes me a beer, so you can go first.'

This place was a risk. Every step they took was a risk. Bastien was in danger and she didn't know if she could protect him. Not the way this was turning out. Lara seemed to be going out of her way to separate them. She could be right about appearances protecting them all, about not starting a war with Valenti or turning the population of the kingdom against them. But that didn't make it any easier.

Bastien went off to his room without a word, but paused at the top of the stairs, glancing down at her, just for a moment. The look left Grace more confused than she could say. A warning not to follow? Did he think she'd run off after him? No. She wasn't running after anyone. Ever.

Let him go off up there with his new wife.

The empty hole inside her stomach wasn't just hunger. It was something else, sucking all feeling and energy from her, feeding on anger and sorrow. It twisted away.

The Deep Dark had done something to her. Every so often she felt it, when misery or pain made her weaken her resolve. Like now. It was that whisper in the back of her mind, telling her that every doubt was true, that she had already lost him.

That whisper was getting stronger. And so was whatever it had planted in her when it infected the warrant. Whenever she reached for her magic, something else came, too. She ought to tell Bastien, she knew that. But the words wouldn't form. Why give him another excuse to push her away?

True, he'd been drugged and his memories wiped. He'd been ordered to murder her and he had almost succeeded. It hadn't been his fault.

But Grace couldn't seem to forget or put it behind her. He wanted Rynn with him in Thorndale, thanks to whatever vision he thought he'd had. She had royal blood, as did he. Rynn made more sense as a queen or a consort, much more than Grace.

Maybe she should return the ring. She knew she should. She just… didn't want to.

Why give herself another excuse to give up and let it consume her?

'Beer,' Ellyn said, catching a glimpse of the mood inside her. 'Remember?'

'Yes. Beer. Excellent call.'

The taproom wasn't busy. Grace and Ellyn picked a table where they could sit with their backs to the wall, watching the main door, with a good view of the bar and the other ways into the room. The fire was low and lit the room with its flickering light and, as the daylight outside started to fade, the barman lit thick candles on each table and those impaled on spikes set on a heavy iron ring hanging from the ceiling.

'Makes a change from palaces and balls,' Ellyn said. 'Almost like home.'

'Almost like the Larks' Rest, you mean.' Kurt Parry's tavern was the nearest either of them had to a home apart from the Academy. Misha set up by the fire, tuning his harp. Never one to miss the opportunity to play to a willing audience, that one. Grace wondered if he should after the incident on the ship but Bastien had assured them that his magic was back in balance and Misha himself had promised that he would just play, not use his magic at all. Lyrics probably didn't come through this way too often and it wouldn't do to draw attention. The border was dangerous.

The door opened and closed behind three men. Grace gave them a covert once-over. Locals by the look of them, no sign of travel, and they knew the place well. Two took seats while the third called out a greeting to the barman and headed up to order.

The night dragged on. Jehane joined them and finally Daniel did too as Grace got up to take her turn checking the perimeter. Admittedly that involved little more than walking around the exterior of the inn, via the yard at the back. She wandered through the stables, where the horses whickered and shifted in the straw-filled stalls. It was quiet here. The sort of place where nothing happened. People came and went, but this town – not even a town really, a crossroads with an inn and some houses – this town was just passed by. It was almost tragic. Nothing seemed permanent except the walls of the inn. But the people, the horses, the carts and the cargoes, everything travelled on.

But the night air was soothing, calming. There was some kind of scent from the flowering bushes along the road that was strangely familiar. She pulled one of the small white flowers off and lifted it to her nose.

It felt like inhaling memories, sweet and bitter all at once.

It grew in the garden, at the rear of the forge. Her mother loved it and refused to cut it back as much as she should. And the evenings were full of it as the flowers clustered around the open window of her little room.

Grace dropped the flower and took a rapid couple of steps back. She stared at it accusingly as it lay in the mud of the road. What was that? A memory?

'Captain Marchant?' Jehane appeared in the inn's doorway. 'Did you want dinner? Bastien and Rynn are having a meal sent up, and Lady Kellan said to order what we wanted in the taproom.'

Bastien and Rynn. The ring felt heavy on her finger, his ring. She twisted it around and around as if it was a magic charm, as if it could take the pain away.

Grace waved Jehane off. 'I'm fine. I'm not hungry.'

She was better off out here, in the dark, in the peace and quiet. The lights of the inn were warm and inviting, but the one in the upstairs window just reminded her of what she was about to lose. What she had to let go.

The darkness inside her spread a little more, devouring that pain, thriving on it. She swallowed hard on the lump in her throat.

'We can talk, if you want,' Jehane said, coming closer.

She didn't need his sympathy. Or his pity. 'Talk about what?'

'Whatever you want. Him? Your… your relationship?'

'No thank you.' The thought of spilling her intimate fears out to Jehane made her suddenly uncomfortable. It was too much, too familiar. And she wasn't sure what she would say anyway. Not now.

'I… I don't mean to intrude. I… just… you're hurting. It isn't fair.'

'Life isn't fair, Jehane. It tends to make that pretty clear very quickly. Better get used to it, and fast.'

He sat down on the low wall, his long legs dangling, his arms stretched out on either side. 'I know that as well as anyone, my lady.'

She frowned. 'Don't "my lady" me. I'm not a lady.'

He smiled, an easy, gentle smile. 'But you are. You hold the warrant. The king gave it to you, so that Bastien would be safe. And it protects you. It's unique, the one thing that can command his power, command him. You know, some people would say that warrant should make you the queen.'

That caught her wandering thoughts. She snapped up to attention, staring at him in horror. 'What? No.'

But Jehane shrugged as if it was the simplest thing in the world. 'The monarch holds the warrant,' was all he said.

'That wasn't what Marius intended. He was trying to protect Bastien. I was the only person there who could do it.' But that wasn't true either.

Grace knew that. There were all kinds of people who could have done it. There were any number of Royal Guards. But Marius hadn't been sure who to trust, who had what agenda, and how many Aurelie had gathered to her cause. So he had chosen her. She had just been convenient. She'd thought he was insane at the time. Now she was sure of it.

'Bastien even gave you his ring.'

She covered the ring with her other hand. It didn't mean anything. Not now. It couldn't. 'I'm an Academy officer, Jehane. Just… no one.'

He smiled at her, an understanding, but sad smile. 'You aren't no one, my lady…' He caught the glare starting in her eyes and corrected himself, still smiling. 'Captain.'

She sat down on the wall beside him and stared off down the road.

Beside her, Jehane pulled at the same white flowers and then somehow spun them together with shadows. They rose into the night air and then came to rest on her head, tangled in her hair. A crown of flowers.

'Shadows aren't all bad. You owe me, remember?'

Back on the canalside, when he'd first saved her, he'd told her she owed him her life. He'd been joking, so arrogant and amused with himself. Like a different man.

'My life, I believe.'

He shrugged. 'I'd settle for friendship instead.'

Grace couldn't help but smile then. The laugh was unexpected, that was certain, but she couldn't help that either. Friendship. Yes, after all they had been through she could offer him that.

Not that she could just say it outright like that.

'Stop it. Maybe you're a Charm rather than a Shade, Jehane.'

His grin didn't fade, not exactly. But it wasn't the same. 'It would have been easier, wouldn't it? Charms don't face the same things

Shades do. Like Flints. People expect us to be destructive, difficult, or dangerous. My family certainly did. Oh, they couldn't get rid of me fast enough.'

Grace frowned. It was a familiar tale. 'They threw you out?'

'They didn't have much choice. The town didn't want a Shade around. Bad for the crops, the herds, everything. They figured it was only a matter of time before I did something awful. So… I ran away. I ran as far as Rathlynn.'

'Where you became a…?' She couldn't say *spy*.

He gave a rueful grin, understanding anyway. 'Eventually. I found a new family, in service to the crown.'

Like her. She didn't know if he'd almost been killed before he ran away but somehow she figured he might have. Same story, almost exactly. But he'd kept his magic. Hers had been stolen. Now it was back, it felt like a parasite inside her. Maybe it was.

She turned to look at Jehane to find he was watching her, his gaze fixed on her. For a moment she thought he'd lean forward and try to kiss her. She didn't know what she'd do, how she'd stop him. She'd offered friendship, but nothing more. And he wasn't Bastien.

She leaned back, pulling the flowers from her head. When her hand crushed them that scent returned, overwhelming her senses, blocking everything out.

Jehane didn't kiss her though. He wrapped his hands around hers. 'They're called snowflowers. They say the scent can calm a fever, send good dreams and ease a troubled heart.'

'I remember them. From when I was young.'

'Maybe you lived nearby then. They only grow here, in the mountains. Do you have family here still?'

She shrugged. Not a memory she wanted to dwell on, however curtailed her memories of that time were. Even if they hadn't been wiped away like chalk from a blackboard, the snatches that she had recovered were traumatic. Seeing your family home burn, your parents murdered, and then being drowned tended to do that. But she didn't want to tell Jehane the details either.

She slid off the wall, back onto her feet, still holding the flowers only because she didn't seem able to let them go.

'Put them under your pillow,' Jehane said, with that same flirtatious grin. 'Maybe you'll dream of me.'

'I doubt it.' If she hadn't seen him weave shadows to his will she'd be sure now that he was a Charm instead of a Shade. Perhaps the two were related.

'One day, Captain,' he teased. 'Other girls would take me up on the offer.'

She cast him an arch look. Teasing was easier. It was almost like being back at the Academy, with the banter and camaraderie she loved. She was on firmer ground again. 'Better go and find those other girls then, hadn't you?'

'My current options are Ellyn and a princess and I don't think either of them are particularly interested in the likes of me.'

'Oh, so I'm your third choice. Flattering. Just as well I'm not a queen then, isn't it? Thanks.'

'Never. You're the moon, my lady, the star in my sky.' He stood up, one hand in the air, declaiming his bad poetry.

'Jehane, you'll wake the dead. And they won't be happy. Especially not with that imagery.'

'At least you're smiling, my queen. Should I sing instead?'

That made her laugh. 'Dear divinities, no. Keep watch. Stay out here and be quiet. If I'm the moon and the stars and everything else' – she couldn't say a *queen*, couldn't use *that* word – 'you can follow my command and do what you're told.'

Grace left him standing there, still smiling to herself and walked towards the inn. She glanced up and saw the figure standing at the window. Bastien. She knew him instantly, even from his silhouette in the candlelight. He'd been watching them, had seen everything.

And even though she couldn't see his face, she knew he thought the worst.

The humour drained out of her. Only pain remained.

And the gnawing pit deep down inside her, eating away at everything she held dear. She hadn't meant to, but somehow she felt she had betrayed him.

Chapter Twenty-Two

Grace's second watch was uneventful to begin with. She checked the perimeter first, then she climbed the stairs to check upstairs. The corridor was empty and there wasn't a sound from Bastien's room. She stood there for the longest time, her hand pressed to the surface of the door, ready to open it and go to him, but she couldn't bring herself to do it. She closed her eyes and once more forced herself to be strong.

A noise behind her made her turn. Rynn stood in the doorway dressed in a scant, silken robe. Where she'd got hold of that, the goddess alone knew. She couldn't have looked more shocked or horrified to find Grace there if she'd tried. No pretence in that look.

'Your highness,' Grace said in as calm a tone as she could manage.

'Oh. I was just… um… I thought you were—'

Bastien, obviously. Maybe Rynn was ready to consummate that marriage after all. So long as she got the protection she wanted. Problem was she only had to ask him. He'd protect her. He had a heart that would look after this whole world even if it killed him.

'I see.' What else could she say? It was pitifully obvious.

Rynn glanced towards the door to Bastien's room. 'What were you…?'

'Checking security, your highness,' she said in even tones. 'I'll let you get back to sleep.'

Well, she didn't have to give her an open invitation. Grace turned and made her way down the stairs but Rynn followed her. There was no shaking her off. Grace wondered momentarily if this was how Bastien felt. But no. Clearly not. Bastien had just turned off his feelings again, focused on whatever it was he had to do in Thorndale. Pushing her away.

For a brief moment, on board that ship, with him, their bodies entwined, she had cherished a brief hope that they could be together. Since they set foot on Larelwynn soil, that was gone. Evaporated like morning mist.

And still Rynn was wittering on.

'Captain Marchant, I didn't… I wouldn't…'

'So you said.' Divinities, why wouldn't she go away?

'Under the law—'

Grace turned on her, straining not to draw a knife. 'Oh, I know all about the law.'

That was when Ellyn came out of the guardroom, bleary-eyed. Her mouth opened, her gaze fixed on Rynn. 'Divinities, don't you own any clothes that actually cover you up?'

Rynn's face made a sort of pained, embarrassed wince, and turned scarlet with mortification. Abruptly, Grace felt sorry for her. She didn't want to, really didn't, but there they were.

'I was just… I wanted to talk to *you*, Officer de Bruyn.'

Ellyn scratched her head, her hair falling out of the plait. 'Me?'

'Well… yes… You're Valenti too, and you're of noble birth.'

Grace raised her eyebrows and Ellyn shot her a filthy look.

Rynn went on. 'Your family—'

'Are all *dead* now. Mainly thanks to *your* family.'

The princess closed her arms around herself. 'Well yes. But you said – you said you'd help me. And you – I wanted to talk to you.'

'Dressed like that?'

The frustration showed on Rynn's beautiful features. 'My clothes are part of the problem. I have some from the ship but… I was hoping…'

But Ellyn was taller and broader than the princess, a form made for fighting and—

And suddenly Grace got it. Oh, she'd been so stupid. Rynn wasn't looking for Bastien, sneaking around in the middle of the night. She had a perfect right to go to him whenever she wanted under the law, as she said. She was his wife. But she'd opened that door when she heard a guard, hoping, no doubt, it was Ellyn.

'Oh,' said Ellyn, her grey eyes going wide. Her gaze trailed over the young woman and she flushed a little. Then they narrowed again, suspiciously.

Rynn began to retreat. Grace took pity on the two of them. Well, more on Ellyn than the princess but she'd known her longer. And liked her more. Ellyn had never seen the point of fixating on just one gender, she'd often said. She saw beauty everywhere. And Rynn was indeed beautiful.

'Officer de Bruyn,' Grace said in her best Academy voice. 'You did volunteer to help her, as I remember it.'

'You do?'

'Distinctly.' Grace shook her head, trying not to smile. 'Always told you not to volunteer but you never listen to me.'

'I never… Grace?' The look of panic was comical.

Daniel was going to laugh so hard when she told him. And Bastien—

The thought of him made her stop.

Her heart, briefly buoyed up, sank again like a stone.

'Grace.' Ellyn hadn't moved and her voice was suddenly more urgent. There was a noise outside. Grace fixed Rynn with a firm look and lifted a finger to her lips. Then she gestured to Ellyn to take her upstairs. Grace slipped through the doorway to the guardroom.

'Daniel? Jehane?' she whispered and they stirred, waking just as quickly. The tone of her voice did it. Misha sat up too, blinked groggily, nowhere near as awake. 'You stay here,' she told him firmly. 'There's someone outside.'

'Where's Ellyn?' Daniel asked.

'Upstairs. Warning the others and getting Rynn hidden.' Or at least she had better be. That was the drill when protecting someone.

Grace nodded to the door of the guardroom, grateful she'd slept down here. She slid across the room and opened the door a crack. Three figures, all clad in black, their heads hooded, all armed, had entered the inn. A man's body sprawled by the main door, blood pooling around him. The innkeeper had either let them in or had tried to stop them. Whichever, it had ended badly for him.

Jehane slipped by her, out the door, heading for the taproom, and seemed to become shadows himself.

With a quick series of hand signals, Grace directed the squad to back her up and Misha to stay put and hide.

Then she heard them, coming right for the guardroom door.

'Get the guards. Especially the redhead.'

She knew that voice. Shit.

Seven hells erupted on the other side of the taproom. Shadows poured out from behind the bar, swirling around the nearest attacker and bringing him down in seconds. But Jehane couldn't stop them all. The second and third came towards her. The main door to the inn stood open and more figures flooded in. It was impossible to tell how many, too dark and too much movement. She was under attack. They all were.

Worse, she was a target. Their leader had singled her out.

Daniel headed for the door, his knives flashing as he moved. Jehane leaped on top of the bar and reached for another figure. He went down, gasping for breath, strands of shadows wrapped around his throat. Then the Shade sought Grace out and she saw the look of alarm pass over his handsome face. 'Grace, look out!'

Something slammed into her, pushed her against the wooden panels on the wall. Her head glanced off the surface, leaving her dizzy for a second, a second too long. Her attacker's rough hands grabbed her shirt, feeling for the warrant.

'Figured you'd be upstairs fucking his lordship,' the man drawled. 'Lucky me, you made it easy.' His hand closed on the warrant and his face lit up in triumph. 'I got it, boss!' he yelled.

'No!' A deeper voice, cultured and angry, shouted from the stairs. How had they reached the stairs already? 'I said don't touch it. Just—'

But the warning was far too late. The man holding her burst into flames.

Jehane was right. The warrant protected itself. No one could take it from her by force.

'Yeah,' Grace muttered. 'Lucky you.'

She swiftly kicked his burning body away and the man crumbled in front of her eyes. The ghastly fire illuminated the room. Dozens of them, hooded figures, overpowering her team, already up the stairs and too many to deal with, far too many.

A huge man, twice the size of anyone else there, seized Jehane by the leg and pulled him off the bar. His head slammed into it as he went down and in that instant all the shadows faded. The fire from the corpse illuminated the room, but as another man stepped forward and stretched out his hand, water gushed over the flames, dousing them. A

Tide… and the other one was a Brawn… They were mageborn. There were others too, a Flint maybe. Not all of them, but enough. And they were powerful. Too powerful.

'Enough!' A familiar figure hauled Misha out of the guardroom, a knife at his throat. Going for the weakest of them, and their weakness. 'Stand down,' said Asher Kane. The knife pressed closer, a line of red trickling down the harper's throat. 'You two, weapons down.'

They were outnumbered, surrounded. Daniel dropped his blades instantly. Divinities, he never learned. Grace's own knives were still firmly in her hands. She had no intention of obeying Kane.

Kane pushed Misha forward onto his knees and one of his compatriots stepped up behind him. Misha's eyes were huge, pleading with Grace as the sword tip pressed to the base of his skull. A soldier's execution stance, quick and brutal. All the bastard had to do was fall forward and Misha would never survive.

'And what do you want here?' she said, trying to keep her voice calm.

'My king, of course, and his bride. Her family are beside themselves. Oh, and I want the warrant. Naturally. Hand it over, there's a good girl.'

Condescension never made her willing to cooperate. She would have thought someone would have worked that out by now. Not Asher Kane, clearly.

'I can't do that.' She'd only taken it off once, to give it to Bastien and recreate the crown which turned him into the Hollow King. He'd given it back. She didn't even know what would happen if she gave it to someone else now. Especially not with the touch of the Deep Dark on it.

'Can't or won't?'

Grace shrugged. Either way, she wasn't giving it up. Kane stalked towards her and his guards fell back, letting him approach her alone.

She couldn't do anything. If she stabbed him, Misha was dead, and Daniel and Jehane seconds later. Divinities alone knew where Ellyn was. Guarding Rynn, she hoped. There was no sign of Lara at all.

And as for Bastien...

'Drop the weapons, Marchant. It's over. Learn when to give up.' Grace loathed that tone and knew it too well. Kane actually smiled. But his pulse jumped in his throat, giving a lie to his confidence. She watched it, thinking about how easy it would be to slam a knife right in there. It would only take seconds. And then... then they'd all die, of course. Those following him didn't seem the type to just back down without him.

Grace sheathed the knives and Kane smiled, self-satisfied and loathsome. He was so sure of himself.

She was going to wipe that smug expression off his face. Maybe not now. But soon. Of that she was determined.

He reached out, stroked her face and she suppressed a shudder of revulsion. 'Remarkable,' he murmured. 'Orphan, street child, Academy brat... but look at you. Marius was a canny man, of course. He knew, I suppose, the moment he saw you, how Bastien would react and how you could use that to control him. Our Lord of Thorns always was entirely predictable. Where is he? Upstairs with the princess?'

She kept her eyes fixed on his, although the temptation to glance up was almost overwhelming.

Had Lara got him out? Had they escaped? Ellyn was up there too with Rynn. Had they managed—

Kane grabbed a fistful of her hair and wrenched her head to one side. 'Come along, Captain Marchant. Let's go and see our reluctant king, shall we? Maybe he can persuade you. Or you him.'

He all but dragged her up the stairs, kicked open the door to Bastien's room and flung her inside. She'd hoped it would be empty, that while they'd been fighting downstairs, Bastien and the others would have escaped through the window or something. But he had done nothing of the sort. Of course he hadn't.

Bastien stood there, arms folded, waiting, all alone.

'Asher,' he said in a voice as cold as arctic wind. 'I'd appreciate it if you didn't harm her. I'll be very put out if you do. Did Aurelie send you?'

'Aurelie, the Dowager, Celeste… what is it with you and powerful women, Bastien? You really know how to piss them off.'

Bastien bent down and helped Grace gently to her feet. 'Sorry,' she whispered. 'There were too many of them.'

'It's not your fault.' Like she'd spilled something. Like it didn't matter at all.

She scanned the room. Four more of Kane's guards came in behind him. Three wore collars, she could see that now they'd discarded their hoods. Their eyes were dark. Nightborn.

He was working with the nightborn…

Seeing her notice, Kane's hyena smile widened. 'Celeste and I came to an agreement with the Deep Dark. It's very persuasive. And the nightborn are its creatures.'

Across the corridor, the door was closed. Was Ellyn in there with Rynn? She had to be. And where was Lara? Damn it all, they were too few, scattered and at this bastard's mercy.

'What do you want, Asher?' Bastien asked.

The cruel smile spread over his face. 'Why, only a Larelwynn on the throne of course. And you, Lord of Thorns, in your rightful place. But first I need obedience. Real obedience this time. And to get that I need the chunk of gold around your lover's pretty neck.'

Bastien's hand closed on Grace's arm and he moved her gently to his side, and then behind him. 'That is not negotiable.'

Asher grinned. 'Oh, I think it is. She needs to learn her place in all this.'

The guards rushed them. Grace didn't even have time to get the knives out. Bastien's hands closed on the nearest mageborn, tearing the magic out of him before he could even use it. The man cried out and fell, his body convulsing.

But they weren't just mageborn. They were nightborn, their wild magic racing through them, making them stronger and faster. More dangerous by far.

The Brawn seized Grace, his arms wrapping around her, lifting her off the ground. The grip crushed her arms against her sides, and beneath them her ribs into her lungs. She couldn't catch her breath, no matter how she squirmed and kicked. He absorbed any blow she managed to land, each one making him even stronger. The world turned blurred and dark, patches of light eating away at her vision.

'Enough, or we'll work out how to take the warrant from her corpse,' Asher Kane shouted. 'We don't actually need her. Just the warrant. Do as you're told, Bastien.'

Bastien fell still, staring at her, and she knew… He'd give up. For her. She could see it in his eyes.

She was his weakness.

'Where is the Valenti girl?' Kane asked.

'Gone,' Bastien said firmly. 'She wasn't actually too keen on marriage as it turned out. Not when your spell broke.'

Asher shook his head. 'She was a sharper little thing than I thought. I'll enjoy breaking her when I catch up with her, rest assured. I think the Larelwynns have always set too much store by that ridiculous potion anyway. We can try it again when we get to Rathlynn. But there are other ways to exert pressure on you, Bastien.' He leered at Grace. 'We all know that.'

So they hadn't found Rynn, or Ellyn. If things had been different, Grace would have breathed a sigh of relief, but that wasn't an option right now.

Asher waved his hand and the Brawn crushed Grace in his grip until she felt like her ribs were about to crack.

Bastien gave a choked cry and lurched forward but Asher blocked his way.

'Now, we'll start again. Grace here is going to suffer every time you defy me. And you *know* the things I'm capable of doing.'

'Let her go. Please.'

Bastien could destroy Asher Kane with a touch. All he had to do was reach out. But he didn't. Because of her… He could get out of here. She knew the power he could command. Even now, even diminished with the torc around his neck and the warrant around hers. He was the strongest mageborn she knew.

But he wouldn't…

'Give me the warrant, Bastien,' Asher said.

The grip on her tightened. Painful now. She couldn't breathe. White spots danced in front of her eyes.

'Grace,' Bastien murmured. And she suddenly knew what he was thinking, what he was prepared to do to save her. Because he would always try to save her.

'Don't do it,' she gasped. She could barely get the words out. But she had to. 'That's an… an order. Don't you dare put this thing on him.' She felt the power of the warrant wind itself around them both, more clearly than she had ever felt it before. That should protect him, shouldn't it? It had to. It was all she could do now.

'Grace… I'm sorry,' he said. *Sorry?* He had nothing to be sorry for. She had failed him, not the other way around. Her one job had been to keep him safe.

The Brawn let her go and she dropped to her hands and knees. But before she could recover he kicked her in the stomach, lifting her off the ground. She rolled away, gasping in pain. The other guards laughed quietly, snickering among themselves.

The Flint had taken up position outside the doorway. But he wasn't alone. A slight figure slid like a shadow behind the Flint and, before Grace could blink, he stiffened, opening his mouth to cry out. But he made no sound, gasped and buckled. The figure caught him and pulled him silently out of sight.

The Brawn turned and pulled her up again, onto her knees, facing them again. They hadn't seen, Grace realised. They hadn't seen a thing. She wasn't even certain that she had. Not in this state.

'I won't tell you a second time,' said Kane, all his attention fixed on Bastien. He reached out and stroked Grace's hair, like he was examining silk, but he didn't shift his gaze from Bastien's appalled face.

'Don't…' Grace tried to say again. 'Don't…' She had to stop him, had to distract them all. She had to tell him, *command* him. The others were coming. Somehow. Lara and Ellyn would save them.

There was only one thing she could think of. She grabbed the Brawn's arm and, reaching into the void inside her, she dredged up her own magic and let it loose. She didn't know what it was now, or where it came from, but it was all she had. Flames blazed from her hands and the Brawn screamed at the unexpected shock of it.

She tore herself free, but she wasn't fast enough. Asher grabbed her – out of the air, it seemed – and slammed her down onto the floorboards. His boot came down on her chest, winding her and holding her down. 'I might have guessed. Mageborn yourself, and uncollared too. A touch hypocritical, Captain Marchant. Oh, but this is even better.'

He pressed down harder. Divinities, were they just going to crush her to death for their amusement, flatten her as leverage against Bastien?

'Lar,' he said. 'Come here. Show us how to deal with fire.'

The Tide swaggered forward and grinned a rotten-toothed grin as he reached out his hands. His eyes glittered darkly, like a cavern in the depths of the ocean. Instantly Grace felt water coalesce on her skin, every droplet from the air around her, every bead of sweat and every tear. Her mouth dried but then abruptly filled again. It crawled up her face, pushed past her lips and up her nostrils. Panic took over. She coughed up liquid, her body desperately trying to save itself. She was back in the river, hands and feet holding her down. She was in the lagoon, drowning before she reached the boat.

'Stop it!' Bastien yelled. 'Please!'

Asher lifted his foot and Grace rolled onto her side, gasping for air as the water she vomited up splattered onto the floorboards. She tried to stop the convulsions racking her body, tried to persuade her aching lungs it was all right to breathe again. Someone laughed. The Tide, she thought.

God and goddess, she'd throttle him herself given half a chance. She'd enjoy it. No, she'd burn him. She'd incinerate him like kindling.

Bastien stood in front of her, blurred by her tears. He looked so afraid, his mask completely stripped away now.

'I'm sorry, Grace. I can't… I can't let them kill you.'

Before she could recover he reached out to take the warrant, lifting the chain with it.

Deep inside her the darkness surged. Bastien's eyes widened, shock turning his skin to chalk. He dropped the warrant but it was too late. She knew it was too late. Something raced through her veins, from her toes to the top of her head, screaming along each nerve. A soft, silent concussion shook the room. Her mouth opened, but no sound came out. Nothing. Her vision went dark, twisted around and turned in on itself.

A sigil cut through the air, more effective than any knife. It struck the Tide standing over her. He cried out, struggling to dislodge it. His magic smothered, he staggered, and then something slammed into the side of his head, bringing him to the ground.

All around her chaos broke out. It was like watching it through deep water, from the bottom of a dark pool. Figures lunged together, flew apart. Swords whirled and flashed and she knelt in the centre, unable to move, barely able to breathe. Bastien pounced on the nearest guard, wrestling the sword from his hands and jamming it up through a chink in the armour. The dying breath rippled around her as he fell to the floor at her feet.

She breathed it in, relishing it.

The Brawn came at him and the Lord of Thorns unfurled his power. Once they'd thought he was a Leech, and that was what he used now, draining every iota of magic from the hulking nightborn.

Bastien staggered back, breathing hard. Grace couldn't help but watch him. He was alive with magic, glowing with it, his skin iridescent.

'Where's Asher?' he yelled. 'Where did he go?'

Lara stood in the doorway, a cudgel in one hand and another sigil ready in the other. Behind her, Ellyn had both swords out.

'Clear downstairs,' she said. 'Rynn's safe. Daniel and Misha are okay. They're seeing to Jehane. The others fled. Divinities, Asher bloody Kane can run fast when he needs to.'

'Get after him.' Bastien's voice rippled with magic, his rage as dangerous as one of the nightborn.

'We can't. We don't have the manpower,' Lara told him. 'Jehane is hurt and he's the only one with a chance apart from—' She stopped as she looked at Grace, still kneeling there like a statue, watching them all as if through thick smoke. Her face fell. 'What did he do?'

Darkness rippled through Grace, making her blood run faster, her heart beat louder. She reached out both her hands and Bastien, dropping the weapons he'd so recently seized, took them in his own. He was trembling, hidden from everyone else but not from her. Suddenly the strength in him was gone. Strange, she'd only ever seen him this shaken once before. When she had been dying…

'Grace?' he whispered. 'Let me take it off. Just…' He reached for the warrant.

Take it off? Why… why would she allow that? It was hers. Marius had given the warrant to her. And with good reason.

The warrant glowed with its own dark light, a light so cold it burned the air itself. The room darkened around Grace as if night was falling and she smiled. Bastien's grip on her hands tightened. Premonition washed through her. Everything seemed painted in shadows and gold.

'*No*,' she told him. Her voice was a low ripple. And her body felt so strong. Strong and made anew, as if all the hurt had been washed away. No one would lay hands on her now, no Brawn, no jumped-up Tide, not Kane, not even Bastien himself.

Anguish filled his eyes. 'Listen to me… something happened to the warrant. You need to take it off. You're a conduit—'

'*I'm already a conduit*,' Grace said, her amusement flooding the words. '*When you brought me back through the Maegen from the jaws of death. Didn't you realise, Bastien?*'

His features glowed with inner light. She could see it swirling within him, along his veins, pulsing with his heartbeat, so strong. The light of the Maegen, the power of magic itself. He was so powerful, drenched in magic, both his own and that he had stolen from the nightborn he'd taken down. Powerful and at the same time weak. Even like this, at her mercy.

'Grace, no,' he whispered.

There was another voice, one from somewhere deep inside her, that emptiness that had been there ever since her rebirth. The voice used her mouth to speak and she didn't care any more. There was no point in fighting it. She didn't want to. '*She was always our way out. We dwell in her. She reached for us, embraced us.*'

'You're using her. When she reached for her magic… you used her fear.'

'*She still reached.*' It laughed at him, as if he was a mother fussing over a child. '*She won't suffer, Bastien, we promise. We will hold her as precious as you do. She'll live in power and glory. Our glory.*'

The rush of pleasure, the spike of adrenaline and endorphins, made her body glow with dark fire. She was whole again, after so long, so many years. She was powerful, endless, as immortal as he was.

Grace looked into Bastien's eyes, so dark they were a mirror, and saw her own eyes reflected there.

They were black, jet black, entirely, as if they were all pupil. They were windows into the void. Her smile widened further.

'No,' Bastien said. 'Grace, listen to me. Please, my love. Please, this isn't you.'

Grace released his hands and shoved him aside as if he was nothing more than an obstacle to be moved.

The laugh that came from her was as empty and draining as the voice inside her. The voice now almost completely in control. It was part of her, fusing with her. And she wanted it to. She'd never felt like this. So strong, so powerful, so free to do exactly what she wanted, to *be* exactly what she wanted.

'*Listen to you? We are chaos. This body doesn't contain us. She welcomes us.*'

All around her magic rippled through the air. The captive nightborn gazed at her in adoration and something in her thrilled to see it. They smiled as she glanced at them. Offering themselves.

She reached out and pulled the remaining scraps of magic from them, a burst of energy rushing through the air, vanishing into the abyss inside her. Bastien had almost emptied them. But it didn't matter. They knew what they were offering. They just didn't care. The magic gone, she drew on their strength and then life itself. They crumpled up like old sacks, falling heavily to the ground.

One source remained, one person with more power inside him than anyone else. Bastien. Her mouth watered at the thought of the magic flowing in his veins, bright as sunlight.

'*My poor faithless Lord of Thorns,*' the other voice said, dripping condescension. '*You think you can hold her? You think you can bring her back? She's a sacrifice. Grace is gone. It was the boys before, those two poor boys, so full of love and blind belief. Honour and duty. And what did it get them? Don't you remember?*'

'Grace… what boys?'

'*Larelwynns,*' the Deep Dark said through her, stopping right in front of him. '*Don't you know your own stories any more? She doesn't either. Your Grace. She's mageborn. She's from the kingdom. She's…*' Grace inhaled and a memory of the two of them entangled, lost in each other, surged forward. Her eyes went wide with the flush of pleasure that rippled through her. The Deep Dark purred with delight. '*She's your mate. I smell her all over you. When she kills you, will you weep, little king? Will you cry? Or will you willingly be her sacrifice?*'

It was like she tripped over something, like a punch to the stomach knocked her breath from her.

Kill him? No. She wasn't going to kill Bastien. That was not the plan. Grace tried to scramble for some element of control, something to cling to, to figure this out. Just a moment, a moment to think…

'What sacrifice?' he asked. 'Answer me.'

Her mouth smiled, and now Grace didn't feel like joining in. This was wrong. She didn't want to answer, she wanted this to stop. But the Deep Dark was not finished, not yet. She fought back, but there was nothing more she could do. It was so strong. Like water, deep, dark water, pulling her down. And all she had was a faint fire of magic. She was drowning all over again.

'*There is always a sacrifice,*' said the voice that was not her voice. '*There are always two of them, one to live and one to die. No one can take on that much power and survive, not if they are to let the Hollow King in. When you deal with the oldest gods, the primal powers, there always has to be an offering. Blood. Life. She's your weakness. She always will be.*'

Bastien was strong to begin with but now, for the first time ever, Grace was stronger. Even consumed by the power of the Hollow King, part of Bastien had still been the man she loved. He stared down into her eyes and she felt the gaze of other, terrible things, crawling inside her looking out, studying him.

'Grace, come back to me.'

He lifted a hand to stroke her hair, the touch so gentle. And she wanted to. She wanted him. But she couldn't find the strength. Not any more.

'*No,*' the Deep Dark said. '*You deserted her. There is no forgiveness. There is nothing. Nothing but us. And you belong to us, heart and soul. Just as she does. Or will. Time is difficult. Three times dead. Twice entombed. Let us show you.*'

The power possessing her body grabbed him, her hand a fist at his neck pulling his mouth down to hers in a bruising kiss. The other hand closed on the warrant and she wound the command it exerted around him, bound him to her will.

No. Not her will. The Deep Dark had control now. Total control. This was its will.

Bastien resisted for a moment but he was weak. She was his weakness. And the Deep Dark knew it. The collective mind of his ancient enemy relied on it. In concert, it reached out and dragged Bastien into its embrace.

Chapter Twenty-Three

The chamber was cavernous. It had never been this large in reality but in his dreams, in his memory, it was endless. Bastien's footsteps echoed as he walked forwards. The boy was waiting, sitting on the throne. He looked the same. Not a year had passed for him. Caught forever in his teenage years, not quite boy, not quite man. The sword lay across his lap, still too big.

'They found you then,' he said.

'Lucien?'

The first Larelwynn king looked exactly as Bastien remembered from the first time he had ever laid eyes on him. All those years ago in a cave very much like this one. Not as vast, perhaps. And there was no sign of the Maegen. But this was the boy with whom Bastien, the Hollow King, had made the pact. They had both been trying to save their people and Lucien had persuaded him. He'd been desperate. It had seemed like the only way at the time.

Now he wasn't so sure.

'I missed you,' Lucien said.

'What's happening?'

'You're lost. But… here we are.' Lucien stood up, putting down the oversized sword, and he walked to Bastien, embracing him. 'Who did they use as a sacrifice? Someone you care about?' He studied Bastien's face. 'Oh, I see. I'm so sorry, old friend.'

'What did you do, Lucien?'

'Me? I did nothing. It was you.'

'I don't…'

Lucien frowned. 'What do you remember?'

The cave… this cave but not this cave. The Maegen. Being ready to die. Either by Lucien's hands or by giving himself up to the Maegen and the monstrous power that presided over it. The words, those words on his lips… 'It is my honour to serve.'

'Bastien?' Lucien called his attention back to him. 'Bastien, what *do* you remember?'

'I remember you and the cave. The pact…'

'But before that?'

'Before?' There was no before. There was just… he'd been the Hollow King, the first of the mageborn. He'd battled nightborn and the Deep Dark. 'When I was the king?'

Lucien's hands rested on his shoulders and he stared deeply into Bastien's eyes. 'No. Before that. Before the Hollow King. Before Thorndale. When you were just Bastien. When we were… we were friends.'

'Lucien… we were never—'

Darkness swirled around them, pulling at him, dragging him down. It wasn't cold and hungry like the Deep Dark. It was something else. Something ancient and grim, determined.

Bastien closed his eyes. His memories blurred, resolved themselves again. He remembered the blade at his throat, felt the metal dig in and he welcomed it. He knew it had to happen and he was ready for it. The wild ecstatic sense of love had swept through him.

'It's okay, Lucien. It's okay. It's for you,' he had said.

But Lucien had sobbed, helpless, devastated. 'Please. Please don't…
don't…'

Bastien forced himself to stillness, made his eyes open. It was the
old cave, much smaller, the boiling glow of the Maegen churning
before him, throwing light up onto the ceiling.

*One boy stood by the broken obsidian throne. The other knelt in front of the
pool with a figure towering over him. The knife at his throat glimmered,
reflecting the light of the Maegen.*

Bastien moved closer.

What do *you remember?*

*Both boys were on the cusp of manhood. Perhaps fifteen. So young and
their eyes were fixed on each other, desperate, devastated. But the other
one, even while tears gilded his face, made no move to help. Bastien knew
him. It was Lucien. Lucien as he had been then, before he became a king,
before the pact, before he ruled.*

Just a boy.

*'I will always be with you,' the other boy said with Bastien's own
voice. 'It has to be this way. A sacrifice.' He looked at the reflection of his
murderer in the pool, a face made of stone and fire, a face that couldn't be
real. And yet it was. 'I'm willing to die for him. It is my honour to serve.'*

*And the knife bit deep. Blood fell in the Maegen, swallowed by it, and
behind the boy the man froze, light spilling from his eyes. The colour faded*

from his body, stone climbing up his limbs and torso like vines, petrifying him until only a statue was left behind.

Lucien didn't move for a moment. On the other side of the pool he sat cradling a broken crown, trying to force himself to keep breathing.

'Bastien?' he whispered.

There was no answer.

He watched the other boy get up, his face a mask worn by an unfamiliar power. He stepped into the pool, blood still pouring down his chest. The Maegen boiled around him, drinking him down, swallowing him whole, and then he emerged at the other side, drenched in power, in life, reborn. He stopped in front of Lucien Larelwynn.

The boy with Bastien's face knelt in front of his king, light spilling from him. 'Majesty, I am yours to command. Now and always.'

Moving like a puppet, Lucien jerked the broken crown towards him and the boy who had become the Hollow King – a god now sheathed in a human form – took it. Divinities, what had they done?

Was this part of the pact?

The smaller part of the broken crown melted in his cupped hand, until it was a golden disc, the size of a coin. He handed it to Lucien Larelwynn who closed his hand over it. The warrant. Then the rest of the crown transformed, twisting and reshaping itself in his hands, and Bastien felt the weight of the torc nestling around his throat.

'I'm sorry,' Lucien whispered from behind him, his voice broken. Not Lucien then. Lucien now. Whenever now was. 'Three times dead, it said, twice entombed. And you thought it meant you. We'd been through so much. You'd died, or almost died, we both had, and then… It was a mistake. We should never have done it.'

'There's always a sacrifice,' Bastien said. 'And it was me… whoever I was.' He couldn't doubt it for a moment, looking now into the face of the man who had been the first Larelwynn king.

'There was no other way to bind a god. You said… you said it was your duty. Duty and honour. That mattered to you more than anything. He said it was the only way. That he'd sleep and live through you, biddable, obedient… But he's awake, Bastien. The Deep Dark is out and he's awake. He can bind the Deep Dark again if you only ask him. He's waiting.'

'For me?'

'For both of us.'

'But you're dead.'

The smile that flickered over his face was heartbreaking, lost. 'Yes. Yes I am. Which means he'll want someone else. Another life. Another sacrifice.'

Behind them a fire roared into being, a column of flames without any sign of fuel. He stared at it for a moment, at its swirling shapes. Slowly it resolved to a figure, a woman, with long red hair and golden-brown eyes. A woman more beautiful than he had ever known. More beautiful to him than anything he had ever seen. He loved her. All he could do was love her. She was everything.

The expression on Lucien's face said it all and Bastien recoiled.

'No. Not her.'

'She holds the warrant. And your heart. She's more like you than you know. The Deep Dark is making her its own right now.' Lucien studied her, the way someone would look at an experiment or a work of art. 'She's so angry, Bastien. She's in so much pain. All that misery, all those years of not knowing who or what she was, and then you come along. You with all your power, all your broken memories, just like hers. And she loved you. By all the powers, she loved you more than anything. More than life itself. Perhaps she still does. But how do you repay her?'

With danger and death, with grief and pain…

Three times dead, twice entombed… but that didn't apply to Grace. She had died and Bastien had brought her back. She'd been buried in the collapsed building in Rathlynn but… she didn't fit. She simply didn't… He could not allow this to happen. Not to her.

He backed away, forcing himself from his memories, from the things he didn't want to remember. Memories that were not his. The boy who he had been, the life he had sacrificed, the king before him. Then and now.

'No.'

'There are others. They even have my blood, my descendants. They're few and far between but they are still there. Some stronger, some weaker. Make one of them take her place.'

Grace would never forgive him. He knew that. 'No.'

'I'm so sorry,' Lucien said.

'I don't need your pity.'

As he retreated Lucien's voice drifted after him. 'Perhaps not. But you have it nonetheless, my Bastien. You always will.'

*

His body felt numb and uncertain. The world around him was muffled and wrong somehow. Bastien struggled against the night that pressed close, the smothering blanket of darkness that surrounded him. Pain lanced through him, tearing into his consciousness and dragging its barbs along his veins. It was right somehow. Like he deserved this. It was retribution. It was justice. He'd die for her. She'd live. It was better this way.

He opened his eyes and saw her, saw Grace. The searing pain around his throat, crushing into his skin, far tighter than the torc had ever been before… and Grace, Grace killing him…

He was helpless before her. The warrant gave her complete power over him and she had only ever used it with the lightest touch. He knew that now. Compared to this, compared with what she could do, what she did now…

Wild rage slammed through him, a violence such as he had never known. He couldn't escape her. With the warrant corrupted, she was at the mercy of the Deep Dark, a new goddess containing its power, its puppet, its host. But he wasn't. And he would not allow that. With every ounce of strength he had left to him, he pushed that rage down through his body, through his touch and his kiss and into her. It went like a fire, roaring through his veins and ignited the Flint in her.

Her eyes blazed, the black transformed, illuminated from within. The darkness inside them burned away and they were golden again. More than golden. Incandescent with light, like newborn suns. The heat of her touch seared his flesh but he didn't care. If this was what it took to save her, to drive the Deep Dark out of her, then he would endure it. He would be her sacrifice.

Grace drew back a fist and punched him. The pain blinded him, sent him reeling. So he wasn't invulnerable. It was almost a relief.

Divinities, she packed a punch though.

But it was her. Just her. He saw it in her face, in her fury.

He staggered away and Grace lunged at him. Before she could touch him again, strong arms seized her, pinning her arms expertly behind her.

'I've got her,' Ellyn shouted.

Inside Grace the Deep Dark rose up again, holding her hostage inside her own body. He could see it through the haze of pain like a tangle of black briars under her skin.

But it didn't lash out at Ellyn. Grace wouldn't let it.

He saw that, the conflict in her eyes. It was one brief glimmer of hope.

Everyone spoke at once, a cacophony of voices. Lara, Ellyn and Daniel. Even Misha and Jehane, joining them…he didn't know when they'd arrived. It hardly mattered.

'We've got to get it off her.'

'Don't touch it. You saw what she did.'

'How do we get it off her? How do we get her back?'

They were talking about the warrant. But they couldn't touch it. It would kill anyone who tried.

Bastien stood there in the middle of it all watching Grace struggle against Ellyn. But she couldn't tear herself free. Something in the other Academy officer held her. He narrowed his eyes, studying them. Light in their veins, in both of them. Light and darkness, tangled together, and not just in Grace.

And then another voice, soft and scared, not the voice of a warrior at all, not like the rest of them.

'I'll do it.'

Rynn. It was Rynn. And no one else was listening. Not well enough. She walked through the chaos, sidestepping them as if they were background elements in a painting. She had a light in her, pulsing with the beating of her heart. But it wasn't strong enough. Bastien knew it even as he looked at her. It would never be strong enough.

'Don't,' he whispered. His voice grated against the inside of his throat. 'Don't do it, Rynn. Please. It will… it will hurt you. If it doesn't kill you. Larelwynn or not.'

If he sounded pathetic, so be it. He wasn't afraid for himself. He could feel the malice the Deep Dark pumped through Grace, feel its hunger and rage. The things it promised to do to Rynn if she touched the warrant.

Find another to take her place, Lucien had said in his memories. Find another Larelwynn. Another sacrifice to replace Grace. But how could he make a decision like that? Pick someone else to save her? She'd never forgive him.

And now he saw it was all for nothing.

Rynn had Larelwynn blood but it was not enough. It never would be. Not for the Hollow King. Not for the warrant.

The Valenti princess raised her hands, bit her lower lip and reached for the warrant. Grace – or the Deep Dark possessing Grace – bared her teeth.

'*You think you can wear it?*' the Deep Dark snarled at the princess. '*It'll flay the pretty flesh from your bones. We will swallow you whole and keep you screaming for eternity. You'll burn for all the long days and all through the nights as well, you vapid, selfish bitch.*'

Rynn flinched, her face bloodless. But then she stretched out her hands again.

'*Go on then,*' Grace shouted at her. No, not Grace. It was not Grace. She'd never be like this. '*Go on. Take it. Like you take everything else. Take what isn't yours and claim it always was yours by right. Your birthright, by virtue of your royal blood, like your kind always do. Even if you don't want it. Take it and see what we will do to you. We will burn you, and freeze you, we'll drown you and tear you apart. We'll put you back together and do it all over again, repeating it for ever. We'll make you weep and beg, and curse the day you were born.*'

'No!' But it wasn't Rynn who cried out.

Ellyn yanked Grace away from the princess. Bastien let out a cry of warning but Ellyn didn't listen. She grabbed the warrant, tearing it free from Grace's throat before Rynn could lay her hands on it.

Grace twisted around, turning on Ellyn to attack, even in the instant that the power of the Deep Dark released her, momentum carrying her on, and then all strength left her. Bastien caught her as she collapsed, folding up like a paper doll. She weighed almost nothing in his arms, her skin bloodless, her body so cold. She gazed up at him like she didn't know him, her mouth making little shocked gasps.

Ellyn staggered as if she had been kicked in the guts. Then she straightened, clutching the warrant in her hands. It was still dark but the darkness only contrasted with the transformation in the Academy officer. She was aglow with light, illuminated from within, blazing like a newborn star. Light surged through her body, along her veins, so much brighter than Rynn had been. There was no doubting what it was, Larelwynn blood making itself known.

And then, all Bastien could hear was her desperate scream.

Chapter Twenty-Four

Daniel was the first to reach Ellyn. He didn't hesitate, heedless of the danger. He wrapped his arms around her and attempted to shake the necklace from her hands, holding her close and calling her name. Grace tried to pull herself free but Bastien didn't let go of her. When she reached for Ellyn, Daniel snarled at her.

'Don't you dare touch that *fucking thing* again! Back off, Grace. Now!'

He'd never talked to her like that. Never. He must be terrified. And furious.

What had she done?

Laughter echoed in the recesses of her mind, in the darkest, most primal parts.

The warrant fell to the floor between them with an empty thud, cold and tarnished, ominous. Ellyn slumped in Daniel's arms.

Rynn dropped to her knees in front of her, ignoring both Bastien and Grace. 'Is she okay? What did it do to her? What did it—?'

Daniel shook Ellyn gently, trying to wake her. 'I don't know.'

'Bastien,' Grace said, her heart and her head pounding violently. Her voice grated against her throat. 'Bastien, you can help her. Please. Do something.'

His grip loosened, just for a moment, but he was still reluctant to let her go. Dear divinities… what had happened? 'Don't move. Promise me.'

She nodded. She'd do anything, anything at all. So long as he made this stop. So long as Ellyn was okay again. 'I promise. Just do it.'

He stood up and when she mirrored him, he stopped, glaring at her. 'Jehane,' he said, in the cold voice of command. 'Make sure she stays here.'

Jehane took his place, drawing Grace back towards the doorway, his touch gentle but firm. She didn't doubt that if she showed even the slightest wavering moment he would overpower her. Blood covered one side of his face, bright and sticky. She let him hold her, afraid of what the others would do if she struggled now.

The warrant lay on the ground. She could still feel its touch, an echo of it still hanging around her neck, the place against her chest where it used to sit painfully cold.

It called to her, murmuring promises and threats in the rear of her shattered mind, until tears made her vision blur. She had to force herself to look away from it. That wasn't the warrant. It was the Deep Dark.

Bastien knelt down beside Rynn, studying Ellyn's face.

'May I—?' He held out his hand but waited for permission. He wanted to help though, that was the Bastien Grace knew. No matter what they might be going through, that was the man she loved. Daniel nodded and Bastien pressed his palm to Ellyn's forehead, frowning as he did so.

'What is it?' Rynn whispered. 'What's wrong with her? What did it do?'

Grace felt the magic flowing in him, more clearly than she had ever felt it before, and through him into Ellyn. He had control of so many branches of the mageborn powers but she could already tell he wasn't as strong as he usually was. Whatever happened when Grace had touched him had drained him.

'Be careful,' she warned him but he wasn't really listening. Or if he was, he didn't care. Again she was reminded that Bastien's intense loyalty extended to her squad as well. They were his people too. He'd said so.

'I am, I promise.' He was such a liar sometimes. 'She's transmuting it, I think, as best she can. But it's—'

Agony. Grace could see that in every wince and twitch in Ellyn's face.

'We don't have time for this,' Lara interrupted. 'We need to get out of here. Asher will have reinforcements on the way. If they find us here—'

'Not now, Lara,' Bastien said. It was the voice that would brook no argument. 'Go and secure the place. Take Jehane and Misha and make preparations. Now.'

It was the most regal Grace had ever heard him sound.

Lara walked off, muttering to herself, stepping over the bodies of those she had killed and those Grace had. Dead mageborn, stripped of magic and stripped of life itself… What had she done? Grace could remember it, but hazily, as if she had been watching someone else from far away. The door snapped shut behind them. It left Grace with just Daniel, Bastien, Ellyn and Rynn.

Bastien looked up into her eyes, back at Ellyn slumped in Daniel's arms, and then at her again. The weight of a question he didn't want to ask lingered in his eyes. Finally, he lifted his hand and Ellyn stirred, her eyes fluttering open.

She groaned, rolling out of Daniel's arms and holding her head. Rynn tried to help her stand, almost holding her up. For once Ellyn didn't pull away. Perhaps she didn't have the strength.

'Did you know?' Bastien asked.

'Know what?' Grace asked. Daniel looked just as confused as she felt. But he wasn't asking them.

'Ellyn?' Bastien asked again, endlessly patient and endlessly determined. 'Did you know?'

What was he on about? Grace shook her head, staring at him as he got to his feet and turned to face her. He looked more like the Lord of Thorns than he had in months and it chilled her. Withdrawn into himself, suspicious, and deeply troubled.

Ellyn looked like she'd been on a three-day bender. She held her hand out as if she could fend him off but when Grace looked she saw tears streaming down her friend's face.

'Know what?' Daniel asked again, sounding as bewildered as Grace felt.

'She's a Larelwynn,' Bastien said.

'No I'm not!' Ellyn spat the words out like a curse.

'Ellyn…' he sighed. 'I saw you. There's more Larelwynn blood in you than there is in Rynn. It's like a light, in your veins. I could see it so clearly. You need to tell me the truth. Who are you?'

She drew herself up, letting Rynn help her to her feet. 'I'm a Valenti water rat, that's all, the daughter of a fallen house, a refugee who grew up in Rathlynn. I'm nothing.'

'Don't say that!' Rynn interrupted. 'You know it isn't true.'

'Stop it, Rynn. I don't know what you want from me but I'm not your family.'

Rynn made a face of disgust. 'I know you're not. You're another line. The de Valens and the de Bruyns were never—'

'What are you talking about, Bastien?' Grace said over the sound of Rynn and Ellyn's bickering, as they made their way out of the room and downstairs, followed by a hesitant Daniel.

'You saw her, didn't you? You were right there. You saw the reaction she had to the warrant, and the way it attacked her.'

'I saw her screaming.' That was afterwards, after Ellyn took the warrant. But it hadn't killed her. Anyone else who had tried to take it by force had died in flames. But not Ellyn.

The pendant was still lying on the floor, the chain sprawling around it. Grace didn't want to touch it.

'Did you *see* her *glow*?'

Light. Yes, there had been light. 'The light inside her?' It had been beautiful, but she hadn't known if it was the Deep Dark making her see things or something else.

'Yes,' he said. 'Just like I used to see…'

Bastien wilted in front of her eyes, the strength leaving him. She grabbed him before he could fall. He'd never forgive himself if he collapsed now but he was exhausted in every way. Exhausted and in pain. And it was her fault.

'See who?'

'Lucien,' he whispered, like it was a guilty secret. He didn't meet her eyes as he said it and she knew something was terribly wrong. What was going on?

'Larelwynn?' she asked, dreading the answer. But she forced her voice to gentle again. She couldn't afford to turn this into a fight. 'Bastien. What happened? Tell me. Please. You remembered something?'

'I was *made* to remember… far more than ever before.'

There were still bodies around them, the Tide, the Brawn, the Flint, and the other guards. Bastien had all but stripped them of their magic, but Grace had taken their lives. She hadn't meant to, but the Deep Dark had been hungry and they had been close at hand and, as nightborn, more than willing to give up everything to her… no, to the

Deep Dark. Not her. She recalled all that magic rampaging through her. She had turned it on Bastien.

She choked on a sob, but forced her iron will around it. She couldn't break now.

'Please, I can't stay in here,' she whispered. She needed to get out of the room, away from those accusing eyes. She needed the open sky above her and no walls closing in.

His shoulders stiffened. He was staring at the warrant. 'We can't leave that there.'

She winced. 'I can't…'

'You have to. It's yours. I can't take it. Neither can the others. It would kill them.'

'But what if it—'

She felt his powers kindling inside him, fell the wave of it building around her. 'I won't let you hurt anyone.'

What else could she do? He was right. They couldn't leave it there for someone else to find. She couldn't give it to someone else with the Deep Dark infesting it. She had to be ready for what might happen and so did he.

'If you're sure,' she whispered, knowing there was no choice. Only Ellyn had a chance against it. And she couldn't ask that of her friend. It was her burden.

When she picked the warrant up it was cold and dead, depleted. Not even a hint of power in it. She put it back around her neck and tried to breathe evenly. Bastien held out a hand and she took it. Together, they made their way down the stairs and out into the early morning's cold light. They walked across the yard and Grace waited. Waited for something to happen. Waited for him to speak. Eventually they sat side by side on the low wall as the dawn slid up in the sky behind the inn.

'I saw Lucien Larelwynn,' Bastien told her. 'I spoke to him. I remembered. I saw what happened to me. Grace... I wasn't always the Hollow King... I was human, once.'

Her heart lurched inside her. It was a distillation of every nightmare he'd ever confessed to her, since they had discovered what he had once been, and what the Hollow King's crown could make of him again. 'Of course you're human, Bastien.'

'No... I mean... I *was*, I was a boy, Lucien's friend and... and maybe more. And I was killed. The Hollow King killed me as part of the pact because there had to be...' His voice trailed off and he choked on the words.

'A sacrifice,' she whispered.

'Someone... something to hold all that power. The Hollow King. Me. Or whatever... whatever I am.'

Grace pulled him into her arms. He buried his face into her shoulder and she held him for as long as she could.

She didn't want to let him go.

And she didn't want to think about what had just happened to her. She didn't want anyone to ask. If he had become the Hollow King, what did that make her?

The Deep Dark had overwhelmed her so easily but it hadn't only come from the warrant. That was only its way out, the door. The darkness had come from inside her.

Silence swept over them, awkward and unsure. The breeze turned cold.

Grace couldn't shake the feeling of being watched, of something lurking behind her, following her every move. Bastien's arms around her should have been a comfort. But they weren't. His hands slid down her shoulders, along her muscles. She couldn't handle tenderness from him, not now.

He hugged her and didn't let go. 'We will find a way, my love.'

My love. Those two words meant more to her than she could possibly articulate. 'What are we going to do?'

'I don't know.'

'It's not gone, Bastien. The power in the warrant might be dormant for now but I can feel it still inside me, waiting for a chance to get out again.'

He smiled at her. A heartbroken, regretful smile. 'So do I.'

He bent to kiss her, his lips soft but demanding, and she responded, indulging in this forbidden pleasure.

'This isn't an answer,' she told him when she could catch her breath.

'It's a question,' he said, and kissed her again.

It couldn't last. They needed to move on. Jehane and Misha appeared first, then Lara, handing them orders about the horses.

'You should check on your wife,' Grace said. 'We need to get moving.'

'Grace…' he breathed. For a moment she wondered if he wanted to argue that Rynn wasn't his wife, that this was all a misunderstanding, that he loved her… but he didn't. 'Thorndale isn't far now.'

She shook her head, pushing her hair out of her face. 'Don't try to make promises, love. We don't know how this will turn out.'

He frowned. He had to understand, he had to. She couldn't say it out loud, but she didn't believe in fairy-tale endings. Not any more. She was dangerous to him. Dangerous to all of them. She was barely holding onto herself by her fingernails. And if she lost control again…

When she left, he didn't come after her. And that was what she wanted, wasn't it? Asher was right, she was his weakness. Now more than ever. The Deep Dark knew it too.

She was about to go through the door to the guardroom when she heard Ellyn speaking.

'It wasn't her fault. I felt it when I took the necklace off her. I *heard* it inside me. All those voices, all that power, constantly clawing at me… Divinities, Danny… it was… it was a fucking nightmare.'

'I've never seen her like that. Do you think… do you think Bastien can fix her?' Daniel didn't sound convinced. *Daniel*, of all people, who had always been on her side.

'Him?' Ellyn scoffed. 'He causes the problems rather than fixing anything. Anyway, it's not about *fixing* someone. There's no way to fix that.'

'He can do it. You didn't see—'

'I saw everything you saw. And more… I felt that power. It burrowed under my skin like acid. It almost destroyed me. How long has she been wearing it? There's something wrong with her, Danny. Don't tell me you—'

Grace cleared her throat and they both looked up, guilt spreading all over their faces the moment they saw her.

Ellyn sat on her bed, and slowly dropped her head into her hands with a mortified groan. Daniel sat beside her, his arm around her, and, as Grace watched, his eyes closed in dismay.

Her friends. Her oldest friends. The only ones she thought she could always rely on.

'Sorry, Grace,' he said. 'She didn't mean…'

Grace heaved in a breath. There was no point in having an argument. Ellyn was probably right. She usually was. She won every bet she ever made.

'It's okay. There is something wrong. I'm trying to keep it under control. It's not far to Thorndale now. Bastien says he can stop it there.'

'Stop it, how?' Daniel asked. 'Wave his hand and make it all go away?'

'It's where it all began,' Ellyn replied. 'Where Larelwynn made the pact…'

Thorndale, the pact and the sacrifice Lucien Larelwynn made with Bastien… Grace didn't share her own doubts about that. Neither did they. But they were still going there, as if the place drew him inexorably home. All of them perhaps. Or at least she hoped they were still coming with her.

Ellyn frowned.

'I'm sorry, Grace. This stuff… magic and royal blood and—' Ellyn began and stopped when Daniel laughed. She glared at him. 'What?'

'Our Ellyn's a princess.'

Ellyn couldn't have looked more shocked if he'd kissed her. 'No I'm not. Fuck off, Danny.'

The mood shivered into something almost familiar. Grace sat down on the other side, the three of them perched on the narrow cot.

'Shush now, you shouldn't use language like that when you're a princess,' she chided.

From somewhere she found a smile. A real one. So did Daniel. Her friends, the ones she needed more than anyone else.

Ellyn threw back her head with a guttural groan of dismay. 'I'm not a… Divinities, you're never going to let this go, are you?'

'No. Absolutely not,' Daniel said with a grin. 'Princess Ellyn. What is Kurt going to say? A princess and a duchess. I'm moving up in the world. Wait, can I be an earl? No… a count…'

'Something like that anyway.' Ellyn shoved him away, but gently, half-heartedly. 'My dad… my dad was always saying one of his great-grandmothers was – *ugh*, it's ridiculous. Look at me.'

'Yeah, look at you, gorgeous Valenti specimen that you are,' Daniel told her, nudging her side. 'From what I've seen you'd shake their stupid monarchy to their foundations. That would be worth watching, wouldn't it? They're all inbred and weird anyway. Like Rynn would break if you—'

Someone cleared their throat pointedly in the doorway, just as Grace had done. Bastien was standing there, with Rynn right behind him.

'We're ready to go,' he said, coldly. Rynn stared at the floor, avoiding eye contact, her cheeks red. Bastien took her arm and they swept on outside. And just like that the good humour was doused with a new wave of ice-cold guilt.

'Where was she last night?' Daniel asked. 'While it was all going on? Where did she get to?'

Ellyn got up and grabbed her pack, avoiding meeting his eyes as completely as Rynn had. 'She was hiding in her room, under the bed.'

'You know that how?'

'I told her to slide underneath it and stay there. She… she's okay. Leave her alone.'

Daniel stared. 'She's what now?'

'She's okay. She's terrified. Her family are all bastards. She doesn't want to cause trouble, and she hates what she's done to you, Grace, but… let up on her, Danny.'

'I thought she bothered you,' Daniel asked.

'Stop, Danny,' Grace said. He never knew when to stop. She understood now what Ellyn thought of Rynn, and why she bothered her.

'That's what she said,' he protested.

'Yeah. I did.' Ellyn pushed out of the door past them and they could only follow, Daniel utterly bewildered. 'But I know what she was hiding now. And it's not so terrible a thing. Maybe it is to her family. Not to me. Besides, we all have secrets. Don't we?'

*

The road they took headed through rolling hillside, and beyond it the mountains on the border loomed closer, snow remaining on the tops. There was a chill to the breeze but the winter was some months past. One more day, Lara estimated, and they'd reach Thorndale.

What then? Grace didn't know. She didn't want to ask.

Bastien rode ahead again, with Rynn beside him. All appearances were restored, everything back in the perfect image of royal procession that Lara insisted upon. Ellyn followed them closely, keeping an eye on both. *Larelwynns*, Grace thought. All three of them. Even if Ellyn denied it. But none of it sat right. Why was that bloodline so special? Why did everything keep revolving back to them and why did so many people die around them?

One thing was certain, whatever happened at Thorndale, it wouldn't be pretty. Grace just needed to keep them alive. Now more than ever since an unkind fate had dragged Ellyn in.

'Grace?' Daniel and Misha came up on either side of her, their horses huffing away at the brief exertion. 'We were talking.'

She glanced from one to the other. 'That's ominous.'

'About what Bastien said. And the… the thing in you… what it said. About there being two boys, not just Lucien Larelwynn. But Bastien as well.'

Grace didn't want to think about that either. Blood, sacrifice, Larelwynns… all the things that were troubling her. 'And?'

'There is a story,' Misha said. 'A song really. From that time. But it wasn't encouraged.'

'What do you mean?'

'The royal family made it pretty clear that singing it and sharing it would be punished. Early on. They had some pretty imaginative ways of dealing with performers who disobeyed. Tongues cut out, fingers chopped off, charming stuff.'

'But you still learned it?'

He gave her an amused smile. 'Not just me. Do you know what harpers are for, Captain?'

'I imagine the clue is in the name?' Daniel laughed, but Misha tilted his head to one side, watching her, waiting.

'What are harpers for then?' Grace said, humouring him.

'To preserve memory. Even the things some people would prefer forgotten. That's easiest with songs. They can be passed on, shared, never really stamped out. One day such information might be necessary. Like now.'

'What do you know?'

'There's a song – "The Prince and the Guardsman". It's from the mountains, from this very region. In it the prince goes on a quest to save his people and his faithful guardsman goes with him. They're both young and the prince is often foolish but the guardsman is loyal and does his duty, time and again, saving the prince. He cheats death twice. He's buried alive as well. But each time he comes back, to serve and protect his prince. They fall in love. But when they reach the end of the quest, there has to be a sacrifice and only the two of them are there. It can't be the prince. The guardsman gives his life. It's an amazing verse.' He hummed a melody and then sang in his sweet voice. '*For this is my final wish, to lay my head beside yours, to bend my knee before you, to spill my blood on the cold hard ground, three times dead, twice entombed.*'

Something cold and hard in equal parts knotted inside Grace's chest. It crawled up through her body to make a lump in her throat and squeeze at her stinging eyes. It was so sad. So horribly sad. She remembered the tune, remembered Misha singing it in Iliz and a few other times. And those words…

'But it doesn't say it's Lucien Larelwynn,' Daniel said. 'The prince, I mean.'

'No. But his family were the ones to suppress it,' muttered Misha. 'His son Anders, actually. Anders the Great… well… Anders the Bastard more like.' Given Anders was Lucien's son and must have been the first to change the nature of the pact to Bastien's unknowing enslavement, Grace was inclined to agree. But there was more information hidden in that song, things which explained what Bastien had seen.

'They killed the guardsman and the Hollow King took his body,' she murmured. 'Or the body became the thing to hold the power of the Hollow King. And because Bastien couldn't remember, Lucien lived with that all his life. He lost his love, but not his memories. He spent his whole life looking at Bastien, knowing that. Knowing the man who loved him was dead and a god walked in his body instead.'

'That's the romantic view of it, I suppose,' said Daniel. The bitterness in his voice made her look at him again.

'And the unromantic?'

Daniel shrugged. 'He was a guard, a grunt, same as you and me. Dispensable. His job was to die when his king required it of him. Like us. So he did. At least he got to choose when, I suppose.'

The words made Grace shiver. She looked ahead again, at Bastien's back. She wanted to ask him. She wanted to know what he thought but, honestly, she didn't dare. She was terrified of the answer she would get.

And another darker thought occurred to her. Bastien, the Lord of Thorns, the Hollow King, was heading back to Thorndale with two women bearing the same blood as the king who had trapped him in that form. Whose family had wiped his memory time and time again and hidden what he really was from him for their own ends. Would he let one of them die to save her? Not the Bastien she knew, surely. But this one, this new king, this man who had seen the darkness in her and others, who had purged it and now felt it his duty to save the world from the nightborn and the Deep Dark? She was beginning to wonder if there was anything he wouldn't do to stop it. No sacrifice he would not make.

Of all the people here, she, Daniel and Misha were definitely dispensable.

She'd died for him. She'd been buried.

Maybe… maybe the Hollow King had plans of his own.

Chapter Twenty-Five

Zavi, the Master Atelier of the Academy, stood very still, with his arms folded, staring at the pile of glittering treasures on the workbench.

'Well?' Kurt asked.

'Well what?' Zavi didn't offer Kurt so much as a glance. From the doorway opposite, Melia rolled her eyes but said nothing. Kurt had expected more gratitude from Master Atelier Zavi after they'd rescued him from the Temple, at least. Perhaps even a little interest?

Syl shifted on his feet, looking more nervous than Kurt had ever seen him. 'Can you use them?'

Zavi glanced once at Syl, who turned scarlet, then back to Kurt. His expression was unreadable. 'Use them to do what, Mr Parry?'

The *Mr Parry* thing rankled. It always did, no matter who said it, but Zavi's tone was the worst of all. He didn't need to sound so much like a school master. Kurt – in the few brief years he had bothered with what passed for a formal education in Eastferry – had not taken kindly to teachers. Daniel was the one eager to learn. Kurt had already been sure he knew everything there was to know. He was usually right.

Now he was not so sure.

'It's everything we could gather that has some way of controlling mageborn. Some of it's really old, or really rare. Some of it… well, we had to get inside the palace and the Temple for it.'

Zavi nodded. 'And luckily you found me as well. Those were sewers we escaped through, weren't they?'

Kurt shrugged. He didn't need gratitude. He wasn't sure he was likely to get it anyway. 'People forget what's underneath this city.'

'But not you, I see. And this is how I repay you, I suppose. Give you ways to enslave mageborn?'

Oh. That was what he thought.

'Master Atelier, no! That's not—' Syl began but Zavi lifted a single finger and Syl's voice fell away. He lowered his gaze, stricken.

For a moment Kurt couldn't think of a thing to say in response, either to the accusation or Syl's cowed obedience. Once a master always a master, Kurt supposed.

'Your reputation goes before you, Kurt,' Melia said, the tone just teasing enough that it broke the shock.

He let out a long breath and fought to keep calm. 'That's not what I'm looking for. I'm trying to help people here.'

'Of course you are,' the Atelier replied in a tone that said he didn't believe it for a moment. 'But which people?'

Damn it, when had he acquired a reputation for enslaving mageborn? Mostly he hid them, helped them or got them out of this godforsaken shithole. Silently, quietly, without a trace. And because of that he was some kind of monster?

'Grace never said you were as bloody-minded as she is.'

Zavi frowned at the mention of her name. 'Grace? Grace Marchant?' He sounded surprised.

'Of course Grace Marchant. How many other Graces do you know as stubborn as a mule with a sore head? Danny's my brother. You did know that, didn't you? I thought the whole Academy knew that and never let him forget it. Or has imprisonment made your memory as rusty as your skills?'

The old man scowled at him. That was more like it. Real anger, real emotions. He'd been locked up in the dark for so long Kurt had been worried he'd lost his mind. Or had it tortured out of him. It happened to more than a few of them, especially the mageborn. Celeste had been experimenting, or so the rumours went, using them to try and break whatever spell Bastien had laid on her. And the Master Atelier himself had made the sigil that had bound Celeste Larelwynn. Zavi Millan should have been the greatest prize of all. Kurt had never met anyone he couldn't get any sort of agreement out of before.

Except maybe Grace.

'You still haven't explained what you want of me. The queen had many demands. So did the Lady Celeste. Their ideas were… less than palatable.'

Kurt could imagine. Aurelie wanted her addiction fed. Celeste had wanted power too, power and control. She had wanted her freedom, something no one in their right mind would allow. They were both of them insane in their own ways, and terribly dangerous. Just one of them now, he supposed. He hoped.

The news that Celeste Larelwynn was dead had come as a surprise.

They all knew Kurt hadn't killed Celeste but no one else was owning up so he was getting the blame. And the story was that Aurelie had taken the severed head home with her. What for remained to be seen. Maybe madness was catching.

Aurelie had killed a goddess. A broken and crazy one, sure. But still… What did that do to someone? Kurt shuddered at the thought.

'Look,' he tried again. 'There's something happening to the mageborn in the city. I don't know if it's them, or if it's something else but – surely, some of the imprisoned ones went crazy too? Far more powerful, but not like someone who has gone hollow. Worse. They know what they're doing. They don't care any more. It isn't insanity. It's malice.'

Zavi chewed on his lower lip and tightened the grip on his folded arms. His shoulders tensed.

'Nightborn,' he said. 'We call it nightborn. A lot of people think it's an old story, a myth. The Lord of Thorns always kept it under control. But the story persisted. A warning from long ago.'

'Well the Lord of Thorns is gone. And if the queen has her way he's never coming back. She's sent that Asher Kane after him. And others too, I don't doubt it. And if they do bring Bastien back, he's going to be her creature, at her beck and call. We can't rely on him. It's up to us now. No other bugger is going to save us, are they?'

Zavi walked forward, studying the workbench with its clutter of treasures, royal and mundane. Kurt had told his people to scour the city for whatever they could find, if it had a story or even a half story attached to it, if it had ever done something odd or someone had reacted weirdly to it. And then there were the things Syl and the mageborn escapees had snagged from the Treasury after her royal psychopath had finished with him.

'Half of this is rubbish,' Zavi said at last. 'But…' He sighed and brought his hand up to squeeze the bridge of his nose, like someone trying to dispel a headache. 'There are some things here which could help some of my people. Or stop them. It's possible…' He turned to Kurt then, his gimlet gaze fixing him to the spot. Honestly, in all his life, Kurt had never met anyone who made him uncomfortable like this. Except Grace.

Now he figured he knew where the Duchess learned that glare.

'Possible, *but*?' Might as well offer the opening. This was going to be a delicate balance, managing this man. Syl had told him that the Master Atelier was difficult, but he had given no indication how difficult. And Grace Marchant was the only person he listened to. Kurt couldn't even play that card because everyone knew Grace had no patience with him at all. They were not friends, but there was no one he respected more. Especially now.

'Parry, how do I know whatever I make will not be used *against* my people? The queen wanted such tools. I refused. She was displeased. But I still refused.'

They'd tortured him. Kurt knew that. Killed people he was close to. Tortured anyone even remotely connected to the Academy. The few surviving cadets they had freed had been candid enough about it. There were scars, visible and invisible, marking all of them.

Some of them had broken down and wept. Most were just kids.

But still Zavi had refused.

'Master Atelier.' Kurt kept his tone as calm and respectful as he could. Melia stared at him as if she didn't think he was capable of it. He'd have to have words with her about that. 'We have to find some way to protect our people. All of them, mageborn and quotidian. Most of the threats I can deal with.'

'Oh, you can, can you?'

'Yes.' There was no point in demurring. He didn't have the time. Besides, *most* of them, he *could*, one way or another. 'The nightborn are something else. They're people's family, their children, their friends. Or they were, until… until they weren't any more.' All the words that occurred to him were not quite enough to describe it.

But Zavi continued for him. 'They're beyond dangerous. They don't care who they hurt. They don't care if they die. They exist only to serve the Deep Dark and they only want to kill.'

That pretty much summed it up. But he could add his own details too.

'The other day there was a teenage girl who set fire to everyone she came close to in the marketplace. I locked her in a metal room and she burned herself alive. Her parents and her sister came to beg for her life. I couldn't even let them see her because she'd have killed them too. Do you know what they did afterwards? *They thanked me.*' Well, the mother did. Bella though, the sister… *if you can't get* him *back, what good are you?*

What good was he, indeed?

Zavi's eyes closed, the thought of it paining him. Kurt knew that feeling. He was still disgusted with himself.

'And then,' Kurt went on, 'they asked me to get Bastien Larelwynn back here. So he could sort it out for us.'

The Atelier thought about that for a moment and then shook his head. 'Bastien Larelwynn is not the answer.'

At last, something on which they could agree.

'No, he's not,' Kurt told him. 'We are. Are you willing to help us?'

Chapter Twenty-Six

The road crawled up the ridge and then dropped away, down into a lifeless valley. Thorn bushes covered it, tall as houses, black as charcoal, as if they had recently burned. A path ran down between them, narrow and ill-omened. They stopped at the edge of the grim forest. Grace reached out to touch a branch but instead of old burnt wood, she found it smooth and hard as glass. Her horse skittered to the side, spooked by something, and she snagged her finger on an ancient, petrified thorn. Her blood splashed onto it, bright and glossy.

Thorndale. They had finally reached the valley where the Lord of Thorns had been born. Somewhere in there lay the ruins of his home, and the cave containing the Maegen. Once it had been the Valley of Roses, until the Hollow King came, until the Magewar, when the nightborn had marched on his last hiding place and burned it, transforming it into this wasteland.

'It's not far,' Bastien said. 'I'll ask no one to come with me the rest of the way.'

Grace looked at Ellyn and Rynn. There was no way she could remain behind without him, but this was their chance to back out. She only hoped they would take it.

'We're going with you,' said Daniel. 'All of us.'

Common sense seemed to have taken its day of leave.

'It could be dangerous in there.'

Daniel laughed. 'Just like everywhere else then. We've already discussed it, Larelwynn. We're with you. Let's go.'

Trust Daniel to make a vote of support sound like an insult.

So that was that. Bastien turned the horse's head downhill, and they plunged into the half-light of the petrified forest.

The further in they travelled the darker it got. There was no sound but that which they made. Nothing lived here. What was there to live on? Grace shuddered as the shadows pressed closer. The Deep Dark seemed nearer than ever, and stronger inside her. So strong in fact she was sure she could sense it peering out from behind her eyes. She was surprised the others hadn't tied her hands together but for some reason they left her free. She would not have been so trusting.

The warrant was cold as ice, all the time. It weighed her down, dragging at her senses. But it hadn't stirred, hadn't tried to seize control of her again. Perhaps it didn't need to. Perhaps she was doing what it wanted anyway.

The atmosphere darkened around them with the fading light. The curling branches of black thorns blotted out the sun overhead. Within them Grace began to imagine she saw movement, heard other noises, laughter, soft cries. She was certain now that this place was haunted. How could it not be?

The things that had happened here, the death, the sheer, raw magic unleashed on this land…

They were less than halfway there when Misha began to sing. Hesitant at first, shaking off the oppressive atmosphere, his voice rose clear and bright, and for a moment she thought a host of glories had descended. The song wasn't one she knew but that didn't matter.

It wasn't the song itself that mattered but the magic behind it. The morose atmosphere lifted with the sound.

When he finished, Bastien glanced at him. 'Keep going,' he said. So the harper did, swinging the harp around so he could play as well. Daniel snatched up the reins to lead the Lyric's horse in case it bolted or stopped and Misha closed his eyes, singing and playing tune after tune.

Just as suddenly as he started, the harper stopped.

'Bastien?' he said. No 'your majesty', or 'my lord'… Bastien looked back at him, frowning.

'What is it?'

'Something's coming.'

The ambush came from both sides. Figures lurched up through the branches, flinging themselves forward heedless of thorns and stone. Their eyes were black and the skin clinging to their bodies putrefied. Dead creatures, human and otherwise, launched themselves at the group.

With a cry of terror, Bastien's mount reared up, but he clung to it grimly as it danced around, kicking at this new threat. The other horses bolted down the track and Grace raised her hands as something came at her from the upper branches. With a sickening crunch it took her from the saddle. The ground hit her hard and then there was nothing she could do as the dead thing pinned her down. Her instincts took over.

Fire ripped through it, igniting all along the animated corpse, so intense and bright that one moment she was staring into a long-dead face that was more than half skull, and the next ashes were raining down on her.

She twisted around, drawing her sword and her knife as she rolled to her feet. There were more of them, tearing their way through the branches, the dead rising, dead from countless years ago and newly dead and everything in between. Her horse was gone and she didn't blame it. She wished she'd had the wits to hang onto it.

Her sword seemed to take on a life of its own in her hands. The impact of bodies on its blade shook down her arm and she fought through, desperation making her keep moving. To stop was to die. Clawed hands grabbed her hair, raking along her scalp, and the stench of the dead and decaying made her throat close. But she had to keep going. Lunging, twisting, hacking through them, body after body. The only blood was her own and still they kept coming.

Like they were coming for her and her alone.

'Grace!'

Thunderous hooves drowned out the beating of her heart, the gasps of her breath. Her limbs burned, but still she slashed at the things coming for her. A huge black beast trampled through them and, from its saddle, Bastien stretched out his hand.

A desiccated grip closed on her throat. She drove her knife through an eye socket, the creature reeling away from her, clawing at it.

Damnation, she thought, I loved that knife. But she grabbed Bastien's arm, his hand locking above her wrist, and swung herself to relative safety behind him. Wrapping her free arm around his waist, she kept slashing at those still attacking her.

Bastien yelled something at the horse and dug his heels into its sides. Its muscles bunched and released, a huge leap forward, taking them down the path at a gallop. The poor animal heaved and strained, running for its life and carrying them both with it.

They burst out of the thorn forest and into a clearing in front of great tumbling ruins of black stone, sheer as glass and dark as obsidian. The others were there, all of them, shaken and scared, but alive. That was all that mattered. She slid from the horse's back as it slowed, but

Daniel caught her deftly. Grace pulled herself free of him, understanding now what she had to do.

She drove the sword into the ground. She didn't need it now. It was no longer the best weapon for this task. She knew what she needed. It coiled down deep inside her, dark and insidious, waiting. It knew her, knew her needs and her drives, knew that when the situation became desperate enough, when her friends were in danger or when she had no other choice, she would reach for it. She hated herself that she was so predictable, so transparent to the evil inside her. And yet, she still did it. Grace reached for the power of the Deep Dark and it laughed as it tangled its way up through her and poured out into the world. Standing her ground in front of the forest and the wave of the dead surging through it after her, she unleashed every iota of magic still inside her.

The white-hot flames leaped up at her command. They roared along the trail, incinerating anything in their path. The dead died again without a sound except for the rushing wind of incandescent flame.

Grace dropped to her knees, crushing the magic back inside her before it could slip free of her control, smothering it with every scrap of strength she had, and Bastien was with her, his hands on her shoulders. When she opened her eyes he was studying her face again.

She swallowed hard, waiting to see for herself if she'd gone too far, but after a second he gave an apologetic smile.

It was an unexpected relief. The warrant was still cold and heavy, but it wasn't in control. Not yet.

'Still me,' she told him. 'Just about.'

'You can't keep doing that.'

'No one else was going to.'

He smiled at that. 'No one else could, love. Not even me.'

She almost laughed but it was a broken, rusty sound she didn't quite recognise.

'What were they?'

'The dead. All those who died here in the Magewar, I think, and since. Mageborn, nightborn and everyone else.'

'Didn't like me, did they?'

He shook his head. She could guess why. It was some sort of defence mechanism, a spell to stop the Deep Dark getting anywhere near the source of magic. And she was still carrying it. She couldn't doubt that, not with the Flint in her stronger than she would ever have thought possible. Even if it didn't still whisper to her, laugh at her, make promises of what could be…

The warrant was a curse.

She pushed the thought away. 'Are we there yet?'

Bastien helped her stand again, steadying her before turning her around to face the ruins of Thorndale Castle.

'Home sweet home,' he said with that sardonic tone that masked his inner pain. Grace knew him too well now. It wasn't bitterness or cynicism that made him sound like that. It was regret and loss.

The castle had been huge once. More than a castle, she realised as she looked at what remained of its towers and pillars, those still standing and those which had fallen spilling black rocks across the scorched and dead land. It would have been beautiful, she could see that too. Before the destruction, the ruin and decay. But it wasn't a palace. It wasn't a fortress or a stronghold. The layout was strangely familiar and for a moment she couldn't tell why. The idea that it might be a memory from the Deep Dark made her shudder, but then she realised it wasn't that either.

She knew it from Rathlynn.

It had been a temple, an exact mirror image of the Temple of the Little Goddess where Celeste was imprisoned.

'Your home,' she whispered. Not to Bastien. He had never lived here, not really. They knew that now. This was the realm of the Hollow King.

Bastien swallowed hard, the movement in his throat the only indication of his mixed emotions at standing here, in this desecrated place.

'Its towers reached to the sky,' he murmured suddenly. 'Red pennants flew from each one. The roses all around it reflected in the walls and when the rising sun hit the surface in the morning… it was magnificent.'

He did remember then. Or rather, the being inside him did. Grace didn't even know what was Bastien Larelwynn, what was the Hollow King and what was… whoever he had been before it all. When he'd been just a boy who was loyal to a fault. Someone who would give his life for those he loved. That had never changed, had it?

But she couldn't let him do it again. Not this time. Bastien was hell-bent on sacrifice and she now had a suspicion who he intended that sacrifice to be. Because of course he would do it himself rather than ask anyone else to lay down their life.

'Where now?' she asked.

'There's a tunnel, under the ruins. It leads to a cave.'

She was ready to hand out orders but Lara was there ahead of her. The marshal had already staked out a perimeter, Daniel and Misha were seeing to the exhausted horses and everyone seemed to have a job except the two of them.

'Bastien, we should go. Just the two of us. Now. There's no need to drag them along with us.'

'I saw Rynn down there with me.' His vision. She'd forgotten about that. She cursed softly and he pressed his hand to the side of her face. 'I wish it could be different, Grace.'

'So do I.'

She couldn't let him do this. Not to Rynn. Not to Ellyn. Not to himself.

With deft and sudden movement, she scooped his legs out from under him. He went down with a cry of alarm and she ran for the ruins. True, she had no idea where she was going but that didn't matter. She just needed to reach the tunnel before he did.

The cries of pursuit were quicker than she would have liked. She could feel Bastien reaching out with his magic, trying to locate her as she dodged through the fallen walls and crumbling arches. The layout of the Temple back at home was familiar, a circular complex with the great domed central building surrounded by towers and gardens.

'*This way,*' something whispered to her. And though she knew that listening to the voices in her head was a really bad idea, she followed the instructions. What choice did she have? This had to be done, and fast. Before Bastien could stop her.

'*Left,*' it came again, a laugh behind it, as if they were playing some nightmarish game. '*And right.*' She dodged down the passageway as instructed and then she saw it, a hole in the ground that had once been a sunken garden. And in the centre an archway leading underground.

She plunged into the darkness beneath Thorndale.

Chapter Twenty-Seven

'Grace!' Bastien's own voice echoed back at him, taunting him. The passageway was narrower than he remembered, the stone smoother, and everything was darker. But he pushed on, certain Grace had to have come this way. What was she thinking? Was she thinking at all?

Or had the Deep Dark claimed her again? Her magic was more powerful than it had the right to be, even had it not been stolen and broken repeatedly over the years of her short life. The Deep Dark had done something to the warrant, connected to it somehow and tied it to Grace. It fed her magic, he was sure of it now, and fed on her fear. Both were getting stronger all the time. He hardly dared summon more than a glimmer of flame himself in case she turned it against him.

He was losing her. No matter what he did, no matter how he tried to preserve what they had, she was slipping through his fingers and, curse him, he wasn't strong enough to save her. He'd been so torn, so desperately concerned with who could take her place, who he should sacrifice and how he could make such a decision… but he should have known she would never allow that. Not Grace.

Pushing through the last stretch of tunnel, he almost fell out into the cavern. The pool spread out before him, larger than his visions and his twisted memories. It didn't glow as the Maegen glowed, it didn't boil with magic and life. It was just a pool, the surface black and unbroken, a perfect sheen reflecting smooth black rock overhead, and the single point of light in the cavern.

Grace was standing there, aglow with fire. It rippled over her skin, played among the strands of her hair. The pool reflected her as she stood at the edge, right beside the broken throne, and light illuminated the roof of the chamber. But the light was hers, not the Maegen's, and thankfully her eyes were still her own. Her own, but she was not quite herself. She was struggling to hold on.

'Grace?'

She looked up from the water, and tilted her head to one side.

'Where is it?' she asked.

'What?'

'The Maegen. It should be here, shouldn't it? Bastien—' A sob of dismay shook her and she clenched her hands into fists. 'I can't hold the Deep Dark in much longer. Where's the Maegen?'

He didn't know the answer to that. He'd expected it to be here as well. Not this cold, empty place. But there was the broken obsidian throne on which the Hollow King had sat. There was the water that had reflected his face. The pool that had drunk down his blood all those years ago when he was a boy.

But it wasn't glowing now. It was dead and empty. All it could do was reflect the power in her.

'I don't know.'

'You don't understand. I have to put an end to this. I need to give the warrant to the Maegen. The Deep Dark is going to come out again and I can't—'

The statue stood at the edge of the pool, opposite the remains of the throne. Bastien hadn't seen it at first, but suddenly it seemed to command his attention. Stone carved so cunningly in the likeness of a man that he thought at first it had to be a real person. It wore a crown, an ancient style, with long slender points, the largest at the front as sharp as a blade. He knew that crown. Grace caught the direction of his attention and turned to stare at it as well.

'It looks like you. Like you when I first met you.'

'It does?' That was news to him. It was cold and terrifying, the stern face and the frown, the clenched jawline.

'I was so afraid of you. I thought you were a monster…'

Her voice softened suddenly and before he knew what she was doing she started to walk towards the statue.

'Grace, stop.' She didn't listen. With one hand, she reached up and pressed the palm against its cold cheek. The ripple of magic travelled through the air and Bastien gave a choked cry.

Suddenly it was as if two images swam together, a double vision of her standing there, looking up at him and from a distance. He could see her from the eyes of the statue as well as his own. His body froze, trapped in stone like the statue, and, at the same time, the statue opened its eyelids, golden light spilling from its depths.

'*Beloved*,' it whispered. It wasn't Bastien's voice. It didn't even sound like him. And yet somehow it was.

The statue turned its head to look at him, stone grating against stone, and Bastien saw himself through its eyes. Weak and pathetic, trapped, a mere mortal who had dared to steal the power of the Hollow King… But it had agreed. He knew it had agreed. Perhaps it thought…

It had thought it was the one in control. Or that it would regain its power with Bastien's death. It had reckoned without Lucien and his sons.

'*Where are they?*' it asked. Grace gazed up at it in wonder. '*The Larelwynns… She is not one of them. Where are they?*'

'They're… they're gone.' Bastien blurted out the words, terrified Grace would answer instead. Whatever it had done to her, she seemed enchanted, so deeply under its spell now that he wasn't sure if he would be able to break her free. But he had to try. 'They're all dead. All of them. Gone.'

The statue of the Hollow King smiled and shook its head like it pitied him. '*I remember you, Bastien. You were so eager to die for Lucien Larelwynn. You should have tried living instead. You would have had more thanks. He cheated us both, you know.*'

That, at least, was true. Lucien Larelwynn had trapped the Hollow King in Bastien's form, and it should have been for a single human lifetime only. But the Larelwynns devised a way of stripping Bastien of his memories time and again, of keeping him trapped, of using him to control the mageborn, making them do their will, and keep the threat of the nightborn at bay.

'He did what he thought was best…'

The Hollow King chuckled, and brought his hands up to pull Grace into his embrace. '*You always were a fool. Especially for those you loved.*'

'Let her go.'

'*I'm not holding her here. The Deep Dark has burrowed through her body and her soul. It's part of her now. They live such fragile, mayfly lives, humans. Gone in the turn of a breath to you and I. She can stay with us forever. It's kinder. She'll stop fighting it then.*'

So she was still fighting. That was something he could use. Bastien edged closer, circling around them so he could see her face.

'Grace, don't give in to the Deep Dark. You'd be with him, not me. You said he reminded you of the way I was when we first met. The monster behind the throne, remember?'

The smallest frown formed on Grace's brow. The Hollow King lifted his hand and smoothed it away with gentle fingertips.

'*What has he brought you but pain, little one? What has he done but made you suffer? What joy has there been since you met him?*'

'Joy?' she whispered, so softly it was a sigh.

But there was joy. True, it was fleeting, and time and again he did something that destroyed it, but there was joy. There was love. There were the moments they stood together, laughed together. The moments when they made love and lost themselves in each other. He had never known joy like that, not in all his long life. It had to be the same for her. It had to be.

'Grace, please...' he whispered. His legs felt frozen, ice cold. His arms reached for her, but he couldn't move. It felt like the stone was climbing from the floor, covering him, sucking the life out of him and transforming him to a statue now.

The Hollow King glowed with vitality and fire, just as Grace did. She was feeding him somehow, pouring magic from her body into his stone form.

'*On your knees, I think,*' he said in that empty, heartless voice and Bastien felt his legs buckle. He fell forward, his hands landing in the water at the edge of the pool, his body unable to resist. '*I'm so glad you came back, boy. I've waited so long. And now I'll take my rightful place out in the world again. The nightborn can be brought to heel and the mageborn too. I should never have listened to Larelwynn. My sister the Little Goddess had the right of it. Humanity was made to serve us. I was a tired fool.*'

He ran his fingers through the glowing strands of Grace's hair.

'Don't hurt her,' Bastien whispered.

'*No, she is a treasure beyond price. She embodies the Deep Dark, or she soon will. Such power encased in such beauty. I'll not hurt her. Not like you. But you can serve a purpose. You can die again, be the sacrifice you were always so willing to be.*'

Even as Bastien watched, the Hollow King formed a sword out of fire and air and handed it to Grace. She turned, eyes blazing with magic, and walked towards him.

'Grace,' he whispered. He didn't want to die, not like this, not unleashing that thing into the world, to wear his face and take his place. 'Grace, please.'

'She can't hear you any more, Bastien. She hears me. Only me. I've whispered words of love in her ears. I've shown her what it will be like, to be loved by a god. I've never hurt her, not like you.' The king leaned forward, his grin skeletal, all his teeth bared, vicious and eager. *'Kill him for me, my beloved. Spill his blood in the pool and call forth the power of the Maegen once more. Larelwynn blood, the purest form of it, the blood that was spilled to make it great. Bring back my full supremacy and set me free.'*

The blade rested, cold and hard against the skin of Bastien's neck, hitting against the torc binding him. His blood would break the spell then, restore the Maegen and set the Hollow King free. But what of the warrant still resting around Grace's neck? What of the broken crown? Didn't the king know about that? He'd been there when it was made. He'd been...

But no. He didn't know. The Hollow King had been drowned in power in those moments, when Bastien had made the warrant and the torc from the broken crown, the real crown, not the one carved from stone the statue now wore. He'd given the warrant to Lucien and placed the torc around his own neck. The crown had become the very means by which to control the Hollow King.

Bastien sucked in a breath, trying to think, trying to come up with a way out as Grace's sword drew back, ready to swing down and end his life. He flinched.

'Bastien,' she murmured, her voice something between bemused and disappointed. 'Don't you trust me?'

She flung the sword at the statue with all her might.

Bastien jerked back against her in shock and she grabbed him, trying to pull him to safety. The Hollow King snatched the sword from the air moments before it would have impaled him. He held it like a stick a child had played with, and then tossed it aside. It fell with a clatter against the rocks and dissolved into wisps of smoke.

'Shit.' Grace cradled Bastien against her. 'That wasn't meant to happen.'

The Hollow King advanced on them, stepping into the water of the pool without sinking. He walked across the surface, never making so much as a ripple. And then, standing before them, he reached for them both.

Something hard and unyielding crashed into Bastien's side. They sprawled on the stone floor, Bastien and Grace entangled, Ellyn lying on top of them both.

'No!' Grace cried out but the Hollow King was quicker.

'Another Larelwynn,' he growled and grabbed her in that implacable grip. Ellyn struggled, unable to break free, and for the first time Bastien had known her, she truly looked afraid.

'Let her go,' Rynn shouted and a rock hit the Hollow King's shoulder. He flinched back, confused rather than hurt, like a giant tormented by a flea. It did no harm to him, stone on stone. She picked up another rock and let loose again. They must have found the way down here themselves.

'Rynn, that's not going to help,' Ellyn yelled. 'Get the others. Get the—'

The Hollow King hurled her down on the stone floor and her body convulsed and then went still. He held out one hand and light coalesced there, shining brighter as it resolved itself into a curved knife, like something from an ancient treasure trove. It was shaped like a claw, and as sharp as one too.

Bastien knew that blade. He remembered it, could still feel the ghost of its touch on his throat.

'Come then, Larelwynn, and die in his stead.' The Hollow King picked Ellyn up by one arm. She hung limply from his fist, her feet trailing in the water, but that didn't matter to him. He brought the knife up, ready to spill her blood in the Maegen and free himself at last.

Bastien did the only thing he could think of. He threw himself in between them. The knife slammed into his stomach and arched up under his ribs. He felt it there, stuck, as the Hollow King tried to pull it free again. He jerked with it, as wave upon wave of pain swept through him. White-hot and agonising, it burst in the back of his mind, stealing his breath.

With a sound of disgust the stone king hurled Ellyn aside and grabbed Bastien instead.

'*This is what you want? To die yet again? I gave you this unending life. I can take it from you just as easily.*'

Somehow, with unnatural strength, he wrenched the knife free and suddenly Bastien was choking on his own blood. There was a scream in his ears, in his head, and all around him. Grace, it was Grace. She cried out as she attacked. She'd got Ellyn's twin swords, he supposed. It didn't really matter. She was far too late.

He tried to tell her but he couldn't draw breath and the blood spilled from his mouth instead of words. It dripped down into the water and as he gazed down, as his vision grew dark, it began to glow.

Bastien didn't even feel the Hollow King letting him go. The water swallowed him down and the last thing he saw was blood, spreading out through the pool like the roots of a flower.

Chapter Twenty-Eight

Grace attacked blindly, rage taking her forward. The knife the Hollow King had conjured stretched as she reached it, becoming a sword to match her own. Behind her Rynn dragged Ellyn clear, back through the tunnel, but she couldn't go with them. She couldn't leave Bastien.

Any second now, he'd get up. Any second now. He'd move, rise up out of the water. Come to her. Help her. She knew it.

Swords clashed and she sent a wave of fire at the Hollow King. He smiled through it and she watched the stone he was made of grow hotter and hotter, glowing with heat now.

'I don't melt, little one. I don't burn. All you do is make me stronger.'

And it was all she *could* do.

The pool rippled behind her and for a moment she felt a surge of hope. Bastien was moving, he had to be moving.

But he wasn't. He floated face down, his hair spreading out around his head, his blood staining the water. It lapped over his still, pale fingers and began to glow.

'Yes,' the Hollow King said as Grace staggered away from him, the swords so heavy in her hands. This wasn't possible. It couldn't be possible.

It was all her fault.

'Bastien,' she whispered. But he couldn't answer.

There was only the Hollow King now. And the Maegen, bubbling up in the pool, surrounding her lover's dead body, feeding on his blood in order to be reborn. Magic, its purest form, neither light nor dark but a combination of both. Inside her she could hear the Deep Dark crowing in triumph.

The Hollow King had forgotten her now. He walked towards the glowing water, and it illuminated his features. He had Bastien's face, perfect and beautiful to her, more beautiful than anyone had a right to be. It was the face of a god and it had been stolen from the man she loved. Again.

What could she do to stop it? It didn't seem possible. She'd got Bastien killed. He'd trusted her, loved her. And she'd got him killed.

'He let himself die,' the Hollow King assured her. Was he inside her mind even now? Or was the Deep Dark feeding her thoughts to him? 'He let me kill him and that was his fate, then and now. He said it was his honour to serve. And he has served, full circle, to restore the magic, and set us free.'

Grace sobbed out Bastien's name, heedless of the power rushing through her, the rage and the pain.

'*Take the power that is yours*,' the Deep Dark whispered. The chorus of myriad voices laughed and jeered. It didn't want to follow the Hollow King. It didn't want to be constrained by anyone. '*Take it and use it.*'

What did she have to lose any more? The Hollow King had taken everything from her. She reached into the Deep Dark, fully cognisant now of what she was doing. She no longer cared. There was nothing to care about. Bastien was gone. She reached out with all that she was and seized everything.

The rage burned through her, and as it erupted, the Hollow King turned to her, a look of shock on his perfect features. His eyes glowed like sunlight, but she burned brighter. Her whole body was fire, her rage flaming through her.

'What are you doing?'

She didn't know, nor did she care. She reached out blindly, the way she had when the Deep Dark first possessed her in the inn. She felt the magic in the air, in him, in the water and the stones, all the power rippling around her, surging, pulsing. And she grabbed it. Drew it into herself. All that magic, all that power. She took it from the Maegen itself. All of it.

'What are you doing?' the Hollow King shouted again, panic filling his voice now. He ran at her, head down, intent on taking her off her feet, on crushing her, breaking her.

She didn't care.

She had lost Bastien. How could she go on without him? Who needed to live forever without the one they loved? Who needed to live at all?

She screamed, releasing the magic all at once, all that dammed-up power, all the rage, all the darkness, all the agony. The Hollow King roared, throwing back his head as the light within him blazed brighter than the sun. The rock that made his form turned to molten lava and he slid away into the Maegen, into that light.

But he couldn't get away from her, not that easily, not that way.

The cave shook and trembled. The rocks cracked. The water that had not yet transformed to the Maegen boiled. And Grace opened her mouth wide to scream over and over again.

All she wanted to do was destroy it all, destroy him, end it. All of it.

And that was when the roof came down.

*

The scraping of stone on stone brought her to her senses. All was dark and quiet and as far as she was concerned it could stay that way.

'Grace?'

Daniel's voice, far off and desperate. She didn't care. She couldn't care. Bastien was dead and she had as good as killed him herself. The Deep Dark had tricked her, manipulated her, and now she had lost him. He was gone.

'Grace, we're coming. Hang on.'

Daniel had pulled her out of a pile of rubble before. But Bastien had been with him that time. He'd refused to let her die.

And now he was gone. If he'd left her in the cave with the Hollow King, he'd still be alive.

Air came in a rush, and the next thing she knew strong arms were grabbing her, pulling her clear. They dragged her out into the open air. The light was blinding and everything hurt. Daniel and Misha hauled her up with trembling hands.

But worse was to come.

'Where are Ellyn and Rynn?' Grace asked.

Daniel stared at her, his face haggard. Then he shook his head.

No. They were still in the tunnel? Had she killed them too? Divinities, this couldn't be happening.

'Grace,' he whispered, his voice stricken. 'We aren't alone.'

Armed soldiers filled the clearing, surrounding them, too many to count. Lara and Daniel had no weapons, and Misha's harp was a shattered pile of strings and kindling on the ground. The horses were gone, scattered. Someone had let them loose. Standing over her, back in the uniform of the Royal Guard of Larelwynn, his armour gleaming, was Asher Kane.

'You look surprised, Marchant. I followed you here. This is Bastien's home, after all. Everyone knows that.'

Everyone was wrong, Grace thought bitterly. Not his home, but his grave.

After what she had just done, the earthquake, the fire, the rush of magical power shaking the foundations of Thorndale apart… well, anyone would come looking.

Asher fixed them with a glare of pure hatred. 'Keep digging. Find the others,' he told the soldiers. No Valenti mercenaries now. These were Larelwynn troops.

'Find their bodies,' Lara told him. 'That's all that's left. They were in the cave when it collapsed. They're dead – Bastien, Rynn de Valens and Ellyn de Bruyn. Have fun explaining that to the Dowager. All your prizes are gone, Lord Kane.'

He smiled that terrible smile but ignored Lara and glared right at Grace. 'Not all of them, Lady Kellen.' Then he raised his voice in command. 'Seize everything. Take them back to Rathlynn. The queen can do what she wants with these traitors but Captain Marchant and the rest of Prince Bastien's leavings are mine, understand?'

'I am still the marshal,' Lara told him, standing firm. 'I demand the right to be heard. And these people are under my protection.'

'You failed, Lara,' he sneered. 'Don't you get that yet? And you are not the marshal any more.' And then he nodded, a clear signal, looking past her shoulder.

Shadows billowed up around Lara, swirling around her, seizing her. It was quick and it was brutal, a knife appearing for an instant before slamming into her back, up to the hilt.

Her face froze, her mouth open in something like outrage, but Lara Kellen didn't even cry out. She fell silently.

Jehane stood in her place. He looked down on her body for the longest moment. It wasn't regret on his face. He'd killed his mentor without a moment's hesitation. Perhaps he'd always wanted to. He waited until she went completely still.

Grace sucked in a breath and felt the last of her footholds crumble.

'As you will, my Lord Kane,' Jehane said. 'I hope I've proved my loyalty.'

'Time and again. Keep her under control, Alvaran.'

Jehane smiled as he met Grace's devastated gaze. She could no longer see the man who had asked for her friendship. She had trusted him. And look where that had got her. Lara had trusted him too, implicitly. Grace met his eyes for a moment and then dropped her gaze.

Jehane's voice was hard, unrecognisable. 'Oh, that will be easy. She doesn't have it in her to fight any more. She's lost everything. Haven't you?'

She didn't deign to give him an answer. He didn't deserve one. Her eyes burned.

'But just in case,' Asher said. 'She has a tendency to get creative. I know her of old. Put this on her.'

He handed Jehane a collar made of linked sigils, the type they had once used on Bastien. It had contained even his power. It snapped around her throat with a sudden and very final click.

It didn't matter. Nothing mattered.

They were all disarmed with cursory speed. Daniel was the only one to put up a struggle. When Jehane stepped in, Daniel spat in his face which earned him a backhand across his cheek. The brief struggle was brutal and one-sided. Daniel might be scrappy but he didn't stand a chance against so many.

'Stop,' Grace said as a third guard slammed his boot into her friend's stomach. 'Stop! We'll cooperate.'

What did it matter now? Bastien was dead. So were Ellyn and Rynn. Lara lay still in front of her. Four of her company, all gone now. Her squad, her team, her found family. She had lost everyone else. She couldn't risk Daniel and Misha. All they could do now was survive. She could keep Daniel and Misha alive, couldn't she? If she was careful. If she played it right. She had to try.

'Reason? From *you*, Marchant?' Asher laughed.

'I can be reasonable.'

'See that you can,' he growled at her. 'Tie them up and get the wagon. The queen and our goddess eagerly await you.'

*

The wagon jolted and rocked, a slow and torturous trek across Larelwynn lands. Except there were no more Larelwynns. Not even Bastien.

Grace closed her eyes, trying to shut out the world. The collar was icy cold around her neck. She'd always sworn she'd never wear one.

The warrant felt cold too, another chunk of ice against her skin, which told her the Deep Dark still lurked inside her, waiting. Letting it out again… well, that wasn't a good idea. She'd bide her time.

'Grace?' Daniel said. She opened her eyes. He was watching her closely, his expression grim. 'Grace, are you okay?'

It was such a stupid question. 'No. Of course I am not okay.'

They had been captured by the man who hated them the most. And Jehane had betrayed them. Did she need to spell it all out for him?

But Daniel wasn't the kind to give up. 'We'll find a way out. We always find a way out. We'll improvise, remember?'

She closed her eyes again, defeated, devastated. There was no point in fighting any more, not even with Daniel. Asher had them. Aurelie would make sure their last few hours were excruciating. But it didn't matter.

She was already dead inside.

The Deep Dark laughed at her, sang to her, taunted her. It would help if she only asked. She could call them to her, the nightborn, it told her. She could make them her servants, use them all. But she'd only done what she had needed to do. She'd defeated the Hollow King. If she hadn't killed him she had at least trapped him in the Maegen. She'd stolen his magic, sucked it into herself and now it was hers. It boiled in her veins and writhed beneath her skin.

That had to count for something, didn't it?

Given all that she had lost, it had to.

She didn't want to think about what it had done to her, what it might still do, what it might mean.

She had been willing to die in that cave. She had shaken off the power of the Deep Dark and the Hollow King and she had been ready to die, to protect Bastien, to protect them all.

Instead, Bastien was dead. Ellyn and Rynn were lost. It wasn't fair.

Once, she had taken a vow to protect the people of Rathlynn, mageborn and quotidian alike.

Now, she could only keep that promise. Back in Rathlynn.

Grace had always known she would die in Rathlynn. Home. And life, especially her life, had never been fair.

They travelled through the night and the day again, a slow grinding trail that jerked every bone of her body and jolted her awake again every time she thought she had managed to slip off into her dreams. It was definitely that, waking her up. Not the nightmares.

Bastien, the knife gutting him, blood and foam on his lips as he fell forwards. The endless black water swallowing him. The Hollow King wearing his face, smiling in his triumph. Her failure, her rage, her anger bringing down the cave around them all.

Ellyn and Rynn, trapped together underground, crushed, dying. It was her fault. It was all her fault…

The fourteenth – fifteenth? – time she jerked back into the misery of wakefulness, she could smell it. Familiar scents, as familiar as anything she knew. She'd known them almost all her life. Sea and woodsmoke, spices and foul water, an undercurrent of sewers that never quite went away… Rathlynn. They had finally arrived.

Not exactly a looked-for homecoming.

Aurelie would be waiting. And Aurelie was hardly going to welcome Grace warmly. Unless that involved fire. Or maybe some molten iron.

Celeste too. Celeste, who knew more about the Deep Dark than anyone else. Who might understand what was happening to Grace. If she cared to share her knowledge.

The power rippled and surged within her, still there, still waiting.

The streets were quiet, unnaturally so. She knew the sounds as they passed through the main gate. They were stopped by a checkpoint at the Temple Square, but with Asher shouting and cursing, his threats increasingly violent, they were quickly waved through.

Grace felt the incline of the Royal Promenade as they were hauled up the hill towards the palace complex. Through the bars she could see the statues looking down at her, face after face the same, only their clothes changing, a Larelwynn face, his face. Bastien, carved in stone like the Hollow King.

She turned away. She couldn't bear to look at him. Not now.

It had all been lies anyway, all their history, all the stories built up around him. All lies to keep him in his place and the Hollow King imprisoned, the Deep Dark in check. Now it was loose in her and she was lost and Bastien was really dead. Killed by the only hand that could kill him. His own.

She wanted to scream, or sob, but she knew if she started either she would never stop.

When the gates opened and the palace devoured them, she was sure she would never see the sky again.

The wagon spilled them out into a yard with high walls and one gateway leading down to the dungeons. There was no way out even if any of them had still had the strength to try.

'Grace Marchant,' a voice rang out and she looked up. Aurelie stood on a walkway overlooking them, straight and tall, clad in scarlet and her long golden hair flowing down her back like an innocent. Grace said nothing. There was nothing to say and nothing Aurelie wanted to hear from her. Not yet. Later she would want screams and begging, no doubt, she'd want to torture her and see her destroyed, but now she just wanted Grace to look at her and know that she had won and Grace had lost. She had no idea how much Grace had lost. 'I have a gift for you,' the queen said and threw something down at them.

The round object smashed into the flagstones, bloody and broken, but still somehow recognisable. Celeste Larelwynn's face stared back at them. She even looked surprised.

No one made a sound. If Aurelie was looking for shock or consternation, she was going to be disappointed. All three of them had reason to wish Celeste dead, but this...

It was Asher Kane who gave a howl of dismay.

As she walked to the cells, Grace decided to cherish that sound for the rest of her, no doubt very short, days.

Chapter Twenty-Nine

He floated between light and dark, suspended there between life and death. The endless nothing surrounded him, and he drifted in it, lost. It was almost peaceful. Certainly better than the pain he had left behind. The panic, the terror, the struggle, the constant suffering.

In the end, it didn't matter.

Nothing mattered.

'*You matter*,' whispered a voice. Her voice. He was sure of it. Who else could it be? '*You will always matter to me. Always.*'

But Grace was gone.

Bastien opened his eyes, staring into the endless void beneath him. No magic, no power, no will to be one thing or the other. The Deep Dark was not there waiting for him. No creatures lurked there, nothing reached out to drag him down, no countless eyes stared back. It was just darkness, endless and empty.

It shouldn't be empty.

'*They're all gone*,' she said. '*They all went away, with her. There's nothing left.*'

Bastien had failed. His one task, his only mission, the thing he needed to do above all else – to save Grace, to trap the Deep Dark once more, to protect the mageborn and the world he loved. But now the Deep Dark had lodged itself within her, and it was free.

'*Bastien, wake up.*'

He shook his head, his long hair swirling past his face.

'*I know it hurts, love, but you have to wake up.*'

Strong arms held him, the touch so gentle.

'Let me stay here, Grace. Let me stay with you.' His voice shook the water around him and rebounded back to him, so loud, so out of place.

'*You can't. You have to go back. Honour and duty. Remember?*' The voice changed, drifting from hers to someone else's. A young man, barely more than a boy. '*You promised me, Bastien. It was your vow. You said we couldn't have the things we wanted, but we could still protect them. You have to go back and protect Grace. You have to stop them, defend the mageborn, but most of all, you have to save her.*'

Lucien's hand brushed against his face. He knew the touch though he couldn't see the body. But the gleaming light that coalesced in front of him was as gentle as Lucien himself had been.

'Remember, Bastien. Remember everything.'

He hadn't meant to love the young prince, but he couldn't help himself. Lucien was so very loveable. It had been easy to lay down his life for him. Much easier than the alternative.

'Much easier than living for me?' Lucien laughed, but it was a tragic sound, the music made by a broken heart. 'But you can rectify that now. We love where we love. Sometimes in the same way, sometimes different. I loved my wife too. Lived a life with her. But never forgot you. We loved differently. And now, you can live for her, for your love, for Grace.'

'Lucien… please…'

Bastien just wanted to rest. It had been so long. He'd lived so many lives, been betrayed so many times, had all his memories wiped out and started again and again. He was tired, so very tired. And now peace beckoned.

Was this how Grace had felt before he pulled her back to life? Had he dragged her out of a peace like this only to plunge her back into his world of pain and chaos, always running, always hunted, the constant torture of their life together?

Every day she must live with the interminable pain of loving someone like him.

'Bastien…' Lucien said, the tone of remonstration almost amused.

Images of Grace flashed before him, her smile, her kiss, the feeling of her touch, the pleasure of life with her, all those moments, stolen or otherwise, the sheer joy of being with her. It was overwhelming, more than he could have articulated himself. She lived each day like it was her last and full to the brim. She grabbed every scrap of joy they had together and cherished it. Every time they parted was heartbreak, but every reunion was a glorious roar of affirmation. Just to see her across a room, or thread his fingers with hers, or lie beside her, body to body, each curve and hollow matching the other… it all made him want more.

'Go back. Save her. Bastien, wake up. Do this for me and you will be free. She'll set you free.'

'Lucien… I can't leave you here.'

'I'm not here. I'm only here because you are, beloved. Because you need me. Don't you know that? I was never trapped. *You* were.' But Lucien smiled. And it wasn't Lucien. It was light and movement, it was power. He frowned, staring into the light surrounding him. It was the Maegen.

'*Bastien, wake up. Please…*'

And suddenly it wasn't Lucien's voice any more. It wasn't Grace's either. It sounded like Ellyn.

*

'He's not breathing. He's healing but he's not breathing. Why isn't he breathing?'

'You have to get his heart started again, and make him breathe.'

'I don't know how to do that! I'm not a Curer, Rynn.'

'Oh, get out of my way.'

Hands pressed on his chest, trying to shove his ribs down, the rhythm broken and uneven but still there. And then there were lips on his, air blowing into his mouth and down to his lungs. Rynn was determined, he'd give her that.

He coughed, bringing up blood and water, unable to stop himself from dragging in another agonising breath. It rasped down his throat and into his lungs, icy and sharp as knives.

Bastien rolled over, gasping like a beached fish, his whole body shivering with shock and cold as they tried to help him without really knowing what they were doing.

An eerie glow filled the cave, or what remained of the cave. Half of it was covered in rockfall, including part of the pool underneath it. But the rest of the water glowed, throwing its reflection up onto the roof like a maelstrom of light.

Rynn hovered over him, her long hair wet, her eyes bright and triumphant. She looked beautiful. Alive. Had she waded in there to pull him out?

'That's it!' she said, ecstatic. 'Breathe, come on. Breathe again.'

He tried to oblige. Divinities, it hurt.

'Give him a moment. He's still healing. He had that knife so far inside him I thought it would still be there.'

Ellyn... Ellyn was alive too.

'Where's Grace?' he asked, his voice a cracked and scraping thing.

Rynn's face fell, just a little. She was still trying to look positive but she was not one of life's actors.

'Honestly?' Ellyn said, helping him sit, her cautious touch still not managing to make it painless. 'We don't know. We were buried in the rockfall when she brought the whole place down. Thought we'd had it.'

'Are we trapped in here?'

That would be perfect, wouldn't it? Bring him back from the brink of death and then leave him trapped in a cave forever.

'Not trapped, no. We can dig our way out, I'm sure of it. There's a weak point over there, just shift a few rocks and we'll be out. But we… we couldn't leave you.'

'I assure you, you could have.' The water was glowing. It hadn't been doing that before… Bastien clearly wasn't dead, now. But… he'd been somewhere else… He stared at the water. 'Did I do that?'

'Yes,' Rynn said as if it was a wonder. 'Bastien… you threw yourself between the Hollow King and Ellyn. You saved her. You sacrificed yourself.'

Again. He'd sacrificed himself for a Larelwynn again. He gave a defeated groan and Ellyn patted him on the shoulder. It wasn't comforting but Ellyn wasn't a comforting sort of person.

'Leave it, Rynn,' she whispered. She clearly felt as uncomfortable about that aspect of it all as he did.

'We used the water to bring you back. That's the Maegen, isn't it? I thought… I thought if it was some sort of alchemical reaction it would heal you, if it still wanted you here. The texts from the time of the Magewar say that it seems to have some sort of conscious will of its own.' Rynn threw her hair back over her shoulder and smiled, the light of it illuminating her face. 'Look at it. It's beautiful,' she said. 'Beautiful!'

It was what he'd seen. In the dream or hallucination with Lucien, when he'd been knocked out during the storm. Blood in the Maegen, and a sacrifice…

He'd thought the vision meant he'd kill Grace. He was such a fool. The Hollow King had tricked him. He was the sacrifice all along.

A conscious will of its own, Rynn said. Was that what he had been talking to? Not Lucien, not Grace, but the Maegen itself.

Do this for me and you will be free. She'll set you free.

Was that really true? Or another lie? Another trick to make him keep going, to use him to bring order to the chaos magic created?

He didn't know. But the Maegen had brought him back for a reason. That reason might as well be Grace Marchant.

He couldn't fail her again.

'Where's the way out?' he asked.

'We were hoping you could help with that,' Rynn said. 'The tunnel we came in through is buried. Back there, I think. Can't you just…?'

'What?'

'You know.' Ellyn waved her hands vaguely at it. 'Use magic. Move it.'

He waved his hands back at her. 'Just like that?'

The glare would have curdled milk. 'You know what I mean, Bastien Larelwynn.'

'My full name,' he murmured at her, a smile he didn't know he could still form tugging at his lips. 'I must be in trouble. All right, I'll just…' and he waved his hands, for good measure. If she wanted a show he'd—

But nothing happened.

No power, no sense of light inside him, no magic. Nothing.

He had never felt so empty in his life.

They stared at him, waiting. Bastien swallowed hard, and tried again, but even as he reached for the power inside him, for the Maegen which had always been at his beck and call, there was nothing. Not even the emptiness of the Deep Dark. Nothing at all.

'I… I can't.'

Ellyn frowned. Rynn's face fell. 'Bastien! Your magic? It's gone?'

'I don't… I don't know.' That was a lie. He knew. He just didn't want it to be true. He took a deep breath, forcing himself to face it, to be honest. 'Yes. It seems my magic has gone.'

What did that mean? How had it even happened? His death again at the hands of the Hollow King or his resurrection in the Maegen? Something else? He didn't know. And his heart hammered at his chest in panic. He'd been mageborn for so long. What was he now?

'Right,' said Ellyn, resigned. Faced with the facts, she just got on with things. That was Ellyn through and through. Divinities, he admired that. 'Better fall back to the first plan and dig our way out then, hadn't we? Get stuck in, you two. I'm not doing all the work.'

'But…' Rynn looked frantic, her lower lip trembling. She gazed at Bastien, devastated.

'Look, Princess,' Ellyn told her firmly. 'It's the only way. Get to work. Or none of us are getting out of here. Understand?'

It was a tone of command that did not brook any argument. He knew it well. She'd learned it from the woman he loved.

Bastien closed his eyes. Grace was still somewhere out there. He had to find her. But first they had to get out.

It wasn't as easy as Ellyn had made it sound. But then, she probably knew that. It was a way to make them work, to get them motivated. As if dying trapped in here wasn't motivation enough. Entombed…

Had Grace been buried as well? He recalled the power surging around him as he lost consciousness in the water, the wild rage, the despair... had that been Grace?

Three times dead, twice entombed. What had happened to her?

Eventually they cleared a gap wide enough for Rynn to wriggle through. It took them a few minutes more before Ellyn followed and Bastien went last, out into sunlight and the open air.

Lara's body was lying near the remaining packs, and she was the only one there. Still breathing, barely, she stared at the sky overhead, the trail of blood telling Bastien she must have dragged herself away from the place she had fallen. It also told him that they were far too late to help.

'Took you long enough,' she whispered.

Bastien dropped to his knees and tried to lift her into a more comfortable position. 'Lara... what happened?'

'Jehane betrayed us. I set the horses loose, before they... Asher took them... Grace, Daniel and Misha... back to Rathlynn. You have to stop them...'

He nodded.

Lara let out a long breath. 'Knew I'd go like this. Something like this. Stabbed in the back. Little bastard...' She tried to laugh, and blood came from her mouth. She spat it out, heaving in an agonising breath. 'Find Grace. You can save her. Your magic...'

Bastien closed his eyes. How did he tell her? How did he confess that now, the one time he needed his powers, they were gone? Tears stung his eyes and he blinked them away.

But when he looked down again, Lara was dead.

'What do we do?' Ellyn asked.

He wanted to say that they should bury her, give her the passage to the afterlife she deserved. Pray for her and send her soul on its way. He wanted to say so many things.

'We head to Rathlynn,' he said. 'We go and rescue our squad. We'll have to find the horses and… gather weapons, find help and… and I don't know what else.'

'Right,' Ellyn said decisively. She held out a hand to him. He laid Lara down on the ground as gently as he could and let Ellyn pull him to his feet. Her grip was strong, unwavering. 'We'll do what we always do. We'll improvise.'

Chapter Thirty

Grace had expected a cell. But this wasn't a cell, at least not the way she knew cells. She'd once thought Bastien's rooms in his tower were more luxurious than anywhere she had ever been, and they probably were. She'd first made love to him here, held him close the night before Marius died. The night before everything fell apart.

Now it was their prison. And Aurelie's cruel joke, no doubt.

At least Daniel and Misha had not been taken from her. She wondered if it was an oversight. Perhaps Aurelie didn't even notice them. Daniel didn't have any magic and Misha was collared with linked sigils, just as she was. What could they do?

Grace sat on the bed and instantly regretted it.

Daniel was the first to move the moment the door locked behind them, opening the windows, checking the walls and even the floor. Grace watched him. There was no way out. She knew that. Some long-ago Larelwynn prince had designed this tower with Bastien in mind. They would never have risked his escape. The Lord of Thorns was kept on a very tight, if mostly invisible, leash.

He had been. Now he was dead. She'd seen it herself, felt it. She might keep believing that at any moment the door would open and in he'd walk, barking orders or brooding. But he wouldn't. Never again.

'No way out,' Daniel said.

'You should be resting,' Misha told him. 'You're hurt.'

The guards had really done a number on him. When they'd been captured, and again when he'd mouthed off to them on the way up here. They might be able to control Grace and Misha with sigils and collars, but not Daniel. So his treatment had been old-school. And vicious.

It was also a warning to her. Of what they could do to the people she loved.

'There's a bath through there,' she told them. 'He probably has running water and a medical kit. Knowing him. Bastien was—' The name caught in her throat even as she said it. 'He was always prepared.'

'Grace, I—' Daniel began but stopped abruptly. She looked up at him and the expression he wore was one of such pity that she had to look away. He knew how she felt. He had to know. He also knew they couldn't say it. Not out loud. Not if she was to keep going.

'Go clean up and make sure there's no permanent damage,' she said. 'Take advantage of this while you can. I don't know what they're playing at but I don't expect our surroundings will be this fancy for long.'

Daniel and Misha closed the door behind them and she heard their hushed, urgent voices from the other side of it. Discussing her, no doubt. Grace sat perfectly still, forcing herself to inhale, reminding her heart to keep beating, letting the air out in a rush. It took every scrap of strength she still had to kick off her boots. Then she lay down on the bed. Curling up on her side, she pulled the luxurious covers around her shivering body. She stared at the ring on her finger, the golden ring, marked with the pattern of thorns. His ring. Closing her eyes she tried to breathe in whatever faint traces of him might remain there.

But there was nothing. It had been months since they hastily left this room together. His clothes were still in the wardrobe. His belongings still on the shelves and the table. But she knew Bastien was gone.

The tears that finally came burned against her skin. They dropped onto the fabric cradling her, glowing softly, and she stared at them until that weird, swirling light faded. She tried to draw on that inner magic but the moment she did the collar tightened, going cold against her skin. The sigils burned with icy fire and she had to force herself to calmness. The warrant did nothing. Nothing at all.

Think, she told herself in her firmest Academy voice. It almost sounded like her old teacher and commander, Craine. *Stop panicking and think, Marchant.*

Bastien had been able to break free of his collar eventually, burning through the sigils one at a time. She tried to focus, tried to grab the magic inside her and direct it on just one sigil at a time. The pain was incredible, leaving her breathless and blind. She took another gulp of air, gritted her teeth and tried again.

The door to the tower room opened with a burst of violence and noise, jarring her awake. She hadn't been aware she'd slept but she must have.

'I thought you'd have at least washed.' Asher's voice was the last thing she wanted to hear. 'You've got an audience with the queen, Marchant. Get up. Put this on.'

He flung a pile of fabric at her. Black, beautiful, embroidered with golden thread she suspected was made of real gold. It bore intricate patterns of roses. Grace had to catch it before it hit her in the face. She stared at it. No way had it been made for her. For Rynn maybe, but not her.

'Yeah. Not going to happen,' she told him.

Asher gestured to the guards. 'They can hose you down and dress you. I doubt you'd enjoy it though.'

As if he'd already invited them to have a go, the guards started forwards, but at the same time Daniel emerged from the bathroom. He took one look and lost his mind, barrelling forwards.

'Danny, no,' Grace yelled.

He was going to get himself killed. Whether they meant to or not. Misha came to the same conclusion and opened his mouth, trying to draw on his magic, but he'd forgotten about the collar. His cry of pain brought him to his knees and Daniel faltered, his face drained of blood. And the fist that smashed into his stomach sent him down beside his lover.

'Enough,' Grace said, leaping to face the guards. She grabbed the nearest one before he could lay another blow on her friend, shoving him back. 'I'll do it. Just… leave them alone.'

The guards retreated, a bit belligerently, but at the same time she saw something in their eyes that looked suspiciously like wariness. Her reputation preceded her.

'You have an hour,' Asher told her. He jerked his head towards Daniel and Misha. 'They can be your handmaidens. And if I'm not happy, they'll know about it.'

Then he was gone and the door was locked again. Grace looked at the dress, still gripped in her fist. It trailed in the dust and she'd managed to stand on it. Great.

'What is it?' Daniel asked. 'What's he doing?'

'A new form of torture, I suppose,' she told him. 'Come on. Bastien must have left some weapons stashed away somewhere in all his junk. I have to wash.'

'He said an hour,' Misha reminded her, picking himself up, the shadow of pain still clinging to his face.

'Oh, I don't need an hour. But I would kill for a sharp knife to tuck away under this thing. Find one for me.'

There wasn't time for her to grieve and wallow in defeat. She knew that now. If she did she was going to get them killed like everyone else. Magic prickled under her skin, ran tantalising fingers down her spine. The warrant was cold and still. The sigils burned their icy fire against her flesh.

And until then, she was going to have to play whatever sick game Asher Kane had in mind.

The gown was beautiful, there was no denying it. It cradled her body as if it had actually been made for her. The black and gold made her hair a fire trailing behind her, once she'd washed it and Misha had helped her dry and brush it out.

And Daniel had been industrious. The little trove of weapons he'd uncovered wasn't much – Bastien had relied on his magic – but there were three knives balanced enough for throwing which she hid about herself, a sword which she didn't have a hope of hiding anywhere, and a stiletto blade which she used to pin her hair once Misha had twisted it up on the back of her head. The collar was almost like jewellery, if you didn't know its real purpose. And of course she still wore the warrant on its gold chain. She held it now, turned it over in her hand and then let it fall against her chest, its weight a comforting reassurance. It shouldn't have been, given the corruption clinging to it. But it linked her to Bastien. Or to his ghost perhaps. Somehow.

She wore the ring as well. She'd toyed with the idea of taking it off. It was bound to infuriate Aurelie. When she realised that she'd die rather than part with it, however, she decided against it. Infuriating Aurelie would be worth it.

'What do I do with this?' Daniel asked, holding the sword. It was a beautiful piece, exactly the sword a prince would own. Probably not the most practical weapon. Grace wondered if it had been a present. It looked like it cost a fortune.

'Keep it,' she said. 'Hide it. If you get a chance, use it.'

She didn't look like an Academy officer any more. Grace knew, from the way she was dressed, and the fact she wasn't already dead or rotting in the deepest pit in the dungeon, that Asher was planning something. He craved power.

Anger and fear, powerful and wild, fed the nightborn, fed the Deep Dark, and made it stronger. She could feel it seething inside her. It whispered a thousand promises of what it would do to Asher Kane once it was free and she was almost inclined to agree.

She had some plans of her own for him. Not only for Asher Kane. For all of them. The Deep Dark picked through her thoughts and purred in approval. And when she braved another attempt at the linked sigils collaring her, she felt its power added to her own.

She just had to keep Daniel and Misha safe. That was all that mattered. Once she was certain of that…

Asher leered at her when he returned. She let him, staring at the wall behind him, right at the point where the sword would hit if she impaled him this very instant.

'Better,' he said, as if it pained him to pay her a compliment. The thought left her with the urge to peel her own skin off. 'But first, stop where you are, arms out. Search her.'

Jehane stepped into the room behind him, and she narrowed her eyes, but she didn't move. The temptation to ram her fist into his face full force wasn't easy to ignore. She hadn't seen eye to eye with Lara Kellen, but she owed her loyalty at least. For the sake of Craine's memory if nothing else.

Shadows coiled around her and this time she didn't struggle. What was the point? She knew she couldn't escape him. He'd proved that more than once.

'Sorry, Grace,' he said softly. 'But you know how it is.'

'When you're a backstabbing bastard? No, I don't.'

He didn't linger as he searched her, all professionalism. He removed the knives, from the one she'd strapped to her thigh to the one down her cleavage. Frankly she would have been insulted if he hadn't found them, like he wasn't even trying.

'I really am sorry, Grace.' He smiled gently, regretfully. 'In another life we could truly have been friends. Maybe more than friends.'

More than friends. Right.

'In your dreams.'

He brushed his knuckles tenderly down the side of her face and she scowled at him. 'She's clear.'

'When you're quite finished…' Asher's tone said he believed anything but.

But the shadows didn't let her go. The Shade's magic clung to her, holding her still. Asher stepped in front of her, his lip curling. 'You'll do, I suppose.' He opened a pot of something reddish-brown and congealed. Grace stared at it. It looked like old blood.

Asher spat in it and circled a finger to mix it to a paste. 'Celeste left instructions for this. I don't know if she foresaw Aurelie's tantrum or if she was planning to shed some of her blood. It's the oldest form of magic, the most powerful as well. Disgusting but she usually knew what she was talking about. Hold still.'

Grace didn't. She tried to recoil, to fight her way free, but the shadows tightened around her, holding her firm.

'Fuck you, Jehane,' she spat. Asher laughed as he smeared the concoction over her cheeks, her eyelids and then brought his fingers up to her lips. He held them over the surface in warning.

'Bite me and I'll have them geld your friends, understand?'

She fell still, shivering as he spread Celeste's blood on her lips. She could taste it, salt and copper. Bile burned in her throat. Her eyes stung but she didn't dare show it.

She couldn't give him the satisfaction.

He smiled, that twisted self-satisfied smile as he finished. 'There. Positively primal. Celeste would be delighted. She loved all things primitive. Fall in around her. If she moves one step out of line, restrain her. Jehane, keep a hold of her at all time. That won't be hard for you, will it? Try and behave, Marchant. Aurelie is dying to see you. And she'll love this.'

Aurelie dying, there was a tempting proposition. Grace didn't reply, just kept staring past him. She didn't want to draw attention to the stiletto still holding her hair in place. Asher frowned. Irritated, she realised. She wasn't paying attention to him, wasn't snivelling or begging. And he really didn't like it.

'And I can't wait to see her,' she replied carefully and was rewarded with a twitch in the corner of Asher's eye. She hid her smile again.

'Grace, what are you—?' Daniel began.

'You're staying here,' Asher interrupted. 'Surety for her good behaviour. If we have to come and fetch you you're really going to regret it. So is Grace. Understand?'

'It's okay, Danny,' she said softly. 'Just look after Misha. This won't take long.'

The palace was silent. That was the one thing she noticed. Every-where, fear lingered. No one laughed or raised their voice, no one wanted to draw attention to themselves. No one made eye contact, but that might just have been with her. Guilt by association was a dangerous thing, after all.

But this place had changed. It had been bad before. It was a mausoleum now. Every corner reeked of fear.

Aurelie had always been insecure about her power. She responded to threats with violence. With nothing now to limit her baser nature, Grace wondered how far she had gone. How many had died?

It was her fault, her responsibility. She'd left with Bastien, instead of staying here and fighting. Well, that was over now. She was home. And, one way or the other, she was putting an end to this.

Carefully, consciously, she sent another little wave of magic towards the collar and felt one of the sigils burn out.

The throne room was almost unchanged from when she'd seen it last, except that Lucien Larelwynn's sword was no longer hanging up above the throne. Bastien had destroyed it when Asher tried to use it on him. And there was only one throne here now. Aurelie sat in it, her pale blue eyes scanning the silent room. She was still beautiful, golden-haired, her spine ramrod straight, her dress even finer than the one Grace had been forced into. As Grace entered, she saw the queen's jaw tighten and her fingers grip the arms of the throne like claws.

Grace didn't bow. Aurelie's eyes narrowed.

Someone – Jehane probably – grabbed the back of Grace's neck and shoved her forward into a semblance of a bow.

'Marchant,' the queen said in the coolest terms imaginable.

'Aurelie.'

If the slight offended her – and Grace was sure it would – the queen held it together for now. She had Grace where she wanted her, after all.

Slowly, Aurelie looked her up and down, her gaze lingering on her face painted with blood. 'And what is the point of you bringing her here, Lord Kane?'

'She wears the warrant, your majesty. It protects her. No one but a Larelwynn can take it from her.'

'Well, we are in short supply of them. Why isn't she dead, Asher?'

He almost smiled. 'She's more valuable alive. Trust me. You want power, Aurelie. She can feed us just as Miranda did. Just as Celeste did. All you have to do is accept her.'

Aurelie looked repulsed.

'Accept Grace Marchant? As what?'

He almost laughed, the light of a zealot in his eyes. 'Not Grace Marchant, my love. Not any more. Our goddess. Are you ready?'

Another sigil went out and Grace closed her eyes. How many more were there? She was almost there, almost. And if not, she still had her back-up plan.

Asher's voice intoned words she didn't know, that no one could possibly know, and yet Grace recognised them somehow. Words of summoning, words of welcome, words that should never be said.

Magic crept over her skin like ice from the warrant, crawling up her neck and face, over her scalp, threading its way through her hair, and then it was burrowing into her skull, freezing her, claiming her, turning the world dark and nightmarish. The warrant came alive again, all that power, all that darkness and emptiness. For a moment it teetered on the edge, then it surged through her in a maddening rush.

Blood burned like acid on her skin, Celeste's blood, triggered by the influx of power.

Grace couldn't help herself. She threw back her head and screamed.

At her throat, the last remaining sigil flared in incandescence and burned out. And the darkness rushed through her like a hurricane.

Chapter Thirty-One

Rathlynn had changed. Bastien sensed it the moment they entered the gates. Eyes watched them as they passed, gazes suspicious and hostile. He wore his hood pulled up, but even so he wasn't sure that he wouldn't be recognised. Or that he hadn't been already. He couldn't shake the feeling of being followed. It wasn't like the homecoming he might have expected. He was sneaking into the capital city of the kingdom he should be ruling. No one came to greet them and no one would miss them if they left.

Grace would though. He couldn't leave without her. And she had to be here. Where else would Asher take her? The palace, or the Temple, one or the other, to Aurelie or to Celeste.

Ellyn led the way unerringly. She knew the streets of Rathlynn better than he did. Rynn followed, a little bedraggled and less princess-like than he had ever seen her. But she didn't seem unhappy about it. If anything she seemed more driven than ever before. Something had happened between the two women, he knew that. They worked as one now. And his so-called wife hadn't looked at him for more than a second since they'd escaped the cave. Her eyes were only for the self-confessed Valenti water rat, who had royal blood flowing in her veins.

He'd once told Grace they weren't missing any princesses. He'd been wrong. They didn't count the ones born to other royal houses.

A grave oversight.

There was a public stable not far from the main gates and Ellyn handed over the horses there. Whatever she said to the stable boys, they didn't demand payment, just nodded and took the reins from each of them.

'We'll have to walk the rest of the way,' she said. 'Riding through Rathlynn just attracts attention, especially where we're going.'

'Where are we going?' Rynn asked, trying to keep from staring at everything around her. Even the straw and horseshit on the ground. She'd never seen anything like it. Certainly not in gleaming, beautiful Iliz.

Ellyn glanced around them to make sure no one was too close.

'Eastferry first,' she replied. 'And then… they said they saw the general coming through early this morning. We're not too far behind them. There's still hope.'

'Eastferry then,' Bastien said. He could guess where. There was only one place.

'I hope you like omelettes,' Ellyn said to Rynn. She grinned wickedly, her recklessness almost infectious. But Rynn just looked bewildered.

They kept their heads down as they crossed the city, reaching Eastferry within the hour, and word obviously went ahead that they were coming. Bastien could feel the eyes from windows and laneways following them as they approached. The overhanging upper floors of the timber houses didn't offer any shelter. By the time they plunged into the deepest parts of Eastferry, they were being shadowed by about five different people.

'Seven,' said Ellyn, when Bastien whispered as much to her. 'I think I know four of them though.'

She probably did, he realised. She looked comfortable here, with her smooth gait and her easy, relaxed gaze. Nothing seemed to faze her. She was home.

The Larks' Rest looked much as he remembered. A few more people hanging around outside and, inside, the paint more ragged and the smell worse, but otherwise it hadn't changed. Every eye in the place was on them the instant they entered and Rynn shrank back behind them, as if she could hide.

But there was no hiding in here.

'Ellyn?' Kurt Parry came straight for them, a terrifying prospect in any other circumstances. The man was a ruthless killer, a criminal and a thug, as close to a king in his small world as Bastien had ever been in his. But the concern on his face was such that there was no doubt that he had heard what had happened. Or some of it. 'Thank all the glories. We feared the worst.'

Ellyn didn't waste time with explanations. 'We've got to get into the palace, Kurt.'

'I know. We're already making plans, I promise. But you need to rest. Look at you.'

They looked dead on their feet, Bastien knew that. 'We can't wait here and—'

Kurt cut him off. 'You're meant to be dead, I believe? That's what Asher announced anyway. Look, my brother is in there too. And I know they're using him against Grace, so he's more likely to get killed than the Duchess. So back down, Larelwynn.'

It was like a bucket of cold water drenching him. Bastien didn't know what to say. Luckily Rynn was there.

'Everyone's on edge, and with those we love in danger, no one wants to hesitate.' She rested her hand on Bastien's arm. 'But he's right. We can't charge in blindly.'

'You're not charging anywhere at all, Rynn,' Ellyn said firmly. 'You're staying here. Where it's safe.'

Rynn glanced around the inn, its murky corners, the bar with the dubious bottles of alcohol, the seedy stairway leading up to seedier bedrooms, and then back at Ellyn. 'Safe. Here.'

'Nowhere safer in the city,' Ellyn assured her, with an indulgent smile.

'Either we have very different definitions of safe or this city is in more trouble than I thought.'

'And who is this?' Kurt asked. Whether he was affronted by her comments on his city or insulted by her reaction to his inn, he wasn't looking happy.

Ellyn choked. There was no other word for it.

'Princess Rynn Elenore Layna de Valens of Gellen, fifth child of King Roderick of the Valenti,' Rynn said, holding out her hand to him. To everyone's surprise, Kurt took her hand and kissed it with all the grace of a courtier.

'Your highness. I believe congratulations are in order.' He smirked up at Bastien and it was his turn to go a mortified shade of burning red. Trust Kurt. He was loving every minute of this. 'And what does the Duchess have to say about this, my Lord of Thorns?'

'The duchess?' Rynn asked. 'What duchess?'

Ellyn took her arm, leading her aside. 'He means Grace. It's a joke. They're old friends. Kind of. He's Danny's brother.'

Rynn still looked perplexed. 'Have I said something wrong?'

Ellyn shook her head fondly. 'No, love. It's just—'

'Ellyn and your new bride?' Bastien glared at him and Kurt smirked. 'That's awkward. She's a fast mover.'

Bastien didn't dare to ask which one Kurt meant. Parry was enjoying this, Bastien realised. Every barbed word and snide remark. And every glare or affronted silence was just going to make him worse. Kurt Parry talking to him like this was almost friendly.

'Are we going to keep this up or are we going to rescue them?' Bastien asked at last.

Kurt shook his head. 'I never thought you'd be back here. And I don't think you should be here either. You're a danger to our people, aren't you? If Aurelie gets her hands on you again—'

'She won't.'

'I'll see to that for you, if you want.' It wasn't a promise, it was a threat. And at the same time…

'See that you do.'

Kurt nodded and some kind of tension seemed to evaporate between them.

'Like I said, plans are in place. You can join us. I admit, you could be useful. But don't get in the way, your majesty.'

He didn't even sound sarcastic when he said it. That was as close to respectful as he'd get from Kurt Parry, Bastien knew that. All the same, those two words made his heart drop. He wasn't here for the crown. Only Grace mattered now.

*

A circumspect knock on the door jerked Bastien out of a nightmare-infected doze. In his dreams, Grace battled the Hollow King on the edge of the Maegen pool. And in them, she was not winning.

'Enter,' he said, straightening up in the chair. The meal on the table was cold now, a congealed stew that had seen better days to begin with. He didn't want to ask what the meat portion of it actually was; he was pretty sure he wouldn't like the answer. The room smelled heavily of stale perfume. But he had at least been alone. For a while.

He could almost breathe. But when he did, he thought of Grace imprisoned, so near and so far away. His chest contracted as if bound by steel bars.

The door opened to an older man, broad-shouldered and silver-haired, his face haggard in that way only someone who had seen torture could be. He had an ancient leather collar around his neck and, when Bastien stood to greet him, he bowed.

'Your majesty,' he said. 'It is my honour to serve.'

Bastien swallowed. He didn't deserve any of this, not the title or the service. 'How can I help you?'

'I am Master Atelier Zavi Millan, lately of the Academy.'

Bastien's eyes widened in surprise. 'Grace spoke of you often.'

Zavi's smile was brief and fleeting. 'She is the best of us, that girl. I could do with your help, if you will give it?'

'Of course,' Bastien said. It had to be better than being cooped up in here, waiting until Kurt Parry did whatever he was planning to do.

'Come then,' said the Atelier. He led Bastien down the stairs to the main taproom, where all eyes turned on him and every gaze followed him hungrily. Down they went again, into the cellars and down again to the secret chambers beneath. He and Grace had hidden there once. It seemed like a lifetime ago.

The corridor and the rooms off it had changed, no longer a hiding place but a workshop, every wall shelved and stacked high with endless things. A workbench dominated the centre, and spread over it was a variety of sigils, each one beautiful and powerful, the work of a master.

'It's not ideal,' said the old man. 'I have to send to the blacksmith for some of the work. There's no forge down here, although I have a few kilns which almost do the job. We've cobbled together what we could from the various treasures of—'

Bastien paused, staring at a necklace made of silver and starstones. He knew it, knew it of old. It had belonged to the youngest sister of King Riah, a powerful mageborn in her own right. '—Treasures of the royal palace,' he finished, picking it up and turning it over. 'Kurt Parry has been busy.'

'We all have, my lord. There was little else we could do. It was that, or give up and die.'

Bastien laid the necklace down again. The tales said it was cursed, but he presumed Zavi knew that. He'd already prised one of the starstones from it. Now it graced a sigil lying in the middle of the workbench.

'You'll use them all?'

'Their power is formidable. We need them, and their like, to defeat the nightborn, to bind them, or to drive the darkness from them. Sigils, and weapons. During the Magewar—'

'Such things were used, yes.'

He knew far too much for Bastien's comfort. But then, you didn't get to be a master Atelier as renowned as Zavi Millan without finding out more than a few secrets along the way.

'Parry has asked me to arm his people against the nightborn. Do I… do I have your blessing?'

Bastien knew what Zavi was asking. If they used the sigils and Zavi's other creations, so many mageborn could die. Just like on Iliz.

Nightborn, yes, but what were they but mageborn first? They were still his people, the ones he had failed. And now he had no magic to help them, not any more.

'Yes,' said Bastien, even though it broke his heart to do so. There was no other way.

The Master Atelier fetched a long case from a shelf and set it on the table, opening it to reveal a sword. It was made of a curious, dark grey metal which Bastien recognised at once. It had been bigger, of course, so long ago. A ridiculous thing, oversized, far too long for the man… no, the boy, who had carried it. Lucien had never been a swordsman. He had struggled to lift the Godslayer sword in its original form. But this was the sword that they told the world stopped the Hollow King. Bastien knew now that was not true. It was a symbol of kingship and once it had hung over Marius's throne, until Asher had tried to kill Bastien and Grace with it. Filled with the power of the Hollow King, Bastien had crushed it.

But still, it had power. Unlike him.

He lifted it reverently. Now it was smaller, lighter, a more elegant blade.

'The Godslayer,' he said, naming it and knowing it. The Atelier took one of the starstones from its setting and waited until Bastien presented the hilt to him. He positioned it on the pommel. Light flared beneath his hand as he pressed it into the metal and the hum of magic filled the air, rippling down the blade. Bastien felt it in his bones, but magic was like an alien thing to him now. His heart ached with loss for his powers which seemed to be gone forever. Zavi released it.

'It will serve you now,' said the Atelier. 'Protect you. The sword of the king. Do you understand?'

'I'm not the king. I can't be.'

'Yes, Bastien Larelwynn. You can. Now you are no longer mageborn.'

So the old man knew about his lack of magic.

'And what if I don't want to be?'

Zavi smiled, a soft, sad smile. 'I don't think kings get to choose. It's one of the few areas where you're as bound as any man. I have another… not a gift, not really, but…' He held out his hand. In it was a sigil, the likes of which Bastien had only seen once before. It was intricate and beautiful, more skilful than any he had seen produced by a lesser hand. It even made those on the workbench, those powered by ancient artefacts of rare power, pale in comparison. It was made of the Godslayer too, parts of it. And other things. Each element was familiar, and yet completely new. The patterns of the etchings and the way the metal shimmered made his eyes hunger to keep looking at it. The components making it up drew the eye in and held all his attention effortlessly. It was a work of art. It was like looking at the Maegen itself.

'It's more than just a sigil…' he murmured.

'I sometimes see what is needed. Not why, not how, but I know what must be made. You need this one, my Lord of Thorns. And I fear… I fear I know how you will have to use it.' Zavi frowned and looked down at his work again. At any moment Bastien thought he might close his hand over it and snatch it back. And Bastien wished he would. The power ingrained in the sigil was so great, and it felt… so very final. 'It will contain her. I think.'

And the sword… the sword could kill anything. Even a god. Or a goddess.

Bastien bit his lower lip hard, forcing himself to stay silent. He wanted to tell the old man no, that he wouldn't take them, that he would never use that sigil on Grace and how could he suggest such a thing. But knowledge like his was a gift from the divine, a manifestation of the Maegen itself working through a mortal mind.

And if it was too late, for the good of all, how could he fail to act? She would never forgive him if he failed. He could picture the sidelong look, the glare.

He took the sigil. It felt so very warm in his hand and he closed his fingers over it. The edges bit into his flesh.

'My thanks, Master Atelier,' Bastien said and bowed. It was all he could offer.

'I remember you,' Zavi said. 'And your father before you. You're a better man, I think, if you don't mind me saying so.'

Bastien drew in a breath. The man Zavi remembered as his father was just him in another life, before the Larelwynn royal family had wiped his memory and lied about his identity. Not only to him, he now realised. To his people as well.

'We all strive to be better than that which came before us,' he said. It was an old adage, one which was rarely used these days, but the Atelier nodded sagely.

Then he looked down at Bastien's hand clenched around the sigil again. His face was strained.

'Try not to hurt her, my lord,' he said, and turned abruptly away.

Bastien didn't have the guts to tell him that it was already too late for that.

*

There were far more people in the inn when he and Zavi emerged from the cellars. People outside too, people gathered around the doors and windows, peering in. The moment Bastien entered the hall and stopped in the doorway to the taproom, conversation fell silent and every eye turned on him.

Ellyn stood up from the table where she'd been sitting with Rynn and Kurt. She bowed to Bastien and he felt all the blood drain from his head at the gesture.

'There's no way to avoid this, is there?' Bastien murmured to the Atelier.

'Not really, my lord,' Zavi said softly. 'All the city knows you're here. And they want to follow you. Why wouldn't they?'

He could think of at least a dozen reasons right away. Most of them he couldn't or wouldn't share.

'A few months ago they were terrified of me. They thought I was a monster.'

'Some of them. Not all of them. And sometimes we need our monsters.'

He didn't want to think about that. He didn't want anyone to follow him and he didn't want to be a monster. He never had. He just wanted to get Grace back, unharmed and unscathed.

'Monsters won't help, Master Atelier. There are more than enough monsters up in the palace.'

There were murmurs of agreement, whispers and a soft laugh or two. Bastien had been speaking quietly but in the hushed room, with all attention on him, they'd heard him nonetheless.

Kurt narrowed his eyes, watching, taking in everything. Calculating.

Bastien steeled himself and walked to their table. Some people bowed as he passed. Some of them didn't bother to get up but they were fewer. It didn't matter, he told himself. Whether they wanted him as a king or not... it didn't matter. Only Grace mattered.

As he passed the mood changed. From respect and speculation, to awe. The sword, he realised. They saw the sword strapped across his back. They saw the starstone glimmering in the hilt. What they saw marked him.

He carried Godslayer, Lucien Larelwynn's sword.

He sat down, shifting the sword to one side, and faced Kurt, his second Melia, and Ellyn. Rynn grinned at him.

'Scarlet?' Kurt said, breaking the silence and addressing the woman behind the bar. 'Would you fetch us some wine? Or whatever you want, your majesty. We lifted it from your wine cellars so you might as well drink some of it with us.'

It was like he went out of his way to provoke outrage, like he couldn't help himself. Maybe he couldn't. Bastien knew better than to rise to it.

'That sounds fair. But maybe later. I can't wait here, Kurt. Not any longer. I need to go to the palace. This has to be stopped.'

'You only want to find Grace. What if they've killed her already?'

Then he'd get revenge. But it couldn't come to that. He wouldn't let it.

'The same could be said for your brother. They took him too.'

Kurt glared at him. 'Attacking the palace now is suicide. This whole city is designed with it as the heart. Believe me, I've thought about it. There are some ways in, sure, but they're too small and too dangerous for the numbers we'd need. The only other way in without someone inside is through the main gates and they're locked tight now. Attack them and the whole Royal Promenade becomes a killing ground.'

Bastien grinned, humourlessly. 'We can open those gates for you, Kurt. I know the palace like the back of my hand.'

'And you'll just let us in? All of us? All the scum of Rathlynn to pillage our way through your home?'

But Bastien shook his head. 'All the *people* of Rathlynn, if they want. It's not my home. Never was. Well? Will you help me?'

'Me?'

'They'll follow *you*, Kurt. You and Ellyn. They know you, trust you. You won't get them killed. I'm… I'm a Larelwynn. It's more or less all we do.'

Kurt stared at him like he was mad. Perhaps he was.

Ellyn fixed him with as stubborn a look as Grace ever wore. 'You aren't going without me, Bastien. My people are in there.'

There was no arguing with her. He knew that right away. 'Fine then,' he replied.

She looked startled. 'Really? I was expecting more of an argument. Right then. What do you have in mind, your majesty?'

He really wished she hadn't called him that, not with so many of the Rathlynnese listening. But there was nothing he could do about it now.

*

Bastien set off as the Vigil bells chimed out, echoing across the rooftops, Ellyn by his side. The city was silent as a graveyard. No one stirred. Rathlynn was trapped in the grip of terror and it came from both the nightborn and the palace, from those who ruled and those who lived among them.

After Iliz and its constant parties, the quiet was unnerving. It reminded him of Thorndale – dead and empty. The sword was a strange sort of comfort, as was the sigil from Zavi. But his magic still eluded him and, for the first time in all his supernaturally long life, Bastien felt truly vulnerable. The entrance to the Rats' Path was still intact, still hidden, and they slipped inside, ghosts on the ancient stone steps.

'Follow me,' he told Ellyn.

'The others will be waiting. We don't have much time.'

'I know. And we'll do our part. But, Ellyn… once we've dealt with the gate…'

A smile flickered over her lips. 'You're heading on in, aren't you? Going after Grace on your own.'

'I can't risk waiting.'

He wasn't surprised when she shrugged. 'Well then. No plan after all. There's a surprise. You two are more alike than you know.'

He tried to take it as a compliment.

Once inside the palace complex he knew the way like he knew the veins in his own body. Bastien had lived endless lifetimes here and now he could remember them. All of them. They didn't make for comforting memories, but at least he could make his way through the quickest and most obscure route up through the underground levels. Kurt had wanted to send more people with him but Bastien had refused. Just Ellyn, because he trusted her. And because too many feet down here would make too much noise. And maybe, just maybe, there was still some sort of loyalty left in him to this place and its secrets. Even if it was only a survival instinct, he didn't want Kurt Parry to know all his secrets.

They encountered no one on the lower levels. The palace was like a mausoleum. It always had been. It wasn't until they were almost on the ground level, near the old gatehouse, that they ran into a small patrol.

Ellyn brought her hand up in a swift signal, then stepped out in full view before he could stop her. She was brazen, reckless, but he had to admit, if she wanted to throw them off, she was doing her job.

'Hey there, I'm a bit lost. Which way to the crazy queen?'

Bastien launched himself at them. There was no magic at his disposal, no quick and easy way to deal with this. He had never had to fight, not really, not when it truly meant something. His blood pounded in his ears and his limbs burned as he attacked. Ellyn twisted by him, her swords moving faster than he could follow, a technique he could never hope to match. But the Godslayer felt at home in his hands, like an extension of himself. It wasn't magic, not in the way he knew it. This was something else.

What followed was a blur; brutal, bloody. He'd trained with the sword alongside the Larelwynn kings and princes. They were probably testing themselves rather than him. It must have been a thrill, fighting an immortal, a being that was the key to their power and could destroy them in an instant if he so desired. They used him. All his long life or lives or however you numbered it. They used him.

Suddenly there was no one left to fight. He stopped, breathing hard, standing over the corpses.

'You okay?' Ellyn asked. She didn't even seem tired. She wiped her swords on one of the bodies with swift and ruthless efficiency before she sheathed them once more. 'Find out where they are?'

One guard was still breathing – one of hers – a young man, huddled against the wall, bleeding, traumatised. Bastien hauled him up.

'Where is she? Grace Marchant? The prisoners?'

The man stared at him like he was dazed. Perhaps he was. 'Prince… Prince Bastien?'

He shook him hard. 'Answer me.'

'The queen ordered the woman brought to the throne room. The others…' *Don't be dead. Please divinities and glories, don't be dead…* 'They're locked up in the tower under guard. Your tower. Your rooms. Please… please don't…'

The sound of the guard's begging made Bastien's stomach drop. He sounded terrified. His eyes darted frantically to the bodies of his comrades.

Bastien knocked him out with his hilt and watched him fall. He'd be okay. He hoped.

Daniel and Misha were safe for the moment. If Ellyn went now, she could rescue them before anything else happened. Whereas Grace… If Aurelie had her, he could be too late already.

'You want to split up,' Ellyn said before he could say a word. 'You know that's a terrible idea, right? It never works out well.'

She was right. He knew that. But it didn't change anything.

'The gates first,' he replied. 'Then you go for Daniel and Misha while I get to the throne room. If you can make it back to me, I'd appreciate the reinforcements but if you need to get them out, get them out.' She didn't even argue.

The gatehouse was up another level, and it was deserted. That didn't bode well. At the same time, he felt a wave of relief.

'Are you okay?' Ellyn asked.

'Yes. There's no one here.'

'Lucky for us. Better for them.' Ellyn had no qualms about taking a life when she needed to, he knew that.

The mechanism controlling the gates was locked but that hardly seemed to matter at all to Ellyn. The limiter on the machinery obediently snapped open.

Bastien gazed down into the city. There were lights starting up all over Rathlynn, torches, fires, rallying points. A mob or a citizens' army… only time would tell.

'They're coming,' he said.

Ellyn stared at him, wisps of her white-blonde hair ghosting around her sculpted Larelwynn face. He could see the resemblance now, in those planes and angles, in the structure beneath her skin. Her eyes might be that soft grey, but they had the same steely determination in them. Deep down, she was a Larelwynn to the core.

'The people in Rathlynn are starving,' she said. 'That's not exactly new but Aurelie has made it worse. There's a lot of pent-up anger, and you know they'll want to take that out on this place and anyone they find here. Some of them might want you back, might want a king, but not all of them. Not by any means. Bastien… I don't know if Kurt has a hope of containing them.'

'We'll have to hope he does, won't we? Stay safe, Ellyn. Rynn needs you.'

She nodded, just once. Then she held out her hand. He took it and she pulled him into an embrace. It was unexpectedly comforting. It shouldn't be. Ellyn was hard as nails, a fighter. He'd never appreciated such a gesture before.

They parted, not knowing if they'd see each other again, Ellyn heading for his tower to rescue Daniel and Misha, and Bastien faced with finding his own path.

He couldn't rely on his rage to carry him through. Although the sword might help – it seemed to be working on his stamina and strength in ways he couldn't define. It had been made before, before he'd been the Hollow King. The memories of who had made this sword and why were lost in those memories of the boy he'd once been, the boy who had died. But Bastien could feel the magic in it, older than Rathlynn, perhaps older than Thorndale. Godslayer. But what god?

He pushed that thought away.

He couldn't just sprint for the throne room. The great staircase, the wide corridors… they would be guarded. Although his fears that the palace would be swarming with guards had been unfounded – Kurt would have a free run to the gates. But the rest of the guards had to be somewhere. Waiting.

Servants' stairs, antechambers and one way, one path within the palace that only the royal family knew.

The Larelwynns had kept their secrets close. And if Bastien was their greatest secret, the passageway into the throne room was probably second.

The few guards he encountered on the way died or scattered. He was still the Lord of Thorns here, still the nightmare behind the throne. No one wanted to take him on. He might not want to kill, but he wanted to live more. Needed to live. Needed to reach Grace.

The secret passage opened for him like an old friend. His hands shook as he stepped into the darkness. The steps were narrow, functional and steep. The air was thick with dust and clogged with cobwebs. He forced his way through. The door at the top formed an outline of light, a glowing frame. Beyond it he heard a scream. Grace's scream. It triggered something suicidal in his brain.

Stealth forgotten, he burst through the door.

*

Grace stood in the middle of the throne room, aglow with the cold light of the Deep Dark. Someone had daubed ancient symbols on her face in old blood. Bastien's memory stirred, giving them names and meanings, words in a forgotten tongue, the language of dead divinities. Terrible words with terrible meanings. Celeste knew those words, and he had once. Words of power, words of binding, words of ownership.

What had they done to her? What were they trying to do?

Around her throat a collar made of sigils bound her and she seemed frozen there, standing before Aurelie, Asher and Jehane Alvaran. Bastien had worn such a collar himself once, powerful enough to hold a god. Ultimately, not for very long.

Now all but one of the sigils were dark, and the remaining one glowed brightly, almost blinding in its intensity. Grace shuddered, her whole body reacting to something he couldn't see. But he knew what it was.

Slowly she seemed to regain her control and she stretched out her arms to either side and turned in a circle, like a girl before a ball, trying out a new gown, something Grace herself would never do. When she saw him, she smiled.

But it was not her smile.

'*Bastien Larelwynn*,' she said, her voice filled with strange harmonies and unnatural whispers beneath the surface of it. It jarred against all his senses and his blood turned ice cold. He knew that voice, knew it too well. And it was not Grace's. '*It is so good of you to join us. We've been waiting.*'

A wind swept out of nowhere and the door behind him slammed shut. The Godslayer turned too hot to hold and he had no choice but to drop it. The sword clattered to the marble floor, smoking like it was fresh out of a forge. Bastien's legs locked in position, his body held so tight he could barely breathe, let alone move.

Grace walked towards him, Asher and Aurelie watching in stunned silence. Without hesitation she bent down and took the torc from his neck. He couldn't do anything to stop her and the smile she wore made his heart stutter with fear.

It wasn't possible. It couldn't be possible.

She smoothed her hands lovingly across the surface of the golden metal and then tugged the warrant from her throat.

'What are you doing?' Aurelie said, fear infecting her features now.

Grace turned, the black skirt swirling around her, and in her hands the torc and the warrant seemed to melt, spinning together, blending until the molten metal reformed. She held a crown, a golden crown. There was something savage about it, the points more like knives, the ends sharp and gleaming. It wasn't the crown that had formed for him when Grace had given him back the warrant. This was something else. Belonging to another mind, one broken and brutal.

Grace – it wasn't Grace, he could never believe that was still Grace – whirled around with it, laughing in delight and then she settled it on her head. It glittered in her fire-red hair.

'*Now…*' she breathed out the word, a sound filled with anticipation. '*Where shall we begin?*'

Chapter Thirty-Two

Grace's body shook but she was locked inside it, trapped by the Hollow King's crown and the power of the Deep Dark radiating from it.

Bastien was there.

Her Bastien… living, breathing, alive.

Helpless…

There wasn't a trace of magic left in him. She couldn't sense it, couldn't see it. He was only human.

And so very vulnerable.

He struggled, panic making his dark brown eyes wide. Human eyes, without a trace of the Maegen in them. What had happened to him? How was he even here?

She struggled against the bonds holding her, fighting back now. Celeste's laughter echoed through her blood.

'Very amusing,' said Aurelie in her calm, cool voice. 'I'm so glad to see stories of your death were exaggerated, Bastien, but you were a fool to come back here.' She glared at Asher as she walked forward, her long gown swishing hypnotically around her legs. 'I will take great pleasure in reminding you of your proper place.'

The dark goddess laughed out of Grace's mouth again – Celeste's laughter, Grace was sure of it now – and Aurelie turned in shock, her whole affronted demeanour almost comical. Grace gasped for breath, desperate and afraid. Celeste Larelwynn was clawing her way up inside her, driving for the surface, pushing the Deep Dark down in her desire to take control.

The marks on her face in Celeste's blood burned. The power that Celeste had always craved, his crown, her freedom… she had it now. She was free of the Temple, free of the body that had imprisoned her and all the bonds that had driven her insane. She was free of the sigil locking her magic inside her.

Was this what she had planned all along?

'Stop it,' Aurelie snarled at her. 'Asher, make her stop.'

But Asher just gazed at Grace in wonder. No, not at Grace. He was not seeing her at all. It was the Little Goddess who he gazed upon. He smiled slowly, ignoring the queen.

'My goddess.' It was Jehane who spoke, his voice a murmur, his eyes dark with wonder and desire, completely nightborn now. Her creature, Grace realised, Celeste's to the bottom of his soul. 'We have delivered you and given you a new life. As we promised.' She remembered his face when he had first seen the warrant, when he had told her she should be queen. He'd known… he had planned this. Him and Asher Kane.

Asher was watching her with the same rapt adoration, but he wasn't nightborn. His expression was all Asher Kane, greed and triumph twisting him. He'd daubed those symbols on her face in Celeste's blood, marking her for this.

'What is he talking about?' Aurelie snapped at Kane.

'It's not Grace, Aurelie,' Bastien said in a tight and tortured voice. 'Not any more.'

But it was. She wanted to scream it at him. She was still here, still trapped inside herself while this… *thing* was in control.

'Who is it then?' the queen said, disbelief dripping from her words.

'My sister. Celeste.' He was still trying to struggle free of whatever bonds Celeste had placed on him but speaking attracted her attention once again. Grace's arm shot out towards him – she couldn't stop it – and he came down on his knees heavily, pain making him cry out.

'*Don't tell tales, little brother,*' she teased. '*It isn't nice. I worked long and hard to get here, ever since the Larelwynns trapped me in the Temple. I've plotted my vengeance on this wretched place and its family ever since. And you—*' She snarled at Aurelie, who fell back on her throne, white-faced. '*You lied about having a child, and you murdered me.*'

'Asher!' Aurelie cried out. 'Protect me!'

But Asher wasn't paying any attention to her now. Grace would have felt sorry for her, if it wasn't Aurelie. If she hadn't brought this down on all of them.

Bastien dragged himself up from the ground and onto his knees.

'Celeste…' He ground out her name, fighting to keep himself from falling beneath the onslaught of power she continued to rain down on him.

'*I never could fool you for a moment, Bastien,*' she purred. '*She's still in here, you know? Your beloved Grace. She's mine now, mine forever, to do with what I want. Want to see?*'

Sharp points like teeth sank into Grace's consciousness, tearing through her fragile identity. For a moment she was herself again, briefly, enough time to scream in agony.

'Grace!' Bastien's voice wrenched out of his throat and he tried to fling himself towards her. But he couldn't move.

'My goddess, no,' Jehane shouted, his voice unexpectedly firm. 'We need her.'

In that instant, Celeste's control snapped back around Grace and she straightened, looking on him with all the disgust of an empress on a rat. Under the full fire of her attention, Jehane bowed his head. But barely enough to placate her. Celeste scowled.

'*You think you can command me? Your loyalty is fickle, Shade. We should examine that.*'

He flinched like a child seeing a raised hand, just for a moment, but then the cold assassin was back. 'Mistress, goddess…' he began, that charm Grace had noted in him time and again and always dismissed. 'Forgive me. I live only to serve you. But we made a deal, you and I. I saved her life for you. I made her yours. I gave her to you. Pliant, obedient…'

Obedient? No. Grace would never be obedient. As for *pliant*…

Grace fought furiously, trying to break free. If it could be done once, it could be done again. The gap had to be there somewhere. That brief moment of freedom had been enough to focus her mind, to allow her to hope again.

'*You chose well, Jehane,*' Celeste said. '*But I wonder if you ever truly knew her. Pliant indeed. Not Grace Marchant. We don't want her pliant. We want her to fight, to struggle, to fail. Oh, yes, we want her failure, her desperation. And my siblings like to play with her. The Deep Dark is wild and ungovernable. It needs me to control it. It always has. She distracts it. And, as Aurelie so kindly murdered me, I am free. Finally free of that prison they called a Temple and that weak and broken body they trapped me in. Free to do all that I was created to do.*'

'And what is that?' Aurelie asked, still clinging to her throne.

'*Rule, your majesty.*'

'Over my dead body.'

Celeste laughed, her wild rolling laugh, and it was joined by a thousand other voices, drowning out Grace's shout of alarm.

'*That can be arranged, Aurelie.*' The amusement in Celeste's voice was painful to hear. '*This is my crown now. It carries all the power of the*

Maegen in it. Want a taste? I know you do, you pitiful little addict. You've worn enough of my blood to stand it.'

Slowly Celeste approached her, stalking her, and the queen seemed frozen to the spot, her perfect face etched in horror, transfixed. Celeste stretched out one of Grace's hands and touched Aurelie's forehead. The wave of magic sent the queen reeling back, her mouth wide, her pupils dilated to endless black holes. She wilted on the throne, and then shuddered like someone having a seizure. Magic coursed through her, far too much.

'Celeste,' Bastien shouted. 'Celeste, please! Stop this.'

She spun around. He'd made it back to his feet again. Somehow without her attention on him, the power holding him weakened. Grace felt a surge of relief but at the same time she could feel Celeste's insane rage. She wanted him broken. And she intended to do that herself.

Slowly Celeste walked towards him. *'Shall I show you again, Bastien? Shall I let you see her suffer? Or should I leave that torture for her? Grace can see you, you know. She can see everything I do to you. And she is still trying to regain control. She fights and fights, doesn't she? This will be her whole existence now. Fighting forever. My prisoner. My hostage within this body.'*

Celeste reached out, cupping the side of his face with Grace's hand. Grace could feel his stubble, the firm line of his jaw, the tightness… His pain. Divinities, she wanted to touch him, to keep touching him. But not like this. She wanted to help him, free him. She wanted him. Only him.

Celeste drew back her hand and hit him. His head snapped to the side and he couldn't hope to stop the sob of pain and defeat.

'Goddess, we had a deal,' Jehane said again. 'It's time I was paid my due.' Asher hissed at him, but he wasn't listening any more.

Celeste grabbed Bastien by a clump of his hair and dragged him around to face Jehane. The Shade raised his hands in supplication, although his expression said anything but. Celeste tilted her head on one side and studied him, bemused.

'*What do you want, Jehane?*' she sighed, a sound of irritation and disgust. '*Do you fancy you love her too? As much as he does? Should I make the two of you fight for her? Or for me?*'

'No, my goddess. You promised me strength. You promised me power.'

He'd fled his home as a boy, Grace knew that, driven out just like her. He'd fought and struggled and killed, done whatever it took to protect himself, to survive. He was still doing it. The desperation buried in the depths of those heartless eyes told her he'd do anything, betray anyone, for the power Celeste offered. All to protect the terrified child he had once been.

'*I promised you?*' She smiled. She clearly had no memory of making any such promise but it was Celeste. She would have said anything to get her freedom. '*Well, if I promised… If that's what you truly want. I'll make you strong. So strong that no one will hurt you ever again, poor little Shade. I'll give you power. I'll make you mine.*'

Jehane cast a suddenly triumphant sneer at Asher and then looked to her. 'That is my only wish.'

This was a mistake, Grace knew that. Jehane couldn't handle the type of power Celeste offered. And to make him hers? Did she fancy a mad king beside her on the throne? A Shade obsessed with her and all she could offer? Between them, what would they do to Rathlynn? What would they do to Bastien?

Jehane gazed down on her, and she knew instantly he saw her, not Celeste. He had no interest in Celeste bar the magic she offered. But Grace… she was a different story.

'I told Grace Marchant that she owed me her life,' he whispered. 'And that one day I would collect. This is that day, my queen.' The slow smile that spread over his face made her skin crawl with disgust.

Grace reached for Bastien, with a hand that she wasn't even aware she could still control. But somehow she found his fingers threading through hers.

'*Then your wish will be granted, my sweet Jehane.*' Celeste purred his name. '*Join me in the shadows and be mine.*'

Grace shuddered as Celeste's power radiated from her. Bastien's grip tightened on her hand but Celeste jerked Grace away from him like a puppet, her toy. She pulled Jehane to her with a fistful of his shirt, gazing into his lust-filled eyes. Then she kissed him savagely.

It was a bruising, violent clash of mouths and teeth. Celeste was in control now. Grace didn't have a hope of resisting.

For a moment Jehane's eyes fluttered closed, submitting to her entirely, and then they snapped open, jet black as hers, but wide with shock. Celeste drew back as the Shade convulsed and darkness began to pour out of him. He desperately tried to breathe, but the nightborn magic tore through him, taking him apart shadow by shadow. Grace watched, horrified, as he disintegrated, right in front of her.

Part of her felt the justice of it. He'd betrayed her and Celeste had destroyed him. Grace wouldn't have stopped her. Justice had been written on her heart in the Academy. Now it was served.

And for a moment, just a moment, she felt whole again. Celeste reeled back, the outpouring of her power weakening her.

For the first time since Celeste had asserted herself, Grace felt the Deep Dark seething beneath her, distinct, something that wasn't part of her. It was trapped as Grace was and it was not happy. It couldn't break free. No more than Grace could.

Not alone.

It ought to have been unthinkable, but she was desperate now.

Help me, she tried to tell it, to beg it. *Help me stop her. We have to…* *or we'll serve her forever.*

The power of the Deep Dark seized her, hurling her from her body.

Suddenly she wasn't seeing with her own eyes any more, but with its power. She was somewhere else, flying along the corridors of the palace, swooping down the outside of the walls. Rathlynn was full of torches, its people – her *people – racing for the palace, for the gates and the walls, far more than the remaining Royal Guard could deal with. Most of them didn't even try. They turned and ran. She searched the faces, looking for those she knew. Kurt was there, of course, and any number from Eastferry and beyond. She swooped up again, spiralling dizzyingly around the towers of the palace. Ellyn kicked open the door to Bastien's room and Daniel almost took her head off with the sword Grace had told him to use. Ellyn ducked, cursed and then Daniel threw his arms around her. They were safe. Thank all the powers and the divinities they were safe.*

Something hit Grace like a punch in the stomach, dragging her back into her battered body.

Celeste snarled. Had she seen it too? Did she know what was coming?

'Grace,' Bastien whispered again, and she gripped his hand even more firmly. 'You can do this.'

No, she couldn't. Not by herself. But she could have help. If she accepted it. If the Deep Dark accepted her. Help was coming, physical help, that was what the Deep Dark was trying to show her. But it wouldn't be here soon enough.

Help me. Please. Help me and I'll... I'll find a way to help you. Please.

It was a dangerous bargain she was suggesting, she knew that. But she didn't have any choice.

You could be so much more. If you just had the courage to reach out and seize it.

The Deep Dark studied her, deliberating. It seemed as wary of her as she was of it. For the longest moment its myriad energies coiled beneath her, like a great beast ready to spring. It didn't want to be subject to Celeste any more than she did. The goddess was powerful. But the Deep Dark had to remember that it was stronger in all its many forms. A collective consciousness. Stronger than any of them. The Hollow King, Celeste, the Larelwynns...

Terribly strong.

'Be careful love,' Bastien whispered, the sound no more than a breath. 'Don't—'

But before he could say whatever warning he had for her the Deep Dark rose like a tidal wave within Grace, swallowing Celeste up in its rage.

At the same moment Aurelie surged out of the throne and snatched the crown from her head.

Chapter Thirty-Three

Grace stood trembling for a moment, and then all strength was wrenched away from her. She fell like a puppet with cut strings and Bastien's arms closed around her as he gathered her in his embrace, saying her name over and over again like a prayer.

'You have to get out of here,' she tried to tell him, breathlessly. Without his magic, he wouldn't stand a chance. Why had he come? He should never have come… 'You have to—'

Aurelie had the crown. Grace couldn't go anywhere while Aurelie held that crown. And Bastien wasn't going to leave her.

Asher Kane recovered himself first. 'Aurelie, what are you doing?'

She gazed down at the treasure in her hands, turning it around and around to examine it as if it was a longed-for prize. 'Taking what is mine by right, Asher.'

The dilemma showed on his face for only a moment. His wheedling persona returned, all charm and snake-oil.

'Aurelie, let's talk about this. Together we can—'

Pounding shook the doors, shouts and the sound of combat outside. The Rathlynnese had arrived. Any minute now, Grace thought, any minute, they'd take the palace. She had to believe that. She had to.

Kane swallowed and carried on. 'There's a mob out there, your majesty. They'll tear you limb from limb if you don't listen to me.'

Aurelie shook her head slowly. Something in her clearly wanted to believe him, the part of her that needed him, that loved him, or whatever emotion she still possessed that could pass for love. But she hesitated too long. And in that moment, his performance slipped, the master manipulator pushed to the edge by desperation.

'Damn it, Aurelie, do as you're told.'

The glimmer of hope in Aurelie's eyes died. Something else replaced it, cold and vicious. Her grip on the ancient crown tightened.

'They won't get the chance.'

Bastien struggled up, pulling Grace's unresisting body with him. She was too weak and wrung-out to struggle. 'We have to get those doors open.'

As if she sensed the movement, Aurelie turned on them, her eyes ablaze with fury, her hands clenched on the metal of the crown, knuckles white. 'Now, where were we, Marchant?'

Grace's body ached everywhere, the pain of keeping going incredible, but she had to protect Bastien. He might still be the Lord of Thorns but without his magic he was vulnerable, mortal. She pulled free of him, forced herself to stand alone, to defend him as she had promised to do so long ago. Right here, right in this room. 'Get to the doors, Bastien. Get them open and get out of here.'

Grace stood between him and the queen who lifted the crown towards her own head.

'Don't do it Aurelie,' Grace warned. 'Celeste is powerful and not to be trusted. You know that as well as I do.'

Aurelie scowled. 'You think that bitch scares me? You left her weak. You and the darkness. She told me once I'd wear her blood. Well, I did better than that. I killed her. I bathed in it. I can hear her now, begging me. Trapped inside the crown with the Deep Dark and mine to command. All this is mine. You are mine too, Marchant. I will relish taking you to pieces. And Bastien as well. And all of Rathlynn, all this kingdom. It's all mine and I will break it to pieces if I so desire.'

Behind them, Bastien reached the huge double doors and jerked them open. Guards were backed up against them. They almost fell into the throne room on top of him. But they stood firm, blocking him and facing the oncoming horde of Rathlynnese, storming up the main approach.

Rathlynn, Bastien, everything. All those people. Grace knew she still had a duty. Her Academy might be gone but that didn't mean her duty did not remain. Nightborn, mageborn or simply a thief of magic like Aurelie, she had vowed to stop them.

'I won't let you hurt them.'

'Hurt them?' Aurelie glared at the guards and the citizens of Rathlynn who had come roaring up into the edge of the antechamber, but now stopped, a terrified audience in an uncertain stand-off. That one look told Grace exactly how much Aurelie hated them. She'd never really doubted it but to see it so plainly written on her face was harrowing. 'I'm going to do so much more than merely *hurt* them, Marchant. They never accepted me. If they had just obeyed me it all could have been so much easier. But no. They had to be their belligerent, obnoxious, *ignorant* selves. All I asked was obedience, loyalty. And what did they offer?'

Grace smiled thinly. Her wretched, pugnacious city somehow always filled her with pride. They had stood up to Aurelie time and again, and here they were now, still fighting. 'What Rathlynn only ever offers tyrants, Aurelie. Defiance. Did no one warn you about us? We never bow unless we choose to.'

Aurelie sneered at her, an expression dark and loathsome. 'Never? Well, you'll suffer for it now. All of you.'

Aurelie shoved the crown on her own head, pushing it down, just to be sure it would stay there. Then she inhaled sharply and closed her eyes as the rush of power hit her. Grace knew the sensation all too well now. But Aurelie didn't hesitate or indulge the feeling. Not for more than a second. Grace didn't know how she was doing this – a body used to stolen magic, her addiction hollowing her out just enough perhaps, the power or the blood of Celeste Larelwynn saturating her, or else, some echo in her own blood like Rynn and Ellyn… who knew? But somehow the queen held firm with the vast and endless magic that coursed through her.

Aurelie's eyes turned black and she threw back her head, but instead of screaming she roared out her joy. 'This is incredible, Asher. The power. It's better than any purloined magic, better than anything you've ever given me. *Divinities*… this is the power of a *goddess*. *Yes*, this was meant to be *mine*.'

A wave of darkness burst from her, a void which struck like a physical blow. It wasn't the wild rage of the Deep Dark, or the unfocused insanity that Celeste embodied. This was pure malevolence. This was Aurelie. Dark magic consumed the queen. Her hair unravelled from its elegant style, floating like sunlight around her face. When she smiled, Grace saw the echo of Celeste there. But it was so much worse. The people of Rathlynn fell, gasping for air, tearing at their own skin. It didn't seem to matter who they were – guards and citizens alike, mageborn and quotidian – and Grace tried to stand her ground but the surge of malice swept over her, almost driving her to her knees.

Bastien shouted her name. He grabbed his discarded sword and charged at Aurelie. But before he reached her, the queen stretched out one elegant hand and he crumpled to the ground, his back arching in torment, his mouth open in a silent scream. His hand convulsed and the Godslayer fell. Aurelie stalked towards him, stood over him and pressed a foot to his throat. She burned with the darkness, embracing it all, making it part of her.

'Will I kill him, Grace?' she asked. 'Seems a shame after all these years. He's so handsome, a perfect specimen of a man. Perhaps I'll keep him after all. I always wanted him. He was always meant to be mine. He just couldn't see it. Without magic he's no threat.' Her slippered toe flicked his throat and a coil of shadows encircled him, tightening until they formed another collar. She smiled. 'Just so he knows his place.' Then she laughed, delighted with herself and her cleverness. The air shivered with that laugh. 'Asher, that potion of yours, get it for me. We can make him kill her like you promised.'

Asher had dragged himself towards her. 'I'm not your dog to order around, Aurelie.'

'*You?*' Her voice rippled with spite. She turned on him, releasing Bastien. 'I don't think you grasp this situation, this new balance of power. You will do as I tell you, Asher, from now on until I tell you to die. You'll be whatever I want you to be. *Dog.*'

Beneath her, Bastien struggled up, tearing through the shadows. Grace saw the desperation in his eyes. He was using every last ounce of strength he had and Grace knew… just knew… He wouldn't let them drug him. Wouldn't let them enslave him, not again. This was his only chance. He grabbed Aurelie's shoulder, pulled her to him before she knew what was happening. The glow of a sigil flared beneath his hand, the light blinding.

The queen lashed out. The undirected blast of darkness hurled Bastien away. The marble floor cracked where he landed, breath and consciousness driven from his body by the impact.

Aurelie gasped, her hands clawing at her neck, but she couldn't tear the sigil free. She was bound by magic of the simplest and yet most intricate kind, made by a master Atelier. Grace stared, tears starting at her eyes. Zavi's work. It was unmistakable. It was Zavi's...

Where had Bastien got it?

Aurelie shuddered, unable to dislodge the sigil. All that power swirling inside her and the sigil held her, the gemstone embedded in it blazing with light.

Her voice was a shriek of panic. 'What – what have you done? What... get it off me. Get it off!'

Suddenly she convulsed, too much magic dammed up inside her. Her whole body went rigid and then she bent double, dropping to her knees. She folded in on herself before her spine snapped back with a violent crack. She opened her mouth unnaturally wide and screamed, over and over again, like it would never end. The crown glowed, brighter than a sun on her head. Reasserting its dominance at last, the Deep Dark engulfed her, judging her, finding her wanting, and oh yes, punishing her. Because that was what it did. The Deep Dark exacted its terrible revenge on those who would constrain it. And with it trapped inside her, Aurelie had no escape.

Her cry cut off abruptly. She fell forward without another sound, a carcass slipping from its hook. She lay there, staring across the marble slabs, twitching, still gasping for breath after breath. Her eyes rolled up in her skull as the crown rolled off her head.

It made a sound like music on the marble floor, in the ensuing silence, ringing out until it hit a pair of black boots and went still.

Asher stood there over it, breathing hard as he watched his lover's destruction. His eyes met Grace's and he snarled. Bending down, he picked up the crown, studied it for a moment and then returned his gaze to her, the only other person still standing.

'You!' he growled. 'All you've ever done is ruin everything. Every last thing. You miserable nobody.'

Nobody… Yes, she was a nobody, and proud of it. But she knew that Bastien loved her and she loved him in return. He'd brought her back from the dead. He'd come back from the dead himself for her.

He couldn't be dead now. He couldn't. All her instincts screamed. But he wasn't moving. Why wasn't he moving? She edged towards Bastien, trying to reach him.

But she needed to distract Kane, keep him occupied and away from the vulnerable Lord of Thorns.

'All I've ever done is protect people, Kane.'

He drew his sword so slowly, every inch a threat. He cut the air with it a few times as he advanced, mocking her. And suddenly she knew Bastien wasn't the only person Kane hated enough to kill.

Grace dived for the Godslayer and he lunged at her. She rolled as her hand seized the hilt and came up to parry a blow which should have taken her head off.

He was skilled but driven by anger.

And she was exhausted. This was not a good situation.

Grace managed to force him back enough to regain her feet, but he was on her again, a fierce series of attacks raining down on her. The Godslayer hummed in her hands, the power of the ancient blade rippling through her. Not what she needed right now, stupid magic swords distracting her. She couldn't think about that. She could only react, only fight. She blocked it out.

The clash of blade on blade deafened her. She lunged and twisted aside, but Asher feinted and for a moment she thought he had her. Their bodies slammed together, swords crossed, trapped there.

Grace reached back with her free hand, grabbed the stiletto from her hair, and rammed it into the side of his neck.

In the same moment, a spike of agony stabbed her side, deep and deadly, blunt and all the more painful for that. He must have had another knife. She hadn't seen it but by all the divinities she felt it now. And then she remembered, the crown, with its wickedly sharp points. He had been holding the crown. It went deep, so very deep.

She twisted away, tearing herself free of his grip. Asher gagged on his own blood, trying to pull at the stiletto protruding grotesquely from his throat. Grace brought the Godslayer swinging in a wide arc, all her remaining strength behind it, all her will, all her desperate need. The starstone in the hilt gleamed brightly, almost blinding her.

For a moment she thought she'd missed, even though she knew that wasn't possible. Then Asher Kane toppled, his head landing several feet from his corpse.

She stayed, swaying on her feet for a moment that seemed like an eternity. Everything was a high-pitched scream, but she couldn't focus any more. Her vision blurred and she sank to the ground. The fall didn't hurt. The longest, sharpest point of the crown was still embedded in the soft skin of her side, the fabric of the gown around it sodden with her own blood. It sent a lance of pain through her such as she had never known.

She found herself staring across the floor at Bastien as he opened his eyes and saw her, his battered face contorting with disbelief. He was alive. Thank all the divinities. The irony of thanking the gods didn't escape her but when she tried to laugh everything turned to bright agony and white noise. Bastien dragged himself up onto his hands and knees and then tore across the space between them, half animal in his movements, while everything else went grey and slid away around her.

Chapter Thirty-Four

Chaos must have followed. Grace didn't know. She was lost in misty silence, her mind floating and dreading a return to pain and reality. There was no light, no Maegen, no dreams. Whenever she found herself drifting towards consciousness her mind rebelled, sinking down into quiet oblivion where she was safe. She just wanted it to be over. Was that too much to ask?

'Grace,' he whispered. 'Don't leave me. Please, wake up.'

Bastien's voice. It was the only thing that might draw her back. So much of her wanted to stay in this nothingness, to be the nobody Asher Kane had declared her to be.

But Asher Kane was dead and she was still alive. She hoped.

'*Wake up.*'

There were too many voices in her mind. Still there, swirling around like a morass of shadows and spider webs, tangling her thoughts and trying to make her obey. She could ignore them now. All but this one. It overrode them all. She didn't know who it was or what it was, but she had heard it before.

She didn't want to obey. She didn't want to wake up.

Tears leaked from the corners of her eyes. She felt them trickle down her face, and Bastien called her name as he tenderly wiped them away.

He was alive. He was safe. That was all that mattered really. All that mattered to her.

'Wake up, beloved. There's still work to do. Duty and honour, remember? You swore an oath. You made a promise. You swore to serve the crown. My crown. Grace Marchant, wake up.'

She opened her eyes to see Bastien sitting beside her, his head in one hand, his eyes closed. The strain showed on his face, in the lines around his eyes and the tightness of his mouth. He hadn't shaved. He didn't even look like he had washed. He probably hadn't left her side.

'Bastien?' Her voice was a soft rasp and when she tried to move everything hurt. Especially her side. Something in the wound seemed to writhe and twist and she let out her breath in a gasp of pain.

Bastien almost jumped out of the seat as he heard her. He turned, his hands framing her face for a moment, half rose as if to run and then shouted for Daniel.

'Stay still,' he told her in a rush. 'Don't try to get up. Just… just… Danny! Get the Curer. Now!'

'What happened?' she asked.

'It's… it's okay. Danny's coming. He'll explain everything and…'

Daniel would explain everything? Why not Bastien? What was going on?

But the Curer came first, followed by three healers.

'Your majesty,' they chorused as they bowed.

Bastien winced and retreated to let them tend Grace. There was some prodding and poking and they peeled back thick dressings on her side. She felt like a lump of meat but she didn't have the strength to argue. Then they turned to Bastien, ignoring her.

'There's improvement to the fever, and of course consciousness itself is a good sign. The wound in her side is still infected. I've tried to purge it by means magical and quotidian but—'

'I am right here, you know,' Grace growled at him.

The Curer looked over his shoulder at her and his face turned a funny shade of grey. He turned around and peered a little too deeply into her eyes, studying them. 'As you say, Marshal.'

'Marshal?' She glared at Bastien.

He had the grace to look guilty. 'I had to do something. They're writing songs about you.'

'About both of you,' Daniel said from the doorway. He looked tired but unscathed. 'Mostly it's Misha's fault. I tried to get him to stop. He said it was too good an opportunity to pass up.'

Bastien shook his head and turned back to the Curer. 'You can give me an update out here, and let the marshal see her captain.'

He hustled them outside and closed the door, leaving Grace and Daniel alone.

'Captain?' she said. Daniel shrugged. He wasn't any more convinced by the title than she had been when she had it bestowed on her by a king. 'Report.'

Daniel made a face at her. 'I'm fine, thanks for asking, Grace. So is Misha. All good. Ellyn took a few knocks in the taking of the palace but to be honest I think she had the time of her life. I almost killed her but we made up. Good times. Once things settled down here, and you were safe, she went back to Kurt's bar to see if she'd lost Rynn to the girls there forever.'

Her own laugh took Grace by surprise. It was also a mistake because the pain in her side turned white-hot. Daniel held her hand in a grip like iron, his face all concern. He grabbed one of the glasses on the bedside table and helped her drink. It smelled of chamomile, but packed much more of a punch. The pain ebbed, but it didn't go away entirely.

When she could breathe again, she waved him away with it. Too much of that and she'd never think clearly again.

'Danny, tell me what happened.'

He sat down with her, and took both her hands, holding them tightly.

'We almost lost you. Several times. The wound is infected and it's virulent, but they're containing it. They think maybe there's a shard of the crown left inside you but they can't get it out. You've been unconscious for days.'

Days. That was why Bastien looked so wretched then.

Daniel went on. 'When Bastien and Ellyn came after us, word went through the city that he was intent on sacrificing himself to save Rathlynn. Which was... well, it was one interpretation, wasn't it? It sparked something, riots to begin with, and then Kurt turned it into something else. He's good at that, you know?'

'Manipulating people?'

He almost looked hurt. 'Encouraging them. He led an assault on the palace, Grace. You've never seen anything like it. A popular uprising against Aurelie, and in support of the Lord of Thorns. My reprobate brother. There's a turn-up. Don't know what our mum would say. To be honest none but the most devoted to Aurelie put up much of a fight. They held the way to the throne room until... well, you know better than I do what happened in there.'

She did. Some of it at least. Enough.

'And afterwards? What happened to Aurelie?'

'She isn't dead. She isn't exactly... well, *sane* either. They've locked her up in Celeste's tower in the Temple. Probably safest. I don't know what they'll do with her though. But Kane's dead. You might remember that.'

Grace barked out another pained laugh. It was worth it. 'I remember. What's happening politically?'

Daniel rubbed her hand with his. Stalling. Clearly the rest of what he had to say wasn't so straightforward. 'Bastien has been declared king, for real this time. He had some words to say about that – mostly variations on no, and a lot of them not very regal at all; I don't know what you've been teaching him – but, anyway, no one is listening.' He rolled his eyes. 'Portions of the city don't want another king anyway.'

'Your brother foremost among them, I presume.'

'Yes. But he might accept Bastien, under certain circumstances. And then there's Ellyn and Rynn. They have a claim too, and Rynn's his wife. So…' He grimaced as he looked at her, realising what he'd just brought up again. She shook her head. That hardly mattered now. She knew how Bastien felt about her and how she felt about him. 'The noble families, well, they basically ran away, those who were even still here after Aurelie took power. I suppose they'll start slinking back soon, tails between their legs, and start to position themselves as close to him as possible. We're trying to put together some sort of council to sort it all out. But… yeah…'

'And *marshal?*'

He laughed, which was hardly comforting. 'Bastien's idea. He said if they're making him the king he could make you the marshal.'

'The Academy doesn't have marshals. The marshal is something else.'

'I tried to tell him that. All of that. He doesn't listen. He's as bad as you. When we argued, he just made me a captain and then he told Ellyn she has to be commander of the Academy. He wants it re-established.'

The sinking feeling of disappointment twisted inside her.

More mageborn cadets and more days of homage, no doubt. Fix all the mageborn. Go back to how it all was before… But how could he do that now? Her heart fell as she thought about it. She hadn't expected that. It was a betrayal.

'He's definitely the king then?'

'Well, he hasn't let them actually crown him yet, but I don't think anyone is too bothered about that. And even with those who actually want a king, there's still the problem of a king with magic.'

'He lost his magic, Danny,' she said. She didn't know if she was breaking some huge secret or not. But if she couldn't tell Daniel, who could she tell? She trusted him with her life. And Bastien's. 'Doesn't have it any more, not since Thorndale. Almost got him killed.'

Grace's eyes were growing heavy, her brain fuzzy. The tincture they'd given her, no doubt, or just exhaustion. She was still weak and she needed time to recover.

Time she didn't have. She sighed and Daniel's features softened with affection.

'I know, pet. We all do. It's okay. You need to sleep. I'll let you—'

'Wait, Danny…' She grabbed him before he could leave, her grip still strong around his wrist. She pulled him close and dropped her voice to a whisper. 'I need you to get me something.'

When she told him what, he went pale. But she didn't care, not any more. Grace knew what she had to do.

Chapter Thirty-Five

The council, such as it was, met at noon to discuss the coronation yet again. Bastien sat at the head of the long mahogany table, glaring down its polished length as Kurt argued with Ellyn, who argued with the acting commander of the Royal Guard and the first general of the army, who had been recalled from the border with Tlachtlya. The first general glared at Lord Rosse of Wuel, who had managed to drag himself back from whatever rat hole he'd hidden himself in. At the far end of the table, Misha listened carefully to everything and recorded it away in that extraordinary mind of his, making a few pertinent notes on parchment. And Rynn sat by Bastien, her hand on his arm the only thing keeping him from upending the whole table and storming out.

He didn't want to be here. He didn't want any of this, but no one gave a fig. Grace wasn't improving, the infection still running through her system and showing no sign of abating. By this stage, the whole population of the Healers' Halls had seen her, and every Curer Bastien could get hold of. Nothing worked. Misha's music helped more than most of their supposed solutions.

Part of the crown, the tiniest shard, had managed to stay inside her, burrowing through her body, or so they thought. He didn't want to consider what happened when it reached wherever it was going. They had tried everything.

If he still had magic, he could have saved her with just a touch. It wasn't fair.

Sometimes, when he sat by Grace's side, he was sure he saw flickers of shadows in her eyes, black flecks in the gold of her irises. The Deep Dark hadn't gone away. It had winnowed its way into her and it lodged there like a parasite, slowly extending its hold on her ravaged body once more.

'And perhaps a ceremony renewing your marriage vows, your majesties?'

Lord Hale's voice cut through Bastien's thoughts like a hot knife.

'A what?' If a few of them recoiled at the tone, he didn't care.

'A good point, my lord,' said Lord Rosse. 'The marriage took place so rapidly on Iliz that your people here felt bereft. A public renewal would give them something to… to cheer for. Not to mention reassuring the Valenti.'

The Valenti. The last people Bastien wanted to make nice with. They were desperate to cover themselves now. If word got out they'd drugged him and forced him into marriage… well, all the world would turn against them.

But he wouldn't do that to Rynn and Ellyn.

The Dowager, on the other hand, could squirm for a bit. She had played her dangerous game and lost. Iliz was now a disaster area and no traders in their right minds were going there. Her own people were turning against her. He'd rather enjoyed those reports.

'Your marriage was a master-stroke politically, of course,' said Lord Hale. 'A true master-stroke, but… but…' He stammered to silence as Bastien glared at him.

'Give the people a show, you mean?' Kurt cut into the silence. 'Let the ignorant fools cheer and wave, maybe throw some flowers.

Afterwards, they could scrape up the petals so they have something to eat. Or maybe you'd like to hurl them some bread after your feast.'

The room fell into uncomfortable silence.

And then Rynn spoke. 'Perhaps a public celebration isn't a bad idea. But among the people themselves rather than here, and the food from such a feast could be more evenly distributed throughout the city. I'm sure the lords will be more than happy to help provide the necessary provisions.'

Lord Hale looked like he had just swallowed his own tongue. It took him a moment to force a smile. 'Princess Rynn is wise. And we should consider approaching her father in regard to a rebuilding loan to the crown in order—'

'I wouldn't advise it. If you take a penny from my family, Lord Hale, you'll owe them forever. We have money enough here. Mr Parry has some other options. Don't you, Kurt?' She turned her radiant smile on him instead.

Yes, Bastien thought, Rynn might look tiny and fragile as a bird, but she had her grandmother's mind. They underestimated her at their peril.

Kurt stared at her, without any semblance of a polite smile. 'I knew you were trouble the minute I met you, pet. We should never have left you chatting to the girls in the inn for all that time.'

'Saffron's an incredibly good accountant, Kurt.'

'I know that. That's why I hired her. Not to mention how great she is in the sack. Lord Rosse knows all about that, don't you?'

Bastien wondered who would collapse first – those trying to contain their outrage or their laughter.

He pushed himself back from the table and stood up. The accompanying scraping of chairs and the noise as everyone got up as well irritated him all the more.

'Majesty, your coronation—' Rosse tried one more time.

Bastien sighed. 'Just sort it out without me. Or crown Rynn instead. She'd look better anyway.'

*

Grace was up and dressed, which was a tribute to her determination rather than her improved health. She hadn't left the tower bedroom Bastien shared with her. He hadn't had the heart to move to another room. It would feel too much like a statement. And he wasn't going to go anywhere without her now. Let the nobility whisper behind their backs and cast dubious glances at Rynn and Ellyn. None of them cared.

The bandages around her middle were barely visible through the loose shirt she wore over simple drawstring trousers. She was pale, blood loss and the infection still draining all her strength.

She had been busy though. A small table and two chairs had been set up in the space between the door and the bed. It was laid as if for a banquet, with covered dishes, gleaming wine glasses and some of the best cutlery the palace had to offer.

Grace had been looking out of the window when he'd arrived and, when he'd entered, she'd given him the soft smile she reserved for him alone.

That was everything to him.

'I thought they'd try to keep you longer,' she said.

'They tried. There's so much to do and all they want to talk about are ceremonies. It's infuriating.'

'So you ran away?'

'I left Rynn in charge.'

'That's mean.'

'She can handle each and every one of them.'

'I meant to them. You married well, you know, even if you didn't mean to. You don't deserve her.' The teasing tone made the words gentler. He still felt so guilty about the marriage. But there didn't seem to be a way to dissolve it. Not that his people would accept. All he wanted was Grace. She took one look at his face and laughed easily. 'Come,' she said, crossing to the table. 'Sit with me. I asked them for some lunch while I still have a chance to lead you astray. They asked what I wanted, anything I wanted, can you imagine that?'

He looked at the covered dishes. 'What did you ask for?'

'Spicy sausage and bean stew and seven-grain bread. I think they had to go and find a recipe. Your valet went and got the chef to try to work out what it was. I sent Daniel down to them in the end to sort it out.' She lifted the lid and the most incredible aroma billowed out with the steam. The dish was a deep red, with lumps of succulent sausages and many-coloured beans. The bread was thick and rustic, already cut into regimented slices. She uncovered her own dish as she sat down. 'It was my favourite thing we ever had to eat in the Academy. I thought you should try it at least once.'

Her portion was about a quarter of the size of his. She couldn't manage much more yet. As Bastien sat opposite her, she smiled but her eyes looked so sad. Maybe she was thinking of all those they had lost, all her friends who had died since he had come into her life.

He took a mouthful. It was hot and so spicy it made his eyes water in seconds. Grace laughed softly at him again and poured a glass of red wine into his goblet. He drained more than half of it in one go. 'Isn't there any water?'

'Of course, sorry. Here.' She poured water too and then topped up the wine. 'Eat the bread with it. It helps. It's the combination – stew, bread and wine. All of it together. Trust me.'

He'd trust her with his life. He wanted to tell her but he was too busy with the meal. It really was delicious. He wasn't sure he'd ever eaten one better; if so he couldn't remember it. She poured herself some cordial. The healers had forbidden wine for now and Grace was cooperating in the hopes that she'd speed up her recovery.

The light tone was a relief as well. As they ate they chatted about nothing of any great portent, laughing, sharing stories, until his bowl was clear. He mopped up the last scraps with the bread and finished the wine.

Her mood had not been good of late. At night he lay beside her while she slept, the medicinal tinctures Healer Langan made for her causing a deep sleep from which it was hard to wake. They also didn't help with the nightmares. Sometimes he could bring her around. Sometimes he had to listen as she sobbed or screamed and fought against ghosts and memories.

Not all of them were memories.

Voices, she called them. They tormented her. The constant pain made it worse.

When he sat back she smiled again. He'd do anything for that smile. Anything she wanted. But Grace poured him some more wine. 'Drink up. I can't have it but I can watch you enjoy it.'

'If I still had my magic, I could cure you,' he told her, ashamed that it was true. But he didn't have a trace of magic left in him.

'Do you really miss it?' she asked.

'Apart from that? No, not really. To be honest, it's a relief.'

For a moment she looked down at the table and a wave of pain passed over her face. Bastien pushed himself up and stood awkwardly. His legs felt weak, wobbly, and his head swam in a syrup. He swallowed hard on a suddenly dry throat.

When Grace lifted her face, her eyes were glittering with tears.

Bastien swayed for a moment and then sat down heavily in the chair. 'What… what have you done?' His words seemed thick in his mouth, hard to form.

'I'm sorry, Bastien,' she whispered, all the easiness draining from her voice. 'It's for the best. You'll see.'

He didn't have the strength to push himself up again. But he wouldn't just give up.

'Danny,' she called and the door to the study opened. 'Help him. Don't let him fall.'

Strong arms caught him and he found himself half dragged, half carried to their bed. He tried to struggle, to fight Daniel off, but he couldn't.

'Take it easy, Bastien,' Daniel Parry told him. 'I'm sorry, mate, truly I am. But she says it's the only way. And she's still the boss.'

'It *is* the only way,' Grace told him. 'Out you go now, and don't let anyone else in. I need to do this right. No interruptions.' She sat on the bed beside Bastien and waited. She still had the wine glass in her hand. 'Here, drink the rest, love. It'll help.'

His focus blurred but he wasn't sure if it was tears or the horribly familiar sensation of lyriana root sweeping through his system. Grace brought the glass to his lips, lifting his head with her other hand, and helped him drink. He couldn't seem to resist her.

The ache inside tore at his heart, shredding it with claws of iron. 'What have you done?' he asked again, words blurring together.

'Made the right decision for both of us. It has to be done, love. I have to go and you have to stay here. They need you. You're their king, Bastien Larelwynn.'

'The wine?'

'And the soup. And the bread too. I couldn't take any chances. I needed to make sure I got enough into your system. The spices were the best disguise.'

Spices. It had been so spicy he couldn't taste the sweetness.

'Danny got it—'

'Don't blame Danny. He owes me, that's all. He's… he's our friend, Bastien. Listen to me now. Listen, because I don't have much time and we need to get this right. You're going to forget all about me, love. You're going to forget all about me as if—' She choked on a sob, then forced herself to go on. 'As if I never existed. You're going to find someone else to love. Rynn and Ellyn are going to look after you for me, and Danny too. They'll keep you safe, always. And I will never forget you. I'll hold you in my heart forever. But I have to go. If you're ever going to be free.'

She'll set you free…

Her tears fell on his face and she kissed his lips.

'Grace, don't do this. Please… my love…'

'I have to. Look at me. Really *look*.' Her voice dropped low, her eyes so wide, the golden irises flecked with more dark than he remembered. The Deep Dark. He knew it. He had known all along but he didn't want to admit it. That was the infection. That was what they couldn't cure. 'It's still inside me. It's only a matter of time. I can feel it. The shard. I can feel it, almost at my heart. I won't let it take me, understand? Not again. I won't let it hurt you any more. The more sedatives and drugs the healers give me, the harder it is to fight. You see?'

'No,' he whispered. This couldn't be happening. She couldn't be doing this, not making him forget her. She was everything to him, all he had left. She couldn't take that away. If she was gone, not just from his life but from his memories… from his heart… 'I *won't* forget…'

She kissed him again and broke away with a sigh. Her hand brushed down the side of his face like a ghost. 'But you will. You have to. Because I know you. You'd keep looking for me, keep searching, keep coming after me… You'd sacrifice everything and you've sacrificed so much, for far too long. I can't risk you. I love you more than life itself, Bastien. You need to forget me. I need to set you free.'

Do this for me and you will be free, the voice of the Maegen had said. *She'll set you free.*

Not like this. Divinities, not like this!

He couldn't focus any more. The words were drifting in and out of his mind and he couldn't cling to any one thought.

'Forget me,' Grace told him. 'Forget magic. Be the king I know you can be. Never lose the kindness in you. You don't have to hide it any more. You don't have to protect yourself like that. It's my job, love. You're going to be… *such* an amazing king, Bastien. The king they need. Like Marius. Good, kind, just. Please…'

He struggled to sit up, to lift his body, to stop her.

She rested a hand on his chest, pushing him down effortlessly and holding him there with no force at all.

'You're fine,' she told him. 'Don't fight it. No more Hollow King, no more Maegen, no more magic. I'm taking the crown. I'm taking all that remains of the pact and the Deep Dark with me. Three times dead, twice entombed. That's me, Bastien. I've died too many times. Been pulled out of a pile of rubble twice now.'

'You haven't died three times,' he protested weakly.

'Not yet.' She smiled and he knew what she intended. 'I can finish it.'

'Grace,' he whispered but the shadows were clawing at the edges of his consciousness now. The words made no sense. But she was leaving, and he couldn't stop her. With all the power in the world he wouldn't be able to stop her. He never could. His eyes closed. Not even his own tears could stop them as his strength gave out and he knew that the next time they opened the lyriana root would have erased every precious memory of her.

Chapter Thirty-Six

Grace slid off the horse's back. She didn't know how they had made it this far. She'd passed no one on the road to Thorndale, all through the night and the following day, or at least that was what she could remember of it – it might have taken longer. She'd let the horse set the pace, walking, stopping when it needed to, carrying on as it would. She'd slipped in and out of consciousness but all she had to do was point it in the right direction every now and then, and try not to fall off. She was pretty sure something else was leading them anyway.

Once she'd managed to stand on her own two feet, she heaved the saddle off its back and removed the bridle, expecting it to run off then and there. But the poor creature was as exhausted as she was. It just stood there, whickering at her softly, blowing air from its nostrils in a deep sigh.

'Suit yourself,' she told it and her legs gave out.

Everything hurt. Everything. She pulled back her shirt to expose her side and the blood-soaked bandages. Damn, it was bad. Really bad.

Well, she shouldn't be riding long distances while wounded. She could almost hear Commander Craine's disgusted tones.

She unwound them and removed the dressings. What she saw made her wince. Black lines, like veins, came out of the wound, tracing across her skin. She could almost see them crawling onwards as she watched.

'*We will always survive*,' the Deep Dark told her. '*As long as we have you, beloved.*'

'Yeah,' Grace replied, not bothered how insane it looked, talking to the voices only she could hear. There was no one there to listen to her anyway. And the horse didn't care. 'I get it. But you can't get out of me either, can you?'

'*Not yet. In time.*' It moved again, lines like molten metal creeping through her. Grace stifled a grunt of pain.

There was nothing for it. She had to keep going. She had to leave Bastien behind her. He had a new life now. He was safe and she meant to keep him so. Free. Free of all of it. He couldn't even remember her now, so it didn't matter. Giving him that potion had been the hardest thing she had ever done. Filling his head full of pretty lies, letting him go… but she had to do it.

She drank the last of her water. She hadn't brought food because she had known she wouldn't need it. Couldn't have brought herself to eat it without throwing up anyway.

Grace tried to walk to the cave entrance, but ended up half crawling most of the way through the ruins, and down through the half-collapsed tunnel. By the time she squeezed into the remains of the cavern, bathed in the glowing light of the Maegen, she was drenched in sweat and her whole body felt like it was on fire. Still she pushed herself onwards until she collapsed onto the broken throne.

Her blood slicked her hands as she opened the pack, taking out the crown. The Hollow King had once had his own plan, and now it was up to her to fulfil it. Before, he'd broken the crown, given the warrant to Lucien Larelwynn and made the torc to go around Bastien's neck. But he'd broken the crown to destroy it. That was what the story said.

'*What are you doing?*' the Deep Dark asked.

'You mean you don't know? I thought you knew everything?' She laughed bitterly and the voices in her mind growled at her. Pain lanced through her again as it continued its campaign to gain control of her. Deliberate, punishing, vindictive.

Her hands spasmed and she almost dropped the crown.

Breathing rapidly helped her regain equilibrium. It wouldn't work forever.

'*Grace, please…*' It sounded like Bastien's voice. '*Don't do this.*'

She swallowed hard and kept going. It was a trick. It had to be. Bastien was miles away, lost to her, oblivious. He didn't even know her any more.

Forget me, she had told him. And he had.

Tears stung her eyes again. Too many tears. She couldn't seem to stop. Her body was shivering which was, frankly, a terrible sign. Her time was running out. Either the Deep Dark would consume her from the inside out, or she'd die before it could finish its job. Her whole body was caught between shock and determination.

She held the crown in her hands, all the power in the universe in the grip of a dying woman.

'*Put it on, save yourself, save us…*'

Tempting, maybe. To hold such power, the power of the divinities, all the magic in the Maegen. Everything. She could wield the power of creation and destruction however she wanted.

But what would she do with that?

She was just an Academy officer.

Grace pitched herself forward into the glowing water of the pool, taking the crown with her.

Darkness closed over her head. She sank like a stone, into a body of water much deeper than the one in the cavern. On and on she plunged into the abyss, the crown dissolving in her hands. The pain in her side ebbed away, the blood coming from it mingling with the light.

And then she saw him.

The figure formed before her, tall and broad-shouldered, slim-hipped and beautiful, his face etched on her heart and those eyes, those eyes so dark she could lose herself in them. She knew his body intimately, knew the smile he wore when he thought no one was looking at him, when they were alone together.

This wasn't him, though. It just looked like him, an illusion.

The Hollow King's smile was nothing like Bastien's.

'You could have had everything you ever wanted, little Flint. Why give it up?'

His voice reverberated and the currents of magic rushed around her, encircling her and drawing her to him.

'You don't know me.'

'I know you well enough, mortal. You're mageborn, nightborn, and something else. The Deep Dark offered you everything, and all you did was throw it away.'

'The crown was nothing but evil and you know it.'

'Evil?' he laughed. 'You understand nothing. That crown was mine. It's a tool, nothing more. We are power, Flint. Power is neither good nor evil. That can only be assessed by how it is wielded. There was balance between the Maegen and the Deep Dark. Until... until there was not.'

He held out a hand to her. Grace hesitated, but it seemed like a dare, like if she didn't take it, she would fail some kind of test.

He was right. He wasn't good or evil. Neither was power. It all depended where you stood. What you did with it.

'Show me,' she said.

'A command, Flint?' The amusement on his face sent a chill through her. She didn't want to amuse him.

Images flashed before her, quick and bright, like slaps to the face, one after the other. So many images, memories of so many lives, so many pasts. She saw Bastien as he was, saw them together, kissing, the way he'd lain on the bed after they made love that first time, his arms behind his head, smiling up at her. Saw him as the Lord of Thorns, saw him leading Larelwynn armies into battle, saw him on his knees, saw him brought low by Lucien's ancestors. She saw him with his friend, the boys they had been, here in the cavern at Thorndale.

'You stole his life,' she said. 'You will not steal me.'

'He stole my power, and he gave his life willingly to do it. Larelwynn stole his life and many after it.'

And before that… before Bastien… The Hollow King was alone and broken. The nightborn rampaged across the land, and the roses of Thorndale burned with an unholy fire.

'Flints,' he said, and he almost sounded amused. Not what she had expected. 'The most unpredictable and stubborn of the mageborn. And the most destructive. Look at you. You've died and come back twice. You've been pulled out of the womb of the earth itself twice. Three times dead and twice entombed… the old measure of divinity from a time your people don't even remember. This is your third death, do you see? Your feet are firmly set on the path. Grace Marchant, consider all you have done. You've brought down kings and queens and given up everything to be here. Even your beloved.'

'I didn't want to. I had to.'

His gaze turned speculative. 'Did you? What about *his* choice? You took that from him.'

That was her shame, of course. She hadn't let Bastien decide. Because he would have wanted to keep fighting and she couldn't fight any more. She wanted it to be over. Perhaps she was the coward after all? 'I had to.'

'And couldn't you have let him make that decision? You said you wanted to free him. But you wiped his memory in order to have your way.'

The undertone to the words left her chilled to the bone. He made her sound like Aurelie. His truths were hard and bitter, cruel, but truths nonetheless. She had always said she wanted truth. She tried to pull away but the Hollow King was not about to let her go. Not yet.

'It wasn't like that.'

'Wasn't it? I think it was. Maybe you're the Larelwynn after all.'

'I'm not a Larelwynn,' she told him. She didn't have a drop of royal blood in her. She was no one. 'I know who I am now. I'm… I'm nobody.'

'You were never that, Grace Marchant.' His voice was almost kind. He touched her face, just as Bastien might have, a tender caress. She closed her eyes, longing for it to be real, even as she knew that it was not. This being was not her lover. He never would be. 'No one is. Not really. It takes more than blood. Others would have you believe that but power, true power, is always in your own hands. I only surrendered power when I had no choice. But you… you give it up willingly, with nothing to gain from that.'

'Nothing to gain?'

'You're dying, little Flint. Your third death. Don't you realise that?'

'I've been dying all along. It's what being mortal is all about.'

His hand tightened on hers. 'You don't have to.'

She frowned up at him. 'Everyone dies.'

'Do they?' He sounded bemused at the idea. Perhaps he was. Gods didn't die.

She stood there, in the darkness, the Maegen billowing overhead like a glowing sky, its luminous clouds swirling and dissolving. It was part of her, as much as the darkness was. She could see it now, the darkness and the light. Without one it was impossible to see the other. And here she was, suspended between the two of them, her blood flowing into the water, her life ebbing away.

'*Grace…*' His voice. It sounded like his voice and her dearest wish. So far away.

But it couldn't be.

'No,' she said. 'That isn't real. It isn't possible.' The Hollow King framed her face with his hands, tilting it up towards his. She stared into the endless dark of his eyes, devoid of the warmth she knew and loved, his face but not his face. Not Bastien. The Lord of Thorns, the Hollow King, they were nothing without him. They might be magic and power and everything else, but without Bastien himself, there was no heart. No compassion. Not as she knew it.

The Hollow King leaned in, as if to kiss her, but he didn't. His lips, so like Bastien's, lingered just beyond hers, so close she could feel the warmth that came from him, could feel his breath as it brushed her skin.

None of this was real.

It would be so easy to give in. She could become a goddess. But when you stripped away the exterior, the power, the riches, the eternal life… she still wouldn't have Bastien. Not really. And he was all she wanted.

'No,' she breathed again. She had to admit it. 'All I've ever wanted is the truth.'

His hand moved again, cupping her chin, and the Hollow King gazed at her, studying her. And he smiled. And this time… this time it almost did look like Bastien's smile. 'Then you shall have it. All of it. The truth.'

The other hand pressed to her side, right where the crown had stabbed her. Power flooded through her. She arched her spine, her mouth opening in a gasp of shock and water flooded in, choking her, drowning her. The light didn't stop though, like a newborn star bursting into life it tore through her body, driving out the strands of darkness entwined around her heart, winnowing through her veins and purging her. She burned with a refining fire that scorched its way through her and her world turned iridescent.

When the light overwhelmed her, it was a blessed relief.

*

Hands seized her, hauling her half out of the water, smoothing her saturated hair back from her face. She gasped for air, in spite of her determination to be dead, because her body was ever a traitor and it wanted to live.

All around her the Maegen glowed, moving as if it was a stormy sea, and the churning light it threw up hit his face. His beautiful, impossible face. Bastien held her, his expression frantic, his mouth forming her name. She couldn't even hear his voice from the sound of the maelstrom in her mind, the fire that burned through her, roaring out its victory.

And all at once it was gone. The pool went still, the light dimming to a faint golden glow like a reflection, and Bastien held her. He stood in the water, cradling her against him, holding her in his strong arms.

Her Bastien. Even though that was impossible.

'Talk to me. Please… please talk to me. Grace… please…'

'Bastien?' she managed.

With a cry of relief he pulled her into his embrace, wrapping his arms around her and holding her against his chest until she thought he was going to smother her. She pushed back, but only gently, because she didn't want him to let go. Not really.

'How… how are you here?'

He stroked her face, her shoulders, as if trying to reassure himself she was real, that she was healed. And she was. She knew it. The pain was gone, the darkness, the emptiness inside her. All gone.

'Bastien, you're meant to be in Rathlynn.'

She'd drugged him. He shouldn't remember her at all. And even if he did, she had betrayed him in the worst way possible. He should not be here.

'I came after you. I wasn't going to let you—'

'But the lyriana root—'

'Didn't work, love. The healers think I had too much of Rynn's antidote still in my system. And some say it only works on mageborn. I don't know and I don't care. I could never forget you. And you can't make me.'

She'd taken his choice away, the worst mistake she could possibly make. And yet somehow… somehow he was still the same. He had come after her anyway.

'I'm sorry,' she whispered, because the Hollow King had been right and that was her greatest shame. She had taken his choice away. Like Aurelie had tried to do. Like the Larelwynns had done time and again. And she had known what she was doing but she'd still done it. How could she ever make that right? 'Forgive me.'

'Grace.' His voice rumbled in his chest, and she felt it as much as heard it. His heartbeat was so loud, his body pressed to hers. She looked up into his face, so close to her. 'Grace, there's nothing left to forgive. My love… Can't we just start again?'

How could he forgive her just like that?

'Start again?'

Bastien kissed her, his mouth tentative at first, but his lips finding the answer to the question they posed quickly answered. She buried her hands in his long hair, fingers tangling in the black silken strands. Their mouths met, desperate for each other. She couldn't seem to touch him enough, or get close enough to him.

Was it more magic? Another enchantment?

She broke the kiss. The collapsed cavern was empty. Somewhere the stone figure of the Hollow King was buried under rubble, but his spirit was still here, in the water of the pool they stood in, which lapped at their wet clothes, or just in the world around them. Light played like sunset on the roof overhead, light reflected on water. She didn't know where that light was coming from and she didn't want to ask. But she could guess. It came from her. Or through her... Bastien traced his fingers over her skin as if following lines or patterns. The light faded into her, like the setting sun.

'We can't go back,' he told her. 'It isn't safe for you. They'll start insisting that I rule. I can't. I'm not a king. I never wanted to be, regardless of magic or blood or anything else. Marius was wrong about that, but not about you. How he knew, I have no idea, but I'm not leaving you again, Grace. You get into too much trouble on your own. Not to mention the mess you tried to leave me in.'

Her remorse must have shown all over her face. How could she hide it from him? 'I didn't mean—'

His kiss silenced her again. 'I know,' he mumbled against her lips, as if reluctant to pull too far away. 'I understand. But thankfully fate had other ideas, my love, and I will follow this path above all others.' He traced a line of kisses down her jaw and along the line of her throat. Her skin warmed beneath his mouth. 'What happened? Your wound… the Deep Dark…'

'Gone,' she told him. 'The Hollow King drove it out, and healed me. He – I don't know what he did. But… he said the balance was back and that was all that mattered. Not good. Not evil. Just… balance.'

She felt his questing hands surreptitiously testing the area where the crown had punctured her side. He didn't quite trust her to be honest about that then. But she didn't care. All it did was make her shiver with pleasure and press closer against Bastien's body.

'We can leave,' he told her. 'No one knows where we are. We'll go away, just you and me. They don't need us, Grace. Come with me.'

'Where?' she asked, laughing at the urgency in his voice.

'I don't care as long as I'm with you. Somewhere quiet. Somewhere we can be alone.'

'We're alone here,' she teased and the smile that flickered over his lips was wickedness incarnate.

He lifted her and she wrapped her legs around his waist. Bastien traced her body with those clever hands. Her skin shivered in response, the pleasure growing with every touch.

Somehow they managed to shed their clothes, heedless of the water. Its warm embrace lapped against them, cradling them together. His body worshipped hers and what could she do but return such veneration. She sank onto him with a kind of relief, a need finally sated.

'I'll go with you,' she told him, her voice desperate now. 'Anywhere. We can go anywhere. So long as we're together.'

Bastien Larelwynn laughed like a man without a care in the world, kissing her again until she tore her mouth free of his so she could gasp his name out loud.

Epilogue

One year later

The sound of horse hooves echoed down the narrow path through the trees. It brought Bastien's attention up from the vegetable bed he was digging. He wiped the sweat from his forehead with one arm and shielded his eyes against the bright sun.

In the background, the noise of metal on metal rang out of the forge. Birds called out from the trees, the forest thick with life, far away as it was from other settlements of any size. Bastien watched the rider approach, unhurried and relaxed. There was a harp slung on his back. The next village sometimes sent people their way but mainly they were alone.

It was how they wanted to be.

'Hello?' the rider called, his voice naturally musical. Of course it was. Golden-haired and handsome, he hadn't changed. Not a jot. 'Bastien?'

It felt like the world dropped out from underneath him. He hung there, ready to fall and hit the ground hard. And that would be reality once more. A year. They had made it just a year on their own, safe, before the past found them.

Bastien kept glaring at him, waiting until he reached the edge of their land and dismounted. 'Hello, Misha.' He couldn't bring himself to smile or say it was good to see the harper. It wasn't. 'You've come a long way.'

'Well,' said the harper. 'If you will hide yourselves away in the back of beyond.'

'It's not the back of beyond,' Bastien said, a little defensive. He loved this place. They had chosen it together.

'Well, if not, I'm pretty sure you can see it from here,' Misha grinned. 'Can we speak? In private?'

Bastien looked around. There was no one else for miles except for Grace.

'I have, as you say, come a long way to see you,' the harper went on.

Damn it, he couldn't turn him away. Grace would never forgive him. Bastien might want to keep the world out but the world was determined to intervene, it seemed.

'There's a stable out the back. See to your horse. I'll fetch Grace.'

Grace was hammering away at some unsuspecting piece of metal while the forge blazed behind her. Always the right temperature and intensity in her forge. Bastien smiled from the doorway, watching her lost in her work. Maybe it was something inherited. Perhaps she had picked it up from all that time watching Zavi Millan. Or even a natural talent. Whatever it was, when she found someone to take her on as an apprentice, she mastered in months what it took others years. The blacksmith had begged them to stay.

She wouldn't make blades, not beyond kitchen knives and basic implements. But there was no one better with horses.

After a moment she noticed him and set aside the hammer. She doused the metal in the barrel, steam billowing around her. The light glimmered on the sweat dotting the skin of her bare arms and face. She smiled at him and he had never seen her more delectable.

'I heard a horse. Someone throw a shoe?'

'No. It's Misha Harper.'

'Misha?' Excitement made her eyes sparkle. 'What's Misha doing here? Are the others with him? Daniel and Ellyn?'

'No, just Misha.'

'Well come on then.' She grabbed his arm as she went by, pulling him along with her. 'Let's hear all the news.'

'Grace,' he said, a warning tone in his voice.

She turned to face him and her expression grew a little more solemn. 'It's okay, love. Don't worry. Whatever it is, we'll handle it. Together.'

'Together,' he said. 'But it's been a year. The kingdom hasn't fallen apart without us, has it? The council is running things, and Daniel and Ellyn are—'

She stopped him with a kiss. 'Misha won't have come all this way for nothing. And we can't go on hiding forever. Let's just find out.'

'Grace…' he said, but stopped.

'What?'

'I love you. You know that, don't you? No matter what.'

There was that smile again, the one he would do anything for. The one that meant he lost all reason and couldn't deny her anything.

'And I love you. No matter what, my Lord of Thorns.'

A Letter from Jessica

Dear reader,

I want to say a huge thank you for choosing to read *Nightborn*. If you did enjoy it, and want to keep up to date with all my latest releases, just sign up at the following link. Your email address will never be shared and you can unsubscribe at any time.

www.bookouture.com/jessica-thorne

Returning to a beloved world always feels special, even if that world is the world of the mageborn, and there's danger, heartbreak and betrayal around every corner. But there is also passion and wonder, and the final promise of love. Writing *Nightborn* was an adventure in and of itself, especially editing on lockdown during the Covid-19 outbreak. It helped me cope in so many ways and I want to say a special thanks for all the wonderful support from my editor Ellen and the team at Bookouture during this time.

Thanks also to my writing friends, especially the Naughty Kitchen and the Lady Writers, my fellow Romantic Novelists' Association members all over the world, the fabulous Kate Pearce, my family and my beloved husband and partner in lockdown, Pat.

I hope you loved *Nightborn* and if you did I would be very grateful if you could write a review. I'd love to hear what you think, and it makes such a difference helping new readers to discover one of my books for the first time.

I love hearing from my readers – you can get in touch on my Facebook page, through Twitter, Goodreads or my website.

Thanks,
Jessica Thorne

 JessThorneBooks

 @JessThorneBooks

 www.rflong.com/jessicathorne

Printed in Great Britain
by Amazon